SARAH WAS DREAMING OF SUCCESS, KNOWING SHE WOULD DO ANYTHING TO ACHIEVE IT...

"Mademoiselle Taylor." The liquid voice interrupted her fantasy. Octave Rivarol, standing beside the staircase in the foyer, looked up at her. "It's late. You'll need an escort to your rooms."

"Thank you, but I walk home with friends every night. They'll be waiting."

"We could discuss your interpretation of Nicklasse. I have ideas that can help you."

"It's not possible," she said, refusing to pretend she was sorry. "I can't disappoint my friends."

As she started down, planning to skirt around him, he stepped up closer. "Mademoiselle Taylor," he said silkily, "you don't want to disappoint me."

LA BELLE AMERICAINE

BARBARA KELLER

Published by arrangement
with Palace Books Inc.

HarperPaperbacks
A Division of HarperCollinsPublishers

This is a work of fiction. The characters, incidents, and dialogues are products of the author's imagination and are not to be construed as real. Any resemblance to actual events or persons, living or dead, is entirely coincidental.

HarperPaperbacks   *A Division of* HarperCollins*Publishers*
10 East 53rd Street, New York, N.Y. 10022

Cover art by Jim Griffin

First printing: November 1990

Printed in the United States of America

HarperPaperbacks and colophon are trademarks of HarperCollins*Publishers*

10 9 8 7 6 5 4 3 2 1

To Jim—editor, researcher, critic,
comforter, husband and best friend.

CHAPTER ONE

Paris, September, 1888

SARAH TAYLOR CROSSED THE BUSY PLACE DE L'OPERA AS IF she knew just where she were going and why. With each of her brisk movements, the folds of her long skirt flipped about the heels of her elegant black boots. The feather in the hat perched on her upswept red-gold hair bobbed jauntily in the midday sunshine. But when she reached the wide marble steps that ran across the front of the Théâtre de l'Opéra, she slowed, losing the appearance of assurance. She mounted the steps, passing through the arches into the shaded loggia, and stopped, nervously pressing her gloved hands together.

Although Sarah was twenty-one and wanted to think of herself as worldly, the failure of her three previous attempts to talk to the Paris Opéra's director had intimidated her. Only he could give her the chance she was determined to have, indeed had come from Boston to have—to sing in the Opéra chorus. She must try again today, with a different plan.

1

From the boulevards converging on the Place de l'Opéra came the clop of hooves, the rumble of carriage wheels and the jangle of bells on horse-drawn trams. They sounded as if they could be saying, "Hurry, hurry. Don't miss your chance." With renewed spirits, she crossed the covered loggia to the entrance door.

Inside, her footsteps echoed on the marble floor. The vast stairwell was empty of bejeweled women and formally suited men, and its only occupants were Sarah and the bronze statues that held the candelabra. A polished marble wall panel reflected her slender figure. Nervously she wondered if her dress, a tight-fitting topaz silk faille suit trimmed with tiny jet beads, made her appear too girlish. No, she reassured herself, it looked fashionable and sophisticated. She skirted the grand staircase, which curved upward, dividing as it led to the auditorium, and entered the passage to the offices. The third door on the right was open. After one last moment of hesitation, she stepped inside.

A man wearing a coat of a nauseating green color looked up from his desk. Sarah smiled and said, in French, "Good afternoon, Monsieur Lebeau. Is the director in today?" Though Lebeau had not even been polite on their third encounter the day before, she still hoped her dimpled smile might resurrect the charm she had used happily at home.

But Monsieur Lebeau rose angrily. "Mademoiselle Taylor, why do you bother me again? The director is in, but he will not see you—today nor any day!"

"Please, Monsieur Lebeau, I'll take only a few minutes of his time. If he hears me, I know he'll give me a chance."

Monsieur Lebeau turned red, his face and coat bizarre Christmas colors. "What effrontery! For the last time, the Paris Opéra does not engage singers without experience! If we did, we would be besieged by young women like you who think beauty is enough. Furthermore, your French is atrocious. The director abhors American accents, and so do I."

That stung! "I had a French governess, and I probably speak French better than you speak English."

"I *never* need to speak English," he said icily and advanced around the desk with the obvious intention of shoving her out the door.

She retreated into the passageway, but only as far as an alcove where she could watch anyone leaving without being seen herself. Detestable man! He thought he had defeated her, but she wasn't finished yet.

The previous evening she'd spent twenty-five francs of her diminishing money on the least-expensive seat in the top gallery of the opera house. The interior of the building at night had dazzled her, from the guards at attention along the staircase to the opulent gold decorations and red velvet upholstery of the boxes below her. The performance was Gounod's *Faust*. Sarah had loved it all and wept when Marguérite sang of her drowned child. But her principal reason for going was not entertainment. The presentation was a much-advertised new production, and she had guessed that Monsieur Gailhard, the director, would be there. He joined the singers onstage after the finale, and she learned what she had gone for—what he looked like.

Now it was two o'clock, time for people to go out for lunch, and she was going to wait for Monsieur Gailhard. Previously she had observed that Lebeau always went out alone, so she hoped the director would also be by himself.

Very little air moved in the corridor, and the jacket of her faille suit seemed too warm. Her boots began to feel uncomfortable, and she shifted her weight from one foot to the other as she practiced saying "Monsieur Directeur" in her best French. Promptly at two o'clock, Lebeau left. If ever anyone was misnamed, she thought crossly, it was that sour-faced man. Finally she heard more steps and peered out. A short man with a thick mustache and tiny goatee was striding energetically along, swinging a walking stick. The director.

Feeling like a wound-up spring, she stepped out into his path. He stopped, looking startled, and she tried the smile that hadn't influenced Lebeau. "Monsieur Director," she said carefully, "I am Mademoiselle Taylor. More than anything in the world I want to be in the Opéra chorus. If you would give me a chance to sing for you, I think—"

"Mademoiselle," he said in a tone that made Lebeau seem cordial, "I do not audition singers in hallways. I do not listen to them at all unless they are famous." His glance raked her and then dismissed her. "You, mademoiselle, are not."

With the barest nod to acknowledge that she was, if not a famous singer, a female, he swept past.

Humiliation and anger brought waves of heat to Sarah's face as she followed slowly, so that she wouldn't run into him again. The anger was directed at him, but also at herself. How foolish she had been to dream of singing at the Paris Opéra. No, not foolish to dream, but thinking that she could achieve such a fantasy without years of experience was believing in a fairy tale. It was time for her to be realistic. At home everything had come to her easily—too easily—because of Papa. But she wouldn't think of him. That was too painful.

As she began to feel calmer, her resolution strengthened. She *would* have a singing career, and she would begin here in Paris. The question was how to get a start.

Outside, she stopped again on the steps of the Théâtre de l'Opéra and looked up. The domed building towered above her like a huge, tiered cake, decorated by a committee of bakers who had quarreled about whether they wanted it to look Greek or Roman. Though completed after the Germans and Parisians together had sent Napoleon III into exile, the style recalled the gaudy brilliance of the Second Empire. Apollo played his lyre on the pediments of the second-story columns, while from each corner a winged Pegasus struggled to lift his stone body. On the facades, marble musicians, poets and playwrights competed with the dancers who had scandalized some Parisians and delighted others by their voluptuous vulgarity.

Sarah knew that studying the architecture of the building again was only an excuse for delay. Reluctantly she decided to set aside her pride and look for the only person she knew in Paris. Ted Kearns was more like an uncle than a family friend, and maybe he could give her advice. She fished out of her purse the address of the Crédit Lyonnais, the bank where Ted received his mail from home.

As she walked along the Boulevard des Italiens toward number fifteen, her spirits revived. Though the sounds of cracking whips and shouting drivers and the smells from horses could be Boston, the wide, tree-lined boulevard with tables in front of cafés presented a new and different charm. Just being in Paris was an adventure.

The foyer of the Crédit Lyonnais looked like a ballroom, with tapestries and a high, decorated ceiling. When she asked to see the manager, she was shown to a room that she recognized as a bank. The man who came out from behind the cages had a thin mustache and a smile to match. He did deign to speak English and was more gracious than Lebeau, but no more helpful. "I'm sorry, Miss Taylor. We do not provide addresses. If you wish to leave a message, we can give it to Mr. Kearns when he calls for his mail."

She smiled at him hopefully. "That could be several days, or longer. It's important I reach him soon."

The agent's veneer of courtesy thinned. "No, we cannot help you." This time he didn't say he was sorry.

Sarah sighed and sat down at a small desk to write a note. As she finished and rose, a young woman in the white shirtwaist and plain skirt of a clerk came past, carrying a box filled with envelopes. She stumbled beside Sarah's chair, and the box slipped sideways. Its contents scattered over the floor. Sarah crouched down beside the clerk and started gathering up envelopes.

The manager hurried over. "Miss Taylor, that's not necessary." He turned to the clerk, and his face became cruel with anger. "Mademoiselle Floret," he hissed in French, "you are stupid and clumsy. We will not need you in this office any longer."

Sarah couldn't stand the young clerk's stricken face. She put her hand on the angry man's arm. "Oh, no, please. It wasn't her fault. I bumped into her as I was getting up, so I am to blame." He made a shift to amiability and accepted Sarah's apology, but she was glad to leave her note with him and depart.

Halfway along the boulevard she heard a breathless voice saying, "Mademoiselle," and turned to find the young woman clerk. "Thank you," the clerk said shyly, "for helping me. Mr. Kearns lives at seventeen Rue Boursault."

She was gone before Sarah could say thank you in return.

Hansom cabs, as well as larger, more elegant carriages, rattled past along the Boulevard des Italiens. Empty cabs waited at the fiacre stand in a nearby square—not a square, Sarah reminded herself—a *place*. She would have liked to hire a cabriolet and ride in the open air, lounging elegantly under a lace-trimmed parasol. But she didn't have a parasol, and just that morning she had realized how fast her money was disappearing—too fast to consider frivolities.

At the first place in line, a gray horse stood patiently between the shafts of a black hansom cab. The driver lounged beside the cab, pipe smoke curling up under the edge of his worn cap. Sarah chose him and told him the address.

He helped her in, climbed onto his perch behind the cab, and they started off. After rattling along the Rue de Rome and the Boulevard de Batignolles through increasingly shabby neighborhoods, they turned off into a narrow street. The cab splashed through a puddle of water the origin of which Sarah didn't want to guess and stopped in front of an ancient six-story building.

The driver opened the small trap door in the roof and called down, "Here you are." After he yanked on the creaking pulley to open her door, she stepped out and handed up the fare.

Until a few weeks previously, Sarah had lived in a cocoon of Boston wealth. Looking around, she felt distinctly out of place. Could the cab driver have misunderstood her schoolroom French? She turned to him where he sat on his perch, relighting his pipe. "Are you sure this is the right address?" she asked.

He took the pipe out of his mouth long enough to say, "Seventeen Rue Boursault."

Sarah looked back at the building. Below each iron window grating, rust stains dripped down pock-marked stone walls. Would any friend of her father's, even Ted Kearns, live in this dingy place? The question pricked at the wrapping she kept on her emotions, reminding her how little she knew her father, and threatening to call up feelings of betrayal.

Three young men in rough jackets and black knitted caps sauntered toward her along the narrow, brick-paved street. As they passed, they watched Sarah with insolent curiosity and made laughing remarks to each other. Across the way a shopkeeper rearranged a box of pale green pears and chased off a ragged boy. Two women whose gaudy dresses and painted faces suggested their occupation strolled past. A woman leaned out from an upstairs window in the next building and screamed, *"Ordure!"* at a man coming out the entrance. He raised his finger in an obscene gesture before stomping away.

The cab driver still hadn't driven on. He glanced around and then at Sarah, as if comparing her youth and expensive clothing to the bleak surroundings. "You sure you don't want me to wait?" he asked.

Sarah wavered. In this unfamiliar section even the indif-

ferent cab driver seemed like a friend. He could return her
to the world of hotels with linen tablecloths, and silver bud
vases that flaunted out-of-season roses. But she reminded
herself of a time when a school friend had promised an older
brother to take a message to an entertainer he was pursuing.
The other girl and Sarah escaped from school and delivered
the note at an address in a poor section of Boston. The
neighborhood had looked worse than this, enough to make
the excursion an exciting combination of fear and daring,
but nothing dangerous had happened. Nothing would happen now. Besides, Sarah couldn't afford to be timid; her
money was going too fast. If Ted weren't here, she could
surely find another cab.

"No, thank you," she told the cab driver, "don't wait."

Lifting her skirt, she pushed open the rusty gate into a
small courtyard where a single nondescript tree drooped
beside a well. On the other side was a weathered door. Inside
the entrance hall she searched for a name plate marked
portier or *concierge*, but there were only anonymous numbers
on the doors on either side and a narrow stairway ascending
to a dark landing. As she hesitated, a boy carrying a red ball
clattered down the stairs. "Excuse me," she said, enunciating
her French carefully. "Can you tell me where I can find
Monsieur Kearns?"

The boy stopped, considering, and asked, "What does he
look like?"

"He's American. Tall, very thin."

"With glasses?" The boy didn't wait for her agreement.
"The fifth floor. Third room on the left."

"Merci," she said, but he had already dashed past. She
heard his ball bounce on the stones of the courtyard as the
door banged behind him.

She started up the stairs. On each floor a little light seeped
through a grimy window on the street side; in between, the

stairwell was so dark she had to feel her way upward. Several times she stumbled over litter, and the odors of stale cooking and too many inhabitants surrounded her. By the time she reached the fifth floor, she couldn't believe she would find Ted there. Another thought occurred to her: the building hardly looked like the kind of place where the tenants kept servants. She had assumed there would be servants to chaperon her.

Stop it! she told herself. This was Paris, not Boston. There were more important concerns than worrying about the propriety of being alone in a man's living quarters. She was going to be an opera singer!

The door the boy had indicated was brown, with a darker brown splatter at the bottom, as if someone had spilled soup in front of it. Before Sarah could knock, she heard an unfamiliar male voice from inside. Hurriedly she retreated a few steps down the stairwell. The door opened, and a man came out. It wasn't Ted. This man was young and not quite as tall, with wavy brown hair and a mustache. His expensive-looking gray suit appeared reassuringly more respectable than the clothes of the people on the street.

He paused, looking back into the room, and said, "You don't have to hurry about returning the books."

A man, still inside, said, "I've been wanting to read the new Zola and the de Maupassant. Thank you, Pierre."

It was Ted's voice. Relief eased Sarah's grip on her purse. As the visitor walked toward the steps, Ted appeared briefly in the doorway. Looking up through the iron bannister, Sarah could see his tall, thin figure, graying hair and thick glasses, all comfortingly familiar. He called, "Good-bye," and went back inside.

Sarah started up the stairs just as Ted's visitor started down. She hesitated, and he stopped, looking surprised, as if her being on those stairs were somehow inappropriate. "Excuse me, mademoiselle, can I help you?"

"No," she said, "I'm just going to see Mr. Kearns." She was flustered that she had explained anything to a stranger.

His eyebrows raised in a momentary look of surprise. "You are almost there," he said politely and bowed, then continued down the stairs.

She went on up to the hallway and gave herself a moment to calm down, then knocked on Ted's door. When it opened, she said, "Hello, Ted."

Ted Kearns had fled a career in a family-owned Boston bank years before for Paris, where many things delighted him and few surprised him. But now he was astounded. It wasn't possible, he thought, and yet—the red-gold hair and unwavering hazel eyes, the dusting of freckles on the straight nose, the stubborn mouth. "Sarah? Sarah Taylor?"

"Yes." She held out her gloved hand. "Oh, Ted, I'm so glad to find you."

He recovered and took her hand, drawing her inside. "I'm delighted to see you, but I'm astonished. I had no idea you and your father were in Paris." He glanced back at the empty hall. "Where is Josiah?"

"Papa's not here."

"He let you come through the city to find me by yourself?"

Sarah looked down and smoothed a nonexistent wrinkle in her gloves. "Papa didn't come to France," she said. "I'm alone."

"Alone!" Ted couldn't keep the shock from his voice. Josiah Taylor, allowing his precious daughter out of his reach!

She looked up again. "He doesn't know I'm here, and I don't want him to know." Her face flushed and her chin lifted defiantly. "I want to be on my own."

Something was obviously wrong. Uncertainly he said, "But, your father will worry."

"Please, Ted, don't say any more, even though Papa is your friend. This is my decision. You've always treated me like a grown-up, and now I am."

Sarah waited, watching while Ted frowned, took off his glasses, pulled out a handkerchief and polished them. His sandy hair had receded, giving him a perpetually thoughtful look. Finally he settled his glasses back on his bony nose and smiled at her. "Very well, Sarah. Now please sit down and tell me what you've been doing."

In her relief she could look around while she removed her hat and gloves. The room was large. An upholstered sofa, round table, and three wooden chairs filled one end. A partly pulled drapery separated a washstand, bed, and wardrobe from the rest of the room. Lace curtains billowed gently in the breeze from a large window. The books she expected to see sat in precise order on a bookcase beside the door. Above them hung a startling painting of a nude woman sitting on a gold chaise, having her hair combed by a maid.

Sarah sat on the sofa where she wouldn't be distracted by the painting. Ted pulled up a chair across from her. "How long have you been in Paris," he asked, "and how did you find me?"

"I've been here two weeks. A woman who works at the Crédit Lyonnais told me your address."

Ted sighed. "They're not supposed to give out information, but you always could charm people into doing what you want. Of course I'm glad she did," he added. Sarah wasn't quite sure he meant it.

"Why did you choose to come to Paris?" he asked.

"Because I've always wanted to sing in opera. I can speak French but not Italian, so Paris seemed the best choice."

"Surely you're not thinking of the Paris Opéra?" He frowned. "It takes years of training and experience for a place there."

She wasn't ready to admit that her failures had already taught her he was right. "Maybe not the Opéra, but in a chorus somewhere. I've had a voice teacher since I was twelve, and I've done lots of singing at home. Don't you remember the stage that Papa had built in the ballroom? I performed there often. And since your visit last year, I've sung in regular auditoriums for three charity benefits. People paid to hear me."

Sarah's determined expression dismayed Ted. He hated to discourage her, but he really must. She had always been so confident and happy—a lively little girl grown into an impulsive, enchanting young woman. A little hot tempered, perhaps, but with a generous spirit. Still, all her life she'd been sheltered by her father and his money. Regardless of how painful it would be, she'd be better off returning to Boston. "Sarah, singing in your home or even for benefit concerts is not like performing in a real theater. And you know nothing about France."

Her chin lifted in the stubborn way he remembered. "I can learn, and I'll find a way to get experience in a real theater."

A trace of uncertainty in her eyes contradicted the confidence in her face, and he weakened. Giving himself time to think, he rose and went to the window where the curtain billowed out in the breeze. He pulled the window halfway shut and stood a moment. He had a few theater connections; he could help her. If he did, would he be taking responsibility for what might happen to her? She should go home, but he had no way to make her. Obviously she wouldn't do what he advised. Josiah wouldn't like his helping Sarah, but he felt more concern for her than for her father.

Reluctantly he returned to his chair. "I do know the director at the Opéra Comique. If you're really determined to stay, I could introduce you to him," he said, and groaned to himself. He was taking on the role of a father, something he'd scrupulously avoided.

"Oh, Ted. Thank you."

"The Opéra Comique isn't the Paris Opéra," he warned.

"Oh, yes. I know that. But it's next best." She laughed in delight. "Some of my favorite operas had their openings there—*Carmen*, and *Manon*. And *Tales of Hoffman*. I especially love that."

"Well, I suppose it's all right, as long as you know what you're getting into."

"I won't depend on you for anything but the introduction. I can take care of myself."

He felt both relieved and piqued that his fatherhood had lasted such a brief time. "Could I take you somewhere for tea?" he asked.

"Thank you, but I'll go back to my hotel."

"I'll escort you. Where are you staying?"

She hesitated, then said, "The Hotel Valois. It was highly recommended by a woman on the ship coming over."

"The Valois!" He almost winced. "Sarah, that's one of the most expensive hotels in Paris. And I suppose you had a first-class passage on the best ship from Boston to Le Havre and tipped everyone too much. Do you pay any attention to money?"

Sarah felt a surge of anger and guilt, a combination that her fair skin never let her conceal. "I went to New York and sailed from there," she said, knowing it was not a defense but wanting to correct him on the only thing he'd gotten wrong.

Ted made a gesture that encompassed his room, the building, the neighborhood. "Why do you think I live here?"

"I wondered," she was annoyed enough to say.

"It's cheap, and this way I've been able to have my trips to Boston and still live in Paris all these years without a job."

After her protestations that she was grown up, it would be too humiliating to let him know how foolish she had been. "Grandmother left me some money on my twenty-first birthday."

"Your father's always provided for you," he said in an

exasperated voice, "but you'll find it's different on your own. Your grandmother's money won't last forever. You really should go home and try to make a career there where you'll have more security."

Sarah stood up and picked up her gloves and hat. Ted rose also. She jammed her hat on top of her piled-up hair, thrust the hatpin in and jerked on her gloves. "I will earn money myself."

He looked taken aback at her tone, and she felt contrite. "I'm sorry, Ted, for snapping at you. I'm very grateful that you're going to introduce me to someone at the Opéra Comique. You're a good friend, and I know you're saying what you think is best. It's just that . . ." She stopped. She couldn't talk about Papa.

Someone gave two sharp knocks on the door, and a man's voice said in French, "Monsieur Kearns? Are you there?"

Ted took his watch out of his pocket and looked at it. He called, "Just a minute," then said to Sarah, "Would you please excuse me for a short while? That's an artist who lives upstairs. I forgot that I promised him I'd look at his new painting. He wants me to help him decide whether he's asking the right price. I won't be long."

"Of course. I don't mind waiting."

After Ted left she walked to the single window and looked out. Far below were railroad yards. Whistles blared and faded as trains entered a tunnel beside a station. Ted's room was more pleasant than she'd expected, but a curious place for someone with elegant tastes to live. Still, it wasn't fair to be critical of Ted's choice. After all, she didn't want anyone ever again to decide what she did or where she lived. Her father had done that for too many years. Yet, without a way to earn money, she was beginning to realize, she didn't have as much freedom as she thought.

But she would *not* be discouraged. She'd make the most

of Ted's introduction and find an inexpensive place to live.

Ted returned, interrupting her thoughts. "That's taken care of," he said. "I'm sorry to keep you waiting. We can leave as soon as I change my jacket."

He went to the wardrobe and took out his jacket. As the door swung back, Sarah glimpsed the ruffled edge of a garment, pale orange and filmy—certainly not a man's clothing. Ted pulled on his coat, but before he closed the wardrobe door, she also saw a flash of a red silk skirt.

Startled, she turned away so that he wouldn't see her staring and was facing the painting of the naked woman— so different from anything in his family's Boston home. Though she'd known Ted all her life and called him Uncle Ted when she was a child, now she felt confused. Still, she reminded herself, he was her father's age. And she certainly hadn't known what Papa was really like.

In spite of her uncomfortable feelings, Ted's hand was pleasant under her arm as they descended the dingy staircase. She wondered whether she would have to live someplace like this. The thought made her uneasy. To prove that it didn't really bother her, she insisted on letting him walk with her only as far as the Boulevard de Batignolles where he hailed a cab.

When she was settled in the cab, he said, "I'll come around to the hotel tomorrow afternoon and take you to meet my friend."

"Thank you," she said, and waved good-bye.

As the cab made its way along the boulevard, she thought about Ted's admonitions concerning money. First thing the next morning, she would look for somewhere else to live. When he arrived at the hotel, she could tell him, she was moving and—

No! She sat up straight, dismayed. She'd sworn she would be on her own, accountable only to herself. Yet here she was, about to substitute Ted Kearns for Papa.

Papa. The word pulled at her, summoning vivid images of a July night in Boston that she wanted to forget and couldn't.

CHAPTER
TWO

I T SEEMED TO SARAH, REMEMBERING, THAT EVERYTHING HAD gone wrong that warm night in late July. She had been spending a week with her friend, Jane Morrison, at the Morrisons' cottage on Cape Cod. On Wednesday evening, Jane suddenly became ill with a fever and sore throat.

"Sarah," Jane's mother said, her plump face worried, "you must return to Boston."

"But, Mrs. Morrison," Sarah protested, "I want to help take care of Jane."

"No. I'll have enough help here. Lawrence will take you home. There's been diphtheria in the village, and I don't want either of you staying here longer."

So Sarah left with Lawrence, Jane's older brother, driving the family carriage. They had been underway for only a short time when Sarah noticed a certain carelessness in his handling of the matched bays. In the light of the two coach lanterns his fair skin looked flushed and his grin somewhat silly. "Lawrence," she said, "did you spend the afternoon at the Thirsty Sailor?"

He laughed. "Yes, but don't worry. I can handle horses

better after a few whiskeys than when I'm sober."

Sarah, gripping the side rail and the edge of the seat, chose not to comment. It seemed like a long ride until they finally turned into Boutwell Street, deserted and quiet. Sarah guessed that it was well after midnight. Lawrence pulled up the horses, but he didn't get out to come around and help her down.

A little surprised, she said, "Thank you for bringing me home. Please let me know as soon as you hear how Jane is feeling."

As she started to open the door, Lawrence grasped her shoulders, pulling her clumsily toward him. His mustached mouth, smelling disagreeably of stale alcohol, landed on one corner of hers. She wrenched herself back. "Lawrence, stop it!"

"Oh, come on now." He had hold of her arm, trapping her in the carriage. "Just a kiss or two."

When men tried to kiss her, she usually teased them out of it. Or kissed them if she felt like it. A drunken kiss had no appeal. "No! Let me go."

He struggled with her, holding her against the seat, and laughing as if it were a game they'd agreed to play. For a panicky moment she felt his weight bearing her down before she managed to dig an elbow into his side and break away. The door wouldn't open under her hasty fingers, and an involuntary "Damn!" escaped her. It finally gave, and she scrambled down. She started angrily along the path to the dark house when she remembered her portmanteau and turned back.

Lawrence was sitting, looking down at her. "May I have my bag please?" she said stiffly.

"I don't see why you pretend to be so innocent and prudish," he grumbled. "I know you and Jane looked at all my *Pearl* magazines and my pictures from Cuba. She admitted it when I caught her putting them back."

Sarah was glad it was too dark for him to see the wave of red color that filled her face. It had been several months since she and Jane had read with shocked fascination the stories and looked at the pictures, but she still remembered the details. "I'm certainly not prudish," she said hotly. "That doesn't mean I want to kiss you. If Papa knew about this, he'd be furious."

"You'd never be kissed if he could help it. Josiah Taylor doesn't like any man who's not decrepit even talking to you." He leaned down a little unsteadily and pronounced judgment. "You're just like a canary, singing for your supper. If you don't get out of that cage he keeps you in, you'll end up an old maid."

A canary in a cage! How dare Lawrence Morrison say something so ridiculous! "I don't intend to stand here arguing with you when you're drunk," she snapped. "Will you please hand down my bag?"

For a moment she thought she would have to climb back up and get it herself, but he reached behind him and picked up her portmanteau. When he got out, she stepped back warily, but he set it down in front of her and resumed his place in the carriage. Finally he clucked the horses into motion, and the jingle of the harness and clop of the horses hooves faded into the hushed night.

Taking deep breaths to calm her anger, Sarah looked at the dark house. No lights had come on in any of the rooms of the three-story mansion. At least the quarrel with Lawrence hadn't waked Papa or the servants. She picked up her bag and walked up the curving path to the covered front porch. After easing open the heavy oak door, she tiptoed through the entrance hall and set her bag in a corner to retrieve the next morning.

As she passed the open double doors into the parlor, she noticed moonlight slanting across the portrait of her and her mother, hanging on the wall behind the square grand piano. It had been finished for Sarah's tenth birthday, just a few months before her mother died. Sarah stopped, looking at the painting. If Mama had lived, she could have explained about the pictures Sarah and Jane had looked at with such tingling excitement, matching them with the giggled conversations of the "fast" girls at school. And tonight there would be someone to tell about the unpleasant scene with Lawrence. The wish called up a sadness and loss that Sarah thought had faded away.

In the silent darkness, she felt almost like the grieving child of ten. Every night then she'd gone to her mother's room and climbed into the empty bed, finding comfort in the scent of her mother's clothes and perfumes. Sometimes she had heard her father in his room next door, sobbing the grief he didn't express in front of others. It had been a frightening, needful sound that she couldn't acknowledge except by being a loving daughter during the days.

In the years since, he had made her feel loved and special, encouraging her singing and arranging performances. Often he'd told her that he could endure the loss of his wife because she so much resembled her mother. Believing this literally, Sarah had waited for years to find the same oval face in her mirror as in the portrait. But she had her father's hazel eyes. Except for the red-gold hair, Sarah looked more and more like her father, her nose too straight and her jaw too determined for her mother's soft beauty.

The importance of his wife's memory hadn't faded for Josiah. Five years previously Mabel Hewes, a widowed distant cousin, had come to replace a series of unsatisfactory housekeepers. Sarah had thought that her mother's dresses should be given to Mabel. The silks and ruffles didn't really suit Cousin Mabel; she was thin and pale, like a withered flower, but she had few clothes of her own. When Sarah suggested the gift, Josiah's face had whitened and his eyes grown cold. His "No" had been charged with an anger that she still remembered.

After a last look at the portrait, Sarah slipped off her shoes and started noiselessly up the stairs. As she passed her mother's room, she stopped and impulsively went in. Silver-backed brushes lay on the dressing table, along with cut crystal flagons in which the perfume had shrunk to an amber stain in the bottom. Out-of-fashion clothes with faded streaks along the outside edges still hung in the wardrobe, ghostly reminders.

Sarah sat on the bed where the moonlight slid past the draperies at the window, but the room didn't bring her mother any closer. It had been too long. She stood up, embarrassed by the impulse that had brought her here, and heard a sound—a soft cry—coming from her father's room. For a moment it seemed, like the dresses, a ghost from the past. She was listening again to his sobbing.

No—that couldn't be. But Papa could be crying out in a dream—or he might be ill. Alarmed, Sarah tiptoed quickly to the door of his adjoining room. She grasped the knob gently so as to turn it without making a sound and eased the door open. Through the crack she could see the bed clearly, with the moonlight falling on her father's dark hair. He appeared to be collapsed, face down. Her fear growing, she started to push the door open farther when he rolled over, and lay on his back. In the moonlight she saw another face beside his. It was Cousin Mabel.

Sarah stood, her hand frozen on the edge of the door. Josiah turned again, the blanket crumpled around his bare shoulders, facing away from Sarah. Cousin Mabel looked across, directly at her.

A cry stifled in Sarah's throat. She turned and fled, back past the betrayed symbols of her mother and along the hall to the sanctuary of her own room.

She stumbled to her bed and sat down, clutching the scrolled post that held the canopy. The image of the two heads repeated in her mind, like reflections in facing mirrors.

They became mixed with images from Lawrence's pictures.

Papa with Cousin Mabel! How could such a thing have happened? Cousin Mabel must have gone into his room and begged him, and he wasn't strong enough to refuse. No— that explanation didn't fit. Cousin Mabel was timid, and Papa wasn't a weak man.

Sarah lay back, trying to sort out her turmoil. It was the hypocrisy that enraged her so much, she told herself, not jealousy. No—it was jealousy, too. She couldn't pretend it wasn't. But most of all she felt betrayed. While her father had kept up his pretense of grief-stricken love, secretly he'd replaced her mother.

Soft footsteps sounded in the hall, coming toward her room, and then a tap on her door. She recognized the steps and delicate knock—Cousin Mabel.

Sarah gripped the bedspread in tight knots. Her first impulse was to keep silent, to avoid speaking. But a feather of hope put her on her feet. Maybe, in spite of what she'd seen, she was mistaken. The urge to know warred with the fear of knowing. She lit a candle and went to the door.

Cousin Mabel looked all gray—her robe, braided hair and unhappy face. She advanced with hesitant steps, holding the robe tightly around her, like a shield. Sarah closed the door, and she and Mabel stared at each other, the only sound the agitated chorus of their breathing.

"I must talk to you," Mabel said in a shaky whisper. "I want to explain, make you understand."

So it was true. There was no mistake. Sarah's confusion boiled up, tumbling out her accusing thoughts. "How can you take my mother's place?"

Mabel put out a supplicating hand. "Please don't say that. I'm sorry you're so upset. I told Josiah that someday you would find out."

"Someday! What do you mean?" Even as Sarah asked, she understood, and her throat felt so choked she couldn't ask the next question.

Her eyes downcast, Mabel answered anyway in her timid whisper. "It started years ago, soon after I came here." She looked up. "But Josiah doesn't know you saw us. He always goes to sleep right away."

The intimacy of that "always" made what Sarah had seen more real than the evidence of her eyes.

In spite of her distress, Sarah's sympathies were moved by the older woman's sad face. And her own thoughts were becoming clearer. She took Mabel's cold hands in hers. "I have to talk to Papa. This isn't right. Papa and you should marry."

"Oh, no." Mabel's expression became agitated. "It's out of the question. Josiah would never agree."

"Do you love Papa and want to marry him?"

Tears glistened in the corners of Mabel's blue eyes, making them appear larger, pretty. "Yes."

"Well then. I'm going to talk to him. Tomorrow morning."

For an instant Mabel looked hopeful, but then she shook her head. "It won't do any good. You're the one he cares about. I'm happy enough this way." She loosened her hands from Sarah's and slipped out of the room.

After Sarah changed into her nightgown, she took down her hair and brushed it, hoping the familiar routine would calm her. But when she was in bed, questions still whirled painfully in her mind. Everything she'd been taught, at the Unitarian church where she and Papa went together, in the private schools where he'd sent her, told her that it was wrong for a man and woman to lie together unless they were married. She remembered when the widowed mother of a friend was discovered having an "intimate connection" with a man. The family had to move away because of the scandal.

And what about her? Had Lawrence been right? Had her father's love been a silk cage, keeping her happily at home? Then that love had imprisoned him as well, keeping him from remarrying. For all their sakes, she must find out.

Finally she dozed, dipping into sleep so lightly that the first stirring of the servants downstairs waked her. Before she could waver, she dressed quickly and went to her father's room. Her anger toward him had shrunk to a knot of nausea, and she wasn't sure whether her voice would work. Then the image of two pillowed heads sent her hand up to knock on his door.

Josiah opened it as he was pulling on a dark jacket. He stopped, his hand in one sleeve. "Sarah! What's happened? Why are you home?"

"Jane got sick yesterday, and Mrs. Morrison had Lawrence bring me home last night."

He shrugged into his jacket, his dark eyebrows coming together in a distressed frown. "Are you feeling all right? Is it something contagious? Why didn't you wake me?"

His question strengthened the resolution she needed. If she'd roused the house, he'd have had to get Cousin Mabel out of his room in a hurry. Maybe he'd had lots of practice doing that. "I'd like to talk to you, Papa. Could you come outside to the gazebo?"

Josiah's face changed, became wary, uncertain—an expression she'd never seen before. Without waiting, she fled downstairs and outside, across the dew-wet lawn. When he followed her to the white-latticed building, she faced him, too tense to sit down. She really wanted to scream, but she kept her voice low so no one else would hear. "I went into Mama's room last night and looked into yours. I saw you and Cousin Mabel."

He sucked in his breath, and his mustache flattened over his compressed mouth. "What are you talking about? You must have been dreaming."

"I wasn't dreaming. I know what I saw."

His face flushed red, and he responded defensively, in the lecturing way he used when he was upset. "You don't understand. You're thinking this reflects on the memory of your mother. But it has nothing to do with her."

"I'm not thinking of Mama. It's you and Cousin Mabel. You must marry her."

The muscles of his jaw stretched tight, but his voice was still controlled. "Your mother will always be my wife. Anything between me and Mabel is not your concern."

"If you'd married Cousin Mabel," she cried, "I would have understood and respected you. But not this way." She knew her words were cruel, but in her pain she wanted them to be.

He reacted with the fierce anger she'd seen directed at others but never before at her. "I didn't marry Mabel because of you. The way you idolized your mother, it would have upset you too much."

"That's not so! *You* made memories of Mama sacred. Partly to keep me here." Her own words were revealing a reality to her she must have known but hadn't acknowledged. "That's why you made fun of all the boys I was in love with."

He pointed his finger at her. "And you didn't object. Being *in love* never lasted very long. You didn't want to leave me for any of them."

The truth was as sharp as the shard of a crystal goblet she'd once broken. Then, her finger had been pierced; this time the blood didn't show, but it was there. Though she still wasn't sure how she felt, she knew what she had to do. She clenched her hands to keep them from trembling and said with all the force she could put into her shaky voice, "I'm leaving. Today. I'm going to make my own way, as a singer."

"You'll find out it isn't easy when I'm not providing the audience," he said furiously.

Those words released her, to run to the house where the servants' faces hastily disappeared behind window curtains. She spent the rest of the morning sorting the possessions she would take with her and reassuring herself she was doing the right thing. Anger carried her along, letting her ignore the pain underneath.

While she was packing, Cousin Mabel came to the bedroom. "Sarah," she said diffidently, "are you sure this is wise? Josiah is very upset and angry. I don't want to cause any trouble."

"I don't know whether I'm being wise. But you were right about Papa. If I go, he'll likely change his mind about marrying you. You must make him." Sarah gave Mabel a hug and hoped that this faded woman could manage.

An hour later Sarah left in a cab without seeing her father again. She went to the Morrisons', explaining candidly that she and Josiah had quarreled, though not why. Mr. Morrison, with the little attention he spared from his business, welcomed her, and the housekeeper clucked over her. For the next two weeks she stayed there, waiting for news of Jane and making plans.

During the days she was busy, saying good-bye to her friends and her voice teacher, withdrawing her money from the bank, and making travel arrangements. But the nights were painful. At times when nothing seemed important enough for the estrangement from her father, tearfully she would decide to go home. But in the morning, her resolution was strengthened by pride and the belief that for all their sakes she must make her own way.

Lawrence was an unintentional help. He didn't refer to their disagreement the night he'd taken her home, and he treated her respectfully, but occasionally he looked at her with a sly knowledge. One day at the end of the first week he stopped her in the hall. "Jane's going to be all right," he said. "She didn't have diphtheria after all."

"I'm so relieved!"

"What are you going to do now?" he asked too innocently. "Have you heard from your father?"

She could feel a revealing flush. "No, and I don't expect to."

"I guess he thinks you'll change your mind."

She looked at Lawrence with an aloofness that wouldn't acknowledge his accuracy. "Papa knows I'm too much like him to give up when I decide something," she said.

So she had come to Paris—to her painful lessons at the Paris Opéra, and finally to see Ted Kearns.

The cab pulled up before the ornate iron railings at the entrance of the Hotel Valois, interrupting Sarah's memories. She decided that she would accept this one favor from Ted, and that would be all.

As she descended from the cab, a woman wearing a ruffled blue dress came out of the hotel. Sarah thought of the gowns hiding slyly among Ted's suits and shirts. Did all men conceal something about themselves? Very well. Here in Paris she, too, could have a secret life.

CHAPTER THREE

I N 1888 WHEN SARAH ARRIVED IN PARIS, NEARLY THIRTY bridges spanned the Seine River. Many of their names memorialized French history: the Pont d'Austerlitz celebrated Napoleon I's great victory over the Germans and Russians; a roll of the officers who died in the battle was inscribed on ornamental plaques hung along the outside. The bridges named for Louis Philippe and Napoleon III honored the last Bourbon king and the man who replaced him.

The Pont au Change, which Sarah and Ted were crossing to reach the Opéra Comique, had been named, he was explaining, for the money changers who set up their shops on the bridge during the Middle Ages. "An Italian performer once strung a high wire between Notre Dame Cathedral and a house here. When the new French queen was riding across, he slid down and put a crown on her head."

Ordinarily Sarah would have listened with fascination, but her thoughts were on the interview ahead and the impression she hoped to make. Would she be able to choose what she sang for an audition? If not, would she know the piece the manager chose? A breeze pulled a strand of hair from her chignon, and nervously she patted it back into place. That morning she had put on three different dresses before she settled on a light blue walking suit. The jacket had midnight blue velvet cuffs that matched the velvet ribbon around the high collar of her lace blouse. Her skirt pulled tight across the front to a side drape but didn't have the bustle that stood out like a shelf in back. She hoped her outfit was the proper combination of fashion and restraint.

They arrived at the Place du Châtelet. Two theaters faced the square. Ted gestured toward four marble figures grouped around an ugly fountain in the center. "The statues commemorate the first victories of Napoleon I." Sarah's lack of attention didn't prevent him from continuing enthusiastically, "The Théâtre du Châtelet just ahead is on the site of the Grand Châtelet prison. Prisoners were taken there to be questioned by means of torture."

Suddenly Sarah was listening. "Torture?"

"Yes. The screams could be heard across the bridge. The Question Ordinary came first. The jailers put a funnel in the prisoner's mouth and poured gallons of water down it. If that didn't work, the Question Extraordinary—"

"Please," she interrupted, "just tell me—is the Opéra Comique in that theater?"

"No, the Opéra Comique is using the Théâtre des Nations. But that's only its temporary home. The regular theater burned last year." He gave her a doubtful look. "You're a little pale, Sarah. Are you all right?"

"I'm hoping to work in a theater, which is in a square famous for torturing prisoners. The company just moved from a building destroyed by a fire. I'm not superstitious, but you aren't making me feel calmer."

Ted laughed and took her arm as they went up the steps of the Théâtre des Nations.

The lobby was much simpler and smaller than the Opéra,

but it had its crystal chandelier hanging above red-carpeted stairs. Ted escorted Sarah around the stairs and along a narrow passageway that was lined with bilious yellow doors. He knocked on the last one.

Don't be nervous, Sarah admonished herself. *Be charming and confident, and speak your best French.*

"*Entrez*," someone inside called out.

Ted opened the door and let Sarah precede him. A bespectacled man who looked about fifty rose from behind a desk. He was bald, with white side whiskers that flared out in two great wings over his high collar and dark gray cravat. The whiskers reminded her of a friend's father, a Boston banker. Until Sarah learned not to stand too close to him, he used to pinch her bottom. A giggle rose in her throat. In stifling it, she lost some of her nervousness.

"Good afternoon, Monsieur Cesbron," Ted said in French that sounded flawless to Sarah. "I hope we're not interrupting something important."

Monsieur Cesbron smiled and came around the desk. "Ah, Monsieur Kearns. Every day is a crisis in the theater, but I am always pleased to see friends."

"Mademoiselle Taylor," Ted explained after the introductions, "has just come to Paris from the United States. She has a fine voice and hopes to sing professionally here. It would be a great favor to me if you would consider her for a place in the Opéra Comique chorus."

Monsieur Cesbron's eyebrows twitched upward behind his glasses, and he glanced from Ted to her and back to Ted. A worldly smile lifted his whiskers outward, as if he were about to take off in flight. "Of course. I cannot promise a position, Mademoiselle Taylor. We are supported by a subsidy from the French government, so our standards must be rigorous."

"Yes, I see," she said, nervously wondering whether it made a difference that she was American.

Apparently not, because he smiled jovially. "But I am delighted to audition any friend whom Monsieur Kearns recommends." His voice slid across the word "friend" with a delicate understanding.

While Ted expressed appreciation, Sarah decided, half-shocked and half-intrigued, that the manager assumed that she was Ted's mistress. As they walked along to the practice room, she considered this astounding idea. The prospect that she might be a mistress instead of a wife had never occurred to her. Still, this was Paris—a different life with different standards. Why should she be shocked?

Her speculations were sufficiently absorbing that Monsieur Cesbron was ushering her and Ted into a large empty room before she became thoroughly nervous again. The sight of the piano in one corner made her stomach do crazy whirls. As she lagged behind the two men, the narrow heels of her boots drummed on the polished hardwood floor like warnings to turn back. But she took a deep breath and ordered her stomach to settle down.

"What range do you sing, Mademoiselle Taylor?" Monsieur Cesbron asked.

"I'm a mezzo-soprano."

"Splendid. We happen to have need for the lower voices in the chorus just now. Do you know 'L'amour est un oiseau rebelle' from Carmen?"

Sarah smiled with relief. "Yes. I do." With the director accompanying her on the piano, she sang as if she were the fiery gypsy Carmen, flirting with the soldiers, taunting them that love is a rebellious bird no one can tame.

When she finished, Ted applauded. "That was lovely, Sarah," he said, with a hint of relief in his voice.

"Yes, your voice is pleasing," Monsieur Cesbron agreed, getting up from the piano, "and your accent is not too noticeable. You sang that music very well."

Tense with hope that his compliment meant an acceptance, Sarah managed to say, "My voice teacher in Boston admired Monsieur Bizet's operas. She had me learn all the arias."

Monsieur Cesbron smiled benevolently. "We will try you in the chorus." He made a little bow. "Doing a favor for my dear friend will also benefit the Opéra Comique."

Sarah could have whooped with exhilaration, but she managed to restrain herself to "Thank you, Monsieur Cesbron. I'm delighted with the opportunity." Though it was obvious from the artificial gallantry of his voice that the manager was hiring her because of her supposed connection with Ted, she felt sure no job would have been offered to a poor singer. And her French was bound to improve the longer she stayed in Paris.

Monsieur Cesbron pulled a gold watch from his waistcoat pocket and flipped open the lid. "I'm afraid I have an appointment, so I will have to excuse myself. Ordinarily I would ask you to dance for me, Mademoiselle Taylor, but you are a very graceful young woman. I assume you will have no trouble with the dance."

Dance! "Oh, no," she said hastily, her excitement dwindling. "No trouble."

"Well, then, it is settled. I will be busy tomorrow. Please come back day after tomorrow and we'll discuss the details."

After Ted expressed his appreciation and she reiterated her thanks, they left. As they emerged into the Place du Châtelet Ted said, "I didn't know you studied dance. I remember a story about something that happened when you were fifteen or sixteen. Didn't you want to take lessons from a teacher who trained dancers for the stage? And Josiah was upset."

"Yes. Papa was furious." She giggled at the memory. "President Hayes happened to be in Boston. Papa knew him, and he took me to see the president, who lectured me about how wicked dancers are."

"Did Josiah give in later and let you take lessons?"

"No, but two of my friends studied at a dance school. They showed me everything they learned. So I haven't had lessons or actually performed, but I'm sure I can." She hoped she sounded more confident than she felt.

She stopped and looked back at the Opéra Comique theater. The poster in front listed *Orphe aux Enfers* for the evening performance. "I know! *Orpheus in the Underworld* has lots of dancing. I'll go tonight and watch, then practice all the steps for the next two days."

Ted shook his head. "How can you expect to learn steps by watching?"

"I can if I have to. At least enough to get started. Actually, we once had a French maid. I badgered her until she taught me what she said was the cancan."

"Even if that would work, I wouldn't be able to take you tonight. And you can't go to the theater by yourself."

"Can't! Why not?" She didn't intend to give in to prohibitions that might interfere with her extraordinary chance at the Opéra Comique.

"Only women who . . . aren't respectable would go to the theater without an escort."

He meant only courtesans went alone. "But it's important to me to see the dances. And this is Paris. Surely things are freer here." She resisted the temptation to mention the female clothing in his wardrobe.

"You would very likely receive unpleasant overtures," he said stiffly.

Her determination to sing at the Opéra Comique wouldn't let her give in to the uncomfortable feeling in her stomach that he might be right. "I'm twenty-one years old. I've had practice discouraging 'unpleasant overtures' in Boston."

He shook his head again, but this time admiringly. "Yes. I believe you." He paused, and frowned again, as if weighing two choices and not quite approving of either. "There is another possibility. I'm to meet a friend at the Café d'Orsay. I had planned to leave you at your hotel first, but would you like to meet him? He might be free to escort you to the performance tonight."

She wavered, wanting to assert her independence, but not wishing to be ungrateful to Ted. Also, his hesitation in proposing the meeting intrigued her. "Yes, that would be fine."

As they walked across the Pont Royal toward the Quai d'Orsay, she asked, "Who is your friend?"

"His name is Pierre de Tourbey. He writes for several journals, including *Le Figaro* and *La Justice*, Clemenceau's journal."

"Who is Clemenceau?"

"One of the Republican leaders in the Chamber of Deputies." Again Ted paused. "French men aren't quite the same as the young Americans you're used to. Pierre says what he thinks most of the time."

"You mean," Sarah said, amused by Ted's discomfort, "he might make . . . an improper suggestion?"

"No, certainly not. Even if he were . . . interested in you, he would accept your refusal and not press you. You can absolutely trust his word."

Sarah laughed. "A candid suggestion might be better than silly looks and pinches in the dark." Besides, she planned to have lots of new experiences. But she didn't think Ted would care to hear that.

When they reached the Café d'Orsay, the man who rose from one of the sidewalk tables to greet them looked familiar. It was the visitor who had been leaving Ted's room the day before. Ted said to Sarah, "May I present Pierre de Tourbey? Pierre, this is Mademoiselle Taylor, from the United States."

Pierre de Tourbey looked twenty-eight or -nine. Though his elegant tan suit suggested he was a man of means, he had the broad shoulders and chest of a workman. His face didn't fit her image of either a gentleman or a worker. Short brown hair, parted on the side, had been smoothed on top, but it curled defiantly over his ears. He had a full mustache and clean-shaven square jaw, with a suggestion of cleft in his chin.

Pierre bowed over her hand. "*Enchanté*, Mademoiselle Taylor." Tiny lines about his vivid blue eyes and a faint quirk to his mouth looked as though he liked to laugh. It was a bold face.

"I am pleased to meet you," she responded. He was looking directly at her, but he gave no sign he remembered her.

They took chairs, and Ted began explaining about the evening.

Sitting across from Sarah, Pierre listened with half his attention. Could Mademoiselle Taylor, he wondered, be Ted's mistress? Hardly likely, but he could understand why a man might change his ways for this woman. That red-gold hair, the milky skin with a dusting of freckles, and those eyes with their direct look. The American accent that gave her French a sensuous sound. Most of all her mouth. So softly curved, with the lower lip slightly larger than the upper one, as though expecting a kiss. A man would do a lot for the promise of those lips.

When Ted finished, Pierre said, "I'd be delighted to escort Mademoiselle Taylor to the Opéra Comique this evening. Or anywhere she'd like to go."

"Mademoiselle Taylor," Ted said a little formally, "just wants to observe the Opéra Comique. She will be singing in the chorus there."

"I know someone who writes a gossip column," Pierre said. "I could give him a story about you, Mademoiselle Taylor. I could describe your beautiful eyes with a fascinating mixture of gray and green and brown. And your charming American accent. He'd be sure to write about you. It might help your career."

Sarah could feel the heat rise in her cheeks and knew

from the amused sparkle in his eyes that he noticed. The idea of seeing herself mentioned in the popular press revived the prohibitions of her upbringing. Even in the remarkable freedom of Paris, that was too much. "I prefer that no one writes about me. I'm sure I'll get along fine without that. I'm a good singer."

"Then I won't suggest it. I'm sure you do many things well." His expression challenged her to recognize what other things he might have in mind. She felt taken aback and at the same time intrigued.

Ted adjusted his glasses and pulled his shirt cuffs down with a snap, a sign Sarah recognized as meaning he was upset. She guessed he was reconsidering his reassurances to her about Pierre's character. Ted rose and said, "I think Mademoiselle Taylor and I must leave. Sarah, shall we go?"

"If she wishes to stay, I'll be happy to be her escort."

Despite, or perhaps because of Pierre's challenging glances, Sarah was having too good a time to leave. "Thank you, Ted, but I think I'll have coffee."

"Very well," Ted agreed, looking a little like a disapproving uncle. "I'll be coming by to find out how you're getting along."

"Good-bye, and thank you for everything."

Sarah watched him go, then looked back at Pierre. He smiled at her across the table, reviving her earlier sensation that they shared the same unchaste thoughts. "Now," he said, "we can get better acquainted. That was you on the stairs yesterday, wasn't it? Or don't you want me to mention it?"

"Yes, I was visiting him. Are you suggesting that was improper?" she challenged.

"No, not at all. I can't think of anything more pleasant than having you come up the stairs to my room."

In this man's room! Again a quiver of excitement skittered over her skin. Before she could decide how to respond, he asked, "How do you come to be in Paris?"

Uncertain how much she wanted to say, she parried, "First you tell me about yourself."

"Very simple. I write journal articles. I live modestly, though not quite so modestly as I would have to if I supported myself entirely by my literary talent. My parents, who are unfortunately dead now, saw to that. I love good friends, good food, good conversation, exciting ideas, and exciting women." His eyes boldly admired her, telling her he included her in that category. "I enjoy riding a bicycle too."

In spite of her desire to appear sophisticated and unruffled, she was a little shocked. According to standards of proper behavior, she should be insulted at his double meaning. But his easy manner disarmed and amused her, and she liked the feeling of being daring. "I think you also enjoy being provocative."

He laughed. "I'm found out immediately. It's true. I like to set things in motion and see what happens. Now tell me about you."

"I'm from Boston. It's different from France—more proper, I think. I sing, which is what I love to do best."

He made an exaggeratedly dismayed face. "But you've told me nothing. What else interests you?"

"I like all kinds of performances. My worst fault is that I want to be the star in everything. I like to do things I haven't done before."

"That's why you came to Paris?"

She hesitated a moment. "Yes, partly. I love to read, especially newspapers."

"Good. Writers love readers." His eyes seemed to be saying, I find you desirable, and I know we share the same improper thoughts. A quiver ran along her backbone, and she found that she was breathing more quickly.

She could feel a blush coming on. Then he smiled, and his look changed. Now the message was, Trust me, and she

relaxed, feeling as if she could safely say anything she wished
to him. "I'm fascinated by politics," she went on. "If I were
a man, I might go into government. Of course, I'd want to
be a star there too." She felt a little startled at herself for
confiding an interest many people would laugh at. Something about him reassured her that he wouldn't.

"To be a prime minister or president," he said, "you would
have to be a man. That would certainly be a shame."

Sarah had never wanted to be a man. This man made her
feel especially glad to be a woman. It was a slightly discon-
certing feeling.

The afternoon sun had slanted across the café until they
were sitting in shadow. Sarah thought of the time. "I must
go back to my hotel."

"I only forgive you for leaving because I'll be seeing you
this evening." Though he spoke lightly, she was sure he
meant it.

She was surprised how much the idea pleased her.

That evening when Sarah and Pierre were seated in a box
at the Opéra Comique, she saw why Ted had objected to
her attending alone. Unattached men congregated in the
stalls, the rows at the front of the auditorium. They stood
with their backs to the stage, calling up to the women without escorts and making loud comments to each other. The
women, sitting two or three to a box, responded with laughter. One woman in a crimson velvet dress tossed a note to
a tall, thin dandy with long hair worn in an eighteenth-
century queue. He made his way through the throng in the
orchestra and reappeared beside her in the box. The miniature scene was repeated, with more men moving to boxes.
When ushers turned down the gas lights and the orchestra
prepared to begin, other members of the audience had to
protest before the less successful patrons still in the stalls
finally quieted.

In the darkened house, Sarah found the intimacy of sitting beside Pierre both exciting and distracting. Then the music caught her up, and she felt as if she were singing with the performers. Several times the audience laughed at references she didn't understand. After one burst of laughter Pierre leaned his head close to hers. "When Offenbach wrote this piece," he whispered, "the gods and goddesses were parodies of Napoleon III and the members of his court. The Empress Eugenie was jealous of her husband's constant affairs, just as Juno is jealous of Jupiter. Parisians enjoy remembering any kind of scandal, even old ones."

"Yes, I see," she whispered, conscious of a spicy fragrance from something he used for shaving. It increased her feeling of knowing him better than seemed really proper.

Sarah drew her chair a little away, as if to see better, really so that she could concentrate on the dancing instead of him. Most of the dances appeared to have steps she could master quickly, except the cancan at the end. It was more active and revealing than the version of the dance she'd learned from her family's Boston maid. Sarah was sure she was agile enough to perform it, with practice. She was more uncertain about how she'd feel—displaying herself so boldly in ruffled petticoats and pantalettes! But other women did it. Only strangers would see her.

Pierre moved slightly, and she realized that he might come to a performance. The blush that embarrassed her so often spread across her skin. She was glad it was too dark for him to notice. What foolish thoughts! Ted had helped get her a chance others worked years to achieve. She must make the most of it, no matter what kind of dance she must do. And who might be watching.

After the performance, Pierre suggested a visit to a café, but she demurred. His company had unsettled her as much as she wanted for one day. She needed tonight's rest. In the morning she must look for a cheap place to live as well as practice dancing.

When Pierre left her in the hotel lobby, he bowed over her hand, then held it an intimate moment longer. "I still haven't learned much about you. Unfortunately I have to be away from Paris for several weeks. When I come back, we must do lots of things together so that I can discover your secrets."

Secrets again. She watched him leave, his evening cape swinging jauntily behind him with the force of his walk. As she went up the stairs to her room, she tried to sort out her reactions to Pierre. The invitation in his smile suggested he was less interested in secrets she already had than future ones that might include him. It also suggested life shouldn't be taken too seriously—that it should be enjoyed.

She lifted her skirts and ran up the stairs and along the corridor. Inside her room she discarded her cloak and whirled around, ending with an exuberant cancan kick. Paris! Anything could happen here.

CHAPTER FOUR

S ARAH STARED AT THE OPERA COMIQUE'S DIRECTOR, SEATED
behind his cluttered desk, and wondered if her French
was still faulty. She had been singing in the chorus for only
a month and now—

"You want me to sing Nicklausse in *Tales of Hoffman*?"
she asked.

"Only for the Tuesday and Thursday performances next
week, Mademoiselle Taylor, when our regular Nicklausse
will be away. You do know the part?"

"Oh, yes. I studied it with my singing teacher at home."
The trousers role of a young man was an important sec-
ondary part. Two performances to show what she could do!
And at the Opéra Comique, where the opera had its first
performance. Her luck seemed too astonishing to be real.
Sarah wanted to shout and twirl—to throw her arms around
the director.

She managed to restrain herself to "Thank you, Monsieur
Cesbron, for giving me this opportunity."

Color crept up Monsieur Cesbron's face until his white
side whiskers looked like the fringe on a pink flower. He

took off his glasses and polished them, then resettled them on his nose. "Monsieur Rivarol has noticed how well you sing and urged me to offer you this chance."

Sarah's grateful desire to embrace Monsieur Cesbron vanished. She didn't need perfect French to understand what he was saying. The current star tenor of the Opéra Comique had noticed her—but not for her singing.

She started to protest but stopped. Her joy surged up again. What did it matter if Rivarol had his own motives for promoting her? She knew she must be especially careful here because she didn't have the protection of family respectability. In the past month she'd teased three eager men from the chorus into being friends rather than zealous pursuers. Though keeping Rivarol at bay would be more difficult, with care and tact she could still take advantage of this miraculous opportunity.

"Of course," Monsieur Cesbron said, "this will depend on whether you demonstrate that you can fill the part. We'll have a special rehearsal Friday." He was too shrewd a director to risk a bad performance, even to keep his star tenor happy.

She smiled gleefully at the director. "You and Monsieur Rivarol won't be disappointed." At least about the singing, she added to herself.

However, the next two days strained her certainty and her composure. The Opéra Comique had to use every inch of the cramped backstage area in the Théâtre des Nations. Props and scenery stood in corners and corridors where cursing stagehands stumbled into only slightly less profane singers. Nearly every time Sarah was in one of the narrow passageways, Octave Rivarol appeared. Although a tall, heavy man, he could come upon her almost silently. Then he beamed through his black beard and brushed against her as he passed. She resented the way he took advantage of their relative importance, but she didn't let it ignite her temper.

On Friday when she arrived for her special rehearsal with the conductor, her stomach felt as if a tight fist had gripped it and wouldn't let go. Her hands were damp inside her gray gloves. The chorus provided anonymity; now she would be exposed. She paused with her hand on the auditorium door. Don't think about the outcome, she told herself. Pretend this is just an evening at home when friends are coming to hear you sing.

Halfway down the narrow aisle to the stage she stopped. Octave Rivarol stood on stage with the conductor and Monsieur Cesbron. The director said, "Monsieur Rivarol has consented to go through the selections with you."

Consented! Insisted would be more truthful, she thought. She should have expected it.

The obnoxious tenor actually did Sarah a favor. The anger aroused by his presence, and by the way he took every chance to put his arm across her shoulders, distracted her from her earlier nervousness. When she finished her arias, Monsieur Cesbron, several chorus members who were standing backstage and the conductor all applauded. Sarah knew she'd sung well, and on her way back to her room, her confidence soared. She could handle the part and the tenor too!

Sarah had rented a room over a wine merchant's shop on the edge of Montmartre. Several singers from the Opéra Comique lived in the building and had recommended it to Sarah. Her room was sparsely furnished with a narrow bed, a scarred wardrobe, a table not much larger than a candle stand, and two chairs. Its one luxury was an almost full-length oval mirror, left by the previous occupant, a ballet dancer. There was enough space for her to practice dancing if she was careful.

As she was just closing her door behind her, she heard someone calling. Helene Lebout, a petite blond girl from the chorus who lived a floor above Sarah, was hurrying up the stairs.

When Helene caught up, she gave Sarah a hug. "You sang beautifully at the rehearsal," she said generously, then warned, "But you'd better watch Rivarol. Madame Morand will be back from Champrosay next week, and she doesn't like anyone trespassing on her property."

"Good. She can keep him away from me," Sarah responded, but she remembered stories about the soprano's rages. It would be better to dissuade Rivarol from his pursuit before his mistress returned. Exactly how, Sarah wasn't quite sure.

At a second rehearsal the following day, Rivarol touched Sarah at every opportunity, "accidentally" brushing her breasts several times. By the end of the afternoon when Sarah went outside into the Place de Châtelet, she had to stomp around the fountain to calm herself. "I can't stand Rivarol," she stormed to the statue that represented Justice. The unmoving stone face seemed to reproach her outburst. "You're right," she admitted, "I didn't have to accept. I really knew how he'd act. I just have to keep my temper." The statue seemed to her to look more approving. Sarah's confidence and excitement returned.

That evening's presentation was a new Lalo opera, *Le Roi d'Ys*. In the last scene Sarah knelt with the other chorus members to sing a prayer for the soul of the dead soprano, but it was difficult to be as subdued as the music demanded. Afterward, dreaming about her triumph to come, she was slower than usual to change to her street clothes. The building was almost deserted, and she went out through the front lobby. Descending the red-carpeted stairs under the crystal chandelier gave her a feeling of elegance, like the performances she had put on as a little girl, dressed in her mother's jewels and feathers. Partway down she paused, imagining the applause that would reward her in *Hoffman*.

"Mademoiselle Taylor." The liquid voice interrupted her fantasy. Octave Rivarol, standing beside the staircase in the foyer, looked up at her. "It's late. You'll need an escort to your rooms."

"Thank you, but I walk home with friends every night. They'll be waiting."

He took a step partway up the stairs. "We could discuss your interpretation of Nicklasse. I have ideas that can help you."

She knew what sort of ideas! The same ones his marauding hands had suggested for two days. "It's not possible," she said, refusing to pretend she was sorry. "I can't disappoint my friends."

As she started down, planning to skirt around him, he stepped up closer. "Mademoiselle Taylor," he said silkily, "you don't want to disappoint me." More quickly than she anticipated that he could move, he reached out. She felt his hand under her petticoat, touching her leg above the top of her boot and sliding up toward her knee.

Resentment flared into temper that didn't consider consequences. A long hatpin fastened her small blue straw to her upswept hair. She snatched out the pin and jabbed it through her skirt into the intruding hand.

Rivarol screamed in a tone high enough for the climaxes he sang on stage. He jerked, tearing the skin of his hand before Sarah could move, and howled again. Horrified, she pulled out the pin. He staggered backward, the motion of his arm knocking her sideways. As she fell, she grabbed for the bannister railing to keep from sliding down the stairs. Moaning and holding his hand, he slumped down on the marble floor.

Shocked voices came from the front entrance where a few of the chorus members stood gaping. A doorman pushed through and rushed to the wounded tenor. One of the men at the entrance came to the stairs and extended a hand to

Sarah. Trembling, she retrieved her hat and stood up. She could see that he was trying to look concerned but really wanted to laugh.

The others who had clustered around the tenor were saying, "Are you all right?" and, "Here's my handkerchief," but Sarah could see that they, too, were struggling not to enjoy themselves too much. If Rivarol needed sympathy, she thought hysterically, he shouldn't have been injured in such a ridiculous way.

The enraged look Rivarol gave her as he shrugged off help sobered her hysteria. He stomped out, holding his wrapped hand.

After a night of troubled sleep, she arrived at the theater before rehearsal time, hoping to talk to Monsieur Cesbron. He was pacing the lobby. When he saw her, he said icily, "Please come to my office," and left her to follow behind. She didn't see Rivarol, but the director's rigid walk and pale face warned her that the tenor had undoubtedly already had his say.

As soon as the yellow door closed behind them, she began in as unflurried a tone as her anxiety permitted. "Monsieur Cesbron, I regret what happened last night, but please let me explain how—"

"Mademoiselle Taylor," he interrupted, "I need no further description of your disgraceful behavior."

"My behavior! But—"

"You are dismissed. As of today. For conduct that reflects on the good name of the Opéra Comique."

She took a furious step toward him. "That's not fair! I wasn't the one who behaved disgracefully. Ask the others there what happened."

He glared across the tops of his eyeglasses. "Mademoiselle Taylor, you Americans think Paris is a city where you can do anything. That's not so. We are as respectable as anywhere in your country. Your private life is your business, but incidents like what happened last night lead to unfavorable publicity. I explained to you that the French government subsidizes this organization. We cannot have publicity that reflects on our singers."

"But there's been no publicity."

His side whiskers quivered righteously. "I have heard enough. My decision is final."

Shaking with anger, she turned and left, slamming the door behind her. She could have reminded him that opera singers in general didn't have the best of reputations anyway. It wouldn't help. To avoid his mistress's ire, Rivarol had to present the incident in the best light for himself, no matter what witnesses might say.

In any case, she lamented, her marvelous opportunity was gone. It was luck, not her singing, that earned the chance, but that didn't make the loss less painful. She hurried past the gathered company members. Most of them looked curious, and there were one or two expressions of jealous satisfaction. Several called out sympathetic greetings. She felt too devastated to more than nod in response.

Back in the shelter of her room, she alternately raged and cried. Since she had left home, she'd tried not to think about her father. Now the longing to see him affected her so intensely that she started to drag out her trunk to pack. He wouldn't let something like this happen to her!

She stopped. All the reasons for her being in Paris cut through her distress. If Papa had his way, she would not have been at the Opéra Comique at all—not have adventures, either good or bad. Her turmoil calmed, and determination returned to overcome this hurdle too.

The next morning Ted Kearns came to her room. "I heard what happened," he said, shaking his head over her dismissal. "I wish I could help you, Sarah, but I did all I could in getting you the place."

"I don't understand why Monsieur Cesbron was so upset.

He probably has to placate Rivarol. But he blames me for risking bad publicity. I'd think he would want publicity."

"Last year there was a bad scandal," Ted explained. "President Grévy's son-in-law had been selling medals. Even the Legion of Honor. Decorations are very important in France, so people were furious. There were riots, and Grévy had to resign. Since then, anyone getting government subsidies has been careful not to offend public sensibilities. Monsieur Cesbron is probably being more cautious than he needs to be."

"And he's the one in charge," she said dejectedly.

Ted looked at her sympathetically but sternly. "You should go back to Boston. I could borrow enough money for your fare."

"No, Ted. You're kind to be concerned, and I appreciate your offer. I have enough emergency money set aside to go home, but I want to stay here and sing. I'll find something. Maybe in a music hall."

Ted's eyes, magnified behind his thick glasses, looked shocked. He frowned, intensifying his concerned-guardian look, reminding Sarah that in spite of his Parisian life, he was her father's generation. "A music hall would be very unsuitable. Promise me, Sarah, that you won't do anything until I see what I can do."

Ted didn't know how short her money had been, and she didn't want to cause him anxiety. In the month she had worked, she'd learned to get along on her salary and even to save part of it. She could manage for a while. "All right," she promised. "I won't look for a place in a music hall yet." He went away looking relieved.

Sarah counted her money and decided she could last a month or two, maybe until the beginning of 1889, if she were very careful and had some way of earning a little money. Tutoring English—that was a safe enough occupation that would improve her French as well. After con-

sulting Helene, she put a notice in a small local paper, listing
herself only as S. Taylor, to be contacted at the wine shop.
She also posted a sign in the window of a milliner's shop
owned by Helene's cousin. This done, she decided to divide
her time between perfecting her singing and dancing and
learning more about Paris.

Every morning she practiced singing and the dance steps
she could manage in her small room. Then she indulged
her passion for newspapers and read five or six every day.
Scandals received extensive and disapproving coverage; even
the dismissal of a police magistrate in a provincial town who
was discovered with a youthful mistress was reported. Maybe
Cesbron wasn't as unreasonable as she'd thought. Writers
of opposing views carried on violent quarrels in their articles
and occasionally challenged each other to duels. The political
future of a General Boulanger seemed to be the most con-
tentious issue. One journal, *L'Intransigeant*, was particularly
inflammatory. It's editor, Henri Rochefort, seemed ready to
fight a duel with anyone who disagreed with him. She followed the activities of the prime minister, Floquet, and the
complicated news from Madagascar and Africa.

Though she always included copies of *Le Figaro* and *La
Justice* in her reading, she looked unsuccessfully for articles
with Pierre de Tourbey's name. It had been almost six weeks
since he'd accompanied her to watch the cancan at the Opéra
Comique. He hadn't contacted her in that time, and she was
disappointed. She thought of him often, probably, she decided, because she knew so few people here.

On the fourth day after placing her notices, a note came
from a Madame Bourget, inquiring about tutoring. Sarah
sent an immediate reply, and at the time set was waiting in
the back of the wine shop. Madame Bourget was a thin-
lipped bony woman who talked in a rapid voice. She introduced her son, Emile, a nervous young *lycée* student, hardly
more than a boy.

After Sarah explained that she was American, she suggested they go up to her room. "It will be quieter there."

When they arrived upstairs, Madame Bourget looked around suspiciously, then established herself on the bed, as if to make sure this American woman had no chance to lure her son into it. Since he sat on a chair and hardly raised his eyes above the floor, Sarah thought it unlikely he even knew what she looked like.

"What are your charges?" asked Madame Bourget.

Sarah had learned that a wage of three francs a day was considered good. That was the same as sixty cents in American money, which seemed like a startlingly small amount. "My fee is three francs an hour," she said boldly.

Madame Bourget fixed Sarah with a frown. "That's rather expensive."

"I was educated in the very best Boston schools," Sarah said, meeting the disapproving look steadily.

"Very well, but Emile already knows quite a bit of English. I will expect him to progress rapidly."

"How old are you, Emile?" Sarah began in English.

"He's fourteen," Madame Bourget replied.

Sarah said to Emile, "Why do you want to learn English?"

His mother answered. "It's necessary in our business."

"Madame Bourget," Sarah said. "Your son will not progress at all unless he speaks. Now, Emile, please tell me where you go to school."

Emile glanced at his mother, then said in a whisper, "The Lycée Michelet."

As Sarah continued the lesson with simple conversation, he repeated her words, never above a whisper. At the end of the hour, Madame Bourget indicated they would come twice a week. Sarah felt sorry for Emile, but she was glad for the money.

Recalling Ted's admonition, she didn't go out alone in the

evening, but in her free daytime she wandered over Paris. One rainy day she strolled through the Bon Marché, not intending to make a purchase but finally unable to resist a straw hat with a large, curving brim and a russet bow that almost matched her hair. Afterward she scolded herself for extravagance and was particularly careful to find the best bargains in cheese and vegetables for her meals, but she loved wearing the hat. During clear, bright afternoons, the street jugglers and magicians provided entertainment for only a single *centime* dropped in a hat. She longed to try the *théâtrophone*, one of several new telephones scattered around the city. On it she could have listened to music from the Opéra, but it was too expensive, and she would have had to go out alone in the evening.

Often at three o'clock she watched the parade of riders and carriages with their gilt-trimmed coats of arms come out from the Faubourg Saint-Honoré and turn along the Champs-Elysées toward the Bois de Boulogne. One afternoon she saw a woman wearing a sumptuous costume of such dark green velvet it looked almost black. The woman sat haughtily on a beautiful black mare with trappings trimmed in gold. Four grooms, in elegant uniforms of a lighter shade of green and top hats decorated with cockades, rode beside her.

A man standing near Sarah said to his companion, "That's the Baroness Adolphe de Rothschild." Sarah wanted to ask the baroness how it felt, being so well-known that people pointed her out in the street.

Two more pupils responded to her notices. They were Yvonne and Delphine, sisters in their early teens. After an initial interview with their bored mother, a maid delivered them four mornings a week. They giggled and simpered and spent much of their efforts in trying to persuade Sarah to teach them risqué English words. The payment for their lessons eased Sarah's concerns about money, but she began to wish she hadn't promised Ted not to try for a place in a music hall. She missed singing for an audience.

On a Sunday in late October Sarah went on an excursion with Helene and Helene's lover, Marc Simon. They walked to the Quai du Louvre where they caught a horse-drawn tram. Helene and Sarah rode inside, while Marc hung on the outside. At Billancourt, just outside the line of the old Parisian fortifications, they got off. It was a crisp day, with bright sunshine and a wind chasing puffy clouds across the sky, as if October couldn't decide whether it looked back to summer or ahead to winter. Marc rented a boat and rowed on the Seine while Helene and Sarah trailed their hands in the water. Sarah would have liked to row; she had done a lot of that at home, but she thought Marc might be insulted. Afterward they sat on the bank under an acacia tree and ate slices of cold mutton and pears, then finished with pink-iced cakes and a bottle of Madeira.

While Marc stretched out and napped, Sarah asked Helene about the Opéra Comique.

"Rivarol and Cesbron have been fighting," Helene reported. "Yesterday they were shouting at each other for nearly half an hour, and someone heard Monsieur Cesbron say that Rivarol's voice is slipping."

"That's encouraging. Maybe I have a chance to return to the chorus. I miss it so much."

"I think Rivarol won't be there long," Helene said encouragingly.

Sarah went home from the outing, sunburned and more relaxed about her promise to Ted.

The following Tuesday when she was beginning to feel too restless to be a spectator much longer, a note arrived from Pierre de Tourbey. It read: "I just returned to Paris. I'll be at the Café d'Orsay this afternoon about four. I hope you can meet me there."

Pierre's face—particularly his mischievous smile—came

vividly to Sarah's mind. The image produced a breathless excitement. She scolded herself for being as silly as Yvonne and Delphine, but she couldn't suppress an almost giddy feeling. After dressing with special care in a cinnamon-colored wool suit, she brushed her red hair until the gold highlights gleamed.

When Sarah arrived at the café, Pierre was seated at one of the small tables across from the circular bar. He stood up, his strong movements reminding her that he looked more like a workman than a journalist. But his "Mademoiselle Taylor, I'm delighted you came," the kiss on her hand, and his seductive smile were the sophisticated Parisian gentleman.

Unbidden and unexpected, the thought came: what would he look like without his clothes? She startled herself so much that she stumbled over her "How nice to see you, Monsieur de Tourbey." She prayed he didn't notice the warmth she felt in her face as he pulled out one of the cane chairs for her.

When he had taken his seat, he said, "I'm disappointed. You don't look different."

"What did you expect?" she asked, feeling more composed.

"Yesterday, my first day back in Paris, I heard an interesting story from a music reviewer at *Le Figaro*. About a woman who bested the very large and pompous Rivarol—with a hatpin, if the story is correct."

"It was a very large hatpin."

"Then the story is true." He looked pleased. "After such a battle, I expected some change in you."

She laughed. "Did you think I would look depraved?"

"It would be pleasant if you were, but I don't see any evidence of that." He sighed, but his eyes laughed. Then he said more soberly, "I understand you were dismissed from the Opéra Comique chorus. I'm sorry. I wish I'd seen you perform. My six weeks away were at the worst time."

She remembered her fantasy about his being in the audience when she did the cancan and again could feel the damnable blush that showed mercilessly in her fair skin. "Was your trip successful?" she asked hastily.

Pierre noticed the flush of color in Sarah's face. The blush made her look innocent, but she had the sensuous mouth of a seductress. An erotic combination. He wondered if she was aware of the effect she had. He was. And she didn't mind bantering words with him. He'd love to find out just how untouched she was. Naked, in bed, with those wonderful breasts and the thighs he could guess at from her walk. *Par Dieu!* He'd be aroused right here if he weren't careful. Better to talk than imagine.

"I had better luck on my trip than you did at the Opéra Comique," he said. "I could still ask a friend to write about you. It might help get you another place."

Sarah frowned. "The answer is no, and I'm not sure it would help. I lost the position because Rivarol was furious, I'm sure. But the director told me I was fired because there might be publicity. Ted explained Monsieur Cesbron was nervous because of some scandal about medals."

"Ted's right. The public was outraged about the medals. Still, I doubt your director needs to be that cautious."

"Maybe so, but he fired me."

"Since you aren't working now, there's an advantage for me. I can show you more of Paris. And we can get better acquainted. You might let me call you Sarah." He let his eyes and grin say how much better he would like their acquaintance to be.

Sarah understood Pierre's unspoken message. Ted had assured her Pierre would respect a refusal from her. But how would she feel if he were the one touching her breast or leg? A streak of tension tightened her stomach, like riding a fast horse that might get out of control. A pleasurable uncertainty. Yes, she wanted to see more of Paris—and of him. "You may call me Sarah, and I'd like to see Paris with you."

Over the next three weeks, Sarah spent several afternoons with Pierre. They went one cold but sunny day to look at the tower that Gustave Eiffel was building for the May opening of the 1889 Universal Exposition. So far it resembled a giant spider, lumbering on ungainly legs to capture the Hotel des Invalides, framed in the background. "It looks . . . odd," she said, avoiding the word ugly.

Pierre grinned. "One of the proposals was for a tower that was an enormous garden sprinkler. To wet down Paris during a drought. Another man wanted to build a three-hundred-meter-high guillotine."

"Why build a tower at all?" she asked. "Isn't the exposition to celebrate the centennial of the French Revolution?"

"Yes, and our industrial progress," he said more seriously. "The tower illustrates French skill at building with iron. Eiffel is a master at that."

"Will it really be ready in five months?"

"That's what Monsieur Eiffel promised."

Two elderly men sitting on a bench nearby were busy condemning the partly finished structure. "A monstrosity," grumbled one. "It will make the city vulgar."

"It's bound to be a disaster," contributed the other. "The mathematicians tell us it can't rise over six hundred fifty meters high without collapsing."

"When it falls, it's bound to crush everyone in the vicinity," Pierre said in a loud voice.

The two men exchanged alarmed looks, glanced once back at the tower, and hurried away. Sarah laughed as Pierre escorted her to the vacated seat.

Another afternoon Pierre suggested they go bicycling. "I can borrow a lady's bicycle for you. It's one of the newest models, with pneumatic tires," he explained. "I have a Rover safety bicycle, with hard rubber tires. It's faster, but bumpy."

She wondered whom he would borrow the bicycle from, and chided herself for what felt astonishingly like jealousy. "Yes, I'd love to go."

When he called for her, he had on a loose jacket and knickerbockers that came just below his knees. She envied his freedom. Men were lucky not to have to put up with the constraint of corset and petticoats.

They went to the Bois de Boulogne and joined other bicyclers on the trail between the Jardin d'Acclimatation at the south entrance and the Longchamp racetrack. Men and women were getting in their last rides before colder weather, some on shiny new bicycles and a few elderly women on tricycles. One man wobbled along on an ancient cycle that had one high wheel in front and a small wheel in back.

Pierre was a fierce bicyclist; he left her behind several times, circling around to rejoin her and then forging ahead again. Though she hadn't ridden since she left home, she kept up with most of the other riders in spite of her restrictive clothes. Toward the end of the course Pierre's attention was distracted by an argument between two cyclists who had collided. She peddled furiously, loving the feeling of speeding under her own power, and reached the starting place ahead of him. He arrived and said, with surprised admiration, "I didn't expect you to beat me. Congratulations!"

"I like to win," she said jauntily. "As a prize for beating you, I want to ride in a carriage pulled by an ostrich."

At his laughing agreement, they went to the Stables in the Jardin. Pierre paid the fifty *centimes* for Sarah to ride around the lawn behind one of the large, ungainly birds.

During those weeks Helene kept Sarah informed about continuing friction between Rivarol and Cesbron. One Friday when no performance was scheduled for the Opéra Comique, Sarah went to the Place du Châtelet. As she approached the theater, she saw a carriage outside that she thought belonged to Rivarol. Retreating to the Pont-au-Change where she could watch boats passing underneath on the Seine and keep the theater in sight, she waited. Finally the tenor emerged, stomping to his carriage in a stride that looked angry even from a distance.

When the carriage had left in a hurry under the coachman's whip, she went to the theater and found Monsieur Cesbron sitting grumpily in his office. After they exchanged restrained greetings, she asked, "Is there any possibility that I might return to the chorus? Nothing has appeared in a paper about me. I really feel I was not to blame for the difficulty with Monsieur Rivarol, but if you can reinstate me, I will be very careful about my temper."

After two "humph's" and several taps of his forefinger on his desk, Monsieur Cesbron said, "Although I cannot absolutely promise you anything, the situation here may be changing. Come back to see me in a month."

Sarah left, feeling as she had as a girl when school let out for the Christmas holidays. She would leave her notices for tutoring posted, but if she didn't get more than the three pupils, she could enjoy her time with Pierre while she waited for the month to pass.

When she met him that afternoon, she told him about the conversation with Cesbron. "Then we must celebrate," he said. "A new play is opening at the Odéon Théâtre on Wednesday. *Germinie Lacerteux* by Edmond de Goncourt. I'll be out of Paris the next three days, but I'll be back then. Would you like to go?"

"Oh, yes!" A new play, and an attractive Frenchman as her escort. She felt sophisticated and very Parisian.

When Sarah dressed for the play, she was glad her rose silk dress was almost new. It had a high neck, tucked bodice, long puffed sleeves, and was drawn into fashionable gathers in the back. She felt suitably elegant for the occasion—and, she hoped, for Pierre. She had missed him for the three days. Though they didn't meet every day, knowing he was out of Paris made it seem lonely—a feeling that made her a little uncomfortable. She might be too attached to him when he was only casually interested in her. Still, she decided not to let it lessen her pleasure in the evening.

When Pierre called for her, he looked formal in his evening clothes, except for his hair. It still sprang out in unruly curls. His grin, however, had its usual impertinent admiration. He surveyed her as he held her cloak and said, "Goncourt will be in despair. Everyone will look at you instead of the stage."

She laughed at his extravagance, and shivered when his hands brushed the side of her neck as he settled her cloak around her.

As the carriage made its way through the Latin Quarter to the Rue Tournon, he explained that the Odéon was one of the oldest and most prestigious theaters in Paris. "Sarah Bernhardt established herself in roles there. Berlioz says it was the 1827 Shakespeare season at the Odéon that inspired him to write his music. Occasionally the plays offend the ministers and bankers of Paris. The book this play is based on was condemned as vulgar when it came out twenty years ago. We'll see how things go tonight."

In front of the brilliantly lit theater, carriages discharged formally dressed men and elegant women. Sarah and Pierre joined the throng and made their way inside to a box in the first tier. When they were seated, he pointed out a man at the back of a box across the way. "That's the author, Edmond de Goncourt, in Porel's box. Porel is the theater manager. They're waiting out the audience's verdict together." Goncourt was a plump man, with a wide, bushy, mustache and a nervous expression. Pierre rose and made a bow of greeting and good luck. Monsieur Goncourt smiled and nodded, then resumed his anxious expression.

As the performance proceeded, Sarah understood why the author might wish to be inconspicuous. Soon into a dance-hall scene between the working-class heroine and her shopkeeper lover, members of the audience began to hiss. Pierre retaliated with loud applause, and others joined him. The auditorium, with its tiers of ornate boxes facing each other, lent itself to the contest. The struggle to dominate the response continued. When one character called the heroine "a trollop," a fight broke out down in the stalls. Sarah, accustomed to restrained Boston audiences, was astonished.

"This is one of the first plays to show the lives of poor people as they really are," Pierre explained heatedly. "That woman in the third box to the left, Marie Colombier, who started the hissing, is a whore. Everyone knows it. And Vitu. He's here with his mistress. Konig over there started his career as a lover of rich old women. Those hypocrites pretend to be offended by the language onstage. We can't let them close down the play!"

Pierre was so agitated that Sarah couldn't follow his identification of the culprits. She was startled by his frankness. Did the same things go on in Boston, but under the surface? As with Papa and Cousin Mabel. Paris seemed so different, but maybe it was just more open. Perhaps she had been too harsh in her judgment of her father. It was a new and uncomfortable thought, and she was glad to turn her attention back to the play.

At the end, Pierre jumped to his feet and applauded wildly. But when the leading actor stepped forward to announce the author's name, the hissing became so loud that he had to wait for a lull to shout, "Goncourt."

"Hypocritical bastards," Pierre spat, then looked at her. "I beg your pardon, Sarah. Excuse my language, please."

Considering his anger, she forgave his language, but she did wonder if they would leave without his getting into a fight with someone. However, he recovered and ushered her from the theater without more than scowling at the offenders.

In the carriage she said, "I think you are very serious when it comes to literature."

"Naturalism in literature must be nourished," he said soberly.

By the time they arrived at the Café de la Paix on the Rue des Capucines near the Opéra, his usual insouciance had returned. The café matched the elegance of the neighborhood, with tall Venetian mirrors along the walls, ornate flocked wallpaper, and potted palms in the corners. Sarah's attention was caught by the jeweled women in their silk and satin gowns. The women's tuxedoed escorts carried opera glasses and programs, advertising where they had been.

"People from that monstrosity of a building where you'd like to sing," Pierre commented.

"Yes, you're right. Sometimes I daydream that if I work hard and am lucky, I'll sing in the chorus at the Opéra."

"Or be the star?"

"I don't think I'm good enough for that."

"A modest woman." He looked at her, his mouth shaping an intimate smile, the challenging expression strong in his eyes. "Maybe this café isn't the best choice. I prefer that you think about me, not the Opéra. Shall we find another café?"

She wasn't ready to go back to her room, but the opera patrons did make her a little envious. "Yes."

Outside on the Rue des Capucines, a group of young men and women hailed Pierre. After some confused greetings, he turned to Sarah. "Some of these scoundrels are my colleagues. They insist we join them. Are you willing to put up with them?"

"Of course."

They were swept into the group and along to a small, much less elegant café on a side street away from the boulevards. In the confusion Sarah didn't try to remember names. Toasts were drunk to Zola, Goncourt, Flaubert, and realism in literature. A small man in a workman's cap and a checked suit sang a mournful song about a man who hanged himself over a lost love. As the evening grew later and rowdier, one of the men offered a toast with the last of his second bottle of wine. "To the lady who impaled Rivarol, instead of the other way around."

Uncertain whether she felt offended or flattered, Sarah pretended not to understand. But when Pierre caught her eye, she laughed and blushed at the same time.

Eventually the others straggled away, and she and Pierre were left. The café quieted to only a few nodding drinkers, and she felt a comfortable lassitude from the evening's excitement and the wine. Pierre leaned forward at the table and let his white gloved hand rest close to hers. "We do know each other better now, but I'm not sure I've discovered any mysteries. You say you don't sing well enough for the Opéra. I can imagine that you would be very good at other things." He stroked one finger across the top of her hand.

Her hand tingled. "You should control your imagination."

"But it's such pleasure. And could be even more if we weren't just thinking." He pulled his glove off, turned her hand over so that it rested palm up, and began to unfasten the mother-of-pearl buttons at the wrist. It all seemed part of the evening, a Parisian evening, a different world from Boston.

Her more prudent self knew she should keep a rein on her feelings. "Ted warned me that you might make an indecent suggestion."

"I would certainly like to." He slid one finger inside the opening of her glove, caressing her palm. She felt warm from the wine and his touch. He smiled, his eyes a soft, smoky blue in the haze of the café. "And what did Monsieur Kearns advise you to answer?"

"He was sure that I would refuse."

His fingers rested now on hers, stretching the glove so that it held them close together. "Is that what you want to do?"

His eyes held hers, suggesting unknown pleasures. Their joined hands, the atmosphere of the café, gave her freedom, like the safety of a long friendship, for errant thoughts. What would it be like to be touching even more intimately? Dangerous speculation! "I might not want to refuse, but I will."

"How can you disappoint me—disappoint both of us so much?" He looked both comical and serious.

Reluctantly recalling her proper self, she pulled her hand away and began to button her glove. "Ted also said that I could trust your word that you wouldn't press me when I said no."

"But let's not settle this now. Wait and see how you feel later."

"No." Being with him was comfortable—and enticing—but she couldn't abandon so easily all that she'd believed in for the twenty-one years before she came to France. Still, she didn't quite trust herself with him. She wanted his word. "Promise that we'll be friends only."

He sighed in an exaggerated way. "Ted has given me a reputation for dependability I'm not sure I want. All right, I promise. But I warn you that if you change your mind and make an indecent suggestion to me, I'll be much weaker than you and give in immediately."

"You're safe," she assured him. She was Sarah Taylor from Boston. Surely that Sarah would never make an indecent proposal to anyone, even as tempting a man as Pierre. Paris wouldn't change her that much.

CHAPTER
FIVE

SARAH WONDERED WHETHER, AFTER REFUSING PIERRE'S OVertures, she would see him again. However, two days later a note arrived, inviting her to go bicycling again in the Bois de Boulogne. This time, she decided, she would not wear a corset. Her brown wool dress was heavy enough to keep her warm and conceal her lack of proper undergarment. She dressed happily, humming the melody from *Carmen* with which the gypsy welcomes her soldier lover.

Pierre was waiting when Sarah arrived in the tiny courtyard behind the wine shop. As she walked the last steps to meet him, his attentive gaze made her more aware of the unrestricted movements of her body. Suddenly her dress didn't seem like concealment after all.

His eyes laughing, he said, "You look . . . particularly attractive this afternoon."

Her skin seemed more alive, brushing against her camisole and drawers. Even so, she loved the embarrassing freedom. "Thank you," she said. Straightening her back, she marched ahead of him to the cab.

The same two bicycles were tied on the back. As they

rode toward the Bois, her need to know overcame her reluctance to recognize that she might be jealous. "Your friend doesn't mind letting me use her bicycle again?"

"No, she's happy to do me a favor."

That wasn't a satisfactory answer. She wished she hadn't asked.

As if he knew what she was thinking and took pity, Pierre said, "She got the bicycle for her granddaughter, but it isn't used much."

The rather dim sunlight seemed brighter.

Few other riders were using the trail, and Sarah found her unrestrained body made her a more even competitor for Pierre. When they finished their ride, she was out of breath but very pleased with herself. Afterward they sat on a bench under the bare linden trees and had a picnic. While she ate cold trout and broke off pieces of a baguette to go with it, Sarah asked Pierre about newspaper work.

"A paper's a noisy, exasperating place. There's never enough time. Everything needs to be done half a day ago."

"But you love it," she guessed.

"Yes, I do." He helped himself to a pear and cheese, then added, with a note of seriousness, "Writing for a newspaper can be a way to promote important causes."

"I admire that kind of purpose."

He shrugged, as if not quite comfortable with her praise. "That's part of it. I like the rowdy life. The crazy things people do amuse me."

In spite of his disclaimer, she decided he took his work more seriously than she'd first thought.

His grin reappeared. "Now if I thought I'd get to sing with you for a partner, I might try to change my profession. If I did, would you stab me with a hatpin?"

Though she already doubted she would repulse his advances so quickly, it wouldn't do to admit it. "That would depend on how you sounded," she said pertly.

"*Ah! te t'en souviendras, Nicolas,*" he sang in an unpolished baritone voice. The song was about a boy who tried to kiss a girl and got a beating instead.

When he finished, she shook her head in mock despair. "It's the hatpin for you."

On the way back to the wine shop, she felt pleased and happy with the companionable afternoon. She'd come to expect and enjoy the undertone of sexual innuendo, like a spicy sauce that enhanced the flavor of their outings.

After he helped her out of the cab, he said, "I won't see you for a while. I have some business out of Paris."

As she climbed the stairs to her room, her disappointment surprised and upset her. She shouldn't become too dependent on his friendship, she lectured herself. Instead she should think about how to earn more money. The lecture didn't erase her disappointment, but it did turn her to planning.

One or two more students would ease her finances. Emile had progressed to looking her in the face while they talked. Perhaps his mother would let him suggest to other students at the *lycée* that Mademoiselle Taylor was a good English tutor. As Emile and his mother were leaving after the next lesson, Sarah brought up the possibility.

Emile said, "Yes, I'll be happy to do that," before his mother could answer for him. Madame Bourget looked taken aback and followed Emile from the room without saying another word.

The next day she met Ted Kearns at the Restaurant Richelieu for their weekly lunch, and noticed unaccustomed lines of tension around his mouth and eyes. "Is something wrong?" she asked.

"No. Not exactly." He took an envelope from his pocket. "I had a letter from Boston—from your father."

"From Papa!" Joy swept over Sarah—followed as quickly by apprehension. "How is he?"

"Concerned about you. He traced you to France through the ship you took from New York. He asks if I know where you are." Ted's glasses seemed to magnify his eyes more than usual. "Do you want to read the letter and answer it?"

Her feelings in turmoil, she stared at the gray envelope in his hand. One emotion came clearly to the fore: she didn't want to return to being dominated by her father. And she wasn't ready to test herself yet. "No."

"I can't lie to him, Sarah," Ted warned. "When I write, I'll have to tell him you're here."

"Yes, I know." She thought of her father's pride. It must have hurt him to admit he didn't know her whereabouts. "That's all right. I'm glad he won't have to worry about where I am. Maybe if he writes again, I'll feel better about answering then."

"Very well." Ted put away the envelope.

Later, as he was leaving her at her room, he asked, "Any word from the Opéra Comique? I'm sorry I haven't been any more help to you."

"No, but I hope to hear soon. Please don't worry about me."

"Do you still see Pierre de Tourbey? He might know of something."

Sarah felt an unsettling response to the name. "I haven't seen him recently."

In spite of her warning to herself that she might be too interested in Pierre, a note from him the following Wednesday gave her a rush of good spirits. He asked her to meet him at a small café on the Boulevard des Italiens.

She left her room early and walked to the boulevard. It was the first of December, the pale sunshine more like winter than fall. A sharp wind pushed dead leaves across the walks below trees whose branches made patterns of brown lace. Five stories above the street, chimney stacks looked like fingers poking into the clouds scooting by. Women in dark jackets and cloaks all seemed to have chosen brightly colored ribbons to adorn their hats, making up for the missing gaiety of flowers around the trees. The smells of fresh bread and cinnamon rolls from a *boulangerie* made Sarah's mouth water.

In spite of being early, she found Pierre already waiting, a cup of coffee and a glass of brandy in front of him. When he saw her, he jumped up. "Sarah, beautiful as ever," he greeted her. He kissed her hand but didn't linger over it. Something seemed to be on his mind; he looked like an excited schoolboy who has just discovered a scheme for getting around a demanding master.

"How did your business go?" she asked when they were seated.

"Very well. Another writer and I are going to start a newspaper."

"Congratulations! That must be why you look so pleased."

"Only partly. I have another enterprise in mind too. You did tell me you like to try new things." He looked as if he would explode unless she agreed.

She didn't hesitate. "Yes."

"And politics intrigue you."

"Yes."

He paused, waiting impatiently until the waiter poured her coffee. "How would you like to help a man get started on a political career?"

His grin as he poured a little brandy into his coffee told her, *I understand enough about you to pose a question that will ensnare your interest.*

She didn't resist. "You want me to help you go into politics?"

"Me? No, never. The man is my cousin, Armand, the Comte de Saint-Maurice. His mother and mine were sisters. His father's dead, and Armand is the only son." Pierre's face took on a serious expression. "His mother, my Aunt Nathalie, rests all her hopes in him. He wants to go into politics, and he'd be very good at it. But she's fanatically opposed."

"Why? Isn't government service respectable?"

"Only the army or the diplomatic service for the *old* aristocracy—people who had their titles before the fall of the monarchy in 1789. Unfortunately for Armand, his father came from the Empire aristocracy whose titles were created by the first Napoleon."

She sipped her coffee, enjoying the rich, bitter flavor and thinking about Pierre's cousin. "But then if he's not old aristocracy, why doesn't he go into politics?"

"He could, but Aunt Nathalie is wild to be accepted as if the Saint-Maurice family had been ennobled in the *ancien regime*." Pierre gave a rueful laugh, as if he should be amused by the situation but wasn't. "She won't do anything that the old noble families would look down on. So she's deadly opposed to Armand being in politics."

Sarah didn't want to hurt Pierre's feelings, but she had to say what she thought. "Would your cousin be any good at helping to run a government if he can't stand up to his mother?"

Pierre didn't seem offended. "You have to know about his father. Armand worshipped him. He died when Armand was eight years old. When he was dying, he made Armand swear he'd never go against Aunt Nathalie's wishes."

"But that's shocking!" Sarah said. "An eight-year-old shouldn't have to swear to something that affects his life!"

"I agree, but Aunt Nathalie uses a combination of calls-to-duty and convenient illnesses. Armand's too concerned about his duty to recognize that she's manipulating him. But except for his blindness about her, he's tough-minded enough to get along. He's been in the army and the diplomatic service, and he believes policies he opposes can be changed only in Paris, not in Tunisia or Indo-China."

In his agitation, Pierre ran one hand through his hair,

letting the curls escape in all directions. Sarah couldn't help laughing. "You look like a wild man," she said, but he didn't smile in response, and she subdued her laughter. "I see your cousin means a lot to you, but what help can I be?"

Now his eyes sparkled again. "Let's walk along the boulevard, and I'll tell you my plan."

They joined the other strollers along the broad thoroughfare. Pierre ignored the people around them and the clatter of horses and carriages. He talked excitedly, almost walking backward in front of her to make sure she understood. "The only thing Aunt Nathalie would hate more than Armand in politics would be for him to make an unsuitable marriage. That's where you come in. I'll introduce you to Armand. He'll be attracted to you—maybe fall in love with you. I'll suggest to Aunt Nathalie that he might want to marry you. She'll decide she'd rather have him in politics."

He wanted to introduce her to another man. Sarah wasn't sure whether she should be hurt or amused, but his excitement had an ingenuous charm that made hurt feelings seem silly. Still uncertain, she said teasingly, "So I'm such a bad marriage prospect that your aunt will prefer politics and your cousin will give me up. I think I should be insulted."

His eyes softened to the invitation she recognized. "If you'll accept my suggestions for you and me, I'll abandon the whole plan."

Now that he'd answered the question she hadn't asked, she could enjoy toying with his outrageous idea. "I don't believe any of this would happen."

"Here." He took her hand and pulled her rapidly along a side street to a bench in a tiny square. "You see," he explained, as if she were a little slow witted not to understand immediately, "an American wife would be unsuitable for a really ambitious politician. If Aunt Nathalie is really worried about you, she'll encourage him to try politics. By the time you turn him down, she'll have to settle for what she has and give up the nonsense about the old aristocracy."

"Why are you so sure your Armand will be attracted to me, much less fall in love or consider marriage?"

Pierre's face took on the sensuous smile that had been the first thing she noticed about him. "Armand and I have similar tastes in women. You're an irresistibly intriguing combination. You obviously come from a good background. Yet here you're living in a disreputable situation. An American woman, alone in Paris, singing at the Opéra Comique. Your speaking voice alone with that American accent would do it."

"Thank you," Sarah said dryly.

"Armand will fall in love with you," Pierre continued, as if he hadn't noticed her ironic tone. "I'll make sure Aunt Nathalie thinks he's interested in marriage."

"You're trying to play God," she protested. "You say your aunt manipulates Armand, but aren't you doing the same thing? Is that fair to him or your aunt?"

Pierre waved aside her objections. "Aunt Nathalie will be better off when she gives up her obsession. Armand will be sorry he can't have you, but in the end he'll be happy with a French girl and a chance to work for his ideas."

Though Sarah was still uncertain exactly how she felt, Pierre's plan was intriguing. "And what about me? Will I be happy in the end?"

"Of course. You'll see Parisian society at either its best or worst, maybe both. All the hostesses will invite you to their salons in the hope of being able to report a scandal."

"What if I fall in love with Armand? What if I were so much in love I became his mistress?" She didn't really think she might, but she was a little piqued at Pierre's eagerness. Some jealousy on his part would be pleasant.

"You aren't supposed to fall in love with Armand. If you want to be in love, you should begin with me. You've already shown, unfortunately, that you can withstand my appeals.

I'm confident you won't succumb to him." Pierre spoke lightly, but with a subtle intensity underneath. It reminded her of music that sounds somewhat gay and frivolous but is in a minor key.

A little flustered but pleased, she laughed. "Such confidence."

"What do you say to my plan? Will you help?"

Sarah bit her lips, considering. She'd left home to escape having her life managed by her father. Would this be the same thing? No. Now she was choosing whether to play this role or not. The idea was crazy, but irresistible. Or perhaps Pierre was irresistible after all. "If your cousin is as conceited as you are, I'm safe from falling in love with him. Yes, I'll do it."

"Good!"

"But," she warned, "I don't agree to continue if I don't like this arrangement."

"Of course. My aunt is having a musical evening next Sunday. I'll take you and introduce you to Armand. Together we'll save him. And maybe France."

"The dress is almost right," Pierre said. "Turn around again."

It was the first time he'd been in her room. Sarah had hesitated about asking him inside. Despite her success at resisting his advances, the prospect of being alone with him in her bedroom was a little too interesting for comfort. However, she wanted his appraisal of her dress before they left for his aunt's house. Perhaps sensing her slight nervousness, his manner had been courteous and circumspect, as if there were no bed in the corner.

Sarah had looked at the advertisements for gowns from the houses of Worth and Laferrière and decided that her only formal evening dress would do. The Genoa velvet was blue green, a color that accented the green flecks in her eyes.

It had a low neckline, tiny sleeves that barely covered her shoulders, a snug bodice and flaring skirt.

While she pirouetted, Pierre leaned back in the one comfortable chair, his thumb absently stroking the corner of his mustache. "It needs a vulgar touch. Animal jewelry is popular—a gold spider, or an emerald caterpillar. I've seen a diamond chicken inside an enameled egg. Do you have jewelry like that?"

She touched the pearl collar at her throat. "This is all I have with me, and I've never owned jeweled animals. I don't think I'd like them."

"Then take off the pearls. Going without any jewelry is eccentric enough."

When they were underway in Pierre's brougham, he said, "Aunt Nathalie's mansion is in the Faubourg Saint-Germain. You'll notice she has petrol lamps, which are a nuisance. She won't install electricity because the old aristocracy opposes change."

An interesting confirmation of his aunt's attitude, but she was more interested in Armand. "Tell me more about your cousin. How old is he? Do men like him? Do women? What is he like?"

"He's four years older than I am, so he's thirty-two. He earned a reputation for courage when he was in the army. So men admire him. They also respect his style of dueling. He's skillful at wounding his adversary without badly hurting him."

"Duels? I thought they were illegal."

"They are, but that doesn't stop them. Most mornings in the Bois de Boulogne, there are two crazy men going at each other."

"Do you fight duels?"

"Are you asking if I'm crazy?" he teased. "Anyhow, we were talking of Armand. Women—yes, they like him. There's something about him that makes a woman feel sympathetic—but you'll see."

The rain that had been falling all day had stopped. The brougham took them past the glistening walls of the Palais du Luxembourg. In the light from the street lamps the bare treetops in the famous gardens looked like spindly arms. They turned into the Rue de Lille, passed the solemn German embassy, and arrived at a mansion guarded by an iron fence. A gate let them into a graveled drive that ran through modest gardens and stopped in front of an impressive four-story building.

Footmen in gold and brown livery were opening carriage doors for men in black overcoats and women in furs. Other men in plain brown uniforms took the horses and carriages away. Sarah wondered if her coat with modest fur trimming appeared "eccentric," and the thought excited her, as if she were stepping onto a stage. Inside, the house unfolded like different sets: first, the cloakroom where other footmen took their coats and Pierre's hat. An enormous red-carpeted staircase wound upward in three turns to a small room where the majordomo directed a servant of lowly status to write their names in a register. Sarah had to stifle an impulse to say she was the queen of Madagascar. They went along a short hall with an Aubusson tapestry as its single decoration to the concert room.

It was long and at least two stories high; three chandeliers, with crystal holders for the many candles, were evenly spaced along its ceiling. Silver brackets fastened to the walls held more candles in front of diamond-shaped mirrors, giving the room the brilliance of daylight. Tall, red-draped glass doors led to what must be a balcony. An enormous tapestry covered the opposite wall; its hunters, dogs and deer regarded each other peacefully in a harmony of greens and browns. Sarah wondered if the elaborate decor represented tastes acceptable to the "old aristocracy."

Guests in evening dress stood in clusters or sat on chairs arranged before a platform at one end of the room. On it a small man fussed over an ebony piano; chairs and music stands took up the rest of the raised space. Servants carrying salvers moved among the guests, offering refreshments.

"Which are your aunt and cousin?"

"I don't see him yet. She's at the far end, near the platform."

As they made their way in that direction, Pierre stopped frequently to greet other guests. Sarah responded to the introductions, but there were too many for her to remember names except to notice that several had titles. When she and Pierre walked on, a pause in conversation followed by the hum of lowered voices behind them made Sarah suspect that the "eccentricity" of her dress had been noticed. A gray-haired general stared at her quite openly through a large monocle, and a marquis's white tie bobbed with agitation after he gave her a similar perusal.

"You're making a stir," Pierre whispered in her ear, the crinkles around his eyes showing her how much he was enjoying himself. She concluded that what she'd already suspected was true—however much he wanted to help his cousin, he was getting equal pleasure for himself from his scheme. His enthusiasm was infectious. She felt like a schoolgirl with a part in her first play.

When they reached the cluster of people near the platform, Sarah finally saw Pierre's aunt. The Comtesse de Saint-Maurice was almost as tall as her nephew. Her brown hair, which looked as if gray had been artificially banished, was piled on the top of her head. The train of her heavy black silk dress fanned out over the carpet. So many ropes of pearls and diamonds decorated her neck that hardly any skin showed above a low neckline. Pink enamel balls nestled in her hair, their surfaces winking with candlelight reflected in tiny diamonds. More diamonds glittered on her black lace fan. Sarah had never seen as many ornaments worn at once except on opera heroines.

At a break in the conversation, Pierre said, "Good evening, Aunt Nathalie."

She turned to him with an austere smile. "Pierre, you surprise me. Though you left a message, I wasn't sure you were coming."

He kissed her hand and then her cheeks. "This is my friend, Mademoiselle Taylor."

"Oh, yes. Your note said she would be accompanying you."

Sarah performed her most deferential curtsey. "Thank you for allowing me to come."

Nathalie looked at Sarah as if she held opera glasses and were studying a singer whose voice displeased her. She and Pierre had similar strong jaws and cleft chins, but whereas his chin gave him an appearance of deviltry, hers made her look haughty. "You are an American," she said to Sarah, in the same way a judge might say, "You are a criminal."

"Yes, but if I were not, I could enjoy being Parisian. It is a beautiful city."

The countess's blue eyes thawed a little, but not enough to look cordial. "Perhaps we can talk of Paris another time," she said dismissively, in a tone that made clear she had no intention of ever having such a conversation.

A dragon, Sarah thought as she and Pierre went on. Armand couldn't be much of a man if concern for that woman ruled him. No—that was unfair. She herself had allowed her father to dominate her too long.

By the time Pierre found two seats and the pianist was ready to begin, Armand still hadn't appeared. "Do you think this is all for nothing?" she whispered to Pierre.

"He'll be here."

The pianist, a tall man with thick black hair, began with a musical adaptation of the Habañera from Bizet's *Carmen*, went on to a furious Liszt intermezzo, and ended with a Chopin Polonaise. During the interval, while different musicians were arranging music and instruments for a quintet, Pierre and Sarah joined the eddy of guests circling the room. The men were like black rocks in a stream; the women swirled around them like floating blossoms—pink and orange, mauve and blue. Bits of conversation floated with them, about people she had never heard of.

An occasional phrase stood out—a woman who'd been identified as a princess was saying, "But the family doesn't have a really old name." Then Sarah heard, "Still, the men of the Empire fought well," from the general who had ogled her earlier. Their words, she surmised, reflected the social distinction between old and new nobility that Pierre had described to her.

She was listening to hear what might be said next when Pierre touched her arm. "Mademoiselle Taylor, I wish to present my cousin, the Comte de Saint-Maurice."

The man who bowed over her hand was tall and handsome, slender enough to look trim in his evening wear but large enough to have an appealing masculine strength. Blond hair, parted in the center, waved softly around his head. His light blue eyes had a suggestion of circles under them, as if he'd witnessed too much sorrow; they gave him an appearance of sad delicacy. Despite his military-style mustache and sideburns, he looked too sensitive for a man with an impressive military record for bravery. She understood why women might feel an immediate sympathy for him.

"I am delighted to meet you, Mademoiselle Taylor." His voice could be that of a singer, deep and musical.

"And I'm glad to be here."

His face relaxed into a warm and gracious smile, still with that hint of sadness, but with pleasure also. "Your voice. I hope you don't mind my saying it's charming."

"I don't mind at all." Sarah had the feeling that she might not mind anything he said.

At a signal from the platform, there was a general movement back toward the seats. Armand said reluctantly, "Please excuse me. I haven't spoken to my mother so I must do that, but I hope Pierre will not take you away too soon."

When Armand had left and they were seated, Pierre whispered, "You see? I told you."

She smiled at him in agreement. Yes, he was right that Armand seemed to be attracted to her. But now she wasn't as sure he was also right about her resistance to Armand's appeal.

The musicians began the lyrical melody of Mozart's clarinet quintet, music that ordinarily would have absorbed her. But her thoughts kept returning to Armand and the role she'd agreed to play. Sarah, she warned herself, you might be getting into trouble. Still, the excitement could be worth the risk.

CHAPTER
SIX

ARMAND STOPPED IN FRONT OF THE OFFICES OF *LE COM-battant*. The paint of the red letters for the name above the entrance still looked wet. It was like Pierre, he thought, to start a newspaper called The Fighter.

Two men in overcoats were standing at the door, reading the newspaper pages fastened to the glass panels. Armand waited for them to finish so that he could go inside. When they left, he entered and climbed a flight of dark stairs and walked along a hall. The waiting room at the end had an atmosphere of hastily assembled poverty. The chairs placed against the walls looked as if they'd been rescued from some-one's attic. Faded brown drapes hung at smudged windows, and copies of *Le Combattant* and several other papers were stacked on a scratched claw-foot table. However the men, most of them young, coming through the room seemed busy and energetic. One was reading a piece of handwritten copy as he walked. Two others in ink-stained canvas overalls carried trays of type. All had airs of going about important business.

Armand approached a young clerk who stood behind a

high desk. "I would like to see Monsieur de Tourbey. Can you please let him know that the Comte de Saint-Maurice is here?"

"Yes, right away."

While Armand waited, a small, dapper man bustled in carrying a page of newly printed proofs. He wore an elegant jacket and trousers, with a silk embroidered waistcoat that swelled out over a small paunch. His hair, bleached a brassy yellow, was combed to a high pompadour. Surprised, Armand recognized Roland Gille. So *Le Combattant* was going to ensure circulation by including a notorious gossip columnist in its pages. Armand wondered whose decision that was. Pierre and Gille detested each other. Maybe Victor Marmontel, Pierre's partner and co-editor, had suggested it. Apparently his and Pierre's concern for their political goals overrode scruples about printing trash.

When Gille saw Armand, he stopped and gave a smile that was both ingratiating and superior. "A pleasure to see you, comte, though I'm surprised to find you here."

"I'm here to see my cousin."

Pierre came in then. He and Gille nodded coolly to each other. Armand was glad to leave the columnist behind and follow Pierre back along the hall.

They passed a large room where several men sat writing around a long table. "These are the editorial offices," Pierre explained. In a smaller one Armand glimpsed two men playing cards. "Not everyone takes assignments seriously," Pierre remarked with an edge of irritation. "But they're useful at covering theater news."

"But you take your work seriously," Armand said.

"Yes, or I wouldn't be here."

They reached a small office, and Pierre waved Armand inside. The room held a desk, two chairs, shelves filled with books and papers, and files with more papers stacked on top of them. A tall window let in sunlight that captured dust motes floating over the desk.

After they were seated, Pierre said, "I'm glad you came by. Anything I can do for you?"

"I'm here for the same reason you and Marmontel started this paper," Armand responded. "The threat from General Boulanger and his followers. The Boulangists are dangerous. He must be defeated in the special Paris election."

"Then you don't believe those people who say his candidacy is a comic opera affair?"

Armand was never completely sure when Pierre was joking. "No, certainly not. And you must not either."

"Well, Parisians do love their comedies." Pierre's face sobered. "Of course I agree with you."

Armand said, "I'd like to provide you with some money in this venture if you need it."

"Thanks for the offer," Pierre said. "We may be able to use the money. Boulanger seems to have a good chance."

"Yes, but why?" Armand spread his hands. "I don't understand his appeal."

"Everyone loves him," Pierre said dryly. "When he was minister of war, he gave the army better barracks and food. Thanks to him, now every captain is allotted a horse, and ordinary soldiers can wear mustaches. He sent troops to break up a strike, then ordered the soldiers to share their food with the strikers. So he pleased both the business men and the workers. He brought back military parades, and he said nasty things about Germany and Bismarck. What Frenchman could resist him?"

"Be serious, Pierre."

"I am. Never more so. Serious enough to use Gille."

Armand frowned. "Was that your idea or Marmontel's?"

"It was Marmontel's, but I agree. A lot of Parisians buy newspapers to read Gille's columns. We need to reach as many readers as possible. The election's only eight weeks away."

"You'd better be careful with Gille. He can be vicious."

Pierre shrugged. "How can he hurt me?"

"He can attack anyone connected with you. Like that American woman you brought to Maman's musical evening."

"Sarah Taylor." Pierre leaned back in his chair, an expression on his face Armand couldn't interpret.

"I assume you do have a connection with her," Armand said a little huffily. It irritated him when he couldn't guess what Pierre was thinking.

Pierre noticed Armand's annoyance—a good sign of his cousin's interest. He debated how much to say. "We're . . . friends. She's a very attractive woman."

"Yes. I would say quite beautiful."

So, Pierre thought, Sarah had made an impression. Armand's standards for female beauty were exceedingly high. "She has a good singing voice too. Or so I'm told. I've never actually heard her. Cesbron at the Opéra Comique let her go because she punctured Rivarol with a hatpin when he made advances."

"A woman with spirit, then," Armand said admiringly. "You're involved with her?"

Pierre leaned back in his chair. "Are you interested in my private life? Or in Sarah's?"

If Armand could look anything but dignified, Pierre would have said his cousin was flustered. "I thought . . . well, it doesn't matter."

Pierre rose and went to the window, where he pulled a drapery partway across, shutting off some of the morning sunlight and giving himself time to think. To his surprise, he found he was reluctant to encourage Armand's interest in Sarah. Maybe the plan wasn't needed.

He returned to his desk. "If you're worried about people like Boulanger, you should get into politics yourself. With your background in the army and foreign service, you'd be a good deputy. Maybe prime minister some day."

"There's no point in another discussion about that," Armand said. "You know Maman would be devastated."

"Aunt Nathalie would be unhappy, but she isn't going to die from disappointment. Or disown you. You're too important to her."

"We'll never agree about Maman," Armand said and rose. "Remember to ask me if you need money." He started to the door, then turned back. "There was another thing I wanted to remind you about. When you oppose Boulanger, you're going up against people like Henri Rochefort. He has no scruples about what he says in *L'Intransigeant*. Or whom he challenges. I don't want you to have a duel with him."

Pierre felt a rush of affection. Armand might look austere and have trouble expressing his feelings, but he'd come with warnings and an offer of help. The scheme for Armand and Sarah might work. For Armand's sake, Pierre decided, he could certainly get over his reluctance to share her attention.

"I'll remember your advice, Armand. By the way, there's to be a Christmas celebration Thursday of next week. At the Café Riche. I expect that Leon Duval will be there. He's working for *Le Figaro* now. Maybe Zola and Maupassant. I know you think my writing friends are seedy, but there's sure to be interesting conversation about Boulanger. Why don't you come along?"

Armand hesitated in the doorway. "I'm not sure."

Pierre came around the desk and put a companionable hand on Armand's shoulder. "I'll invite Sarah Taylor. She's charming and amusing. Conversation about politics, and a beautiful woman to look at. What better combination?"

A smile lit Armand's blue eyes. He looked almost boyish. "Yes, that's true. I'll come. Good-bye, and let me know if you want money."

After Armand left, Pierre felt an unfamiliar discontent. He thought about Sarah, the sparkle that she had when she was enjoying herself. That special blend of innocence, but with the promise behind it of sexual fire. Just the way she moved her body when she walked. By God, he'd like to be the one to help her discover her own nature. What a mistress she would make!

Yes, maybe he did mind sharing Sarah's time, but it was for a good reason. And maybe better for him not to be too involved with her. For now he must get down to work. First he'd write Sarah a note, asking her to meet him at the Café Américain. She liked to go there because the name had a sentimental appeal for her. He would tell her that Armand wanted to see her again and ask her to the Christmas party.

Sarah looked around the café and was surprised not to see Pierre. The clocks in the center of the Boulevard des Capucines read a few minutes after three, the time his message had asked that she meet him. Before, he had always arrived ahead of her, even when she was early, to make sure she wouldn't be in the café alone.

Customers still sat at the sidewalk tables, but the December breeze was brisk enough that she went inside. Also, she felt less conspicuous that way. In Paris, she'd been surprised to learn, "respectable" women were no more free to go out alone than at home. She was still enough of her Boston self to be a little hesitant about breaking the rules, but she wasn't willing to be that restricted. A prim-looking hat and a haughty expression, she'd discovered, discouraged overtures from strange men. So she purchased a severe black straw that she wore when she went out by herself.

Sarah ordered café au lait. Three women also sat alone at small square tables. Each one was brightly dressed, almost gaudy. Sarah speculated that they might be performers from the vaudeville, which was nearby. She would have looked for a job there if it hadn't been for her promise to Ted.

Another woman came in and sat down by herself. She was a plump blonde, fairly young, with a face white with powder, mascara rimming her eyes and thick false eyelashes.

Without asking for an order, the waiter brought her a bright yellow drink in a slender glass. After a few sips, the blonde looked around, smiling in an inviting way. A middle-aged man in heavy English tweeds got up from a bench along the wall and went over to the woman's table. She greeted him with another coy smile, and he sat down. They talked in low voices for a few minutes. Then Sarah heard the man say, in English, "Forty francs!" in a shocked tone. The blonde put her hand on his arm, and they continued in lower voices. Shortly afterward, the blonde gave the Englishman a slip of paper, drained her glass, got up and left. Her customer, as Sarah decided he was, paid the waiter for the drink and followed, avoiding looking at other patrons.

So the unescorted women here were not necessarily from the vaudeville; some at least had another profession. Forty francs to perform what must be the most intimate of acts with a stranger! Sarah was fascinated and dismayed by the glimpse of a life so different from her own.

Through the small-paned window she saw Pierre hurrying along the street, dodging past other pedestrians and street vendors. His hat started to blow off; he grabbed it, and his hair flew about his ears. He came through the door of the café as if bringing the wind with him.

"Has anyone bothered you?" were his first words to her, accompanied by such a fierce look at the men at nearby tables that one elderly gentleman got up and left.

"No, no one has spoken to me," Sarah said, amused and touched.

He sat down and breathed a little more slowly. "I'm sorry I'm late. There's so much to do with the new paper."

She remembered why he'd been away, arranging to start a newspaper. "You've begun then. What is it called?"

"*Le Combattant*." She listened with fascination while he explained about its role in the coming special election. "We should have started sooner. But at first no one took General

Boulanger seriously. The Republicans called him a *Saint-Arnaud de café-concert*. Saint Arnaud was a man who helped engineer the seizure of power in 1851 by Napoleon III."

"So General Boulanger was the music hall Saint Arnaud."

"Yes, but no one's laughing at him now. He and his backers have been very successful. They hired an American who's experienced in political campaigns to advise them."

"I still don't understand why you're so opposed to him. Aren't the elections fair?"

Pierre's jaw was set in a hard line, and his eyes looked fierce. "Yes, but the Boulangists don't really want a republic. They want to change the constitution. We don't need another general to become president and then emperor. He's one of those charismatic generals—like the two Napoleons. That's what makes him such a threat. We must stop him!"

She hadn't seen Pierre so agitated since the night he took her to the Goncourt play. "You sound like someone going to war. Your cousin isn't the only one interested in politics."

Pierre looked a little startled, then relaxed into his usual affable posture. "I only do battle as a journalist. That reminds me of what I wanted to tell you. Our plan for Armand is getting off to a good start. I saw him earlier and he brought up your name. Said he thinks you're beautiful."

He smiled at her, but his expression didn't have the enthusiasm she expected. Maybe the "good start" wasn't quite as good as he'd hoped. "What does that mean? Will he ask to escort me places? Since you're so busy, that would be a good idea." Even as she volunteered the opinion, she hoped he wouldn't agree.

"No, Armand doesn't rush into anything. He finds you attractive, but we'll need to prod him more."

"What do you mean?"

"Are you dressed warmly enough? Let's walk a bit and talk."

Outside the breeze had died down. The air smelled of

dry leaves and approaching winter. The few linden leaves that hadn't been swept away earlier had settled into cracks between the paving stones or hidden under the bottom ledges of the shop windows. Sarah took Pierre's offered arm, and they started in the direction of the Church of the Madeleine. It felt companionable to lengthen her stride in rhythm with his. Pierre didn't begin his explanation, and she was content with the brisk air against her face and the warmth of his elbow seeping through her glove to her hand. Was she greedy, she wondered, to want to keep both Pierre's and Armand's attention? No. Surely an independent woman in Paris should enjoy the company of more than one man.

They came to the Place de l'Opéra, and Pierre gestured toward the elaborate opera house. "Is it still your shrine?" he asked.

"Yes, but I'm not aiming so high now. Just to be back at the Opéra Comique."

They passed the flower market, with its spicy fragrance of carnations, and reached the Church of the Madeleine. It was built to resemble a Graeco-Roman temple, with Greek columns and pediment. The figures, however, represented The Last Judgment, with Saint Mary Magdalene kneeling beside Jesus, asking mercy for the wicked. Sarah sat at the bottom of one of the columns. Pierre stood, his hands in the pockets of his trousers, looking up at the building, which he must have seen hundreds of times before.

Finally he sat beside her. "We must make plans," he said. "Friends and I are meeting for a Christmas celebration at the Café Riche next week on Thursday. Some of them you'd probably like to meet—Maupassant and Zola may come. Armand will be there, and I told him I'd invite you. Will you come?"

The wind seemed colder. Sarah tucked her feet back under the bench and pulled her long coat more tightly around her legs. "Then you'll give me over to him, just like a Christmas parcel?" She intended to say it lightly, but she heard a trace of querulousness in her voice.

"No! Of course not!" His startled look pleased her. "I see I didn't explain something important about Armand. Our strategy will be the opposite. You'll have to act like a woman in love with me. And I'll treat you the same." He rose, bowed to her, took off his hat, and lifted her hand to his lips. His kiss and the way he held her hand while at the same time gazing into her eyes, was a stage stereotype of an amorous suitor. "Am I doing this correctly?"

Though she knew he was pretending, his mock ardor affected her. A constriction rippled through her chest and spread to her stomach. She pulled her hand away, laughing to cover her response. "Yes, your performance is very good."

He sat down, a little apart from her. "Armand has always fancied the women he saw me involved with. From the time we were young. I suppose you'd call it a sort of friendly competition." He grinned and continued teasingly. "Then there's my vanity. I'll be disgraced if my friends think I know such a tantalizing woman and you aren't my mistress. So that's another reason for you to act in love with me."

"You mean—the others there will assume I'm your mistress?"

"Does that bother you?"

Did it? She tried to decide. A year ago she would have been more than bothered. Offended, maybe outraged. Her friends in Boston would be horrified. Still, there was a certain tantalizing temptation to the idea. It would be like playing a role in an opera—Violetta in *La Traviata*. And no one in Paris except Ted really knew her.

"And Armand? Would he think I'm your mistress?"

"That's the point."

Somehow it seemed important to sound as casual and flippant as he. "You're an attractive man. It's reasonable that

I might be in love with you. Yes, I can play the part. To save your cousin and your vanity both."

He leaned back, his hand resting on the bottom of the column, close to her leg. She could almost feel his hand, as if he'd touched her.

Though his pose was relaxed, his face had a closed look, as if he didn't want her to know just what he was thinking. "Of course," he said, "we don't have to pretend. I'd be happy to show you the real joys of Paris. Or more likely, you could show me."

His tone was still teasing, but the warmth she felt confused her. The plan concerning Armand suggested Pierre didn't have a serious interest in her. So seduction was a game he played—had probably played with lots of women. She wasn't certain of the rules, but she did know how to perform a role. "Singers must be actresses too. Pretending to be your mistress will be good practice for the stage."

She stood up, and he rose also. The last light was fading; soon the gas lamps would be lit. She opened the pocketwatch she wore on a chain around her neck. "I must get back to my room. I'm expecting a new student. Someone from the *lycée* whom Emile recruited."

"Let me walk you home."

"No. I'll take a cab."

He hailed one for her and helped her in. "I'll send you a note about Thursday," he said.

As the cab started up, she looked back. He was still standing, watching after her. She turned around so that she wouldn't see him anymore and tried to recover the light-hearted feeling she usually had when she'd been with him.

It must be her vanity, she decided. Probably she was piqued that he seemed ready to relinquish her to his cousin. She should listen to her own advice: playing a role was good practice for her. And it wouldn't hurt her to be a little more humble. That was the one criticism that Papa had sometimes made.

As she thought about Pierre's invitation, her spirits lifted. She'd been dreading the Christmas season, with its memories of decorated trees and rituals from her childhood, and a reminder how far from home she was. A party at a French café would be completely different from a party in Boston. She would use all her acting skills, and Armand would respond to her. He was as attractive as Pierre. It might even lead to other roles she'd want to play for a long time.

CHAPTER
SEVEN

LIGHTS FROM THE CHANDELIERS IN THE CAFÉ RICHE SHONE through its square windows, illuminating the pedestrians outside. The glare reached out between the trees into the Boulevard des Italiens; it competed with the lanterns of passing carriages. Entertainments of the holiday season drew thicker crowds than usual as people headed for the cafés up and down the boulevard. Shops on the side streets kept their windows lighted to display animated woodcutters and other figures from Christmas stories. Even the whores, flipping their skirts to advertise a glimpse of ankle, had exchanged their bored expressions for something approaching gaiety.

Sarah and Pierre reached the corner of the boulevard and the Rue Lepelletier just as a young man approached. He called exuberantly, "Pierre," and ran, catching up with them by the entrance to the Café Riche. Long, black hair fell in curls to his shoulders, its luxuriance matched by a thick, curly beard. His movements were quick, almost jerky.

After Pierre introduced him as Leon Duval, the two men exchanged congratulations, Pierre for Leon's start with *Le Figaro*, and Leon for the founding of Pierre's paper. "Are you still writing for *La Justice* as well," Leon asked.

"Yes, but Clemenceau insists on a very serious, intellectual tone. I think that to defeat Boulanger, we need to reach people who won't read the better papers."

"You must be convinced, to put up one hundred thousand francs to get *Le Combattant* going."

Sarah looked at Pierre, startled. That was the equivalent of twenty thousand dollars. A modest fortune! He must be more wealthy, or more serious about politics, than he'd let on.

They entered, passing the obscurely placed number sixteen, as if to indicate that the Café Riche was too important to serve strangers who didn't already know its location. Inside, white pillars separated the large center room from smaller spaces around the edges. The walls were white, relieved by gold trim on the plaster scrolls. Red plush chairs surrounded the tables, with benches upholstered in more red plush along the walls. Sarah observed that her dark red velvet dress, which she liked to wear at Christmas, almost made her part of the decorations.

Men in tall silk hats and women wearing tiaras or small hats sat at crowded tables around the room. Behind the circular bar waiters in white aprons filled glasses from spigots in the oak barrels that rested on their sides. The barmaids who served drinks already looked tired to Sarah, their smiles rigidly fastened on their mouths. Leon Duval excused himself and went to join a table of noisy patrons.

A waiter came over to Pierre, a genuine smile animating his mustached face. "*Bonsoir*, Monsieur Pierre. Monsieur Delvau will be delighted when I tell him you're here. He's making *sole aux crevettes* tonight, and he knows how much you enjoy them. Are you dining downstairs, or in the *entresol*?"

"In the mezzanine. But we're a little early, so we'll have a table here and go upstairs when the others arrive."

As the waiter started to lead them to an empty bench along the wall, Pierre turned to Sarah. "Would you like to see the kitchen? It's impressive. We'll say hello to the chef."

Pierre was right. The kitchen impressed Sarah. It was like several kitchens together. Smoky haze drifted up and collected under the ceiling, which was two stories high. Huge black ovens filled one corner, their chimneys looking like smokestacks from old locomotives. In a side section poultry and game, including a whole deer, hung along the walls. Beneath them was a large tank divided into sections for live trout, lobsters, and sea creatures that Sarah couldn't identify. Glossy copper pots hung from iron racks over the counters. Cooks in white jackets ignored the black-jacketed waiters, who in turn brushed aside the boys who scurried around with collections of dirty dishes. Pierre introduced Sarah to the chef, who stood with his hands behind his back, his formal frock coat open over his very generous stomach. He looked more like a genial host than a worker, and he seemed delighted to see Pierre.

"You're known for your appreciation of food?" Sarah asked as they left the kitchen.

"When I first started out as a journalist, I used to write about restaurants. I particularly liked this one because interesting people came here regularly. Like Manet. And Baudelaire, though he was before my time." He pointed toward a table in the corner. "Offenbach had a boiled egg and a cutlet every morning over there. Maybe while he was eating, he was thinking up songs you'll perform."

Sarah felt a pang at the reminder that she wasn't singing. Pierre must have noticed her expression, because after they were seated, he asked, "What do you hear from the manager at the Opéra Comique?"

"I went back to see Monsieur Cesbron a few days ago. He was encouraging. I think that after the New Year, he'll probably offer me a place."

"But it's hard for you to wait," Pierre guessed.

"I've never been good at waiting for things," she confessed. "Isn't everyone that way?"

"No. I'm very patient. When I want something." He leaned across the table and briefly touched her chin with one finger, just a slight brush, but it seemed to vibrate along a network of nerves and blood vessels.

She laughed, but she didn't sound quite real to herself. "Are you playing the lover already? Your friends aren't here yet."

"With you, it's a pleasure to practice." His smile caressed her, and her inner network responded again.

The waiter came back. "What would mademoiselle care to drink?" he asked.

"Wine?" Pierre asked Sarah. "They have a good Château Larose here."

"I've never tried absinthe. It must be a very popular liqueur. The cafés near my room have signs for l'heure verte. Doesn't 'the green hour' mean a special time for drinking absinthe?"

Pierre frowned. "Yes, but you should leave absinthe alone," he said with uncustomary force. "It has wormwood in it, along with some other potent ingredients. If you drink very much, it causes hallucinations." He paused, as if uncomfortable with his vehemence and went on more lightly. "Rimbaud claimed that hallucinations are better than real life. But unless you're a poet or partly crazy, don't drink it."

Her impression of Pierre had been that he tolerated all human whims. Maybe she was wrong. Perversely, she felt like ordering absinthe, to see whether he would stop her. Deciding her impulse was childish, she said, "I'll have the wine."

Before she had more than tasted her wine, three boisterous men and a cheerful young woman came in. Pierre rose and waved to them. Sarah recognized Hector Lunel, partly be-

cause he was clean-shaven, unusual among all the mustaches
and beards. She'd met him the night she and Pierre had
gone to the play at the Odéon. The young woman with him,
a small plump blond with a ready laugh, was introduced as
Mademoiselle Barbier. Since Hector was tall and gaunt, in
appearance they made a mismatched pair. Leon Duval joined
them again, and they started upstairs. On the way, Mademoiselle Barbier said her name was Virginie and that she
lived with Hector. Though startled by Virginie's candor,
Sarah liked the happy laugh. And after all, Virginie supposed
Sarah had a similar relationship to Pierre.

The thought disquieted her momentarily, but she reminded herself that she'd agreed to go along with Pierre's
request. To practice her role, she took his elbow as they
reached the *entresol* and looked at him with what she hoped
was an adoring smile. After a blink of surprise, he returned
her look with one of such ostentatious admiration that she
wanted to laugh. His mustached lips curved in a sensual
invitation that sent shivers along Sarah's arms.

She almost protested. It wasn't fair for him to be so skillful
at the outward signs of love when a conquest of her feelings
wasn't what either of them wanted. She released his arm
and preceded him into the private room.

The walls and furnishings repeated the white and gold
paint and the red plush upholstery of the main floor below.
Two windows looked out onto the boulevard. Against the
opposite wall was a large divan, wide enough that Sarah
could imagine it had been used for many passionate encounters. A fire burned in the fireplace, and a table had
been set underneath a gold chandelier where seven white
candles already multiplied their flames in tall mirrors on the
side walls. As Sarah passed one of the mirrors, she noticed
phrases scratched on it—dates, women's names, amorous
avowals. A few words were unfamiliar—she suspected they
were obscenities. The mirror, together with the divan, gave

the room a disreputable but exciting aura of illicit encounters.

"Is Zola coming tonight?" Hector Lunel asked Pierre after they were seated and champagne had been poured.

"He sent back an acceptance," Pierre said.

"Have you seen him recently?" Leon Duval asked. "He's lost so much weight that I hardly knew him when I saw him at the Odéon last week."

"He looks happy, too," Hector added, with the sly expression of someone who has heard some particularly enjoyable gossip. "Perhaps he's fallen in love and has a young mistress."

Norbert Le Pol, a round-faced man wearing a polka-dot waistcoat, laughed. "It would quiet the critics who attacked him for his lack of virility. Maybe he'll leave his wife for someone else. Prove he can perform with a woman and not just write about it. Then he'd really silence them."

"That newspaper article was mean-spirited and vicious," Pierre retorted angrily. "It used personal innuendo to attack him and his writing. We should ignore that kind of cruelty. I think he's too loyal to Alexandrine to leave her after all the years of poverty she's shared with him. If he wants to take a mistress as well, I'll wish him happiness. We should leave his personal life alone."

"Don't be so noble, Pierre," Hector said. "Your new paper has hired Roland Gille—a purveyor of all kinds of trash. And he doesn't hesitate to print gossip just because it's cruel."

"Yes," Pierre admitted. "It's a compromise I don't like, but Boulanger will be hard to defeat. A lot of people can't wait to read Gille's column each day."

The talk turned to estimates of General Boulanger's strength in the coming election, and Sarah gave a startled thought to how much she'd changed. Just a few months ago she couldn't have imagined listening to men discussing another man's virility. Now she had been interested rather than shocked. At least, not very shocked. Pierre's intensity in defending Zola's privacy also surprised her. When she'd first met Pierre, he'd kept his serious concerns well hidden under an almost frivolous exterior. She had an unusual involvement with a man she was only beginning to know.

"What? The party's hardly underway yet?" The speaker, in the open doorway, was a tall, brawny man with thick dark hair and mustache, whose sad eyes and haggard face contradicted his cheerful voice. From the greetings, Sarah concluded this was Guy de Maupassant, another of the writers Pierre particularly admired.

In the past week, she had read several stories and a recent novel each by Maupassant and Zola. The reading sharpened her French and prepared her to meet the authors. Some of their candor still unsettled her Boston bred literary expectations, and she was curious to talk to them both.

As soon as Pierre introduced Sarah, Maupassant said, "Pierre doesn't deserve to claim all the beautiful women," and took Pierre's chair beside her.

"Perhaps women claim Pierre," Sarah responded, and was pleased when he laughed.

"Is that what you're doing?"

"Maybe. Women can choose, too. Do you think all women are as pitiful as your heroine in *Une Vie*? She suffers whatever cruelties her husband cares to inflict."

His expression became serious. "Of course all women aren't like that. Her romantic attitudes and naive dreams lead to her unhappiness, not just the fact she's a woman."

"But in *Bel Ami*, the women aren't naive, and your hero takes advantage of all of them," she retorted. Pierre and Hector were both listening; she felt very bold to be arguing with so famous an author.

Maupassant, smiling again, glanced over at Pierre. "Are you wondering if I took our good Pierre as my model? No, certainly not. True, Bel Ami is a journalist, like our friend. But Pierre would never be so unscrupulous as to advance his career through women."

Pierre grinned, reached for the wine, and filled glasses all around. "Let's drink to my good character," he said. "Now that I have a testimonial to it."

Sarah supposed she believed Maupassant, but she also thought that men probably defended each other.

While she had been speaking to Maupassant, another couple arrived. The dandified-looking man seemed eager to meet Sarah, but the woman, whose name was Jeanne, sat down next to Norbert of the polka-dot waistcoat and ignored everyone else. The door opened again to admit Armand. Sarah's stomach did a small flip of excitement. She realized that she'd been waiting for him to arrive, a bit like waiting onstage for the curtain to go up and the performance to begin.

She'd forgotten how handsome he was. He wore evening clothes, as he had when she'd met him at his mother's house, and she couldn't imagine him otherwise. The formality suited his air of concealed sadness. His blond hair, when he removed his hat, looked as though it had just been combed, and his sideburns and mustache were impeccably trimmed. Nothing out of place or ill considered.

He bowed to Sarah and said, "Mademoiselle Taylor. A pleasure to meet you again."

Sarah heard nothing in his voice except the most formal of acknowledgements. Pierre's plan was hopeless. Armand de Saint-Maurice would never do anything so rash as to become enamored of an American woman living in disreputable circumstances. She felt disappointed. Her performance as Pierre's mistress wouldn't last long without an audience.

Pierre obviously didn't share her conclusion. As soon as introductions were over, he came to Sarah's side and said to Maupassant, "Sorry, Guy. You've had a long enough turn in my place." As Pierre waited for the other man to give up the chair, he rested his hand lightly on the side of Sarah's neck, just above the edge of her high collar. When he sat down, his fingers trailed away in a tiny caress.

Sarah stared down at her own slender fingers, pale tan against the white damask tablecloth, and hoped that the telltale color wasn't creeping into her face. Pierre leaned across and whispered into her ear, "How good an actress are you? Come on. It's your chance to be ridiculously in love with me. Watch Hector and Virginie."

She looked around and saw that the couple had moved to the divan. They were embracing in an attitude that suggested an abundance of drink as much as love. Virginie's left sleeve was halfway down her arm, exposing a fair amount of her left breast. She and Hector attempted a kiss that took two more trials to complete.

Sarah turned angrily back to Pierre, ready to renounce any plan that used Hector and Virginie as an example. He was laughing at her so beguilingly that she knew she'd been taken in. Her anger couldn't resist his mischievous enjoyment, and she laughed too. He poured her more wine, and as they touched glasses, his eyes took on an adoring look. She put her mouth close to his ear and whispered, "If your newspaper fails, you can work as an actor."

"Not fair," Leon said from across the table. "No more lovers' secrets."

Lovers. Though she and Pierre had intended that very impression, hearing the word said aloud evoked disapproving Boston voices in Sarah's head. With her skin burning, she turned away from Pierre, and found Armand staring at her. His gaze held sympathy—and interest.

Another entrance interrupted them. Two men came in, followed by a waiter carrying a large box. The man in the lead was middle-aged, with receding dark hair and a close-trimmed beard that had gray generously mixed in. He directed the waiter to put the box beside the fireplace. The second, younger man was slender with a pencil mustache.

When Pierre introduced them, the older man turned out to be Emile Zola. His companion was Paul Alexis, a journalist and close friend.

Because of the earlier conversation, Sarah couldn't help evaluating Zola's appearance. He was plump for a man of medium height, but not fat. Certainly at that moment he appeared happy and content. He was lifting small packages from the box by the fireplace and unwrapping them. Curious, Sarah went to look. "May I help you?" she asked.

He turned dark eyes on her and gave her a soft smile. "Thank you, Mademoiselle Taylor. I enjoy arranging them myself. You see, these are *santons*, little saints from my childhood country, Provence. A friend sent them to me from the fair in Aix. I brought them to share for the evening's festivities."

"What a generous and delightful idea," she said admiringly.

Under his loving fingers, a *crèche* took shape on the white marble mantel over the fireplace. It was different from the Christmas manger scenes Sarah was accustomed to at home. Around the holy family stood clay figures, not of shepherds in Middle Eastern dress, but of French peasants. One was a gardener carrying flowers and a watering can. A hunter had a dog on a leash and a hare hanging from one hand. "This is the mayor," Zola said, showing her a man in waistcoat and suit, "and here are the peasant and his wife with their basket of vegetables and chickens to sell."

Sarah's eyes misted. In spite of the differences between this *crèche* and ones from her childhood, the scene of the Christmas birth brought Boston painfully to mind. Reasons for being away from her father felt unimportant next to the longing to see him, to exchange gifts that were tokens of loving and being loved. This wasn't a place to give in to sentiment; she concentrated on examining the *santons*.

It was clear why Zola wished to handle them himself and

not trust them to careless hands. Craftsman must have put hours of work into each figure. The detail and color were extraordinary. The knife grinder had his grindstone, and every lacing was distinct on the drummer boy's drum. "Who is that?" she said, pointing to a woman riding a donkey and holding an umbrella.

"That's Margarido." Zola gave her another of his soft smiles. "She's the village gossip—a little like a writer."

It was hard for Sarah to believe that the brutal novel about miners she had just read was written by this gentle-sounding man.

As if the waiters had been waiting for the famous author's appearance, they arrived, balancing large silver platters of food. Sarah saw that Armand was taking a place down the table from her and Pierre. He could see them, but conversation wasn't possible. Just now she didn't care. The smells coming from the dishes being set out engaged all her hungry attention.

"Ah," Zola said. "Oysters. I love seafood."

Sarah preferred the *foie gras*, especially when she spread the goose liver on thin crackers. The promised *sole aux crevettes* was delicious, and she ate almost as much as Zola of the sole and shrimp dish. "I'm glad the chef likes you," she told Pierre.

During the meat course of roast duck and ham, she found Armand watching her; and when she exclaimed in surprise over a raspberry sorbet being available in December, again he was watching her. After that, however, he became engaged in a discussion with Leon Duval. Dried apricots and bonbons were passed around; the final course was a fruit cake in the shape of a yule log.

She observed that Zola, who was sitting almost across from her, listened intently to the conversation of others but said little himself. She wished he'd say something that would tell her about his background. When the coffee had been brought, she couldn't resist questioning him. "In your books, Monsieur Zola, you write so vividly of terrible hardships and privation. The scene in *Germinal* where the two men and Catherine are trapped in the mine, surrounded by water. How do you know about such things?"

"I visited the mines and listened to the miners."

"But you wrote as if you knew just what it felt like." She shuddered, remembering how his description had affected her. "I was sure you had lived it yourself."

He smiled at her sympathetically, but a little amused too. "I would guess that you have never known real hardship. Am I right?"

Had she? Leaving Papa had been painful, difficult. But here in Paris she had been lucky. Feeling almost ashamed, she said, "Yes, you're right."

"I hope that your good fortune continues. And that you only learn about how difficult life can be from my books."

Zola rose, announcing he must leave, and everyone got up. Maupassant said he must go on to another celebration. "At Marie Kann's," someone said, but not until the door had closed behind Maupassant.

"How does he find so many women who are both beautiful and rich?" the dandy asked enviously. "It would help my career too."

Apparently, Sarah thought, advancement through the favors of women was admired. *Bel Ami* might be quite true to life. But whose life?

There was general discussion of the hour and where to go next. Virginie seemed to be asleep on the divan, but Hector managed to get up and unsteadily joined the other men. They were speaking in low voices, but Hector didn't bother. "Let's go to a *maison de tolérance*," he said.

Sarah puzzled over his words. She hadn't heard the term, *maison de tolérance*, before.

Pierre said, "Shut up, Hector," in a quiet voice.

Hector persisted, as loudly as ever, "If anyone has enough money, the Perroquet Gris has a wonderful new Turkish girl. Straight from a harem. Who'll go? How about you, Le Pol? Pierre? Comte?"

"No," Pierre said. He sounded furious. "You're drunk, Hector, and you're being offensive."

He certainly is! Sarah thought, and was surprised at the vehemence of her reaction. She looked at Hector with distaste. How crude he was.

Armand said something she couldn't hear, but it was clearly a refusal. Of course. Sarah couldn't imagine him going to a bordello. He came over to her for the first time since they exchanged greetings. "I apologize, Mademoiselle Taylor, for Monsieur Lunel's behavior."

She smiled at him, appreciating his concern and his dignity. "Thank you, comte. I choose to ignore him."

Zola went to the mantel and began to wrap the *santons* and place them in their box. Sarah followed to take a final look. When he was finished except for one figure, he turned to her. "Mademoiselle Taylor, I'd like you to have this."

The *santon* was a woman, her head wrapped in a peasant's scarf, her face lined, her clothes simple. She carried a bundle of faggots. "As you see," Zola said, "this woman is poor and humble. You will never have to earn your living by gathering firewood, but you may find you understand her."

"Thank you," was all Sarah could manage. This famous writer was nothing like Papa, but she felt cherished by the gift, in a way that she had been missing.

As farewells were said, she went to the window, not wanting anyone to see how moved she was. The brocade drapery partially screened her from the room. Outside, the Boulevard des Italiens was as full of people as ever. Somewhere bells rang in a Christmas carol, the music coming faintly over the air. Across the way the lights of the Café Anglais shone through the bare tree branches and picked up tiny flakes of snow drifting down. Despite the throngs of Christmas party goers, the scene had a lonely sadness. The little clay woman felt cold in her hand, and she held it against her, as if it were alive and in need of warmth.

An arm encircled her shoulders. "Are you thinking of home, *chérie*?" Pierre asked, his voice low and tender. The endearment felt natural, and she responded by turning to him. A lock of his restless hair had fallen forward, and one corner of his stiff white collar had turned down over his white silk cravat. It gave him a boyish, disheveled look, no longer the Parisian sophisticate. His eyes, which so often tried to tease or seduce her, were understanding. "Christmas is a time for remembering home."

He touched the side of her face, brushing back a tendril of hair that had come loose. His fingers stopped on her cheek, and a half-startled look came over his face. As if not quite sure what he intended, he moved closer. His mouth touched hers lightly, his mustache barely brushing her skin, and then retreated. They stood, staring at each other. With a sense of time slowing, she waited with exquisite tension for him to kiss her again.

The arm that had rested so comfortingly across her shoulders moved to her waist and pulled her fast against him. She could feel the beating of her heart, as if it were an echo of his. Their lips met again, his enticing, then demanding—hers responding, to him and to the pleasure swirling in her body.

The kiss ended, and still he held her. "*Joyeux noël*," he whispered. Then he stepped back, releasing her, and was again the insouciant Pierre of the boulevard cafés, her confederate in pretense.

She turned a little unsteadily, and found Armand a few feet away. He had his hat and walking stick, and his cape hung over his arm. The pale skin of his face was slightly flushed. He must have seen Pierre kiss her, but she couldn't tell whether he was embarrassed for her or intrigued.

"I must leave," he said. "Mademoiselle Taylor, I regret that I did not have the opportunity to spend more time with you this evening. Pierre, thank you for inviting me. And remember what I said about funds for *Le Combattant*."

"Yes, I'll remember."

With a bow, Armand was gone. Everyone else had left as well except for Virginie, asleep on the divan, and Hector, who was trying to rouse her. Pierre collected his and Sarah's wraps and escorted her down the stairs. When they were outside, she welcomed the cold air. It helped clear her bemused feelings from the evening's wine—and Pierre's kiss.

Light snow was still falling. Only a few people remained on the boulevard; carriages pulled by plodding horses passed slowly by, the rumbling of their wheels muted as if they too were tired. While they waited for their carriage, Pierre said jauntily, "Congratulations, Sarah. You were superb. Any man who didn't desire you would be only half alive. I'm sure Armand is intrigued. He may not need much more prodding."

Sarah preferred a topic other than Armand's interest in her. "What did he mean, about funds for *Le Combattant*?"

"He's offered to help if we need money."

"I'm curious about General Boulanger. Does he make public speeches?"

"Not speeches, but he appears at rallies."

"Would you take me to one?"

"Yes, if I can."

In the carriage Sarah leaned back, feeling tired and uncertain and not wanting to talk to Pierre. Why had she asked about Boulanger? She was curious, but she wondered uneasily whether she'd responded more to an uncertainty about Pierre. Would he still seek her company? Or would he leave it to Armand to do that instead?

She thought about Armand. Though she hardly knew him,

his dignity and courtesy appealed to her, and he was enormously attractive. At least as much as Pierre.

But something still felt unsettled. She and Pierre had kissed—nothing unusual. It should have been all part of their plan, but it hadn't felt that way to her. Any man would desire her—that's what he'd said. In spite of that, she didn't know his feelings, and it bothered her.

It bothered her even more that she didn't know her own.

CHAPTER
EIGHT

SARAH PACED THE CORRIDOR OUTSIDE MONSIEUR CES-
bron's office at the Opéra Comique. Nervously she
tapped her polished boot on each of the checkerboard
squares of the floor as she paced, thinking of what the director
was surely going to say to her.

Octave Rivarol had left Paris just before Christmas. He'd
gone to London, or to Vienna, depending on which gossip
Sarah listened to. Far enough away not to care about her
any longer. When she heard that news, she'd tried to see
Monsieur Cesbron. He'd had the effrontery to go to visit his
wife's parents in Nantes, not to return until after New Year's.
She wanted to rush to Nantes and drag him back to Paris,
but at least she was hopeful while she waited.

After the party at the Café Riche, she didn't see Pierre
until New Year's. He sent her funny notes, apologizing for
being so busy. They were embellished with cartoon drawings
of a man at a desk stacked with papers, tearing out clumps
of his hair. When she wrote him that Rivarol had left, he
sent her a sheaf of papers, attached so that they folded out,
each one with a theater marquee advertising her starring in

a different opera. She laughed over it and looked at it often.

On Christmas day she'd gone with Helene and Marc to visit Helene's cousin and her family. They arrived early at the flat above the millinery shop, in time to add small gifts of bon-bons to the wooden shoes set out, and later shared the Christmas goose. Being with a family had assuaged Sarah's wistfulness over her first Christmas away from home, and she was grateful to Helene and Marc.

She and Pierre and Ted Kearns celebrated her prospects of good fortune on New Year's Day. Ignoring the cold, they attended a puppet show and had ices at Tortoni's. It had been a brief visit with Pierre, because he'd had to go back to the newspaper. Through the evening she'd wondered if they would kiss again. Ted's presence proved inhibiting. Even so, being with both of the men made the holidays feel complete.

Then that morning had come a message from Cesbron: "Mademoiselle Taylor, can you please come to the Opéra Comique at two this afternoon?" Completely unnecessary question!

The director's office door opened, and the tenor who was taking Rivarol's place came out. "Monsieur Cesbron is free now," he told Sarah.

Finally! She said a quick prayer and entered the office.

Monsieur Cesbron nodded gravely and said in a schoolmaster's voice, "Please sit down, Mademoiselle Taylor."

She sat, trying to feel confident but keeping her back straight and her feet together, as she'd been taught when she was a schoolgirl.

"Mademoiselle Taylor," he began, "I would like to have you in the chorus again." He held up his hand, warding off her exclamation of pleasure, and continued sternly, "But you must understand that there can be no public mention of any sort that reflects on your name."

"Yes, I understand. I'm very grateful for the chance to

come back." Privately Sarah couldn't imagine why anyone would be interested enough in her to notice what she did. But she didn't intend to argue.

"Very well. We rehearse *Carmen* beginning tomorrow afternoon. Please be here."

Her joy felt like a kettle about to boil over. "Yes, I will. Thank you. Thank you so much!"

"One more thing, Mademoiselle Taylor." He hesitated, and then his side-whiskers quivered as his mouth curved in something that was close to a smile. "Perhaps it would be wise for you to wear hats that don't require a hatpin."

A delighted giggle escaped her before she could suppress it. "Yes, Monsieur Cesbron," she said demurely, "I'll take your advice."

They smiled at each other.

Pierre dashed up the steps of the Théâtre des Nations into the empty foyer. Damn, he was late. Sarah's first night back in the Opéra Comique chorus, and he'd missed the opening act of *Carmen*. He checked his overcoat and hat and went to the ticket window. Briefly he considered trying to find a place in one of the boxes, then purchased a seat in the stalls. He'd be able to see better from that section at the front of the auditorium.

In a few minutes people emerged into the corridors for the first intermission. Norbert Le Pol came over to Pierre. Even in black instead of his polka-dot waistcoat, he looked a little like a circus barker in disguise. "I haven't seen you since the dinner at the Riche," he said.

"I've been busy with the newspaper," Pierre explained.

"I suppose you're here to watch your mistress in the chorus."

Pierre didn't like Le Pol's casual assumptions about Sarah. He couldn't object, though, since he'd implied as much by his attentions to her at the Café Riche. He put Le Pol off with, "I like Bizet's music."

After he greeted others he knew, he made his way down the aisle of the auditorium and found his seat in the stalls. Most of the audience were still out for intermission, and he welcomed the time to himself. He needed to relax, but he found he couldn't. Le Pol's remark about Sarah wouldn't leave him.

When he'd first thought of the scheme about her and Armand, it had seemed simple. An American woman, alone in Paris, who had beauty, charm and self-confidence. She didn't have family reputation to consider. By falling in with his plans, she would have entry to a level of Paris society she'd never see otherwise. But now he knew Sarah better, and he wasn't so sure of his assessment. Was he putting her in a position to get hurt? He shifted uneasily in his seat.

The audience returned, and in a few minutes the second act curtain went up on a café with soldiers and gypsies drinking and dining. Pierre searched and found Sarah. She was sitting beside a singer dressed as a smuggler. Her white lace-trimmed blouse and full red skirt were ornaments for her high breasts and small waist. An embroidered scarf partly covered a full black wig. Pierre guessed it was to make her appear more like a Spanish gypsy, but it couldn't compare to her own red-gold hair. He also noticed that she made her flirtation with the supposed smuggler look very real.

While the mezzo-soprano who had the role of Carmen sang of guitars and tambourines, the chorus did a whirling gypsy dance. Sarah's partner swung her around with enough force that the tops of her black boots showed beneath her flaring skirt. She danced away from him, arching backward, holding her braceleted wrists above her, and her partner followed. With a lot more enthusiasm than needed, Pierre thought. He was glad when the chorus joined in the song and the dance ended.

It was impossible for him to hear Sarah's individual voice, but he kept track of her actions. When the toreador made his entrance, she fluttered and carried on as if overcome by admiration for him. Pierre thought the toreador didn't warrant that much attention. He was short and looked as if he'd spent more afternoons sleeping and eating than fighting bulls. After the chorus exited along with the toreador, Pierre only half followed the love scene between Carmen and Don José, even though he particularly liked the tenor's flower song. He decided he didn't need to wonder whether Sarah could convincingly portray a woman in love. With her, a man might not know for sure when she wasn't acting. If she made love with the fire of her dancing, he probably wouldn't care.

On stage Don José made his painful decision to desert from the army and join Carmen and the smugglers, and the curtain fell. After the applause and curtain calls, Pierre made his way into the corridor. He scribbled a note to Sarah, saying he'd be around to see her backstage after the opera, and gave it to an usher. Then he went toward the bar. He felt a vague sense of irritation, probably because of the long hours he'd been putting in at the paper. A brandy would take care of it.

In the changing room backstage Sarah waited for a turn in front of the mirror and read the note from Pierre. It added to her exhilaration. Tonight they could celebrate her return to the Opéra Comique.

She hadn't seen him since New Year's, but in those two weeks she'd been busy preparing to rejoin the chorus. She gave up tutoring, except for Emile. He'd blossomed so much with the lessons, more in losing his shyness than in learning English, that she didn't want to abandon him.

The space in front of the dressing room mirror was finally clear, and she inspected her costume for the third act. The scene was set outside the smuggler's mountain hideout, in the winter. She straightened the black shawl that covered her head and shoulders; along with her dark blue skirt and high-necked blouse, it felt very warm. In the crowded room with the gas jets adding to the heat, perspiration was already collecting under her wig. But she was too happy to care about being hot.

"Sarah, have you seen my shawl?" Helene asked in a worried voice. "It's one of the gray ones."

"No. I'll help you look."

After searching in the trunks and under other pieces of costumes, they found the only shawl, an orange one. "I'll be in trouble," Helene wailed. "Monsieur Georges is already angry at me because I tore my dress the last time we did *Tales of Hoffman*."

The costume designer, Sarah knew, insisted that everyone wear exactly what he dictated, and he had a hot temper and a cutting tongue. In this act, only Carmen was allowed anything brightly colored. "You could borrow a dark shawl from someone," Sarah suggested.

"I've asked. No one has one." Helen was close to crying.

Sarah remembered seeing the mezzo-soprano who had the part of Carmen in a gray shawl. "Madame Auber was wearing a gray shawl at rehearsal. Ask her if you can borrow it."

Helene looked shocked. "I wouldn't dare. She'd never lend it to someone in the chorus."

"I'll ask." Sarah was off down the corridor before Helene could protest.

The star's door was pink with scrolls of green leaves and dark pink roses. Sarah hesitated in front of it. She didn't know the singer and hoped she wasn't making trouble for herself. No matter, this was for a friend. She knocked, and at least the answering *"Entrez"* sounded pleasant.

Madame Auber would have been a voluptuous Carmen for the opening performance fourteen years previously. Now she had to be called stout, but she had large, fiery black eyes and she still sang like a passionate gypsy. Her glance at Sarah in the mirror was amiable. "Yes? What is it?"

"I am Sarah Taylor, Madame Auber, from the chorus."

"Mademoiselle Taylor, of the hatpin?"

Would that never be forgotten? "Yes. Please excuse my bothering you, but I have a favor to ask." Sarah explained about Helene and finished, "If you're agreeable to letting her wear your shawl, she'll be very careful. And I'll return it at the next intermission."

Madame Auber's eyebrows raised a little in surprise, but she smiled politely. "Yes, of course. Eloise," she called. A maid emerged from an adjoining cubicle. "Please find the gray shawl for Mademoiselle Taylor." When the maid brought the shawl, the soprano said, "Wait until after the last act to return it."

"I will," Sarah said, "and thank you. Helene will be so grateful."

When Sarah returned to the dressing room with the shawl, she enjoyed the startled look on Helene's face. "She let you have it!" was her awed comment.

"Yes, she was very nice." Sarah laughed as she helped her friend arrange the shawl. "I suppose I should be discouraged. If the star helps me, it might mean she thinks I'll never be competition for her roles." Sarah didn't believe that herself. Tonight her future was golden.

The last two acts seemed to glide past. By the end, when Sarah rushed with the crowd out of the bullring to see Carmen dying in Don José's arms, she could have begun the opera again. Though she knew the "Brava's" were for Madame Auber, she felt as if they included her.

Backstage she changed rapidly from the flower-trimmed dress she wore in the last act to a blue walking suit. Then she found the borrowed shawl. "I'll return this now," she told Helene.

"I should do it," Helene said, but Sarah could see from her friend's face that she was intimidated at the prospect.

"No, I told Madame Auber I'd take it back. I'll tell her how much you thank her."

"That's good of you." Helene gave Sarah a hug of gratitude.

Sarah found Madame Auber's door open. The star was changing behind a screen, and she had a visitor. The woman lounging on the small divan looked thirty-five to forty, and she was the most beautiful woman Sarah had ever met. Tall and slender, she reclined against the pillows like a queen waiting for her courtiers to present themselves. A necklace of diamonds and emeralds gave her simple black gown an added appearance of regal splendor. Abundant dark brown hair set off a pale, oval face in which gray-green eyes dominated. Her small mouth held a suggestion that she was ready to smile, if anything were sufficiently amusing.

Madame Auber came out from behind the screen. "Mademoiselle Taylor. You are very prompt."

Sarah managed to look away from the visitor. "Mademoiselle Lebout asked me to thank you. She and I are both very grateful that you let her use your shawl."

"Henriette, you must introduce me," the visitor said in a musical voice that told Sarah this must be a singer.

"Of course. Solange, this is Mademoiselle Taylor. Mademoiselle, you have the privilege of meeting Madame Rabaud."

One of the famous singers of the Opéra Comique! Almost as famous as Hortense Schneider in Offenbach roles. Sarah could hardly believe that this was Solange Rabaud. She had to be at least fifty, although she didn't look it; but if she were younger, she would have had to have been singing leading roles when she was a child.

"Henriette, don't be so formal." Solange smiled, her eyes embracing Sarah, who decided every leading male singer must have fallen in love with her. "You must call me Solange, and you are . . . ?"

"Sarah. And I'm delighted to meet you."

"And I already admire you. I detest Octave Rivarol." Solange made a small grimace that only added to her charm. "Oh, dear. I see I've embarrassed you."

Sarah smiled, hoping her blush was fading. "It's just that so many people seem to have heard about that."

"Of course. Because so many people dislike him. And we all love gossip." Solange preened a little, with the obvious expectation that no one would find fault with anything she did.

Reluctantly Sarah said, "I must go. Thank you again, Madame Auber."

Solange rose and glided toward Sarah. "You and I must meet again. I'm sure we'll be friends."

"That would please me very much, Madame Rabaud."

As Sarah opened the door, she saw Pierre walking past in the corridor. He stopped and came toward her, smiling. Then his glance went beyond her, and his smile stiffened.

"Why, Pierre." It was Solange, from behind Sarah. "I haven't seen you for a long time."

"Madame Rabaud." He gave Solange a formal bow, then took Sarah's arm. "Yes, it's been quite a while."

"You are Sarah's escort this evening?" Solange didn't wait for him to answer. She gave Sarah a proprietary touch on the arm. "Well then, Sarah, I know you are in the best of company. So farewell for now." Her smiling eyes included them both in a seductive glance before she made a grand exit into Madame Auber's room, closing the door behind her.

Sarah had to walk faster than normal to keep up with Pierre as they went down the corridor and out the stage door. Piqued by his silence, she said, "Aren't you going to congratulate me?"

He stopped. In the flaring streetlights she could see that the lines of his face looked tight. "Of course. Congratulations on your return. I noticed that your acting is very good.

Especially in the tavern scene."

"You don't sound pleased," she said, annoyed. "That's more like an accusation."

"I'm sorry." He didn't sound contrite. "When did you become so friendly with Solange Rabaud?"

"I met her just tonight." Sarah's irritation increased. "I think she's charming. It appears you know her well enough. In any case, how friendly I might be with her is not your concern."

His face relaxed a little, but his smile didn't have its usual spontaneity. "You're right. It's just . . . but, never mind." He looked around. "Cabs are scarce here. If you're warm enough, let's walk a little until we can find one."

Rain had been falling earlier that day. The wheels of carriages splashing across the Place du Châtelet sent up sprays of water. As Sarah and Pierre walked, he said in a more normal voice, "I'm sorry I didn't sound more pleased about your performance tonight. I really am glad you're doing what you want. But I couldn't actually hear your voice among all the others. Would you sing for me sometime?"

"Yes," she said, glad his strange mood was gone. It seemed such a long time since she'd seen him. She was disconcerted to realize how good it felt. Tonight she was in the mood to enjoy everything—especially being with Pierre. "And I'll still help you with your plan for Armand, if you wish."

"Of course," he responded, but his voice sounded flat again.

No cabs came along, so they went into the Café d'Orléans near the Palais Royal. After the waiter brought champagne, Pierre lifted his glass. "To you, Sarah, and to success."

"Thank you."

He smiled with genuine pleasure as they drank, but then he looked thoughtful again. "How do you put yourself in the right frame of mind for acting? How can you behave as if the toreador is dashing and handsome when he really isn't?"

"I pretend he's exciting and attractive and sing to that imagined man. With some of the men in the chorus it's easier, because they really are good-looking."

"I see."

What she could see was that her answer hadn't pleased Pierre. He looked tired. He had been working long hours. Reluctantly she suggested, "Maybe I should go home."

"All right, if you're sure you want to do that."

It wasn't what she wanted to do at all! She couldn't say that now. Suddenly the fatigue of the performance caught up with her.

They were silent on the cab ride to her building. As Pierre left her at her door, he said, "If you still want to see General Boulanger, I'll take you to a rally Sunday afternoon. Do you want to go?"

She hesitated. He'd been so strange this evening—the ambiguous tone when he mentioned her acting and then the disapproving question about Solange Rabaud. But Sarah did want to see the notorious general—and be with Pierre.

"Yes."

"Sunday at three."

Inside her room Sarah puzzled over the evening. When she'd met Pierre, his easy demeanor had encouraged her to feel as if he were a friend of long standing. Someone she could trust in spite of his provocative remarks to her. Partly because of that she'd promised to help him with his cousin. She wouldn't go back on her promise; that wasn't her way. However, she was discovering sides to Pierre that he seldom revealed. Tonight he'd been like a stranger. She wasn't sure how she felt about this man.

By Sunday the January weather had cleared. The sun probed the bare poplars and chestnuts as if astonished that they hadn't yet produced spring leaves. When Pierre called for Sarah, he looked dressed for a casual country outing.

He had on a soft cap and an ordinary overcoat over a tweed jacket and trousers. His expression was as cheerful as the weather.

"You aren't worried about Boulanger any longer?" she asked.

"Haven't you read my devastating attacks on him in *La Combattant*? How can he win after those? Besides, today I'll be with the most beautiful singer at the Opéra Comique. I can't let politics spoil that."

So he didn't intend to be serious. That suited her, and when he said "Shall we take the omnibus?" she agreed happily and lifted her skirts enough to match his rapid pace to the corner. An omnibus was just approaching, its three horses trotting briskly. After Pierre hailed it, they had to run the last distance. He held her hand, pulling her along, while she clutched her hat. When they climbed aboard the heavy carriage, she was breathless and warm.

"Here," he said after they sat on one of the side benches, "you're coming apart." He lifted a strand of hair off the back of her neck and tucked it up under the coil of her chignon. The gesture was at once both casual and intimate. Pierre was again the familiar companion, but with enough memory of the stranger to make her very conscious of his touch.

The omnibus rumbled along the Boulevard de Sébastopol. They passed groups of men wearing red chrysanthemums, Boulanger's symbol. The men were putting up posters with Boulanger's name splashed across them and a drawing of a bearded man with a cockaded hat and a general's epaulets. "All I see are Boulanger posters," she said to Pierre. "What candidate are you supporting?"

"Edouard Jacques."

When she and Pierre left the omnibus at the Place de Châtelet, she noticed that on the wall of the Théâtre des Nations someone had put up another Boulanger poster. Its stark message competed with the frivolous colors of one advertising *La Belle Helene* at the Opéra Comique. "I think politics and love are all Parisians think about," she said to Pierre.

"What better occupations?" he said, then added with sudden seriousness, "Making a living is what most people have to spend their time doing."

As she and Pierre walked along the Rue de Rivoli, they made their way through increasing crowds. On a signboard near the garden of the Tuileries, a man was pasting a Boulanger poster over one that had the name Jacques on it. Sarah felt Pierre's arm tense under her hand. He muttered an oath. "Sorry, Sarah, for swearing. Boulanger's campaign has people covering over our man's posters all around Paris."

For a moment she thought he was going to try to stop it. But other men and several women had made a circle, watching in apparent approval. Far too many for Pierre to confront, and she was glad when they walked on.

They crossed the Place de la Concorde to the Champs Elysées, and Pierre stopped. "Boulanger's rally will be someplace in this area," he said. "Every Sunday he starts out near here. Then he parades to his headquarters, which is set up halfway between the building for the Ministry of the Interior and the Ministry of War and President Carnot's palace over there."

Looking to her right, Sarah could see the gates of the Elysées Palace on the corner of the Rue St. Honoré. "Why does Boulanger have a headquarters halfway between?"

All of Pierre's earlier gaiety had disappeared. "So that he can send troops to take over the most important parts of the government. Paul Déroulède—"

"Who is he?" she interrupted.

"He was a hero in the war against Germany in 1870. He's organized a league of patriots, and claims that in five hours he can have ten thousand armed men anywhere in Paris to put Boulanger in power." Pierre gave a smile that wasn't quite a smile. "Déroulède also writes mediocre patriotic poetry."

"Would ten thousand people really take up arms against the government?" It sounded like revolution to Sarah's shocked mind.

"Parisians have done it before," Pierre said grimly. "In 1871, fifteen thousand Parisians, mostly workers, were shot by the Versailles government. People haven't forgotten."

"So that's why this election is important, even though it's only for a single Paris district?"

"Yes."

On an opposite corner carriages and horses had stopped around the Théâtre Marigny. Mounted men, all wearing red chrysanthemums, were trying to open up a path through a gathering crowd. A street vendor was hawking postcards. "Three sous for a picture of General Boulanger," he called in a hoarse voice. "Only three sous."

Pierre took Sarah's elbow. "Come on. I think this is your chance to see the great man."

They crossed the avenue, and Pierre, gripping her arm tightly, started through the crowd. Some of the spectators appeared to be shopkeepers, dressed with modest prosperity. Others were working people, the men in clothes that doubled for work, the women in their Sunday black dresses and shawls. Sarah saw quite a few men in frock coats and silk hats with women whose headgear sported feathers and imitation flowers, like tiny artificial gardens. One large man had on a striped morning coat, as if he'd left a wedding to join the throng. Several times people jostled Sarah, and she had to cling to Pierre to keep her footing. Nearly every spectator wore a red chrysanthemum.

Pierre finally reached a low stone wall topped by an iron railing. He lifted Sarah up onto the wall in front of the railing, then turned and stood close to her, sheltering her with his body from the crush of people. The bars of the railing pressed

into her back, but she could see across his head to where
a space had been cleared.

An army officer on an impressive black charger rode from
behind the theater and started through the opening. Shouts
rang out of *"Vive Boulanger!"* The cries rippled through the
crowd. One man near Sarah shouted, *"Vive Tunis!"*

"Tunis?" Sarah leaned down and asked in Pierre's ear.

"Boulanger's horse," he said over his shoulder.

The general advanced only a few feet when the cheering
crowd blocked his way, and he had to stop. From Sarah's
perch she could see him clearly. He was a handsome man,
younger than she'd expected a general to be, certainly under
fifty. Full blond whiskers, trimmed to a military point, covered the lower half of his face. He sat erect, one hand resting
on a sword, resplendent in the medal-covered uniform that
showed off a muscular physique. The sun glinted on the
gold trim of his epaulets, and the white cockade of his
pointed hat swayed with the impatient motions of his horse.
A chain of red chrysanthemums decorated the bridle. The
effect was to make some of the portraits of uniformed kings
look like imitations.

A chant rose: "For France and Boulanger!" Women near
the general tore off their red flowers and threw them at him.

He acknowledged the chant and flowers with a regal nod
of his head. One of the men with him managed to clear
enough supporters away that the general could advance. He
rode a few more feet, then had to pause again. During the
pause he was very close, and Sarah could see a new, red
scar on the side of his throat, just above his high collar.
When he finally was able to move on, he rode toward the
Tuileries. The crowd began to follow.

Suddenly Sarah was conscious of Pierre's body against
hers. His shoulders and broad back pressed against her waist
and chest. Through her clothing she felt his warmth. He'd
taken off his hat so as not to obstruct her view, and the top

of his head came just below her chin. She stared at his dark
hair and had difficulty breathing. A breeze stirred up a lock
of his hair, and without thinking she reached out to smooth
it down.

At her touch he turned and looked up at her. His dark
eyes searched hers with so much intensity that for a moment
she felt as if she could lose herself in them. She shivered.

His expression changed to concern. "You're cold?"

"No. Yes, perhaps." The air did seem more penetrating.

He lifted her down, his touch firm around her waist. She
didn't know whether she felt hot or cold.

"Let's find a café and have something hot to drink," he
proposed. The crowd was moving off, but the area was still
congested. She was glad to be behind him until people began
to disperse into other streets.

As they walked along, she remembered the new scar on
Boulanger's neck. "Has General Boulanger been in recent
fighting?"

"Not for France," Pierre said. "When he was elected to
the Chamber of Deputies last July, Floquet, the prime minister, insulted him. Floquet said that at Boulanger's age,
Napoleon was dead. Of course the general challenged Floquet to a duel. Everyone expected Boulanger to win. After
all, Floquet is over seventy and overweight. But he was
untouched, and he gave Boulanger a cut on the throat."

"So I suppose people said Floquet won," Sarah said with
a shudder of distaste.

"In a way. But apparently the duel enhanced Boulanger's
popularity with several wealthy society women. It brought
a lot of money to his campaign."

"But he was trying to kill or wound Floquet. Why would
that make a man more attractive?" Sarah protested.

Pierre shrugged. "Dueling is part of French life."

"And you approve of it?"

"There are times it can't be avoided. A week or so ago

Hippolyte Lissagaray, who publishes *La Bataille*, wrote an article about Henri Rochefort, publisher of *L'Intransigeant*, a Boulangist paper. Everything in the article was true, but Rochefort challenged Lissagaray to a duel. Lissagaray had to accept or no one would respect him."

"What happened?"

"They both got minor wounds."

"Would you accept if you were challenged?"

He raised his eyebrows in surprise. "Of course. I'd have to defend my integrity."

There was no lightness in his face or voice. She hoped no one ever challenged him.

They stopped at a small café among the worn-looking shops near the Church of the Madeleine. Other witnesses to the general's display had gathered there, as evidenced by the red chrysanthemums pinned to coats and tucked into women's hair. Pierre ordered coffee with brandy for them both. He sat silently; she guessed he was preoccupied with discouraging thoughts of the campaign. When the drinks came, she sipped hers and watched the people around them.

Two couples occupied the next table; each of them wore the red badge of Boulangisme. The women were dressed with the threadbare smartness Sarah had seen on the *grisettes* who worked in millinery establishments. One of the men looked as if he might be a cabby or porter. The other, who was better dressed, was reading a newspaper.

The nearest woman pushed her chair back and bumped into Sarah. She turned and said, "Oh, I'm sorry. Please excuse me."

"That's quite all right," Sarah responded.

"What a pretty accent you have," the stranger exclaimed with a smile. "You must be an American."

"Yes, I am." The woman had a plump face that reminded Sarah of one of her Boston friends. Her smile was so amiable that it emboldened Sarah to a question. "May I ask you something, madame?"

"Certainly."

"Why do you think General Boulanger should be elected?"

The woman raised her penciled eyebrows, as if surprised anyone would ask such an unnecessary question. "It will be better for all of us. He knows how to talk back to the Germans." She gave a little shrug and added, "Besides, President Carnot is so boring."

The man who had been reading the newspaper said, "Listen to this. *Le Gaulois* says that Boulanger is our battering ram. He'll break through the walls of radical power. His force will clear the way for the monarchy to return in triumph!"

There was general approval among his listeners. Sarah looked at Pierre. His hand had tightened around his glass of brandy until the fingers were white. He lifted it and said clearly, "To the Republic," and drank.

When he put it down, the man reading *La Gaulois* had risen and was glaring at Pierre. "The Republic is like the companies who list shares on the Bourse. It exploits the whole country to enrich a few stockholders."

Pierre stood also. "Do you think a monarchy would make any of *us* rich? Or care about our liberties? No, our hope is to govern ourselves. We need the Republic, whatever its faults."

An interested ring of faces was watching from the tables nearby. The other man at the newspaper reader's table was on his feet also. The reader advanced toward Pierre and hissed, "Here we don't defend *la gueuse*!"

Sarah gasped. To call the Republic a slut! She looked at Pierre, fearful of his reaction. His face was pale with anger. The newspaper reader, looking alarmed, stepped backward, but then stood his ground. Pierre, his hands clenched, started forward.

She jumped to her feet. Pierre was intent on the man in front of him, but the second man alarmed her. He had an ugly expression, part snarl and part smile. He began to circle around toward Pierre's back as he pulled out a small knife from inside his belt.

Pierre's walking stick lay on the floor beside his chair. Terrified, Sarah grabbed it and scrambled around the table. Just as Pierre and his opponent collided, she reached the armed man. With all her strength, she brought the stick down on his hand that held the knife.

The attacker cried out and dropped the knife. Pierre and the other man were struggling. Around them women screamed. Three men who'd been watching rushed forward to separate Pierre and his opponent.

As if the first hand on his shoulder brought him to his senses, Pierre pulled back. Panting, he looked around for Sarah. She still held his stick in her hand. The owner of the knife, cradling his wrist, picked up his weapon. After glaring at Sarah and Pierre, he pushed his way through the bystanders, heading for the door. The woman who'd spoken to Sarah followed.

Pierre's face, sweaty from exertion, flushed a deep red. "Sarah, I'm so sorry." His chest heaving with his rapid breathing, he turned back to the next table. He said stiffly, "I apologize, madame and monsieur. We will settle our differences with our votes."

The man with the newspaper didn't look ready for any further dispute. "Yes, you are right, monsieur."

Sarah's legs still trembled, but she was ready to take Pierre's offered arm and leave. When they were outside, she could feel faint tremors running along his arms, and his jaw was clamped tight. They walked without speaking until his stride began to loosen and his face to relax. By then Sarah felt calmer. In front of a small café that had only a few customers inside, he stopped.

"Shall we risk trying for a hot drink again?" His smile looked fragile. "I promise to control myself this time."

Inside Sarah saw only one white-haired customer with a red chrysanthemum. He was nodding at a table that had three empty wine bottles on it. One had fallen over on its side. The place looked reassuringly dull.

After she and Pierre sat down, he reached across to where her hand lay on the table and took it in his. "I apologize again, Sarah. My actions were stupid. It was even more disgraceful because you were with me. I hope you'll forgive me."

"Of course I do."

"You astounded me so much I haven't thanked you for your help. You must have given that man a real whack to make him howl like that." His graceful smile reappeared. "I've wondered why a woman who looks like you hadn't married some lucky American before this. Maybe none of them could stand up to you."

She laughed, glad for him to be teasing her instead of apologizing. "I don't ordinarily hit men."

"I'm glad you did, this time. Remind me to have you along anytime I get into trouble."

He released her hand, and she was sorry. The warmth of his touch together with his admiration had created a special glow that she wanted to go on longer.

"There's something I've been thinking of," he said more soberly. "My plan for you and Armand—I'm not sure it's such a good idea."

He was confusing her again. "You mean that you don't think it will work?"

"No, that's not it. I'm sure Armand is interested. And Aunt Nathalie would object." He frowned, as if none of the words he could think of satisfied him. "But maybe it's not fair to you. I introduced you to several people, with the implication you're . . . that we're lovers."

"And you regret that?" She wasn't quite sure why she was feeling defensive, but he'd better explain himself!"

A seductive smile spread from his mustached mouth to his eyes. "If I were really your lover, I'd never regret it. Unlike you, I have very little resistance."

Her irritation faded, replaced by the response to him that she probably should be cautious about. It warmed her like coals glowing in a stove—making her feel alive and eager to please him. "Isn't the demonstration today a good reason that Armand should be in politics? You wouldn't be working so hard—or have gotten into a fight, unless you think the future of France is important. And that Armand could do some good. Didn't you say Armand is giving you money for your paper? That means he's concerned too. This is the right time."

He leaned back, looking amused. "We seem to be taking opposite sides. Now you're the one trying to persuade me we should continue."

The switch surprised her a little too. "I don't like to give up something I've started. We made an agreement, and I haven't changed my mind. Besides, you promised I would see French high society."

"Yes, that's true." He was silent, considering, but his expression didn't tell her what. Finally he said, "We can attend Madame Dubreuil's salon next Wednesday afternoon. There are always interesting people there. Aunt Nathalie is envious of Comtesse Dubreuil. She always attends so that she can try to outdo her. I'll see that Armand is there also."

"Then that's settled—we go ahead."

He looked at her searchingly, as someone might study the sky to determine the weather before setting out into uncertain territory. "Are you sure you want to?"

She wasn't certain of much since she'd come to Paris. But if she wanted security, she should have stayed home. "Yes, I'm sure."

CHAPTER NINE

"TELL ME SOMETHING ABOUT MADAME DUBREUIL," Sarah said.

The cab in which she and Pierre were riding had just turned into the Rue de l'Arcade. "Jeanne Dubreuil's beautiful and charming. When she likes something, she becomes very enthusiastic. I've heard her called eccentric, but I think that's unkind. She does things in her own style. We'll be there at the beginning of the salon hours, so you'll have a chance to talk to her."

The admiration with which Pierre spoke of their hostess somehow unsettled Sarah. "What about her husband?"

"The Comte de Dubreuil divorced her a long time ago because of family objections. She's never remarried, but she's had famous lovers, most often writers. Flaubert. The younger Dumas."

Pierre related all this as her father might have described the life of the most respectable Boston matron. After four months in Paris, that casual attitude still disconcerted Sarah. "And everyone comes to her salon?" she asked.

"All kinds of people. Artists, politicians, bankers, men

with no profession who live for racing horses. Even journalists like me."

"No women?" Sarah felt a little alarmed.

"Oh, yes. Society women, writers, actresses. Once in a while Sarah Bernhardt is there. And sometimes Réjane, the actress we saw in *Germinie Lacerteux* at the Odéon."

The cab slowed at the iron grill gate of a high wall. A porter waved it through into the courtyard of a three-story house. Though the building was austere, with plain shuttered windows and a simple arch over the front door, the footman who showed them inside wore livery of black silk with silver trim. In the marble entrance hall, another footman took their hats and coats and Pierre's walking stick, and bowed then on to a huge drawing room.

Sarah stopped just inside the doorway, astonished by the room's opulence. White furs lay scattered over a wooden floor polished to a deep red. More furs covered two large sofas on either side of the white marble fireplace. A cluster of black marble fauns filled one corner. Chairs of Louis XIV style were arranged in conversation groups around the large room. Most of the objects were black and white, or, like the silk upholstery and draperies, so pale as not to disturb the color scheme. A large onyx toad sat on the hearth.

The woman who furnished this room surely deserved to be called eccentric, Sarah thought. Except for the floor, there was color only in the stained glass fan lights over French windows and a portrait sitting on an easel. Her face must have given her thoughts away, because Pierre leaned close and said softly, "Her bedroom upstairs is all pink. On the walls and ceiling are plaster decorations of roses and cupids. Some of the cupids look like her. She calls it her fairyland."

"How do you know?" came out before she could stop it.

"Men talk." Neither his amused look nor his answer pleased her. "Come, I'll introduce you to Madame Dubreuil."

He escorted Sarah across the room to a woman sitting in

a high-backed chair next to the portrait. She looked over sixty—much too old for Pierre—was Sarah's first impression. Her next was that the comtesse was made up for the stage. A coating of white face powder, bright spots of rouge, and hennaed hair gave her face the appearance of a mask. But her smile glowed with good humor.

"I'm delighted to meet you, Mademoiselle Taylor," she said graciously.

"Thank you for making me welcome," Sarah said. She felt a little ashamed for having worried—no, surely not worried—having wondered whether Pierre had a romantic interest in the comtesse.

"Mademoiselle Taylor sings at the Opéra Comique," Pierre explained.

The comtesse sighed. "I went often when Octave Rivarol was there. What a glorious . . . voice he has."

Sarah said hastily, "The present tenor is quite good. Have you heard him?" She didn't want to risk any mention of her dispute with Rivarol.

"Yes, but it's not the same." From Madame Dubreuil's nostalgic expression, it was doubtful that Rivarol's singing was what inspired her admiration.

Other guests were waiting to greet their hostess, so Pierre and Sarah moved on and stopped by the easel. Sarah realized that the portrait was of the comtesse when young. If the artist had been true to life, her hair had once been a rich dark brown and her skin pale and shining. The youthful comtesse wore black, whereas her current gown was a flowing tea gown of white lace. Only the beautiful eyes were the same, and a rose so dark red as to be almost black, which she held in both the picture and real life. The comtesse either didn't realize she had changed or was so self-assured she didn't care. Sarah hoped it was assurance; she particularly admired that trait.

The drawing room was filling up. Neither Armand or his

mother had arrived, but Pierre introduced Sarah to several men, all writers. One, a tall thin man, was receiving congratulations for the success of his latest book. "Yes," he said. "I have the Archbishop of Paris to thank. The book wasn't selling well until several Sundays ago when he denounced it in his sermon for being immoral. Now the sales are excellent. I must dedicate my next book to him."

Several couples had come in, and Sarah was glad not to be the only woman guest. A woman who looked like an exotic gypsy was escorted by a large, red-bearded man. One of the writers near Sarah nodded toward the couple and said, "That's a strange marriage. I can't believe she's really in love with him."

"Of course she is," said the tall writer with the successful book. "She's so anxious to please him when they make love that she practices with other men every chance she gets."

Sarah didn't know whether to laugh or pretend she hadn't heard, but she was determined not to look shocked. An American from Boston might, but a singer from the Opéra Comique wouldn't be so unworldly.

Pierre noticed with amusement the effort Sarah was making to keep her composure. He said, "Does the conversation embarrass you?"

Sarah shrugged, a gesture that looked more French than American. She was changing, he thought. "I'm surprised," she said, "at hearing gossip. I expected to hear debate about how literature is going to change the world."

"That's for Sunday evening dinners at Madame Suardon's," he said, "not Wednesday afternoons with Jeanne Dubreuil."

"All salons aren't alike?"

"No. Some hostesses insist on strict rules for conversation. Madame Suardon rings a silver bell when she wants to change the topic. Jeanne's salon is quite informal, so there's lots of gossip. That's why people like Roland Gille are here."

"Who's Roland Gille?"

Pierre pointed out a man with bleached hair across the room. "He writes a gossip column—for my paper at the moment."

Sarah gave Pierre a questioning look. "You don't sound happy about that."

"He and I don't like each other. But lots of people buy the paper to read his column. I'm being polite for the sake of *Le Combattant*'s circulation."

He saw his cousin and aunt in the doorway. "Armand and Aunt Nathalie are here," he said softly to Sarah. "We'll talk to them after they make their greetings to the comtesse."

To mark time, they wandered over to the French windows and looked out into the gardens. Above formal gravel paths and bare flower beds, elm trees held up leafless branches, waiting impatiently for the onslaught of spring. All too quickly Armand and Nathalie had finished greeting Madame Dubreuil. Now that the purpose of the visit was at hand, Pierre felt a surprising reluctance to relinquish Sarah. But his cousin and aunt were approaching—Armand with a smile in which eagerness had eroded some of his dignity. Nathalie's posture was even more rigid than usual.

"Aunt Nathalie." When Pierre kissed her hand, it felt icy. "Do you remember Mademoiselle Taylor?"

"Certainly," she said. Her careful voice conveyed the message that of course she wouldn't recall anyone so unimportant but was pretending to from politeness.

It was time for him to move things along. "Aunt Nathalie, there's someone here who'd like an introduction to you. Roland Gille writes for the newspaper I'm involved with."

Her eyebrows raised. "That vulgar man?" she said, but he could see he'd snagged her interest.

"I think you'll find him amusing." Though none of the aristocracy who meant so much to his aunt would admit it, Gille's column was read secretly but regularly in the great houses in the Faubourg Saint-Germain. It would enhance

Nathalie's prestige if she could mention how unpleasant it had been for her to have to speak to him. "*Le Combattant* needs him. It will flatter him if I introduce him to my aunt. Sarah, Armand, will you excuse us please?"

Sarah watched Pierre escort his aunt across the room and stop beside the small, dandified man with bleached hair. It was up to her to charm Armand, but instead she wanted to run after Pierre like a child who was being left at school on the first day. But that was ridiculous. She turned to face Armand and found him looking after his cousin with an expression of the same discomfort she was feeling.

Why, she thought with surprised sympathy, he feels shy with me. The conclusion relaxed her, and she smiled encouragingly. "Pierre tells me you've been in the army and the foreign service. And that you acted very bravely."

Armand blushed. "Pierre exaggerates."

Poor Armand, Sarah thought. He probably disliked the way his fair skin betrayed his emotions as much as she did. It gave her a feeling of kinship with him. "I think he said you were on an expedition to one of the countries in East Asia, south of China."

"Yes, to Tonkin," he said shortly. Apparently he was too modest to tell her how he had earned any of his medals.

"What is Tonkin like?"

"All of Indo-China is beautiful." He spoke more easily, warming to the less personal topic. "It's a shame that we had to bombard their capital. After that, if the Chinese hadn't interfered, the expeditions wouldn't have been necessary. Our protectorate could have been established with minimum bloodshed."

"And you think a protectorate is a good thing?"

"Of course. We must civilize them and raise them to equality. It also benefits us. Foreign service gives our young men a chance to uphold the glory of France. Our businessmen can expand their markets and provide more wealth."

"For Frenchmen." She could see that her dry tone puzzled him. "Being American," she went on, "I understand people who want to rule themselves. It's only a little over a hundred years ago that we fought for that right ourselves. You French helped us, and then had your own revolution."

His smile was genuine this time, an expression with charm, and a slight touch of condescension. "But modern colonies are different. Take North Africa. Algeria, for example. I was in the foreign service there. The Berbers are only primitive farmers. On the coast they were mostly pirates. Now, thanks to France, there are railroads, hospitals, schools. And farming is very profitable."

Profitable for the French colonists, she thought, but this time she didn't say it. "Still, you gave up the army and the foreign service. Why?"

The melancholy expression that had been so pronounced when she first met him returned. "I became too frustrated and discouraged. The politicians here pay little real attention to our colonies. The ministry of foreign affairs must beg for money." His eyes didn't look sad now. They flared with conviction. "All they think of in the Chamber of Deputies is revenge. But the best revenge on Germany for the 1870 defeat would be a strong overseas empire."

Just the opening she wanted. "Then shouldn't you be in the Chamber of Deputies? You could work to change that policy."

Quickly he retreated into polite dignity. "I see I have talked too much about a dry topic. Please, tell me what the Opéra Comique is presenting these days. I haven't attended in quite a while, but I hope to see something you are performing in."

"I hope you will," she said. "I'll be in *The Daughter of the Regiment* and *Romeo and Juliette* in the next few weeks. Perhaps afterward you'd come backstage."

"Yes, I'd like to. Very much." He glanced across at Pierre

with a certain pleasure in the look.

Sarah sighed to herself. She liked Armand; his shyness when they first began to talk was appealing. What had Pierre said to her? That women wanted to look out for Armand. She understood that. She also admired the strength of his convictions, though she might not agree with all of them. But if he did respond to her, it might only be because he wanted to take her away from Pierre. On the other hand, she wouldn't care to tell him her motives.

Across the room Pierre and Nathalie had finished a stilted conversation with Roland Gille. Pierre noticed that Sarah and Armand looked absorbed in talking to each other. The reluctance that he'd felt earlier for this scheme returned, even stronger. Wait, he told himself, he'd started this. Now he'd better let Sarah and Armand have a chance. At least some of the time. He owed Sarah that.

He saw that Nathalie also was watching Armand and Sarah. Tiny lines appeared between Nathalie's eyebrows and at the corners of her mouth. She looked tired and old, and Pierre felt a renewal of long-held affection. As a small boy, he had thought her infinitely glamorous. When his parents died, she had grieved with him and for him, showing a tenderness that seldom surfaced.

"I can't believe Armand is interested in your Mademoiselle Taylor," she said stiffly.

For a moment he wanted to reassure her, but he reminded himself that her unrealistic ambitions were stifling her son. "Armand always likes to steal my women if he can."

She raised her chin to an imperious level, a queen ordering a courtier to do her bidding. "But you won't allow anything so absurd."

A flash of irritation dispelled the last of his sympathy. "An interest in Mademoiselle Taylor isn't absurd." Realizing that he didn't want to alarm her yet, he added, "Aunt Nathalie, have you so little confidence in me that you think she'd prefer anyone else?"

After a glance that dismissed him as being flippant and not deserving a reply, Nathalie started toward her son.

As Nathalie approached, Sarah could feel her eyes, the way she used to feel the eyes of her governess when she had been involved in some sort of escapade. Nathalie said, "Armand, please take me home. Mademoiselle Taylor, good day."

"Good night, comtesse," Sarah replied, and stared back just as haughtily, a technique that had often intimidated her governess. Not this woman, though.

As Nathalie went over to Madame Dubreuil, Armand said, "I hope to see you at the Opéra Comique," gave her one of his mournful but charming smiles and departed.

"You've made progress," Pierre commented.

"Perhaps."

Conversation quieted across the room. A tall man was crossing the room to the hostess. "Julien," she said, rising and extending a hand, which he took in both of his and kissed.

He had full cheeks above a small goatee and arresting dark eyes. A handsome man. "Who is that?" Sarah whispered to Pierre.

"Julien Lemaire, a writer and critic. He's Jeanne's current lover."

This man was the aging comtesse's lover? He couldn't be forty years old!

Sarah didn't pay much attention to the talk that resumed around her, too intrigued and puzzled about the romantic pairings that seemed so surprising to her but apparently commonplace in Paris. She glanced at Pierre. Had he indeed learned about the pink cherubs in the "fairyland" bedroom from seeing them? It was an uncomfortable question, one she had dismissed earlier. Respectable French society was in a few ways like Boston, but mostly different. She felt at sea again.

After the flurry that accompanied Julien Lemaire's arrival had subsided, Pierre suggested they could leave. Though Madame Dubreuil received their thanks graciously, her attention hardly strayed from her lover.

As Sarah and Pierre were waiting for their wraps in the entrance hall, another man came in. He was tall, with wiry curls of dark hair that stood up from his high forehead like a topknot. When he saw Pierre, he stopped, and his black eyes took on an unfriendly expression. The two men bowed stiffly, but didn't speak.

When they were outside, Sarah asked, "Who was that man?"

"Claude Vernoy. He works for Henri Rochefort."

"Rochefort," Sarah said, trying to remember. "That's the editor of *L'Intransigeant* who dueled with your friend?"

"Yes, and Vernoy is a lot like Rochefort. He uses his articles to attack without regard for truth."

"He looks like a man who would never forget or forgive an insult."

"And not hesitate over how he repaid it," Pierre said grimly. "You've read his appearance well."

By the time they were riding along the Rue de l'Arcade, the gas lamps made pools of light against the early-evening darkness. As the cab passed each light, Pierre's face was alternately lit and then shadowed. Like her impressions of him, Sarah thought, comfortable friend and intense stranger. There must be more sides to him that she didn't know. When he was intimate with a woman, what was he like? What did it mean to him?

Her pulse quickened; she felt like a taut violin string, waiting for one touch of the musician's bow. She substituted a question she could ask for the one she couldn't. "Madame Dubreuil and Monsieur Lemaire are an unlikely couple. When a man takes a mistress, is it because he's in love with her?"

"Are you asking if Julien loves Jeanne? They see each other every day. That must be love."

"I meant, do most men have mistresses because they're in love?"

He laughed. "That's a conventional Boston question. The answer is—not necessarily. Often a man takes a mistress because it's convenient."

It wasn't the answer she wanted. "Is it the same for women do you think?"

"No. Usually it's love. Or sometimes money."

"Ha! Maybe a man just doesn't want to think that a woman isn't in love with him."

He didn't answer immediately. In the next pool of light, she saw that his mouth had an amused quirk. "I think you're accusing me of egotism."

He reached across and touched her chin, turning her face fully toward his. A trail of sparks ran down her throat to her chest. When he spoke, his voice caressed her. "If you were my mistress, I'd be in love with you."

Answers tangled in her mind. She waited for him to lean forward, to follow the caress of his words with his lips. Then the muscles of his jaw tightened, and he pulled his hand away.

She felt an unreasonable disappointment and then was irritated with herself for it. Her annoyance wasn't relieved when he said, "Sorry. I guess it's become a habit, being your ardent admirer. Even when Armand's not here."

Armand again. She wanted to ask why they had to talk about him so often, but she knew the reason.

"If you come to the newspaper office the evening of election day," Pierre said, "you'll see him. We'll be waiting for the results. You can join the celebration—or the wake."

"All right. I'll ask Ted to be my escort." It would be a relief to be with someone she knew well, whose motives and actions she didn't have to guess.

*   *   *

Gas jets lit up the sign for *Le Combattant*. Sarah imagined that the flaring reflection on the red letters resembled the flash of cannons during combat. Ted paused to look at the newspaper pages fastened to the glass of the entrance doors. He read the date at the top. "January 27, 1889. I wonder if this day will be famous in French history. We might know before the end of the night whether France has a new dictator."

Sarah pushed open the door and started up the stairs, too impatient to wait while Ted contemplated history. All day noisy groups of men had roamed the streets, shouting assurances of their candidate's victory. Far more voices had proclaimed Georges Boulanger than cheered for Edouard Jacques.

A boy carrying an armful of broadsheets passed them on the stairs, bounding on ahead. They found the waiting room by following him along the upper hall to a haze of smoke coming from an open door. Inside some men strode nervously about while others snatched the broadsheets and read bits of news aloud. The announcements, which Sarah couldn't quite understand in the jumble of noise, brought groans from the listeners.

Pierre appeared on the other side of the room and made his way across to them. He had an ink stain across the side of his cheek, and his jacket looked rumpled, as if he'd worn it too long. "Come on back to my office," he said. As he led them along another hall, he added. "Things don't look good."

Armand was already in Pierre's office, standing at the window. He turned and greeted them, then pointed downward. "More voting papers being taken to be counted. It must be the last of them."

Sarah went to the window and looked down. Pierre came and stood behind her. In the street below, an officer of the police, his tall black hat with its white plume making him easy to identify, was carrying a large metal box. Two more gendarmes walked in front of him and two behind. Others kept the jubilant crowd back at the edges of the street, so that the one carrying the ballots seemed to walk in the center of a moving circle. A man standing on the steps of the building across the way threw up his arms and shouted, "*Vive Boulanger, Vive l'Empereur!*"

Behind Sarah, Pierre's breath hissed, and his hand, which had rested lightly on her arm, gripped it. She gave a little gasp, and he removed his hand. "Pardon me," he said, "I didn't mean to hurt you."

"It's nothing," she assured him. It was nothing, she thought sympathetically, compared to his distress.

Armand shook his head. "Money. That's what has made Boulanger's campaign so successful."

"Partly," Pierre agreed, pacing the small space, his hands jammed in his pockets. "We have reliable information that the Royalists spent between six and eight million francs."

Over a million dollars! "They haven't spent that money to elect one man just to be in your legislature," Sarah surmised.

Pierre gave her a quick smile, the first she'd seen that evening. "You understand politics."

He brought in a third chair so that she and Ted and Armand could sit down, but he didn't do more than perch for a minute or two on the edge of his desk.

"Paul Gaugin is back in Paris," Ted said cheerily, obviously trying to introduce a neutral topic.

"Gaugin," Armand said. "Is he one of those Impressionists?"

"Not exactly. His work won't be allowed in the Universal Exposition, of course, but he's organizing an unofficial exhibit for what he's calling the Impressionist-Synthetist Group. It's in the Grand Café des Beaux-Arts, just outside the Exposition area for art."

Pierre lifted an eyebrow. "Does he think the people who

come to admire the Eiffel Tower will also appreciate his paintings?"

"They are unusual," Ted admitted.

A boy came in with another broadsheet. After Pierre had read the gloomy news, he took another restless turn around the room, then said to Sarah, "Do you know how to play cup-and-ball? No, of course you wouldn't, but it's very popular in newspaper offices. We do it instead of writing about the news. Especially today."

He took a box from a shelf and produced a ball made of pale yellow oak. It was attached with a string to a shallow wooden cup with a pointed spike in the middle. "Here," he said, "see this hole opposite the string. You toss the ball into the air and catch it on the spike. The object is to see how many times in a row you can do it without letting the ball bounce off."

Sarah managed to impale the ball one time. Ted did better—three times in a row. After several fumbling tries, Armand got up to five. By then Sarah had watched carefully; she tried again, reaching four. It seemed to her a silly game for men to be playing, but it helped ease the tension while they waited. "How many times can you do it?" she asked Pierre.

"Once I got up to twenty-two. Roland Gille has the record at this paper—thirty-nine. The junior reporters all look up to him because of his skill."

A commotion came from the direction of the waiting room. Pierre was out the door, racing down the hall, leaving them in the door of his office. In a few minutes he came back, his face grim. "The count is finished. One hundred sixty-two thousand votes for Jacques. Two hundred forty-five thousand for Boulanger."

None of the men said anything, but their faces were angry. Sarah knew they would have been swearing if she weren't there. "What do you think will happen now?" she ventured.

"I don't know, but I'm going to see," Pierre asserted. "The Boulangists will be meeting at the Café Durand, across from the Church of the Madeleine. I know some of the waiters there. They'll tell me what's going on. Sarah, I hope you'll excuse me. Armand and Ted can escort you home."

"No," she protested. "I want to go with you."

"Sarah, I don't think that's wise," came from Ted.

At the same time Armand said, "It might not be safe."

It was eleven o'clock on election night. Time for a sensible person to be off the streets. Ignoring both the men, Sarah looked at Pierre. "Please. It would be terrible to go home now and miss the rest."

He studied her, weighing the possibilities, then said, "All right. But you'll have to go into the church and stay there if things get ugly."

"I'll go along too," Ted said. "That's just like you, Sarah, never content to be left out of anything." He shook his head, but admiration was mixed with his censure.

"Very well," Armand agreed, "let's all go." Sarah could tell from his slight frown that he still thought it foolish.

When they were outside, she began to wonder whether Ted and Armand were right. Even before they reached the Place de Madeleine, they encountered a mass of people jamming the boulevards. Noise pounded on her ears—screams, whistles, the clang of bells—seeming as loud as though she were inside an enormous drum. The crush became greater. "Take hold of my arm," Pierre told her, "and don't let go. Take her other arm," he shouted to Armand. Wedged between the two men, she still felt buffeted by the motion around them. When they finally reached the Madeleine, they had lost Ted. She hoped he had given up and made his way home.

They pushed through the throng until they were across from the Café Durand. Bright lights radiated from the four windows on the first floor and three of the windows above.

The draperies were closed on the remaining three windows of the second floor. Sarah looked up at the dull red glow of the guarded windows, her chest pulsing with excitement and foreboding. What kind of arrangements were being made there? A dark passageway opened at one side of the café. It fascinated her; she half expected to see a uniformed man on a black horse burst out in a furious charge.

Pierre maneuvered their way closer to the Church of the Madeleine until they reached the gallery at the front and could stand with a column at their backs. He cupped his hands around his mouth and shouted, "I'm going over to the café to see what I can find out. Armand, will you see that Sarah is all right?"

He plunged back into the crowd without waiting for an answer.

Cheers and chants surrounded Sarah and Armand, making conversation impossible. Most of the spectators were men, but the hats and bonnets of women surfaced like gulls on the sea of male headgear. Sarah wondered how long the people waiting there would remain just onlookers if the general appeared. Maybe some of them were armed, part of the ten thousand men the League of Patriots had claimed they could muster. Would Paris wake the next day and find the Republic overthrown? It had been foolish for her to insist on coming, but she didn't regret it. Still, she was glad for Armand close beside her. Just so Pierre was safe.

Bells from the cathedrals of Saint Augustine and the Trinity began to ring, and the crowd quieted. Sarah counted: one, two, three . . . until the twelfth chime reverberated over the hushed throng. A murmur grew, questioning, disappointed. Nearby a man shouted in an angry voice, "Where's the general? We want to see the general." Other voices took up the demand, the crescendo rising. Armand gripped Sarah's arm and looked behind them toward the tall doors of the church.

But like waves exhausted on the shore, the unanswered cries for Boulanger's appearance began to fade. Breathing spaces appeared in the mass of people as disappointment sent shopkeepers and workers, aristocrats and curiosity seekers wearily on their way. "There's Pierre," Armand said. By standing on tiptoe, Sarah saw Pierre making his way toward them, against the current of departing supporters.

When he reached Sarah and Armand, a generous space had opened around them. "What happened? Did you find out anything?" she asked impatiently.

"The victory dinner was just that—a dinner. Boulanger accepted congratulations, but then sat and drank his wine. No call for a coup d'état. I saw a fellow journalist leaving. He'd like another Bonaparte regime, but he told me he doesn't think Boulanger will even take his seat in the Chamber tomorrow."

They stood silently, the men looking as perplexed as Sarah felt. "Boulanger may have more respect for the Republic than it appeared," Armand suggested.

"Possibly." Pierre frowned, considering. "Or just no plan for tonight. There are still the general elections later. He could expect to win everything then, as the second Napoleon did forty years ago."

"Underneath it all," Sarah said, "maybe he really is a music hall general."

Pierre grinned and took her arm. "Cheerful Sarah. You had to be an optimist to come to France alone. But let's give up tonight. Armand, I'll see you Thursday."

Armand looked disappointed. "Shall I escort Mademoiselle Taylor home?"

To Sarah's surprise, Pierre said, "No. I'll do that. Good night." He moved off with her before she could do more than nod to Armand.

She walked beside him, her irritation building. "Why didn't you want Armand to take me home?" she asked. "Isn't that what we're working toward? Or can't you make up your mind what you want to do?"

"Of course I can," he said, but with enough force that she suspected she'd guessed correctly. "But we can't let him think I'm going to give you up so quickly. He does like competition, remember."

"I prefer to choose my escorts for myself. He asked you and you decided without consulting me."

He stopped suddenly, leaving her a half step in front of him before he caught up again. "Sorry. I forget that you're an independent woman."

"Please don't forget again."

They had to walk for some distance to find a cab. The air was cold, the moonlight adding to the wintry atmosphere. As the streets emptied, the chill quiet seemed austere but peaceful and Sarah lost her annoyance.

When they were finally in a cab, she asked, "Is the fight against General Boulanger over?"

"There are still the general elections. We can't let up at all. And you and I need to proceed with our project. I've arranged with Armand to have lunch a week from Thursday. Early, before you have to be at the Opéra Comique. You'll join us?"

"No," she said with some pleasure in having plans that didn't depend on him. "Solange Rabaud has invited me to have lunch with her that day."

"I didn't know you'd seen Solange again." He sounded unfriendly.

"I haven't, but I intend to."

The cab stopped in front of the wine shop. Pierre helped her out and asked the cabby to wait. Inside, he walked up the stairs with her and stopped outside her door. She put out her hand to him. "Good night, Pierre. I'm sorry Boulanger won, but maybe—"

"I think you shouldn't have anything to do with Solange," he interrupted.

Her irritation returned, growing into anger. "I can't imagine what you have against her. You seem to know her well enough. And you've introduced me to men and their mistresses and let them think you and I are lovers."

"Solange leads an . . . artificial life, not one for you, Sarah."

This was too much! It had been an unhappy night for him, and he was probably exhausted, but he was going too far. "You're not running my life, Pierre. I want to see Solange Rabaud. I think she's interesting. And I'll damned well do as I please."

In the dim light from the gas jet on the landing, he looked startled. Good. She seldom swore, but she hoped she'd shocked him for a change. She jerked open the door to her room, then turned back to add a defiant "And if she offers me absinthe, I'll try it."

Only consideration for the other people sleeping in the house kept her from slamming the door. Inside she listened and finally heard his footsteps receding.

The room was cold. She considered starting the tiny stove and decided to hurry into bed instead. As she undressed, she was trembling, more than the temperature warranted. A quarrel with Pierre—it gave her an unpleasant feeling in her stomach. But she was right to resist his dominance. She intended to try everything. Well, no, not everything. Hallucinations would scare her. But she intended to find out whatever there was about Solange that Pierre didn't want her to learn.

CHAPTER
TEN

I RON RAIL FENCES AND SMALL GARDENS SHELTERED THE
buildings on the Rue de Chazelles from the street. Gray
stone ledges outlined the windows and doorways, giving
the connected houses an anonymous similarity. Only the
draperies showing through the window panes suggested the
tastes of individual occupants. Most were dark green or
brown. At number eleven, Solange Rabaud's address, they
were a bold red, outdoing the early-afternoon sunlight.

Sarah pulled the bell beside the entrance and looked back
at the street. It was quiet, the only sound the rattle of the
hansom cab that had just deposited her. Several doors away
a black-uniformed maid with a shopping basket walked
briskly along. The neighborhood looked bourgeois and prosaic, not the place a disreputable woman would live.

The maid who let Sarah into the foyer had the peasant
face and body of the *santon* Zola had given Sarah. The drawing room, where the maid left her, had white wainscoting
and wallpaper of narrow red and white stripes. Potted green
plants were everywhere; bric-a-brac and framed pictures
cluttered the tables. A clock decorated with alabaster cupids

sat on the mantel along with several boxes encrusted with seashells. The only unadorned object was an upright piano. The room was too messy to be dignified. Sarah felt as if she'd arrived at the home of a comfortable friend.

When Solange entered, her appearance reinforced the room's informal atmosphere. Although she was as beautiful as Sarah remembered, she wore an elegant but informal lavender tea gown, with soft flowing lines. It made Sarah aware how restricting her own corset felt.

Solange held out her hands and grasped Sarah's in welcome. "I'm delighted you could come. As you see, we're lunching tête-à-tête, so please, let Berthe take your hat and gloves."

Sarah complied happily and settled into a soft overstuffed chair while Solange sat on a red velvet settee and talked. "We must get well acquainted. I'm a person who makes up her mind instantly. From the moment you came to Henriette's dressing room, I knew we would be friends. I'm also very changeable. That's one of my faults." She said this with the charming smile of disclaimer Sarah had noticed the night they met. "You're sure to notice many others, but you mustn't tell me."

Sarah couldn't imagine she would want to criticize this dazzling woman. "I admire what I've heard about you from other singers. Do you still sing publicly . . . Solange?" She almost said Madame Rabaud. With their thirty-year age difference, the formal address had come naturally to mind. But she was positive that would offend the older woman.

Solange's expression grew mournful. "A bad throat infection. I never recovered my voice."

"I'm sorry. I wish I'd heard you sing."

Solange got up and took a large picture in a silver frame off a table. "Here's a picture of me in my gown for *The Grand Duchess of Gerolstein*."

A young Solange, a crown on her luxuriant dark hair,

looked imperiously into the camera. She wore a dress stiff with brocade and jewels. A satin cape with white fur trim spread behind her in a train that must have required three or four pages to carry. After Sarah admired the photograph, Solange went around the room, identifying the role she'd played for each picture; all of them were of her in costume. Someday, Sarah fantasized, she might have a similar array.

Solange sat down at the piano. "Please, you must sing for me. What will it be? I know—something that miserable Rivarol kept you from performing." She began the music for Nicklausse's song from *The Tales of Hoffman* about a mechanical doll that fell in love with a mechanical bird. Sarah felt intensely self-conscious, but Solange sent her such an encouraging smile that she relaxed and sang easily.

When she finished, Solange applauded, then rose and embraced her. "Brava, Sarah! You will not stay in the chorus. Some day I will go to the Opéra Comique—no, to the Opéra itself. And I'll hear you sing that very song."

It was extravagant praise, and too generous. But hearing her hopes predicted by someone else thrilled Sarah.

Berthe announced lunch. In the dining room warm colors predominated, yellows and orange, with the same abundance of plants, small statuary, and candles in elaborate holders. Berthe had a difficult time squeezing dishes of food onto the side table.

Over lunch Solange talked about herself, beginning with her childhood. With the asparagus soup, she told of living in a provincial town west of Paris and going to a convent school. The pink-fleshed trout, which Sarah thought the most delicious fish she'd ever eaten, took the story through Solange's marriage to "an impossible navy officer."

"He took my virginity so quickly I hardly knew what had happened," Solange reported matter-of-factly while she helped herself to a roll. "Then he neglected me. So I took my first lover."

Next came Solange's account of her escape and flight to
Paris. Despite the shiny crust and delicious yeasty smell of
the roll Sarah was pulling apart, she ate without being aware
of its taste, too startled and enthralled. An artichoke and a
salad of three different kinds of crinkled green leaves received a similar lack of attention. When the apples and soft
white cheese were served, Sarah recovered enough to appreciate them, and to ask, "When did you start singing?"

Solange paused, a bite of apple halfway to her mouth.
"Not when I first got here. Let's see. I think it was—yes, it
was after the politician. He gave me my own horses and
carriage," she said in a chatty aside, accompanied by a little
shrug. "Great heaven he was boring—so I left him. My next
protector was a director at the Théatre-Francais. He wanted
to put me on the stage. Unfortunately I couldn't act. But I
had a natural voice. He introduced me to a man who had
helped finance the careers of several composers—Offenbach
for one."

Solange laughed, clearly enjoying her memories. "That
one was an old man, and not in good health. I let him see
me naked. In return he paid for voice lessons and saw that
I got a start."

Sarah couldn't think of a response. No one, not even the
"fast" girls when she was at school, had ever talked about
being naked in front of a man. Fortunately, Berthe interrupted to say that coffee and liqueur were ready in the
drawing room. By the time Solange and Sarah were seated
with coffee and cut crystal glasses of brilliant green char-
treuse, Sarah's shock had faded. Boldly she asked, "You've
had many lovers?"

"I was poor, and beautiful. And I had no skills to earn a
living until I discovered I could sing. I tried giving piano
and English lessons, but that barely fed me. I saw how other
women made their way, and it was easy. A little mad, perhaps. Once a priest reproached me, and I assured him I had

never been a thief or a murderer." Again her glance invited complicity, that she could never do anything really wrong.

"I wasn't like some women," she continued. "When I was very young, the most notorious star of the demimonde was Coral Pearl. She was crude. She used to tell stories about all her lovers." Solange was watching Sarah with a sly smile, as if to test how outrageous she was being. "She used to describe them according to their endowments—straight, crooked, quick to rise or almost hopelessly resistant. I would never say such intimate things about my lovers."

When Sarah felt her inevitable blush appear, Solange looked pleased.

To Sarah, Solange wasn't just a different nationality. She was a person from another world, one that seemed more like a forbidden novel than real life, and Sarah was enchanted. "I've been giving English lessons," she said, offering this as something they had in common.

Solange clapped her hands delightedly. "I knew you and I have souls that are alike." She put aside her coffee and curled up against one end of the settee, indicating the other for Sarah. "Come, sit here where I can hear you best. I have told you about me. Now you must tell me your story—how you came to France. Everything."

Sarah began diffidently with Boston, her voice teacher, and the maid who taught her French dances. When she came to her reasons for coming to France, Solange's complete attention and sympathetic eyes made it natural to talk about the night she discovered her father and Cousin Mabel together. "And so, for Papa's sake and to be independent, I decided I must go away," she finished.

Solange looked incredulous. "You mean you left home because you found out your father has a mistress?"

"Yes, well, I . . ." Sarah knew she was blushing again, and that made explaining even more difficult. "Since I've been in Paris, I see that the way I acted must seem foolish. But

Boston is so different. Things aren't done the same way."

"Men don't have mistresses in the United States?" Solange asked skeptically.

"I suppose they do. But where I lived, no one ever talked about it. And I was taught that if a man and woman are . . . intimate, of course they must be married."

"There's some of that kind of pretense in France, too." Solange sighed over such a sorry state of things.

The cupid-encrusted clock on the mantel chimed four times, and Sarah rose. "I must leave so that I can get ready to go to the theater. Thank you so much for lunch, and the conversation."

Solange rose also, smiling brightly at Sarah. "It was a pleasure to have you here. We will visit again soon. I see that I must educate you so that you will understand better the way men really are."

For a few seconds Sarah thought of her childhood friends and teachers and what they would say of Solange. For surely she was one of the *grande courtisanes*, the kept women of the Paris demimonde. But that remembered disapproval couldn't match the pleasure of Solange's company. She smiled and said, "I would very much enjoy visiting again."

"Good. And you'll sing for me again too." Solange ran her fingers along Sarah's arm in a small caress. "How nice that you're a mezzo-soprano and can sing the trouser roles. You'd make a delightful young man."

"I hope I can some day."

"You will," Solange promised, as if fate wouldn't dare withhold anything she predicted.

While Sarah was putting on her hat and gloves, Solange said, "You must meet Parisian men. They aren't all like that dreadful Rivarol. You already know one interesting man. Weren't you with Pierre de Tourbey the other night?"

"Yes. I met him through a family friend who lives here. Pierre also introduced me to his cousin, the Comte de Saint-Maurice."

"Pierre is a good lover," Solange said, as casually as if she were pointing out that the afternoon was sunny. "Armand is too."

Sarah stopped, her hands on her hat, then slowly settled it on her upswept hair and fastened the hatpins. "You know Pierre and Armand well?" she managed to ask in an almost normal voice.

"Pierre was a very young man when we were lovers, but men don't change that much. He's probably more skillful now. Armand was older before I knew him. A generous man."

When Sarah was outside, she couldn't remember whether she had said good-bye properly. A cab passed her, and she didn't notice until it was too late to stop it. She started walking slowly, buffeted by an emotion that felt painfully like jealousy. Solange and Pierre! She supposed it explained his objections to her associating with his former mistress. *His former mistress.*

And Solange had been Armand's mistress too. At least it substantiated what Pierre said—that his cousin pursued his women. That probably meant her task of attracting Armand was easier—if it could be easy for any woman to captivate a man who had been the lover of a woman as beautiful as Solange.

Did she want to see Solange again? Yes, even with this uncomfortable knowledge, she did. Solange fascinated her, and the praise and encouragement about Sarah's future in opera had been more intoxicating than the wine. Also, the prospect of "instruction" was irresistible. However prosaic her life might turn out to be, Sarah wanted at least to know what men like Pierre and Armand did in Solange's bed.

When Sarah returned from an evening performance at the Opéra Comique the following week, she found a gray envelope on the floor just inside the door of her room. The address stared at her even before she picked it up: "Mr. Theodore Kearns, c/o Crèdit Lyonnais, 15 Boulevard des Italiens, Paris, France." The handwriting was her father's.

Scrawled along the top was Ted's note: "I received this letter from Josiah, with an enclosure for you."

It had been two months since Josiah's previous letter. He must have debated with himself, Sarah thought, about whether to write again. But he had, and directly to her. In spite of the distance between her and Boston, she could feel her heart accelerate as she held the envelope, almost as if it brought her father's authority into her room. Chiding herself for letting her confidence be shaken, she sat down and opened the note.

Josiah's words were uncomfortably prosaic, from his "My Dear Daughter" to the "Your Loving Father" at the end. He wrote about his insurance business, his good health and news of several family friends. There was no reference to his and Sarah's quarrel, nor any mention of Cousin Mabel. The only personal note came just before the closing: "I hope that you are getting along well and enjoying your visit to Paris. I would appreciate hearing from you."

Yes, this time she would answer. But what could she tell him of her life that he would welcome knowing? She didn't think of herself as "visiting" Paris—not any longer. He wouldn't want to hear that, and certainly not what had been on her mind since the lunch with Solange.

She rose and went to her bedroom to get ready for bed, composing a letter in her mind as she undressed. Describing some of the sights of Paris—that would be safe. He wouldn't be too unhappy about her tutoring in English. She'd have to include that she was singing at the Opéra Comique; that news would upset him, but she couldn't leave it out.

While she was brushing her hair, she thought back to the

first time she had written Papa a letter. She'd been seven or eight and had gone on a trip to Maine with Jane Morrison and her family. At that time she'd signed her letters in the way she'd been taught in school: "Your loving and obedient Sarah." She still loved him, but she was no longer obedient, and no longer his.

Pierre passed the entrance of the Café de la Paix and climbed to the third floor of the Grand Hotel. He was still uncertain why he was there. The message from the new minister of the interior had arrived at the paper that morning, asking him or Marmontel to a meeting in a private room. Since his copublisher was away, Pierre had come. Partly for courtesy, even more for curiosity.

General Boulanger, for reasons he hadn't stated, had not taken his seat in the Chamber of Deputies. Pierre enjoyed the irony of thinking the general didn't really know what to do with his victory. But with the national elections to come, the situation was still too dangerous for comedy. Alarmed by Boulanger's popularity, the new prime minister, Tirard, had chosen Ernest Constans as a minister of the interior who might be able to stop Boulanger. The ministerial post dealt with judicial proceedings and was a position of considerable power. Constans was known as an ambitious man and skillful politician. Pierre wondered what he had in mind to stop the Boulangists and how it involved a meeting with journalists.

When Pierre reached the private room, he found five other journalists there. Their cigars had already produced a haze, which the midday sunlight coming in the windows could barely penetrate. Hector Lunel greeted him, indicating an empty chair beside him.

"What's this about?" Hector asked after Pierre sat down.

"I don't know, but I see Constans coming in now. We'll find out."

Constans was a short, bald man with bushy black eyebrows that overbalanced a thin mustache. He took a seat and began to speak immediately. "Gentlemen, what I tell you must remain confidential. I've chosen you for this meeting because I am certain you will respect that necessary request."

Nods and murmurs of assent went around the room.

"A few days ago, General Boulanger and your colleague Rochefort had dinner with the top echelon of the Bonapartist Central Committee."

Not surprising, Pierre thought. The general was no Napoleon Bonaparte, but he might imagine himself as another Napoleon III. The mediocre nephew of the first Bonaparte had been dictator for twenty years. It had taken the defeat by Germany in 1870 to get him out and reestablish the Republic.

"That meeting," Constans continued, "means we can't wait. I believe Boulanger is personally vulnerable and I have a plan to persuade him to leave the country. To do that will require the timely publication of certain information. For that I need your help."

"What kind of information?" Pierre asked.

Constans smoothed his mustache. "Among other things, it might include the word 'treason.'"

"Is that true?" Pierre persisted.

"If not immediately, I have evidence that it will be soon."

So, Pierre thought, there were to be rumors and innuendoes, circulated in the press, calculated to intimidate Boulanger. An underhanded tactic, but one that would test the general's mettle. Pierre had never liked to participate in that kind of maneuver. He'd talk it over with Marmontel at the paper.

After more general discussion about the political situation and Boulanger's vulnerabilities, Constans rose. "I'll be in touch with you gentlemen soon."

As Pierre left, Hector clattered down the stairs after him. "Say, Pierre, what do you think of the minister's plan?"

"I'm not sure."

"It sounds straightforward to me. If Boulanger's innocent, he'll fight. If he's guilty, he'll leave."

"What if it's like a farce by that new playwright, Georges Feydeau?" Pierre said. "Misunderstandings and comic poses. People going in and out of the wrong hotel rooms. Maybe Boulanger's all bluff."

"No use talking to you," Hector complained. "You're never serious." He went on ahead past the entrance to the Café de la Paix and outside.

Pierre was about to follow when a waiter touched him on the arm. "Monsieur de Tourbey, a lady in the restaurant wishes to speak to you. Over there."

It was Solange Rabaud, sitting on a bench along the wall. He'd forgotten that the Café de la Paix was a favorite spot for the *cocottes* and *grande courtisanes* to gather. He crossed to her, bowed over her hand and took a chair.

She rewarded him with her seductive smile. "I wanted you to know that I adore your Sarah."

"She's not mine," he cut in, but she went on as if he hadn't spoken.

"Such a marvelous figure. And that brilliant complexion and those enormous eyes. What color are they? Brown or green or gray? I can't decide. And her mouth, so proud looking. Except when she laughs. Then she's delightful, like an innocent schoolgirl. On top of everything, her voice has extraordinary charm, both for speaking and singing."

Though he had put it to himself in more earthy words, those were many of the same thoughts about Sarah that Pierre had. He didn't like hearing them from Solange. "I'm sure you're a better judge of a singer's voice than I am," he said coolly. Good Lord! He wasn't going to discuss Sarah's looks with her.

"I've always wanted to be someone's voice teacher," Solange said. "I think I'll help Sarah with her vocal technique." Her coquettish look invited him to wonder what other techniques she might also want to teach. "And she must be exposed to Paris life. Poor girl, growing up in Boston. I plan to invite her to go with me to the Incoherents' Ball."

Pierre wondered what he had ever seen in Solange other than her beauty. The Incoherents' Ball was usually a riotous business. Masks and costumes gave license to displays of seminudity that would put performers in jail if they appeared that way on stage. Pierre had gone occasionally and enjoyed the ball and the overnight female company generated by the atmosphere. Sarah, for all the independence and sophistication she'd developed in Paris, would be out of her element there. Though he felt his anger rising, he didn't want to show it.

"I must go," he said and stood up. "You look as beautiful as ever, Solange." That truth substituted for the more polite lie that he'd enjoyed seeing her.

Outside on the Rue des Capucines he started toward the Place de l'Opéra, then stopped and looked at his pocket watch. Reversing direction, he started for the Châtelet and the Opéra Comique. He hadn't seen Sarah for almost three weeks, not since election night when she'd been so angry at his remarks about Solange. And she had reason, he had to admit. He didn't have the right to tell her what to do—had warned himself not to become so involved with her. A warning he didn't always take.

And there was Armand. Pierre knew he wasn't managing his feelings about that business very well. After telling himself to stay away and give Armand a chance, he'd sent Sarah three messages asking when they might meet. She'd written that the Comique was putting on a series of operas by Jules Massenet and that she was rehearsing and couldn't get away. It had seemed best to wait until she wanted to see him, but today he intended to talk to her anyway.

The foyer of the Théâtre des Nations was empty except for the porter, who was listening to music coming from the auditorium. The notice board listed a dress rehearsal for a Massenet opera, *Herodiade*. Pierre recalled the story—of Salome and Herod, and the death of the prophet, John the Baptist. Quietly he went upstairs and slipped into the stage box at the front. Jules Massenet, a handsome man with a receding hairline and a bushy mustache, was the conductor in the pit. If the composer himself was taking time from his duties at the Paris Conservatory to conduct his operas, then Pierre understood Sarah's reasons for spending so much time practicing.

The stage set was an Eastern palace, where a banquet was going on. The principal singers, representing Herod and his wife and her daughter, Salome, wore elaborate robes and crowns. Pierre quickly passed them by, locating Sarah. Like the other women in the chorus, she had on a veil, long billowing pants, and a low cut top that covered her arms but not much of her breasts. The music and action suggested an orgiastic revel, and in her eastern costume, Sarah was all the things Solange had said about her. Without clothes she'd be even more beautiful. She was a far more erotic vision to Pierre than the opera's star, Salome.

Jules Massenet rapped his baton on his music stand, halting the music and interrupting Pierre's thoughts. "My dear singers," the composer said, in an amiable voice that still carried clearly, "let us remember that we are all musicians. Pretend there is an audience and that they are on their feet, applauding you. And sing!"

Salome and Herod started over, and the violent action proceeded to Salome's suicide and the final curtain without the composer having to interrupt again. When he announced himself satisfied, the singers began to drift off the stage. Pierre went down the stairs and around to the back, catching

Sarah before she went into the dressing room. "Sarah, may I talk to you?"

When she turned toward him, her expression seemed stiff, like a portrait in which the artist has not quite caught the likeness. Her eyes looked almost wary, her smile without its usual gaiety. It didn't seem like Sarah to hold a grudge for his intemperate attempt to tell her what to do. What had she heard from Solange? Silently he cursed Solange and himself.

"Pierre, I didn't know you were here. How are you?" she said politely.

"Fine. Busy. I saw a little of the rehearsal." He could also see, through the costume that clung to her, her arms, slender and graceful, and the shapes of her breasts. A whiff of her perfume came to him. It smelled like crushed spring flowers. How fragrant would it be just there—between her breasts. With an effort, he looked at her face. "I still haven't heard you sing away from the chorus." Teasing, distracting himself, he added, "I could ask Cesbron for the use of the theater for a special performance."

Her smile relaxed a little. "I think I'm back in his good graces, but not that far."

"Do you have time for something to eat now?" When she hesitated, he said, "I apologize for our disagreement on election night. You were right—where you go isn't my business. I hope you're not still angry."

"No, I'm not." He believed her, though she still didn't seem completely at ease.

"I am hungry," she said. "I don't have to be back here until five. I'll go change."

At a small café just across the Pont au Change, they had hard-boiled eggs and salad, along with bread and wine. Pierre talked of minor incidents at the newspaper, and she described a performance of *Rigoletto* in which the padding that had been fastened to the baritone to make him into a hunchback had slipped until he looked as if he were wearing a bustle.

By the time they got to coffee, Sarah had lost her earlier constraint. "I'm sorry I've been so busy," she said. "Since Monsieur Cesbron took me back, I want to do everything right and I've been practicing constantly."

"How do you feel about that now?"

"Confident again. What about Armand? Should I be doing something more?"

He should encourage her, but instead he found himself saying, "Yes, but before that, there's a ball you might enjoy. Two weeks from Tuesday is the annual Incoherents' Ball."

"Who are the Incoherents?"

"A group of writers and artists who proclaim they admire the freedom of incoherence. It's a kind of protest against order and uniformity. The first thing they did was to put on a show of drawings by people who don't know how to draw. Now they have a costume ball each year."

Sarah laughed. "It sounds crazy."

"The ball gets rowdy sometimes. Not the kind of occasion Armand likes. Would you go with me? I'll look after you if things get out of hand."

It occurred to him that he was suggesting she should have a man to protect her—and that he, not Armand, was the man.

"A rowdy ball." She laughed again, with such enjoyment that he dismissed anything but sharing her pleasure. "I never heard of anything like that at home. Yes, I'd like to go with you."

"You'll need a costume."

"Helene, my friend from the chorus, probably knows how to find one. Or . . . Madame Rabaud may have a suggestion." Her eyes held his, challenging him, but with a trace of uncertainty too. That combination of boldness and inno-cence acted on him like an erotic suggestion. His thoughts must have shown in his face, because her color rose and she breathed a little faster.

"That's settled then," he said. "We'll go. The tenth of March."

"Yes, and I must get back to the Opéra Comique now."

After leaving her at the theater, he walked slowly across the square, thinking of the things they hadn't said. Sarah must have heard something from Solange, but not everything. In Sarah's present guarded mood, it wasn't a topic they could discuss. Not yet.

CHAPTER
ELEVEN

SARAH ADJUSTED A MOROCCAN FEZ ON HER HAIR, STUDYING herself in the tall mirror in her room. Two long curls of her red-gold hair hung on either side of her face, and the edge of soft waves showed below the fez. In back her hair hung loose. She had wondered whether the red felt head-piece would clash with her hair. Instead it looked satisfyingly exotic. A ruffle edged the modest neckline of the sheer white blouse she wore underneath an azure blue silk vest. A heavy brass necklace with a large blue enamel medallion reached almost to her waist. Wide enameled bracelets encircled her upper arms over her sleeves. When she moved her hands, narrow bracelets on her wrists jangled together tunefully.

Laughing, she turned to Helene, who was standing behind her. "I sound like a gypsy who's from some traveling band. The kind you see performing at fairs."

"You look wonderful," Helene said. "Are you happy with the costume now?"

"Yes, I think so," Sarah said doubtfully. The top was fine, but the bottom still concerned her. The full underskirt was pale blue muslin, with an overskirt of blue and red striped silk. The overskirt draped across one hip and tied at the other, leaving the underskirt showing on one side. The skirts came to just below her knees.

A friend of Helene had been wardrobe mistress for a ballet company and had inherited worn or damaged costumes. Helene had borrowed one which had been used in a production of *Coppelia* and helped Sarah mend several tears. Sarah liked her exotic appearance in it—as if she came from Hungary or Romania. However, the short skirts that allowed freedom for the ballet dancer were more immodest than anything she'd ever worn. Helene had helped again by supplying a pair of black tights. Sarah's own high black boots, designed for Boston snows, ended two inches below the bottom of the skirts.

"I've been to two of the balls put on by the students from the art school," Helene said. "You'd be amazed to see what some of the women wear to that. I've heard costumes at the Incoherents' Ball are crazier. No one will notice whether your tights show above your boots."

After Helene left, Sarah started back to the mirror, then sat on a chair without looking at herself. It was the only costume she had, so worrying was pointless. At least she would have the anonymity of a black mask. She'd intended to consult Solange, but the day after Pierre's invitation, a message had come on the noon post, asking Sarah to attend the Incoherents' Ball with Solange and her friends. Solange wanted always to be first choice, Sarah felt sure. She sent the most polite refusal she could devise, and she didn't ask about a costume. Solange's response had sounded cooler than the previous note. Fortunately it also included an invitation for a future visit to Solange's town house.

When Sarah and Ted had their weekly lunch together, he'd seemed unconcerned at the news that she had met Solange. "She's one of the *dégrafées*," he said casually.

"The 'unbuttoneds'?" she asked, then realized why a

woman who took many lovers would have that nickname.

"Yes. Madame Rabaud never had a really outstanding singing voice," Ted had said, "but her technique was excellent. And she gave off an allure that made her exceedingly popular. Her protectors came from the very best circles."

Now, as she waited, Sarah thought again about Solange and Pierre. In spite of his apology for objecting to her seeing Solange, a certain strain to his manner indicated he still disapproved. She was tempted to tell him she knew that he and Solange had once been lovers—to see his reaction. But she wasn't certain of her own motives. Several times, when she was almost asleep, she'd imagined Pierre and Solange together. In these fantasies, they were embracing, naked. The images had disturbed and excited her at the same time.

It was almost midnight when Pierre arrived. He halted just inside the door, looking at her. Helene had been wrong about her costume. From the way his gaze lingered on her legs, she could tell that he noticed the length of her skirts immediately. "Excellent!" he exclaimed admiringly. "I'll have to keep a tight hold on you or someone will try to steal you."

"Thank you," she said.

When he took off his cape, Sarah thought it just as likely some woman would want to snare him. He was a Harlequin, with tights and jacket patterned of alternating black and white diamonds. His wide Harlequin hat turned up in front with points on both sides, and he carried the traditional wooden sword. A mask dangled around his neck. The jacket and tights fit his muscular body closely, and she could observe what his regular clothes partly concealed—broad back and chest, tapering to lean stomach and hips, and strong legs.

Finally she noticed that printed pieces of paper had been fastened to several diamonds on his chest and back. "What are those?" she asked.

"Come closer and read," he invited, grinning.

They were sections of a newspaper article. The top one on his chest had the headline Incoherents Arts Show. It was dated October 27, 1886, and carried Pierre's name. The various sections described exhibits in the show. A bread crumb sculpture was by the Hungarian from Montmartre. The same artist also entered a painting, done in oil on emery board, labeled as one of the Paris boulevards a few years before the birth of Christ.

"The Hungarian from Montmartre," Pierre explained, "is really Toulouse-Lautrec."

"Yes, how clever," she said. At that moment she was too aware of the odor of Pierre's skin and his chest so close to her to care much about the contents of the article. He turned around, and the ridged muscles of his back moved in fascinating ripples. "What do you think of the Monsieur Vénus de Milo?" he asked.

"It's . . . interesting," she said, forcing herself to focus on the newsprint enough to hunt for the reference. It did sound interesting when she found it—an armless, bearded statue. Pierre's article also described a painting of a drunken house and a sculpture of a bidet under a cardboard sun. "What kind of ball are we going to?" she asked.

"I told you it's crazy." He turned, releasing her from her study of his back. "Your costume is beautiful, but I think we should make one change." He went to the window where a row of empty flower pots waited for spring. After a moment's study, he chose one and returned to replace her fez with the dark brown pot. "There. Perfect now."

His hands lingered on her hair before he reluctantly helped wrap her long cloak around her.

She was glad when he put his cape back on, so that she wasn't tempted to more surreptitious glances.

The ball was held in a large building near Les Halles market. As Sarah and Pierre approached, she could smell

the produce that would be for sale at dawn, about the time
the ball would end. Onions, garlic and potatoes mixed their
kitchen odors with the perfume of flowers. Inside, gaudy
streamers hung from the roof. Great swaths of cloth—brilliant yellows, purples, vermillion—made dizzying patterns
on the walls. Along the two long sides were tables and chairs,
most of them already occupied. Stalls for drinks and food
filled one end of the room; kegs of beer and barrels of wine
stood in racks. In between bowls of fruit and plates of
cheeses, pastries sent out tempting smells. Waiters in white
aprons scurried back and forth, carrying trays precariously
balanced over their heads.

The building already teemed with masked celebrants, a
few in costumes she'd seen at balls at home—shepherds,
courtiers from medieval courts, Greek goddesses, a dancing
bear or two. Other, more spectacular, figures surprised and
enchanted her. A bearded man in a ballet tutu had bare legs
as hairy as his face. Two clowns passed her, one a tall woman
and the other a short man, each wearing a clown suit a size
to fit the other. The man had to hold onto his pants to keep
them from dragging on the floor. The woman's thin arms and
legs extended their bare length well beyond the ends of her
garment. A man in a knight's armor had a tall lamp on his
head that gave out light and smoke from its wick. With him
was a woman dressed as an artichoke.

More revelers were arriving all the time, adding to the
crush. With a feeling of relief, Sarah decided that if Solange
were here, it was unlikely they would meet her. She also
realized how discreetly she was dressed. Though most of
the women's costumes were no more daring than hers, a
few wore gowns that clung to their bodies in very revealing
ways. One passing couple caught Sarah's eye. The man's
shirt was open to the waist, displaying his bare chest, and
he had a patch over one eye. A pirate. The woman was
dressed in what Sarah guessed was a harem costume. Green

pants of a soft material were gathered at her ankles. Large dark nipples showed through a beige gauze top. Sarah stared, shocked, and realized Pierre must be noticing the woman's breasts too. She gave him a sideways glance; fortunately he was searching for a free table and looking at neither the harem costume nor her own embarrassed face.

Pierre found two places at the edge of the center area where people were dancing. A platform at the end opposite the food stalls held the musicians, but they had to compete with impromptu performers. Two men cleared a space in the middle of the dancers for a woman with huge gold ear hoops and a crimson dress, who sang and danced to the accompaniment of her tambourine. A man jumped up onto a table and played on a fiddle. Sarah judged from the player's mournful face that it must be a sad song, but she couldn't hear him. She saw two men from the Opéra Comique chorus. One wore the horns of a bull on his head. The other had on a toreador's costume, but the bull held the red cape, and periodically the toreador charged him. Over everything was the noise of talk and laughter, people shouting to friends at other tables, the general hubbub of revelers determined to enjoy themselves.

The din made conversation nearly impossible. Pierre had to lean so close to Sarah that his mustache brushed her ear. She could smell the spicy fragrance of his skin. "Do you want to dance?" he asked.

"I think I'd rather watch at first," she said, with her mouth close to his face.

Before she leaned back, he turned his head toward her, and their lips brushed. For a second or two she felt caught, held motionless, as if there were no space between them. Then she moved back, but part of her still felt as if she were touching him. The sensation spread, until she was aware with each part of her body of the corresponding part of his. Her arm next to his. His thigh resting on his chair but feeling as if it were beside hers. The pressure of her boots seemed greater because they rested near his.

Surely it was an hallucination. But her glass held ruby wine, not the bitter green absinthe that turned milky with water. She glanced at him and saw in his face the same awareness of her that she felt of him. He smiled, his eyes crinkling into the seductive teasing look, but with a kind of inviting tenderness. She felt a message—that this was a night for hallucinations. Tomorrow nothing would have been real.

Yes, she did want to dance—with him. She stood up, holding out her hand. He took it, and they joined the dancers. The musicians were playing fast Viennese waltzes. Pierre held her firmly about the waist, bracing her as they whirled and dipped. At moments she felt as though she might fly off into space without his supporting arm. They danced until she felt breathless and dizzy. When they finally sat down, she realized that she hadn't once worried about whether her skirts had billowed out high enough to show more of her black tights.

Several people greeted Pierre and read his costume. As the evening went on, drinking and celebrating reached a higher pitch and antics grew wilder. More tables became stages for performers. A harem girl began a belly dance, accompanied by whistled music and cheers. She finished near Pierre. "Stand up, Harlequin," she said to him. When he obliged, she stood so close to read his newspaper sections that her quite ample breasts leaned against him. He laughed, but Sarah felt a burning anger and had to clench her fists to keep from pushing the dancer away. When she finally left, Sarah took a large gulp of wine.

A man nearby abandoned his shirt entirely, and almost succeeded in removing his companion's dress. More pieces of clothing were discarded, either by the owner or an exuberant partner. A masked devil whirled out of the crush of dancers. His silky black tights and shirt were so snug

they could have been painted on his body, except for a
stuffed tail that dangled behind him. He grinned at Sarah
and gave an exaggerated bow that made her laugh. His smile
widened, and he grabbed her hand, pulling her to her feet.
"Come," he cried, "and dance with the devil."

Pierre was on his feet instantly, one arm around Sarah's
waist, the other shoving against the devil's chest. "No!" he
said. The devil let go of Sarah and staggered back a little,
but he was held upright by the people behind him. "Not
just now, friend devil," Pierre said in a more good-natured
tone.

After the devil went on to a more willing lady in a Louis
XIV court dress and powdered wig, Pierre said, "He's had
too much to drink."

"He didn't look drunk to me," Sarah said. She hadn't seen
enough intoxicated men to be sure, but it didn't matter.
Pierre's reaction pleased her.

He still held her by the waist. "Dance with a Harlequin
instead," he invited, and pulled her out into the dancers.

The central area had become so crowded that it was impossible to keep a proper distance. Pierre could barely make
the turns of the waltz, and other bodies buffeted them. Over
his shoulder she saw a couple who were both naked to the
waist and pressed together. The woman had her arms around
her partner's neck, and as Sarah watched, their mouths met
in a long kiss. Warmth rose deep inside Sarah, not the blush
that usually embarrassed her but a feeling of growing excitement.

Someone behind Sarah jostled her against Pierre so tightly
that the medallion between her breasts cut into her. She
could feel the buttons of his jacket. For a mad moment she
wondered what it would be like to dance as the couple
behind him, to feel her breasts against his naked chest.
Enough space opened around them that he could turn. Now
he was looking across her head. She twisted a little and saw

the half-naked couple, all effort at dancing abandoned as they continued to kiss. The man's hand stroked the side of the woman's breast, and Sarah's breast tingled as if someone had touched it.

She looked back at Pierre to find him staring down at her. He pulled her outstretched right hand in and cradled it against his shoulder. They swayed still, but it was no longer a dance, only part of an embrace. His eyes behind his mask were midnight blue, shadowy and mysterious, concealing his feelings, but the curve of his mouth was ardent. He leaned down, and she reached up for his kiss.

This was no Christmas kiss, begun in tenderness. It was demanding, passionate, reaching her inner excitement and inflaming it. His lips opened hers and his tongue followed, teasing, tasting. She felt lost in sensations she had only barely known of before. His arms pulled her next to him, giving her a knowledge of his body's arousal that was answered in hers.

The kiss ended. As they drew apart, she felt exhilarated and intensely alive, yet, at the same time, shaken by the strength of her own response. "Sarah?" he questioned, and she wasn't sure what he was asking or what she wanted him to ask.

When she didn't respond, he said, "I'd rather be just with you. Shall we leave?" Answering for her, he made a way for them toward the exit. He put his cape around his shoulders, and fastened her cloak, then hurried her outside. Just beyond the entrance, he pulled her to one side. In the dark corner, he yanked off his mask, then lifted hers off more gently and turned her face up toward his.

This was the kiss of a hungry man, his mouth pressed into hers, his tongue seeking the inside of her lips as if only there could he find sustenance. She clung to him, returning his kiss.

The spark of arousal had only faded, and his touch blew

it to life again. She savored the tremor that began low in her abdomen and raced through her body, responding to the pressure of his chest and legs against hers. His hand found the curve of her ribs, just below one breast. The nipple throbbed, as if there were a fever centered there.

A burst of light and music from behind dragged her back from her dizzying world. A noisy group of celebrants came out onto the street and staggered past them. With the interruption, some measure of sanity began to return. She broke away from Pierre.

His breathing rasped, irregular and hurried. "Let's go someplace—where we can be alone," he said.

"No, wait." This was happening too fast. She wasn't ready for feelings this strong. His passion, and even more her own, frightened her. Frantically she searched for some protection. Something to say that would bring them back to their familiar relationship. "Armand—"

"The devil with Armand," he said and captured her lips again.

Trying not to lose herself, she wrenched her mouth away. "Please, let me tell you."

In the gray beginning light, his eyes were shadowed, but his hands slid slowly away from her shoulders. Still struggling with her breathing, she said, "I have some news about Armand. I forgot to tell you earlier. He sent me an invitation to an evening where Monsieur Eiffel will be speaking about his tower. And he hopes I'll attend the opening of the tower and the Exposition with him."

When Pierre didn't respond, she had to fill the silence. "After the discouraging results of the election, I knew you'd be pleased that your plan is working."

He took a deep breath, but all he said was "Yes, of course."

She couldn't think of anything else to say, as if she were a child again, uncertain of an adult's reaction.

"It's a good first step," he said finally, and he sounded

almost like himself again. She felt both relief, and a contrary and bewildering disappointment.

He took her arm in his usual way, with no extra touch to remind her of their kisses. "We'll need to go to the boulevard to find a cab."

The air felt cold under her short skirt, and she was glad he set a rapid pace. In the cab he was silent, and she didn't talk, trying to sort her confused thoughts. Her life in Boston had taught her that love came before desire—or at least before this much desire. When she fell in love and married, then she would feel passion with her husband. Of course men, because they were naturally lustful, would try to entice women before marriage. And of course women refused. That had been a safe expectation. Not like the frightening desire she'd just felt for Pierre. How had it happened?

The ball, with its licentious atmosphere, had affected them both. He'd been aroused by the sight of the other woman's breasts, as she had by watching the half-naked couple embrace. This was lust, not love. It was a mood that would pass.

Pierre, sitting a little apart from Sarah, was having his own troubled thoughts. Her obvious fear and confusion reproached him. He shouldn't have let himself get so aroused with her. There was too much difference between their experience; she was still unsophisticated. *Dieu puissant!* She was hard to resist, though. And what of his resolution that he wouldn't take so much of her attention? His resolve seemed to last only until he was around her.

In this case he wasn't good at being unselfish. He must let her find out more about Armand, but he wouldn't deprive himself completely. Just keep things from being too intense. That was better for him, too, than a serious involvement with a proper American woman—who was still more like a girl.

He glanced at Sarah. She was looking dejected. "Are you feeling all right?" he asked.

Sarah heard the friendly concern in his voice. It soothed her with its companionable familiarity. She became aware that she did have a dull ache in her head. "I think I had too much wine," she said. "And it's late."

At her building he asked the cabby to wait while he escorted her upstairs. When they reached her door, he surprised her by running his finger along the side of her mouth and then giving her a brief kiss.

"We must keep in practice," he said lightly. "Let Armand think he still has competition."

This familiar, teasing Pierre didn't frighten her. They could go back to being slightly dangerous friends. "Yes," she agreed, relaxing into a smile.

"With repetition, we'll look so genuine he'll never know it's not the real thing."

With a last almost impersonal kiss, he departed, and she went inside, relieved and comforted. She'd vowed to have a secret life in Paris. Well, she did share a secret plan with Pierre. Their ardent kisses tonight had been the result of the ball. Neither his feelings nor hers were the "real thing." With Armand they might even turn out to be real. For now, practice with Pierre, as long as she was cautious and didn't go to another Incoherents' Ball, suited her very well.

CHAPTER
TWELVE

"**T**HAT'S GUSTAVE EIFFEL, TO THE LEFT OF THE PODIUM,"
Armand said to Sarah. They were standing in a
large hall in the newly opened Hotel Terminus. Sarah looked
curiously at the famous engineer who had designed and
built the one-thousand foot tower. His hair curled to one
side, and a well-trimmed beard covered the lower half of
his rather plump face. Such an ordinary looking man to
provide the centerpiece for the grand-sounding "Universal
Exposition of the Products of Industry." No, she was wrong.
Though circles ringed his eyes, Eiffel gazed confidently, even
arrogantly, out at his audience.

"He looks tired," she murmured to Armand, "but as if he
could start to build another structure tomorrow."

"He's considered a genius at building with iron. Quite a
few intellectuals and scientists have criticized the tower.
They claim it's artistically vulgar and scientifically useless.
That's why he asked to address the professional societies
here today. He's had a few troubles. The elevators still aren't
running. Still, he's built the tower on time, for less money
than expected, and only one workman was killed."

"That little loss of life is amazing." Sarah looked respectfully at Monsieur Eiffel, who was stroking his beard and talking to a handsome man with a large mustache. "I think I read that when the Brooklyn Bridge was built, twenty men died."

Rows of chairs held mostly men in dark frock coats, with a few women in brighter colors scattered through the audience. Armand showed Sarah to a seat close to the front. The man with Eiffel called for attention and introduced the builder, who took the podium.

After describing the tower's beauty and some details of the construction, Eiffel assured listeners of its practical value. "In the event of war," he pointed out, "any enemy would be visible for one hundred twenty kilometers around Paris. Weather forecasters and astronomers can make valuable observations from such a height. Scientists will be able to study the effects of gravity and the rotation of the earth." When he finished speaking, applause was warm, and his expression showed satisfaction.

"Monsieur Eiffel's lecture was interesting," Sarah commented. "I'm eager to see the view from the top. I can't wait to find out what Paris looks like from up there."

Armand smiled indulgently. "Yes, women will find the view entertaining. After the elevators are installed, I would like the pleasure of escorting you. You might like to dine at one of the restaurants on the first platform."

Though he was only agreeing with her, Sarah felt a trifle discomfited at his ready classification of her interests. But she did want to see the view and eat in the restaurants. "Why wait for the elevators? It must be exhilarating to climb the stairs."

"It would be too strenuous. There are 363 steps to the first platform, and 381 to the second," he recited. "From there it's 927 to the top."

His precise knowledge silenced Sarah. He obviously had

an excellent memory, but why would he bother to learn the exact number of steps in the Eiffel tower? Maybe he didn't have enough to fill his time. Pierre would probably say such mastery of detail showed Armand would be an effective politician. Pierre would also climb the stairs with her.

As Sarah walked a little ahead of Armand toward the ballroom exit, the man who had introduced Eiffel stopped Armand. "Good evening, comte," he said. "I want to thank you for your lecture to the engineering society. I've never heard the situation in Algeria described more brilliantly."

Armand's face was animated with pleasure. "I was happy for the opportunity to do it."

Before they actually got out of the hotel, three other men spoke to Armand about lectures and other activities he'd been involved in. The obvious regard for his opinion impressed Sarah.

After they were in a cab, Armand suggested supper at the Café Maison-Dorée. Sarah was flattered that he'd chosen one of the most elegant restaurants in Paris. Armand must consider her special to take her there. Even the outside, at number twenty on the Boulevard des Italiens, looked exclusive. Decorative stone carvings formed arches over the lower windows, and elaborate stone balconies ran along the upper floors in front and on the side street.

To Sarah's surprise, she and Armand were escorted upstairs to a small, private dining room. She had heard of the private rooms of the exclusive restaurants, some with separate entrances and stairways so married women could enter without begin seen. The most famous room was the *Grand Seize* at the Café Anglais. The door locked from the inside; aristocrats and visiting royalty dined there in supposed anonymity, and discreetly indulged other appetites. In it the Duc de Gramont-Caderousse had entertained Hortense Schneider, one of his mistresses and, like Solange, a star of the Opéra Comique. Sarah aspired to be a star, but not to participate in such intimate entertainment in a private room.

Uncomfortably she noted that this room had a small divan on one side. However, the round table with cut flowers, heavy silverware, and English china looked reassuringly formal. She was glad her apricot-colored evening dress had long sleeves and a high neckline.

"May I call you Sarah?" Armand asked when they were seated. "Mademoiselle Taylor seems too formal if we are to be friends, as I hope we are." He smiled with the touch of melancholy that suggested hidden cares.

"Yes, certainly," she said, and wondered whether this were the opening for more intimate conversation.

But Armand said nothing that unsettled her. Instead while they ate, he asked her about New England. As they talked, she relaxed. Crayfish and char, a fish from Alpine lakes served with a dry wine from Médoc, reminded her of the many times she had eaten fish and seafood in Boston.

"I've never been to your country," Armand said, "I understand it is beautiful. Americans seem to be an enterprising people. I plan to visit the United States one day."

"I hope you do," Sarah responded, warming to his admiration for America.

As the meal went on, she found more that she enjoyed in his company. There was nothing suggestive about his attitude to her. He was treating her like an elegant woman. In the exclusive Parisian room, with this attentive, aristocratic man, she felt worldly and sophisticated. The naive New England girl she had been seemed left far behind. At the same time his courteous demeanor was what she'd been taught to expect of male behavior. Being with him wasn't dangerous and exciting like the Incoherents' Ball with Pierre. It was flattering and reassuring—and safer.

When they finished the last of the dried figs with brandy and she refused another cup of coffee, he asked, "Will you attend the opening of the Eiffel Tower with me?"

Happily she started to say yes when she remembered what Pierre had said—that Armand responded to their competition. "I would like to, if Pierre agrees. He'll expect me to go with him."

"I'll speak to him," Armand replied agreeably. "Perhaps we can all attend together."

To be escorted by two men. Yes, that was what a cosmopolitan woman would do.

A bright March sun celebrated the first day of spring. It warmed Sarah as she walked briskly along the Champs-Elysées toward the Bois de Boulogne. Buds were swelling into new leaves, and the perfume of flowers overrode the earthier odors of people and horses. Responding to the sunny day, she had on a soft yellow cashmere dress with only a shawl across her shoulders. For the first time she had sent a note to Pierre, using the system of pneumatic tubes that carried messages all over Paris, asking him to meet her at the Jardin d'Acclimatation in the Bois.

She entered the garden and passed the hothouse and mineral spring. On her left ostriches lumbered about in their enclosure, reminding her of the first day she had come here with Pierre and ridden in a carriage pulled by one of the large birds. It was like remembering a different person. How much better she knew Pierre now. Thinking of the last time they'd been together still gave her a shivery feeling. But the evening with Armand and his respectful admiration had reassured her and provided a kind of shelter from the ardent feelings that had frightened her the night of the ball.

Ahead she saw Pierre, his back to her, waiting beside the monkey house. His light gray suit coat curved from his broad shoulders to two buttons at the back of his narrow waist, emphasizing his masculine strength. He turned around and came toward her, looking friendly and relaxed.

"Sarah, in that yellow dress you're a flower out of the gardens."

"Thank you. The day was so nice I couldn't resist wearing it."

He studied her, his head a little on one side. "Are you warm enough?"

"No, but it's worth it to feel that spring is here."

"Then let's walk quickly."

She took his arm as he set a fast pace until they reached a brook. On the linden trees new leaves were just beginning to appear among the fragrant yellow flowers. "Here, let's sit on the grass," Pierre suggested, "and you can tell me your news."

He found a sunny spot and spread out his large handkerchief. When she sat down, he took off his coat and put it around her shoulders, ignoring her protests. It carried the warmth from his body and his own special odor of spicy lotion and clean skin. Wearing the jacket felt as if he were embracing her.

Hastily she said, "Armand has asked me to attend the opening of the Eiffel Tower. I remembered what you said about competition between you. So I told him you would expect me to go with you. He suggested we all go together."

"That's a good idea. I'll talk to him."

She searched for something more to say. "How are things at the paper?"

"Busy. I'm writing articles again for *La Justice* and *Le Figaro* as well as my own paper. How are you getting along at the Opéra Comique?"

"Fine. Everything there is working out so well that I can afford to move. I found a new flat just off the Rue de Lafayette. I'll have three rooms there."

"Congratulations. When do you move?"

"Next week." She waited for him to say something slightly intimate about seeing her new rooms, but he didn't.

A little disconcerted, she gazed out toward the brook as if she'd been waiting to examine the scenery. Farther on, the brook emptied into a pond where ducks were swimming, their blues and greens iridescent in the sunlight. On the other side was a *pigeonnier*, and Sarah followed the flights of pigeons, circling and returning.

Pierre watched Sarah, appreciating her clear profile with its contradiction between the firm chin and sensual mouth. His glance dropped to the high lacy collar and lower to the way the soft yellow material fit over her breasts. By now he knew just how gracefully she lifted her arms, and the way the movement of her hips made her skirt sway. Many times he'd thought of making love to her. Her perfume drifted to him, and the images rose again. He could almost taste her mouth, feel the tender skin of her naked breast under his fingers. Picture the soft roundness of her abdomen and the thatch of red-gold hair.

He half turned away and wrenched his thoughts back from the arousing fantasy. The trouble was, under her outward propriety he was sure existed an erotic nature. He'd love to take her to bed and awaken her sensuality. If she'd been older and more worldly, it might have to come to that before this. But he couldn't forget the fear in her eyes when he'd pressed her to go with him the night of the ball. How she felt had become as important as his desires.

He could almost think he was in love with her. Except that she was too innocent, too different from him—and from the kind of women who generally attracted him. Paris, the scheme about Armand—it was all a new and exciting game to her. No way to tell how it would come out. He'd never liked the role of unrequited lover. Best to remember that. He turned to watch her again. *Mon dieu*, when she looked as beautiful and appealing as today, it was difficult.

When Sarah had her fill of the pigeons and looked back at Pierre, she surprised an expression on his face that made her skin tingle and her pulse accelerate. In the way the lines around his mouth tensed and his eyes looked almost hot she recognized desire. Tension began in her chest, the suffocating excitement that had tantalized and frightened her at the ball. The confidence in her sophistication that she'd gained with Armand wavered under the force of Pierre's expression and her answering sensations. Then his face changed, as if a scrim had dropped, concealing what had been visible before, suggesting it was still there but hidden.

He stood and held out his hand to help her up. "Perhaps we'd better go. I'll be in touch with you before the opening date for the tower."

Sarah rose and handed him his jacket and handkerchief. They walked quickly out of the garden and back to the boulevard, where Pierre hailed a cab for her. As she settled herself inside, she felt a confusing joy. Pierre was holding himself back, but he still felt desire for her. She should take herself to task for being flighty—one minute fearful of his passion and the next fearful of its disappearance. But the day was too fine and she was too happy to scold herself for inconsistency.

"Sarah," Helene called. Still in her flounced costume for *Orpheus in the Underworld*, she was standing in front of the notice board at the Opéra Comique. "Look. We're starting rehearsals for *Esclarmonde* tomorrow."

"So soon?" Sarah joined Helene. "But it's for the Universal Exposition. The first performance isn't until the middle of May."

Helene smirked. "Don't you know why? Sybil Sanderson will sing, and Monsieur Massenet wants everything to be perfect. He wrote the opera for her. So we're rehearsing almost every day."

Sybil Sanderson. That was a name of daydreams to Sarah. As she walked to the changing room with Helene she thought about the soprano with the gold-brown hair and youthful beauty. Sybil Sanderson was American, from California.

Even more significant, she'd been only twenty-two and had no professional experience when she met Jules Massenet. He'd been enchanted by her voice and, according to gossip, by her appearance. She had a famous teacher, Marchesi, but even with that advantage, her story was the kind of fairy tale that fed chorus members' hopes.

"Maybe you shouldn't have used your hatpin on Rivarol," Helene said mischievously. "Think what he might have done for you."

Sarah shook her head. "No career would be worth that. Still, a man as charming and talented as Jules Massenet would be harder to resist."

As they passed Madame Auber's dressing room, Solange Rabaud came out. "Sarah," she said. "I was hoping I would see you. Can you have supper with me and my friend?"

Sarah hadn't seen Solange since she'd offended her by refusing the invitation to the Incoherents' Ball. But Sarah's discomfort vanished under the grace of Solange's smile, and she smiled happily in return. "That will be fine, if you don't mind coming to my flat. I've just moved, and Helene and Marc, her lover, are having supper with me to celebrate my new home."

"Delightful," Solange said enthusiastically. "Then we'll have that pleasure too."

As Sarah changed into street clothes, her curiosity about Solange's friend grew. Perhaps it would be a "protector," a banker or politician. Well-known men like Georges Clemenceau were rumored to have mistresses from among the demimonde.

When they all met in front of the theater, Sarah was let down to discover that the friend was a woman. Eleanore Matrat looked about Solange's age but in every other way different. She was short and stocky, with blue eyes and faded blond hair, and was smoking a thin, black cigar. Something about her expression made Sarah think of people waiting in a train station, tired and bored, not expecting to interest themselves in anything until their trains carried them away.

During the ride in Solange's carriage, Helene and Marc were quiet, as if awed by Solange's elegance. Madame Matrat also sat silently, except that occasionally she laughed with loud heartiness. Solange chatted smoothly about memories of her days at the Opéra Comique. By the time they reached Sarah's new address, Helene and Marc had relaxed and were responding cheerfully.

Though a little shabby, Sarah's flat was pleasant and cost only twenty-five francs a week. Its three rooms opened into each other. The drawing room boasted one faded tapestry, an upholstered couch, two chairs and Sarah's only real extravagance, a rented piano. She justified treating herself to that one luxury by continuing to tutor Emile Bourget. Madame Bourget was less nervous when the room where they met had no bed. The center room was dining room and kitchen, with a table and sideboard, a sink, and a Dutch tiled stove where the stew simmered that she'd purchased earlier at a corner café. The last room was her bedroom.

Over the stew and wine, Solange began telling tales of stage mishaps. She knew of a tenor who had gone to sleep during his soprano's long deathbed aria. Even Eleanore Matrat became animated enough to describe a stagehand who managed to raise all the scenery, giving the audience a view of the street behind the theater. Before long they were all laughing like old friends. After they moved into the drawing room for Brie cheese and a third bottle of Bordeaux, Helene and Marc left.

Eleanore resumed her cigar and her waiting silence, but Solange seemed in no hurry to go. She sat on the couch, leaving space for Sarah beside her. "I've decided," Solange said, "to give you singing lessons."

Sarah hesitated. It was a glorious offer, if she could afford it. Because of the cost of moving, she'd have to figure out how to get enough money.

Solange went on, with a hint of stiffness in her voice. "I'm a soprano, but the techniques are the same for lower voices. I can easily help you with the mezzo-soprano range."

Sarah realized with a feeling of surprise that Solange was anxious about her offer being accepted. "I know you can," she said warmly, "And I'd love to work with you. It's just that I'm not sure whether I have enough money."

"Money!" Solange looked shocked. "I will teach you for my pleasure. Money is not involved!"

The flush Sarah regretted spread over her skin, from embarrassment for her mistake but from happiness too. "You are very generous, Solange. Thank you. I'd love to take lessons from you. I'll work very hard to deserve them."

Eleanore Matrat was frowning. Sarah guessed Eleanore thought she was taking advantage of Solange, but she didn't care.

"Well, now," Solange said. "That's settled. Twice a week. By the way, I understand Sybil Sanderson will be singing in the new Massenet opera, *Esclarmonde*. And that the Opéra Comique director, at Massenet's insistence, is paying her a very large fee. I wonder if she's worth it."

Sarah had read eagerly the details of her fellow American's career. "When she made her debut in *Manon* in Belgium a year ago, the audience and critics liked her."

"Yes, but Monsieur Massenet arranged everything for her in his charming way. You see, I keep up with all the gossip. They spent last summer in Switzerland together. Working on the opera, of course." Solange gave an amused smile, and Eleanore removed her cigar long enough to bark a laugh.

"Madame Massenet," Solange continued, "has the good sense not to make scenes. She spent the summer elsewhere with their daughter. But that's the fate of women who are foolish enough to marry for love."

"You think that's a mistake?" Sarah asked.

Solange touched Sarah's cheek lightly, as if petting a child.

"Love is always the most painful kind of mistake. In marriage certainly, but also in seduction. A woman should lie only with men she's not in love with."

Solange's candor no longer shocked Sarah, but she couldn't accept that opinion. "Being intimate with someone you don't love. That sounds so cold-hearted."

"Ah, *chérie*, you are so innocent. The pleasures of the bed don't depend on love."

"But," Sarah persisted, "love is important for marriage."

Solange sighed. "Sarah, listen to me. If you want to be happy and you think you must marry, do so. But only after you have had many lovers. Then you may be able to marry sensibly."

Sarah couldn't think of any response. Apparently Solange didn't need one. She rose and picked up her wrap. "We must go, but first, I haven't seen all the flat. You must have a bedroom."

The last room in the row had a wardrobe, a dressing table with a mosaic tile top, and a large canopied bed with a tall carved headboard that had numerous scratches. The mattress was lumpy, but Sarah felt almost like the heroine of an opera when she went to sleep there.

"A charming room," Solange said, though she sounded polite rather than sincere. She poked the mattress, like a hotel guest testing to see whether she would stay. "Now you need a lover to share that bed with you. I must think what to advise you about that."

She left in a gust of perfume and smiles, with Eleanore trudging behind her. After Sarah closed the door, she went back to the bedroom and looked at the large bed. She certainly wasn't ready for a lover. And if she were, it wouldn't be one that Solange or anyone else chose for her.

On Sunday afternoon, the thirty-first of March, the elevators still weren't running in the Eiffel Tower. At one-thirty the opening ceremony proceeded anyway. Gustave Eiffel, followed by a few dignitaries, led the way up all 1,792 steps. Sarah, at the bottom with Pierre and Armand, gazed up at the structure soaring above her. From this point its giant feet seemed only waiting to lumber along over all of Paris.

"Notice that the color of the paint gradually changes," Armand said, "from red brown at the bottom to yellow at the top. That's to make it look even higher." In spite of his sober tone, he looked excited.

"Come, Armand," Pierre teased. "This is the tallest structure in the world. Can't you say something more stirring?"

Armand relaxed into the happiest smile Sarah had seen him give. "Yes. It shows what French science, along with courage and perseverance can do."

At the first platform heads began to appear, and a little later more at the second platform. "Not many of them are going to make it all the way to the top," Sarah said wistfully. How she would love the chance to try.

Pierre's grin said he read her thoughts. "Sorry, you'll have to wait with the rest of us."

A few minutes after two, a huge tricolored flag whipped out into the wind from the top of the tower. The sun glinted in flashes off the gold "R F" in the white center section. Cries rose on all sides. *"Vive la France!" "Vive Paris!" "Gloire à Monsieur Eiffel!"*

Pierre shouted, *"Vive la République!"*

Sarah joined the cheering, feeling a thrill of pride in the country and city that she was coming to look on as a new home.

The three of them joined the rush to climb to the first platform for speeches and champagne. Even at that height the wind blew hard enough that Sarah had to hold on to her small hat. The view interested her more than the speeches, and she hung back at the edge to look down on the shrunken bridges of the Seine and the tiny lily pads floating in the pool of the Champ-de-Mars gardens. Monsieur Eiffel gave a patriotic speech, to which Prime Minister Tirard responded by announcing Eiffel's promotion to the rank of officer in the Legion of Honor.

The last of Tirard's words were lost in a fury of wind that slashed across the platform, bringing rain and hail. Retreating to the arcades where the restaurants would soon open gave little protection. Clutching hats and overcoats, the celebrants began the descent. Sarah, her clothes already wet, wanted to stay. The wild force of the storm felt like a last assault of the elements against this man-made challenge. But when a gust nearly lifted her off her feet, she gave in to Pierre's insistent grasp and descended with him and Armand. At the bottom she looked up. The immense tricolor still whipped high above, secure in its mooring.

"Like the Republic," Pierre said. "Still here for now."

"Yes," Armand said.

The two men stood together, and Sarah could see their regard for each other in the warmth of the looks they exchanged.

The next morning a knocking loud enough to penetrate to her bedroom awakened Sarah. At first she burrowed deeper under her covers, not willing to think anyone was really at her door. When the knocks became pounding, she sat up and looked at the small clock on her dressing table. Nine-thirty. It must be some emergency!

Hastily she pulled on a robe and shivered through the rooms to the door. "Who is it?" she asked.

"Pierre. I have some news."

What could have happened? She put her hand up to her hair, disheveled and hanging down her back. The cold floor reminded her of her bare feet. But he sounded so insistent. And he'd come himself, hunting up her new address, instead of sending a message. She opened the door.

Pierre gusted in like the wind of the day before. He looked as if he'd been carelessly put together—hair flying out under the edge of his hat, raindrops glistening on his mustache. He didn't have an umbrella, and water shed in streams from his cape, dripping down his trouser legs. His skin was flushed, his eyes crinkling with pleasure. He looked like a boy on Christmas morning who has just found the bicycle he longed for.

"What is it?"

"Come, get dressed. Armand will be waiting for us at the Café Bonvalet."

"But why?"

"I'll tell you then."

She should refuse. Getting her out of bed. Having her open the door when she wasn't dressed. But his exuberant good humor overcame her resistance. "Very well. But wait in the hall before you make a flood on my carpet."

He glanced down as if surprised to learn he was wet. "All right, but—"

Whatever he was going to say was lost as he looked at her, and she realized that he hadn't actually seen her at first. Now his eyes took in her hair, the ruffled lace of her nightgown at her throat, and the blue wool robe that didn't conceal the lack of corset and petticoats. She became suddenly conscious of her body. Hurriedly she fled back through the rooms that no longer seemed so cold, shutting her bedroom door behind her and leaning against it until she finally heard the sound of the door into the hall closing.

When she was dressed, she paused in front of the mirror to adjust her hat over her hastily coiled hair. Her heart still beat faster than usual, and heightened color flushed her skin. How silly she was being! Whenever she lifted her skirts in the cancan at the end of *Orpheus in the Underworld*, hundreds of men watched. After the first night, that hadn't bothered her. But for Pierre to see her in her robe and nightgown produced a confusion of discomfort and pleasure.

Glad she had no time to wonder what that meant, she found her umbrella and joined Pierre on the landing. After a teasing, "I liked your other outfit better," he pulled her down the stairs so quickly she didn't have a chance to respond.

Umbrellas crowded the narrow street with dark clothing showing beneath them, as if the umbrellas were the pedestrians' heads. Although Pierre held Sarah's umbrella for her, he didn't try to stay under it himself. By the time they arrived at the Café Bonvalet, rain was puddling on his hat brim and making miniature waterfalls from the bottom of his cape. Again he seemed unaware he was wet. He hurried her across to a table where Armand waited, turned out as usual in an elegant dark gray suit but looking sleepy and somewhat impatient.

"Coffee and rolls," Pierre said to the waiter, and then settled back in his chair, obviously enjoying the suspense.

Sarah took her furled umbrella and brought the point down on Pierre's booted toe. He sat up with a startled look.

"Now!" she ordered. "Tell your news."

He grinned. "Yes, mademoiselle. Do you know what day this is?"

Armand and Sarah exchanged puzzled looks. Pierre, his eyes sparkling, answered his own question. "It's April Fool's Day!"

"You got Sarah and me here for a joke?" Armand's handsome face was disgusted.

"Maybe." Pierre's grin became a delighted laugh. "This morning, early, General Boulanger gathered up Marguerite de Bonemains, his mistress—or perhaps she gathered him up. At any rate, together they made a full retreat. They left Paris on the train for the Belgian frontier. By now they should be in Brussels."

Armand's impatience changed to surprise, and then to a

pleased smile. "You mean, he's gone for good?"

"Gone at least for now," Pierre said elatedly.

"Why did he leave?" asked Sarah.

"You can choose your reason. Because he feared arrest for treason. Maybe he loved his mistress more than his career. There are rumors that Madame Bonemains had urged him to give up politics. Perhaps he just lost his nerve. In any case, the Boulangists are without their Boulanger."

"Do you think he was treasonable?" Armand asked.

"Probably, depending on how you define it."

Sarah remembered the crowd at the rally and the crush of supporters in the streets on election night. "What about all those people who cheered for him? Will they give up?"

Pierre's face sobered. "We can't let up on the fight. There are still the general elections in September. Lots of people still want another Bonaparte or a King Louis. But it's harder to make a hero of a man who runs away on April Fool's Day and leaves his followers but takes his mistress."

Armand looked solemn and excited at the same time. "This could be the salvation of the Republic. We can thank God for that."

"Don't forget to thank the Minister of the Interior," Pierre said wryly. "He arranged for the suggestions about treason to be publicized." His delighted laugh broke out again. "A pity Offenbach isn't alive. What a comic opera he could make out of this."

Sarah watched the two men, both concerned with the future of France, but so dissimilar in their responses. The knowledge that stayed at the back of her consciousness sneaked forward. Both of them, according to Solange, had been her lovers. Would they be as different as lovers as they seemed now? An improper question to be asking herself, but one that was too tantalizing to be banished completely.

CHAPTER THIRTEEN

THE 1889 UNIVERSAL EXPOSITION OF THE PRODUCTS OF Industry opened on the sixth of May, a spring day so fair that even the most convinced misanthrope should have been cheerful. Paris looked like a gigantic canvas painted by a wayward but happy child. Bunting and tricolor flags, along with replicas of the Eiffel Tower, hung across balconies and store windows, and embellished even the spires of Notre Dame cathedral. Posters promised fair-goers everything from displays of the latest fashions to music of native Africans. Sarah felt as if all the Fourth of July celebrations of her childhood were collected in one gigantic festival.

With Pierre and Armand, she stood under a canopy of chestnut blossoms on the Champs-Elysées. Pressed into the crowd of Parisians and foreign visitors, she waited for President Carnot to pass by on his way to open the exposition. As two o'clock neared, the first cannon boomed from the Eiffel Tower. At the forty-seventh report, mounted cuirassiers came into view. An open landau followed, its three occupants waving.

"Which one is President Carnot?" Sarah had to shout in Pierre's ear.

He pointed to the serious-looking man in the middle. "A deranged man tried to assassinate him yesterday during a ceremony at Versailles. The shot went wild."

Sarah shivered. It seemed impossible that such ugly things could happen in the midst of so much festivity.

The carriage disappeared across the Pont d'Ilena, and the crowd surged after. Sarah held fast to Pierre's and Armand's arms as the three of them were swept along under the base of the Eiffel Tower, past the colorful uniforms and foreign faces of guards from French colonies, and on to the Central Dome, the entrance to the exposition grounds.

The military band struck up the "Marseillaise." Pierre went inside the Central Dome to take his place with the other journalists. Armand and Sarah stayed outside, where she counted twenty-seven women nearby who were wearing clothing that incorporated the red, white and blue of the French national colors. She had on a blue walking suit with a white blouse and a red ribbon pinned to the lape—America's colors, too.

After Pierre rejoined her and Armand, they walked along the Champ-de-Mars. "With the size of the grounds," Armand said, "we'll have to come back several times." Sarah waited for the numbers, and he didn't disappoint her. "It covers 958,752 square meters."

They went into the enormous Palais de Machines, and she had her first impression of the magnitude of the exhibits. Gigantic iron girders supported a glass roof over an enormous central hall. Wings of almost comparable size intersected it. "It's larger than a cathedral," she said, looking up in awed wonder.

"It is a cathedral of sorts, to the glories of industry," Pierre said.

Armand had a look of concentration. "Without the exhibits, there would be room for twelve hundred cavalry horses to exercise."

"Armand," Pierre said with amused affection, "you don't have to give us all the statistics."

Sarah expected Armand to be offended, but he laughed and said, "You need to be more educated." She reflected that the two cousins, so different in many ways, were alike in their affection for each other.

The three of them climbed up to a platform with a car on it, a kind of rolling bridge that ran from one end of the hall to the other, and managed to see so much that Sarah began to feel numb. Her mind whirled with images of carding mills, machines for reaping, and rods that went up and down or spun around to accomplish tasks she couldn't keep track of. Armand and Pierre lingered at the exhibit of a Benz automobile, the first car to be powered by gasoline. Sarah was more interested in the bicycles, admiring a new Clément model and wishing she could afford its price of five hundred francs. Pierre was intrigued by a new French steam tricycle. "It can go almost as fast as automobiles and climb steep grades," he reported enthusiastically.

Late in the afternoon a sharp cracking sound rang out, followed by a rain of shattered glass from the roof down onto the crowded aisles below. Women screamed, and children set up wails, but when the confusion died, no one seemed to be seriously injured. "It's the temperature change," Armand explained. "The iron supports expand and contract, and the glass panes can't always stand the strain. It doesn't mean the building's collapsing."

In this instance, Sarah appreciated Armand's passion for details.

By the time a cannon sounded from the top of the Eiffel Tower at ten that evening, Sarah was thoroughly tired. But when they reached the Seine, she revived, enchanted by the lighted cruise boats floating down the river as musicians performed on their decks. The cannon boomed again, and lighted flares shot up from the tower's platforms while the beacon on the top flashed alternately blue, then white, then red. During the fireworks that followed, Sarah cheered loudest when one of them was a fiery shower representing Niagara Falls. The display ended with a bouquet that turned into a portrait of President Carnot.

As the sky darkened, Sarah felt a pang of homesickness. Many of the voices around her that day had been English and American. They reminded her that she, too, was a foreigner. Then with Pierre on one side and Armand on the other, she set off through the crowded streets toward the edge of Montmartre and her flat. As they walked, she realized how familiar Paris had become and how pleasant the day had been. Both Pierre and Armand had treated her like a good friend. She hoped that would last.

A week later *Esclarmonde*, the opera Jules Massenet had written to celebrate the Exposition and Sybil Sanderson's talents, had its opening. During rehearsals Sarah had introduced herself to Miss Sanderson, who was too wrapped up in her French debut to be more than marginally polite to a fellow American. Her remoteness disappointed Sarah, but she understood. The opening of a new opera was a gamble. In spite of his previous successes, Massenet, gossip said, had wept after one of the rehearsals, fearful that his music and his protégée would fail.

Under Solange's exacting teaching, Sarah's singing was improving. During rehearsals, she decided she could sing as well as Nardi, the mezzo-soprano who had the role of Esclarmonde's sister. Through the elaborate processionals of the ancient French court on opening night, Sarah pretended that she was Parseïs. When she didn't have chorus lines to sing, she sang Parseïs's melodies in her head. Massenet's music had a lyric quality that Sarah loved; having a solo role in one of his operas was a favored daydream. When frenzied applause greeted the opera's end, she ached for a chance to earn that response for herself.

Afterward she went with Solange to the Café de la Paix. Eleanore Matrat was there, as silent as before, along with two other women and several men. Wilhelm Hotter, a short, stocky man with a German accent, particularly caught Sarah's interest. Except for the obligatory responses to introductions, the only person he paid any attention to was Solange. When she made room for Sarah beside her, he looked upset. Was he the current lover? If so, Solange didn't show it. She ignored him, talking to everyone else.

The discussion centered around Sanderson's performance. "Outstanding voice," was the shared opinion.

"And a beauty too," said one of the men. "I saw her in the lobby of the Hotel Crillion the other day. She wears her clothes very well."

Solange shrugged. "Perhaps, but no one will ever want to copy her dresses." She waited for the titters of appreciation, then continued. "Sanderson reminds me of a singer I once knew who went from one lover to another. After she left them, they were always sorry. But for only a very short time."

Sarah didn't find Solange's comments amusing. She said, "Mademoiselle Sanderson has a magnificent voice."

"Yes, you're right," Solange agreed, and added with the generosity about music Sarah admired, "And her technique is first-rate."

When someone else started on a gossipy story about another singer, Sarah decided to leave. Leaning across to Solange, she said, "I must go home now."

"I understand," Solange said sympathetically. "You must be worn out from all the rehearsals. What a pity that you weren't singing Parsïs tonight. Your voice is perfect for that music. Someday you'll surely have that kind of chance."

A rush of gratitude filled Sarah at having her dream expressed aloud. However unkind Solange might be in other ways, praise from her about music was sincere. "Thank you, Solange. I'll see you at our next lesson."

Solange turned to her German admirer. "Wilhelm, please see that Mademoiselle Taylor gets home safely." She waved away Sarah's protests, and Monsieur Hotter got up instantly.

In the cab he sat silently, and Sarah was amused to compare him to Eleanore Matrat. They were both middle-aged, somewhat overweight, and usually silent. Perhaps Solange chose her friends and lovers so that they let her do all the talking. It would be like being on stage for an audience all the time.

As the cab passed one of the streetlights, Sarah could see that Monsieur Hotter was studying her with a speculative look, just as she had been him. The irony of it struck her and she laughed aloud. He smiled, but it was not friendly. When they reached her flat, his good-night was chilly. Poor man, she thought, to be jealous of anyone, even another woman, whom Solange had kind words for.

The next few weeks Sarah went often to the Universal Exposition with Pierre and Armand. They seemed to have an unspoken agreement that neither would take her to the exposition without the other. In her retreat to a safer self she was content.

The day after the premiere of *Esclarmonde*, the Eiffel Tower had its official opening. When Armand started to the elevator, Sarah protested. "I've been waiting to climb to the top." She started up the steps.

"All right," Pierre said. Though Armand looked slightly exasperated, he followed along as well.

Getting to the first platform was easy. Beyond, Sarah found she had to climb more slowly, holding on to the banister. At the second platform, Pierre asked, "You're sure you want to climb the whole way?"

She didn't answer, saving her breath to go doggedly on.

As she got higher, the wind tore at her clothing. Paris seemed to sink slowly away beneath her. Finally she had to quit looking down for fear of getting dizzy. Reaching the top began to seem more uncertain, but she kept on, putting each foot determinedly on the next step and the next one after that. She glanced back at Pierre and Armand and was encouraged to observe that she was no more winded than they. One last burst of effort took her to the top, thrilled and exultant.

The immensity of Paris viewed from the height awed her. The flag that had looked small from the ground whipped its huge length over her head in explosive cracks. She laughed in triumph; she had earned the feeling.

On the descent, Sarah found she liked the elevators after all. The catch in her stomach when the elevator began its sudden drop was something like the way she felt when Pierre looked at her with a special, intimate expression.

On later visits she took the elevators and did the silly, fashionable thing of attaching a message to a balloon and releasing it from the top. Pierre bought her a copy of the special edition of *Le Figaro de la Tour Eiffel* with her name printed in the corner. She couldn't afford the dress designed to wear at the Tower, the *Eiffel ascensionniste*, with its extra collars "to protect delicate ladies from the cold at such heights." Armand pleased her by a gift of two wineglasses with stems shaped like the tower and pictures of it etched on their sides.

Sarah, Pierre and Armand each had a preference of the other places to see at the exposition. "I'm American, so we must go to the American exhibits," Sarah insisted.

They looked briefly at the typewriters where the demonstrator for the Remington models tried to pique Sarah's interest. "Many respectable young women are working in offices now," he assured her. She smiled politely and didn't say she didn't want to work in an office, nor that she wasn't sure how respectable she was any longer.

Lines stretched out into the aisles to get into the displays of phonographs and electric lighting set up by Thomas Edison. The wait was worthwhile to Sarah; the phonograph delighted her. She listened four times to a recording of the Paris Opéra chorus singing "The Marseillaise" and would have listened a fifth time if Pierre had not dragged her away. "At the next exposition," she fantasized to him, "you'll have to listen to a recording of me."

"I'll be glad to," he said. "But right now Armand and I want to see the firearms at the Winchester Repeating Arms Company display."

She also insisted they visit the American galleries in the Palais des Beaux-Arts. To her surprise, the landscapes interested her most. "Look," she said excitedly, beckoning to Pierre and Armand, "I've been there!" It was an oil, "The Aberjona River, Winchester," by Joseph Cole. The painting of the familiar bridge and placid river affected her with a feeling that was close to homesickness.

"Do you wish you were there?" Armand asked.

She looked at him and Pierre, waiting for her answer. The moment of nostalgia was gone. She smiled. "No, I'm happy here."

Another day Pierre insisted on visiting his choice, a replica of the Bastille. "Don't you have any sense of history?" he complained when Sarah and Armand didn't seem enthusiastic enough. "It's actually an amusement park, but the reconstruction is authentic."

The tall, round towers with crenellated battlements and narrow slits for windows looked too real to Sarah. "It must have been terrible to be a prisoner there," she said.

"Actually, few prisoners were ever held in the Bastille," Armand said, but that didn't make it appear less forbidding to her.

Inside they had cheese and wine at a café, watched colored

light projections that looked like a fountain, and saw a pantomime about a prisoner escaping from the Bastille. It ended with the recapture of the prisoner and his return to a dungeonlike cell.

Afterward Pierre looked at her and said, "I see you didn't enjoy that."

"What could be worse than to be a prisoner?" She shuddered. "I would hate that."

"You'll never do anything to be put in prison," he responded. "Not unless you change your moral character. Of course, that might be interesting." She knew from his teasing eyes that he wasn't talking about the kind of behavior people were arrested for.

The familiar tingle of excitement warmed her. She realized she'd missed it since he was being so polite.

"Come on," he said. "We haven't been to the best part."

Adjacent to the towers were six parallel inclines with tracks, similar to the new roller coasters. Pierre led the way to the top where he paid three fares. An attendant rolled out three wooden horses mounted on wheels and warned, "Just hold tightly to the reins."

"My hat," Sarah exclaimed. "It will blow off."

In answer, Pierre untied his cravat and put it across the top of her round straw hat and brought the ends down. His fingers grazed the sides of her face and paused. Their eyes met and held while the warmth of his hands spread across her skin. It seemed a long, flustering moment until he tied the cravat under her chin and stepped back.

The attendant gave a push to start her horse along its metal tracks. The sensation was like going down a gigantic slide, starting slowly then gaining speed. She let out one involuntary scream as her stomach felt left behind. Clutching the reins, she swooped down one incline, slowed briefly as it leveled, then on down another. The wind pushed against her face. From the corner of her eyes she saw Pierre and

Armand racing along beside her. Because of their greater weight, gradually they moved ahead. Pierre's hat blew off; Armand's still sat firmly on his head, as if too intimidated to disturb the formal picture he made, even on an amusement ride.

The rails finally leveled out at a long flat space. She got off her wooden horse, breathless and exhilarated. "Let's go again," she said to the two men waiting for her.

However, a long line had formed for the ride. After Pierre retrieved his hat and she returned his cravat, they went on to Armand's choice, which was the section on the Esplanade des Invalides that held the colonial pavilions. There, with the dome of Napoleon's Hotel des Invalides keeping watch in the background, an exotic city had sprung up—Algerian bazaars with arched galleries, Moslem minarets, and Cambodian temples. Armand led the way, identifying spices that Sarah could smell in the Oriental pavilions and interpreting the messages of Polynesian flutes and tom-toms from Senegal. At his urging they tried North African couscous. Sarah found the flavors strange, but she enjoyed the taste and the smell left on her hands.

At the Javanese and Tahitian villages, they watched attractive young women dancing. Behind them an indignant man said in English, "It's scandalous. Allowing this kind of licentious behavior."

Pierre glanced back, then whispered to Sarah, "But he's not leaving."

A particularly original showcase was in the Fairyland, most of which was for children. It offered, along with Red Riding Hood and Sleeping Beauty, a blue elephant from "The One Thousand and One Nights." Adults could go inside the elephant to watch an exotic dancer, like the belly dancers in the Arab cafés.

Armand repeatedly quoted precise details. He knew that there were over sixty thousand exhibits and that more than five hundred thousand spectators had attended on opening day. He took Pierre's teasing about his statistics good-naturedly. Sarah found that his knowledge enhanced her enjoyment; on the few occasions he didn't supply special information, she was disappointed.

Pierre seemed to care little about facts and found the people attending as interesting as the displays. When they went to the Café Egyptian, Sarah was fascinated by the dark-eyed dancer with her long rows of beads and tassels that dangled below her scandalously bare midriff. Pierre watched the audience as well. He pointed out to Sarah the man in a clerical collar who looked away and forced his wife to do the same when the belly dancer's performance became too obviously erotic.

Each visit to the exposition ended with a display of the illuminated fountains. Sarah never tired of the sprays of water shooting skyward and then descending in showers of jeweled colors. It seemed as satisfying as her life that spring, full of music and song at the Opéra Comique and the glowing extravagance of the exposition. Going there with Pierre and Armand made her feel more admired than the most popular society belle. Maybe, she thought extravagantly, she would fall a little in love with both of them. Pierre would be the dangerous lover, Armand the safe one.

Among the additional attractions brought to Paris because of the exposition, the one Sarah most wanted to see was from the United States. Since April, posters in Paris had announced the coming of the "greatest attraction in the world"—Buffalo Bill's Wild West Company. One journalist informed French audiences that Buffalo Bill was a kind of enormously strong Robinson Crusoe, of aristocratic lineage. Accompanying Buffalo Bill were Annie Oakley, advertised as the "Queen of the Rifle," and a company of two hundred cowboys, cowgirls and Indians. Almost as many horses and twenty buffalo completed the "Wild West" illusion. The arena on the west side of the city where they performed was always packed, and Pierre wasn't able to get tickets until late June.

Sarah hadn't seen Buffalo Bill when he took his show to Boston several years previously, so the performance was almost as much a novelty to her as to Pierre and Armand. However she accepted compliments on the feats of riding and shooting as if that were what she and her friends did for recreation every weekend on Boston Commons.

Afterward they went to the Grand Café des Beaux-Arts, which had an exhibit of symbolist pictures that had been refused for the Exposition's Palais des Beaux-Arts. The hundred or more watercolors and oils were startlingly different from the ones at the exposition—more brilliant, often with garish colors and stiff figures. At one of the tables a man dressed in a striped jersey with paint-spattered trousers sat drinking and arguing with several other men. Sarah noticed that the handle of his cane was carved into the joined shapes of a naked man and woman. Startled, she whispered to Pierre, "Who is that?"

"Paul Gaugin, the artist who organized the exhibition. That's one of his pieces." He pointed to a painting called, *Breton Girls*, showing two sullen girls with large, very dirty bare feet. To Sarah it was crude but powerful—almost too real, like feelings that she was beginning to suspect everyone had but usually kept hidden. She looked back at the artist with respect for his knowledge.

They saw Guy de Maupassant, who was drinking absinthe, and joined him. Sarah wasn't sure he remembered her, but he graciously claimed that he did after Pierre mentioned the Christmas dinner.

"What do you think of the exposition now?" Pierre asked him. "Have you changed your mind since you signed the condemnation of the tower?"

The waiter brought another glass of brilliant green absinthe for Maupassant and a bottle of Montrachet chablis for the rest of them. Sarah watched with fascination while the waiter put a sugar cube on a slotted spoon, held it over the glass of absinthe, and slowly poured water from a carafe over the sugar cube. As the water dripped into the glass, the green absinthe turned milky white.

When the procedure was finished, Sarah realized that Maupassant was speaking. "Paris is so crowded that you can hardly walk on the boulevards," he grumbled. "No one wants to dine anywhere but the tower. I've eaten in the Alsation Restaurant five times. Getting a fiacre is impossible. The drivers only want to pick up flashy foreigners. Excuse me, Mademoiselle Taylor. I don't mean you. You're practically a Parisian."

For Sarah, his compliment redeemed his criticisms. She liked the idea of being half American and half French.

"But think of what these foreigners are doing to get here," Pierre said. "An American crossed the Atlantic alone in a sailboat. And two Austrians took turns pushing each other in a wheelbarrow from Vienna to Paris."

"Don't you see anything good in the exposition, Guy?" Armand asked stiffly, his expression its most aristocratic.

"I suppose it does show French enterprise to the rest of the world," Maupassant conceded. "But other important things are still going on. Just this morning, Pierre, I heard that you and Claude Vernoy—"

"I think the violin ensemble is going to play," Pierre interrupted. "All the performers are women. It's been very popular."

Astonished, Sarah looked at Pierre. She had never heard him interrupt someone before. He liked to listen to people and usually encouraged them to talk longer than they should.

"Yes, I see." Maupassant sent Sarah a quick glance. "Let's listen to the ensemble."

That was even more strange. Café patrons seldom considered it necessary to stop talking because of music. Conversation was the life blood of the cafés, the reason people gathered there. "Who is Claude Vernoy?" she asked Pierre. The name nagged at her memory.

"A newspaperman." His flat tone cut off any more discussion.

Pierre turned and stared toward the small raised space where the women were tuning their instruments. Armand's face had flushed, and he kept his gaze carefully away from her. She didn't know Maupassant well enough to interpret his expression, but she was positive something was troubling Pierre and Armand that they didn't want her to know.

The following day Sarah still hadn't been able to dismiss the reference to Claude Vernoy from her mind. During the night she'd remembered why his name was familiar. He'd arrived at Madame Dubreuil's salon just as she and Pierre were leaving. A disagreeable man.

As she thought back over the excursion to the Wild West show, it seemed to her that Pierre had been less animated than usual. During the exposition their threesome had become so comfortable that she hadn't paid careful attention to his moods. If something were wrong, it wasn't her affair, but reminding herself of that didn't ease her worry.

It was time for Ted to appear for their weekly lunch. After she moved, she had insisted he come to her flat every second time. When they went to a café, he always paid the bill. Since she suspected he had a limited income, it was only fair to take turns. For this lunch she'd purchased a salad with a special dressing from a café on a nearby corner. Helene had taught her how to prepare the duck stewed with young turnips that simmered on the stove, adding its fragrance to the yeasty smell of a crusty *baguette* from the *patisserie*.

When Ted arrived, she managed to contain herself until they had eaten the duck, with many compliments from Ted, and were finishing a bottle of St. Emilion Bordeaux. "Do you know Claude Vernoy?" she asked.

"I don't know him, but I read an article of his once."

"He's a newspaperman, isn't he?"

"Yes, a scurrilous one. He writes mostly for *L'Intransigeant*, Rochefort's paper, and in the Rochefort style of attacking without caring about the truth. Since Rochefort followed Boulanger into exile, Vernoy's been helping run *L'Intransigeant*."

"What kind of man is he?"

Ted shifted his long frame so he could get to a handkerchief. He removed his glasses and polished them as he answered. "To judge from his reputation, he's not a pleasant fellow. He's a rabid Boulangist and has made threats against anyone who may have forced the general to run away."

"According to Pierre, that could be Boulanger's mistress," Sarah said with an attempt at lightness, but it didn't make her feel better.

"Why are you so interested in Claude Vernoy?"

"I think he's making some sort of trouble for Pierre."

Ted put his thick glasses back on and studied her. "And you're upset about that."

"Not really upset." She got up and took the dishes to the sink, uncomfortable under his scrutiny. "Pierre and Armand both have become good friends. So I'm concerned."

"I see." She turned. Ted was picking up his straw hat.

"Wait," she said, giving up the pretense of calm. "Could you find out what's wrong?"

"I don't think I should. If Pierre wanted you to know, he'd have told you."

"Ted, please do this for me." He started to shake his head, but she took hold of his arm. "It's true, I am upset. If I know, I'll feel better."

He gave her the smile that made his eyes look a little owlish through his glasses. "All right. I'll see what I can find out."

The time went slowly after he left. Sarah was glad that she would be occupied with Emile Bourget, her remaining pupil, who was coming for an English lesson. The shy *lycée* student had blossomed, and Madame Bourget had relaxed to the point that she often napped.

When the bell rang, Sarah found only Emile at the door. "Where is Madame Bourget?" she asked.

"My mother isn't well today, but she wanted me to have my lesson anyway."

Emile's blond hair was parted in the middle and carefully smoothed down. His pale blue eyes were unusually animated. Sarah hesitated, but if his mother approved of his coming alone, there was no reason to disappoint him or lose the tuition. Fewer performances were scheduled at the Opéra Comique in the summer, with none at all for several weeks in August. His fees were insurance.

When he came inside, he said in his careful English, "I have an English book that I would like to read to you so you can correct my pronunciation and explain some of the words. Is that all right, Miss Taylor?"

Though they usually made conversation, occasionally Emile read for her. "Yes, that will be fine."

"Shall I sit beside you on the couch so you can see what I'm reading?" he asked.

She nodded. He took a small book from his pocket and sat beside her. She didn't recognize the title. It seemed to be about a boys' school, and the words were fairly simple, none he didn't know. As he read, her mind wandered to Pierre and whether Ted would be able to learn something.

The words *naked breast* jerked her back to Emile. "Just a moment," she exclaimed. "I want to see your book."

He gave it to her with a hand that trembled. Without her

noticing, he had skipped to the center of the book. The boys' school had become a female academy, where the "hero" was engaged in undressing an obviously precocious pupil.

"Emile, I won't allow—"

In one swift movement, he was on his knees beside her with one arm across her lap. With his other hand, he fumbled at her skirts, trying to lift them. "Mademoiselle Sarah," he cried, lapsing into French, "you must let me touch you."

She gasped, "Emile! Stop this!" He clutched her legs, but she pushed him away and scrambled to her feet.

He slumped to the floor, his face ghostly white. "I thought . . . the others . . ." His voice trembled to a stop. A tear gathered in the corner of his eye, and he turned swiftly into the front of the couch, shielding his face. His shoulders began to tremble.

Sarah was torn between shock and sympathy. She moved to a chair and waited until his trembling stopped. Keeping her voice calm and impersonal, she said, "Emile, please sit up and explain."

Slowly he got up and sat, his knees stiff, as if he were a five-year-old waiting for punishment. Looking down at his hands clutched together in his lap, he muttered, "They said I wasn't anything if I didn't . . ." His voice faded.

"Who are 'they'?"

"In my class—at the *lycée*." He stopped, then continued in a burst. "They said if you were American and came to Paris by yourself, you're . . . *une baiseuse*." His face turned from white to red, and he whispered, "Please excuse my bad word."

Sarah didn't know whether to laugh or berate him and decided neither would do. She walked over to him and put her hand gently on his shoulder. He looked up, and she could see misery in his wet eyes. "I'm . . . I'm sorry," he said.

She stepped back, and he got awkwardly to his feet. "Did your mother really let you come by yourself today?" she asked.

"No," he mumbled, looking at the floor. "I told her I had to study for an examination with a friend."

"Then I think you should go somewhere until it's time to go home. And come back with your mother for your lessons."

His head came up, his expression part fear and part hope. "Then you'll let me keep on with the lessons?"

"Yes, and I won't tell your mother. Of course, I expect you to treat me respectfully."

"Oh, yes. I will. Thank you," he said, his voice still unsteady. He rose and went to the door. With his hand on the knob, he stopped, still facing the door, and said, "They made fun of me because I haven't . . ."

"Yes, Emile, I understand. I think you realize that this was very wrong. We won't bring it up again."

"Thank you," he said and went out.

His book lay on the floor where it had fallen. She picked it up. Poor Emile, to be tormented by the other boys. And yet, he was almost a man. Had he experienced those tumultuous sensations she'd felt the night of the ball? Perhaps he knew as much about sexual encounters as she did.

The small clock on the sideboard in the dining room chimed four o'clock. She put the book in the bottom of a drawer and went to the window. Because the buildings were right at the edge of the street, she couldn't see anyone passing directly below, but she couldn't help watching. Finally she heard steps on the stairs that sounded familiar and hurried to the door. It was Ted, just reaching the landing.

She practically pulled him inside. "Did you learn anything?"

"Yes. Claude Vernoy has challenged Pierre to a duel."

"A duel!" The word was an icy thrust to her chest. "But why?"

"He claims Pierre circulated false rumors that Boulanger was a traitor. The rumors forced the general to flee."

"Can't the duel be stopped?"

"Vernoy issued a public challenge. Pierre accepted."

Her legs felt too weak to hold her. She sat down on the couch and looked up at Ted. "But that is so senseless! Why didn't Pierre refuse?"

Ted sat beside her and took her hands in his. "It's a matter of honor now. You must know that."

Yes, she did. But she didn't want to know it. Her composure threatened to give way; she could feel tears rushing up into her throat.

"Sarah," Ted said insistently, "there's nothing that can be done."

"When is the duel?" He frowned, about to refuse any more information, she was sure. But she had to know. "When?"

"Tomorrow morning."

"Where?"

The frown settled into determination. "It won't do any good to tell you." His voice softened. "I know it's hard when you love someone, but you can only wait."

Love? "That's not it. I don't love Pierre. But I care what happens to him."

He sighed, looking as much older and wiser as she had felt with Emile. "I know. You can't plan love. But there's no good denying it either. We'd probably be happier if we could."

Rising, he looked down at her, the worried frown returning. "I need to go. Will you be all right, Sarah?"

"Yes, I'll be fine."

"You mustn't worry. Pierre's a good shot, and he can look after himself. Most duels aim at barely drawing blood, just enough so the parties can claim they're satisfied."

After Ted left, the word *blood* still reverberated in the air, filling Sarah with terror. Ted was wrong. She wasn't in love with Pierre. But that shaky conviction didn't help her feel any less frightened.

CHAPTER
FOURTEEN

A RMAND HANDED A BUSINESS CARD TO PIERRE. IT READ
"Claude Vernoy, Seventeen Rue de Verneuil." Pierre
put it on the desk in the corner of his drawing room.

Armand's pale face showed strain, the lines under his eyes
deep and his mouth compressed in an unhappy line. Pierre
knew that because of their affection it was hard for either
of them to act as the other's second. But no one would look
after the other's interests better.

"The arrangements are settled?" he asked.

"Yes. We agreed to pistols at twenty-five paces, one shot
apiece. I'm sorry I'm so late getting back, but one of Vernoy's
seconds wasn't available until after eight tonight." Armand
sat down heavily in an upholstered chair. "Vernoy won't
consider an apology. Will you?"

"No. Your duty's done. You've tried to persuade me to
give up the duel."

"It's not just a duty," Armand said wearily, "but I know
you can't back down."

"A glass of Cognac?" Pierre asked.

"No." Armand rose. "I spoke to Gastinne Renettes earlier.

He's personally loading a pair of his pistols. I have to pick up the sealed case tonight. Lunel and I will be here for you in the morning at six-thirty. We'll pick up Dr. Najac first. Vernoy wanted to meet behind the grandstand at Long-champs."

"No!" Pierre interrupted. "I won't put on a show for the voyeurs who hang around the Bois hoping to see someone get killed."

"I knew that's how you'd feel. I insisted on a place south of the Bois de Vincennes. The light will be good when we get there at seven. Is there anything else I can do?"

"Thank you, Armand, no."

At the door Armand turned again. "You've been practicing today?"

"Yes. I used the shooting gallery in Le Pol's cellar. I hit the target every time."

When the door closed, Pierre went to the window and pulled aside the drapery. The night sky was moonless, reflecting only the second-hand light from the city. In the Rue de Bellechasse below a man walking a large, shaggy dog paused under a gas light while the dog urinated against the building. In a few minutes Armand went out the door and strode away. Otherwise the street was deserted.

Pierre let the drapery fall back and thought of the first duel he'd fought. He had been twenty, just finished with his military service and new in Paris. The challenge had been made over an insult in a café to a woman whom he'd been with. All of her that stayed with him after eight years was her first name, Marie, and that she had dark hair. But he remembered vividly the night before the duel. He hadn't been able to eat or sleep, and he could still recall the feeling in his mouth, so dry it was like coarse sandpaper. At that age it hadn't occurred to him he could die. He'd been terrified, not of being hurt or killed, but of appearing frightened.

Now he didn't fear lack of self-control; in the course of the four duels he'd fought since, he'd become confident of that. But he knew he could die. Swords would be less dangerous even though the duel would continue until he or Vernoy were wounded; with pistols he could be killed.

He went to the side table and started to pick up the brandy bottle, then checked himself. Better not to have anything to drink. Instead he wandered restlessly around the room, plagued by a feeling that he'd forgotten something. He stopped beside the white card lying on the desk and realized what was missing—he hadn't written to anyone. Sitting down at the desk, he took a piece of creamy paper from a drawer and pulled forward his inkwell and pen.

But to whom should he write? At the time of that first duel, he'd scrawled a letter to his parents and made out a crude testament, though he had practically no possessions. Now his parents were dead and his lawyer had his will.

Sarah. She was the one he wanted to write to.

For a moment he pictured her, with the intent look she had when she was trying to understand a custom new to her. What could he say to her that would serve anything but his vanity? If he did die, she would have Armand, who could tell her what a proud and foolish man his cousin had been. He put aside the paper and pen.

A soft sound at the door caught his attention. He wasn't sure it was a knock until it was repeated. When he opened the door, at first he thought that he was still imagining her. But she was real, standing there in a blue coat and hat and flushed face. Only Sarah could blush so vividly.

"I—I'm sorry to disturb you," she stammered.

His heart leaped in response. "Please, come in. You aren't disturbing me."

When she came hesitantly in, her unaccustomed timidity made her seem fifteen instead of twenty-one. He searched for a way to put her at ease. If he changed his lounging jacket for a regular coat and vest, this would seem less intimate. And if they weren't alone. "Jacques, my valet, has gone to bed, but I'll have him back in a moment."

"Oh, no." Her face turned an even more impressive red. "No need to get him up. I won't be here long enough. My cab's waiting downstairs. I just . . . I mean . . ."

"Please, Sarah, sit down."

She took the chair nearest to the door and sat stiffly, her elbows clamped to her sides, the tips of her black boots tight together, like a schoolgirl before the headmistress. He sat across from her, leaving what he hoped was a reassuring distance between them.

Her color receded, and she looked directly at him. "I know I shouldn't have come to your home, but I had to talk to you." She sounded determined, but her eyes, blue green in the light from the shaded gas lamps, hadn't recovered their normal self-confidence. "Ted told me that Claude Vernoy had challenged you to a duel."

"That's not quite right. I sent the challenge to him."

The last color drained from her shocked face. "But why? You told me once that you don't believe in dueling!"

"I don't. But it can't always be avoided. Vernoy attacked me in his newspaper. That's not unusual, but he accused me of taking money from the government to spread false stories about Boulanger."

"But that's not true! Can't you ignore him?"

He gave a wry smile. "Thank you for your confidence, but the lie must be silenced. If I don't defend myself, I'll never have credibility in my profession again."

"So it's your honor," she said softly.

"Yes. I'm glad you understand."

She shook her head almost violently. "But I don't."

Trying to strike a less somber note, he said, "Weren't you defending your honor when you used your hatpin on Rivarol?"

"Yes, but it was mostly my temper." She leaned forward, her awkwardness overcome by her intensity. "What good does it do if you're killed? Can't you sue him for slander?"

"No. Only a duel will be convincing."

"Doesn't the government stop duels?"

"It's the accepted way to settle disputes. It keeps men obeying the rules of society."

The skin around her mouth and across her jaw tightened, and he felt a swell of tenderness. She was stubborn, and she had defied propriety to come here out of concern for him. There would be an argument, and he was enjoying every moment.

"Doesn't a really strong man hold out against rules that are wrong?" she charged.

"Maybe I'm weak." He stood up and poured two small glasses of brandy. "Here, Sarah."

Almost without noticing, she took the glass and returned to the attack. "I know you're not weak. There must be something you can do besides go out tomorrow morning and kill someone or be killed yourself. If Vernoy is so despicable, what sense does it make to endanger yourself because of him?"

"Duels aren't usually fatal," he said lightly. "Two reporters I know were so frightened when it was time to start that they both got violently sick. They were so ashamed, that they couldn't look at each other. They charged around wildly without getting near each other with their swords. The seconds finally got tired and stopped the duel. So I may end up with nothing worse than humiliation tomorrow."

"Oh, Pierre." Tears trembled in her voice. "I really do understand about honor. That men believe they have to fight over it. But it just seems so wrong."

His resolve breached by her tears, he did what he'd been resisting. With a quick stride he reached her and pulled her up into his arms. "Sarah, Sarah. Don't worry. I'll be all right."

Her voice was muffled against his shoulder. "I know you think I'm improper, coming here like this."

He stroked her hair and let his hand caress the side of her face. "I wish you were improper. Sadly for me, you're not. But it means a lot to me that you came to talk me out of this duel."

She looked up at him, her eyes large with the tears that threatened to spill over and her lips quivering. With her whispered, "Oh, Pierre," his self-control wasn't enough to prevent the kiss his whole body demanded.

Her mouth softened under his, the trembling turning to an eager response. Her hands went up to his neck, and she pressed against him. Even through their clothing he felt the pressure of her breasts, firm and soft at the same time. Desire shot through him, pulsing in his groin. He wanted to push her down on the floor. Make love to her until passion blotted out everything else.

With a remnant of control he wasn't sure he had, he pushed her away, holding her by the shoulders. "Great heaven! You can make a man forget honor and anything else."

Her breath was coming as rapidly as his, and the bewildered disappointment in her face tempted him almost beyond resisting. But her fear for him made her too vulnerable. Anything that happened tonight wouldn't be fair.

"It's late, Sarah, and I need sleep before morning."

The telltale red stained her face again. "Of course. I'll leave."

"Wait." He couldn't let her feel embarrassed. "It's not that I wouldn't like you to stay. But if you're here any longer, sleep will be the last thing I'll want."

Her head lifted proudly, and he was glad to see an attempt at playfulness in her smile. "So, those times you've tried to seduce me were only when you didn't need your rest."

"You've discovered—I'm a lazy man."

Her smile faded to sadness, and he almost took her into

his arms again. To forestall that he said, "I'll send the cab away and get my groom to take you home." He'd do it himself, but he was too aroused to trust himself.

"That's not—" she began.

"I'm not having you out with a strange cab driver when it's almost midnight. Michel doesn't have enough to do most of the time anyway."

By the time he roused Michel and dismissed the cab, he found Sarah looking composed. Deciding it was better for his self-control to wait below, he escorted her down to the street. They waited in silence the short while until Michel arrived with the brougham.

"Will you let me know what happens?" she asked.

"Yes. Or Armand will bring you news."

The suggestion that Armand and not he would talk to her after the duel hung between them. He took her hand and kissed it, holding it while he said, "Thank you for coming tonight."

He felt her hand tremble before she pulled it away. As he helped her into the brougham, she said, "Be careful, please?" Michel started the horse on its way before he could respond.

After the carriage disappeared around the corner, he climbed the three flights of stairs to his flat, feeling at peace with himself. He would sleep well. When he hadn't known he needed it, Sarah had comforted him.

June's early-rising sun was already lighting a grove of gray-green poplars when Armand's landau arrived at the end of a rutted road. Pierre let Armand and Hector Lunel get out first, then he followed with Dr. Najac. A short distance away a small brook splashed around a barrier of tumbled rocks. A reddish-brown nightingale, still hoping for a mate he should have found in April, warbled from one of the poplars. The smell of dew-wet grass promised a day for lovers to picnic. The hatreds and vanities of men seemed out of place to Pierre. Was it possible this was the last time he would see sunlight and sky? No, he couldn't believe that.

Another carriage pulled up and stopped. Vernoy's two seconds got out first, and when Armand and Hector joined them, the four witnesses walked to a clearing at one side of the poplar grove. Vernoy, his topknot standing up as if he'd waxed it to a threatening peak, stayed in the carriage with a man Pierre assumed was a doctor.

"Are you feeling all right?" Dr. Najac asked Pierre.

"Yes, very well."

Dr. Najac was slightly paunchy, with graying hair and an imperturbable manner. He had served as the doctor in Pierre's last two duels, without having to use his skills. Pierre had been a second in a duel in which the doctor's cool efficiency had saved the principal's life.

Armand and one of Vernoy's seconds tossed a coin, but Pierre couldn't tell the result. Hector and the other second paced off twenty-five steps and stuck their walking sticks into the ground. When he saw the markers, Pierre's throat tightened and his pulse began to beat faster. It was time.

Armand came over. "We won the toss to use our pistols," he reported and reached under the forward seat of the landau for the sealed box that held the Gastinne Renettes. After he broke the seal, he offered the pistols first to Vernoy's second, then gave the remaining one to Pierre.

The barrel gleamed like an ornament; the use it was designed for seemed an affront to its beauty. Pierre lifted the pistol, appreciating the craftsmanship so fine that the weapon bore its maker's name. Its familiar weight and feel calmed him. Armand touched Pierre briefly on the shoulder; his somber eyes held a message of confidence and love.

Pierre walked to one of the upright sticks, which still quivered slightly from the force of the thrust into the ground. Vernoy took his place at the other stick. Pierre sighted mentally, concentrating on Vernoy's right shoulder.

One of Vernoy's seconds stood to one side, half-way between the two principals. "Are you ready, gentlemen?"

"Yes."

"Fire."

It was one motion, lifting the pistol and firing.

Pierre's immediate impressions were also simultaneous—a puff of smoke at the end of his barrel, a similar puff in front of Vernoy, and a fiery pain at the left side of his cheek. At almost the same time, Vernoy spun and fell. Pierre put his hand to his face and brought it back, slick with fresh red blood.

Then Armand and Dr. Najac were there, taking the pistol, insisting he sit down. The doctor had a pad out, pressing it against the wound. Beyond them Hector leaned down, his face anxious.

"Nothing to worry about," Pierre said, but the pain was making him dizzy.

Hector gave him a sickly smile. "If Vernoy really cared about Boulanger rumors, he'd have gone after me."

"How is Vernoy?"

Dr. Najac said sharply, "No more talking. You're lucky the shot wasn't higher, but you're losing blood."

"You hit Vernoy in the shoulder," Armand said. "He probably won't be fighting any more duels."

By the time the doctor had wrapped a bandage around Pierre's head, the poplar trees were beginning to look fuzzy. Armand and Hector helped him to his feet. "Hang on," Armand said. "They've put Vernoy in his carriage, so we have to make it that far. I think he's still conscious."

Of all the barbaric rituals of dueling, the handshake afterward was the most preposterous. But Pierre managed the walk to his opponent's carriage with minimal help from Armand. Vernoy was propped in the corner of the seat, his shoulder and arm wrapped in a bandage, his face like white candle wax. Pierre reached across and offered his hand, which was briefly taken. After that he concentrated on keeping the world in focus until he reached the landau, where Hector and Armand helped him in. He closed his eyes, trying to blot out the pain. Dimly he felt the seat give as Dr. Najac got in beside him.

"It will be just a minute," the doctor said. "The seconds are arranging where to meet later to draw up the official report."

The carriage swayed as Armand and Hector got in, and Pierre felt it begin to move forward. Then pain faded as he slipped into unconsciousness.

Sarah had been awake and dressed since before the sun was up. It was silly, she had hours to wait, but she couldn't bear the prospect of news coming when she wasn't ready to go to see Pierre. Even that idea was probably foolish. But she'd already compromised herself when she dared to go to his flat the night before.

By late morning her kitchen was spotless and everything in her flat had been rearranged and dusted twice. For the dozenth time she went to the window, but she saw only the usual people of her neighborhood—the cobbler going to his shop in the Rue Lafayette. The widow opening her bookshop across the way. A boy from a flat in the next building was rolling his hoop just fast enough that his younger brother couldn't keep up and started his inevitable wail of complaint.

Sternly she took herself in hand and went to the piano. She found the score to *La Vie Parisienne*. It would be revived at the Opéra Comique after the August vacation. But when she opened the score and played the first few bars, nothing would come out of her throat. The notes were wedged there, along with the fear that made her want to weep. Instead she brought her hands down on the keys in a discordant crash, then launched furiously into a Brahms Rhapsody in G Minor. When she finished that, she thundered through a C Minor prelude by Chopin and finally stopped, drained and empty.

She got up and started to the window again when a knock came on her door. She almost stumbled, hastening to answer, until she had her hand outstretched to the knob. Who would be on the outside? What would he say? She had to open her mouth and gulp air to breathe before she pulled the door open.

It was Armand. Her heart seemed to quit beating.

"Pierre was wounded on the side of his face, but he'll be all right." He spoke quickly, as if answering her fear.

"You're sure?"

"Dr. Najac tells me so."

A sigh came out from deep inside her. "May I see Pierre?" That wasn't proper either, but she didn't care. During the long hours of arguing with herself before she went to Pierre's the previous night, propriety had lost a good deal of its inhibiting force.

"Yes. He's at home. It will have to be a short visit, though."

"Of course." She would agree to anything.

The ride through Paris seemed long, the flags and posters for the exposition looking like leftovers from some long-forgotten event. Finally the carriage arrived at the tan stone building, and she was out and starting up the stairs before Armand could help her. When she reached the third floor, she stopped at Pierre's door. Armand was looking at her with a questioning tilt to his eyebrows. She didn't care. If she were Pierre's mistress as he thought, she'd know the right door without looking at the boxes below, as she'd had to do the previous night.

Armand knocked, and a middle-aged man in a black waistcoat and trousers answered the door. "How is he, Jacques?" Armand asked as he handed his stick and hat to the valet.

"Awake. Dr. Najac will be back shortly." Jacques bowed to Sarah. "Good day, Mademoiselle Taylor."

She wondered how he knew her name, but he started

through a back hall, and she was too impatient to think of anything but following him. Armand stayed in the drawing room. Jacques stepped aside at the bedroom door, leaving her to enter Pierre's bedroom alone.

It was a large room with dark wood furniture and tall windows that looked out over a garden at the back. Pierre lay in a high old-fashioned bed. Bandages swathed most of his face, leaving only his right eye uncovered. That eye drooped sleepily, and Sarah noticed a glass beside the bed that gave off the sweetish odor of laudanum. A beige eyelet counterpane came partway up his chest. The top of his white nightshirt was unbuttoned, showing whorls of dark brown chest hair. He looked both vulnerable and very masculine.

When Sarah approached, he held out his hand to her. It felt cold, and she pressed it between her hands, rubbing gently. He smiled groggily at her. "That feels good."

"Oh, Pierre," was all she could say. He was alive. He would get well. Her feelings of joy made her shy.

"Aren't you going to scold me again?"

His teasing reassured her more then Armand's report. "Yes, but I'll wait until you're awake enough to pay good attention."

"Here you are in my bedroom at last. And I'm in no condition to take advantage of you. I suppose it's what I deserve."

She decided to ignore that. "How did your Jacques know my name?"

"I told him if a beautiful red-haired woman with an American accent arrived, it was Mademoiselle Taylor."

A voice harumphed at the door. It was a man with a black bag, followed by Armand. After the introductions, Dr. Najac said, "I'm afraid visiting must wait. Monsieur de Tourbey needs to rest."

As she said good-bye to Pierre, his right eye was already closing. Armand didn't say anything, but from his expression of concern and love, she realized how deeply he cared for his cousin.

When they were in the carriage again, Armand explained that he must leave her and go on to meet the other witnesses. "We have to agree on the report for the newspapers tomorrow."

"Will anything happen to Pierre because of the duel?"

"No. There are prosecutions only if there's no serious effort to reconcile the principals before a duel. Or if one of them behaves improperly, such as grasping his opponent's blade, or firing too soon."

"If someone dies?"

"As long as it was a proper duel, there'll be an inquiry but almost certainly an acquittal."

The process still seemed barbaric to Sarah, but she decided saying so was futile.

Before Armand left her at her door, she asked again, "Are you sure Pierre will be all right?"

"Dr. Najac says so, and he's a good doctor." He spoke with his usual authority, but she could see how tired and drained he was.

"The duel must have been an ordeal for you, too."

He looked a little embarrassed and said only, "Yes." She guessed he didn't like to show his feelings. But he had them, especially for Pierre. She felt a rush of affection for him. "Thank you, Armand, for coming to tell me what happened. And for taking me to see Pierre."

His somber expression lightened and he took her hand. "That was the only pleasant thing that happened today." He raised her hand to his lips and kissed it.

Inside her flat, she listened to his footsteps retreating. Since she'd known Armand, she'd admired his ideas and intelligence, but she had never felt as drawn to him as now. Unintentionally Pierre had created a significant bond between her and Armand.

CHAPTER FIFTEEN

"**I**'M GLAD I FOUND YOU HOME," TED SAID.

Sarah, surprised, stepped back from the door to let him in. This wasn't their day for lunch. Her next feeling was alarm. It had been two days since the duel and her visit to Pierre. "What's the matter? Is it Pierre? Have you heard that he's not getting along well?"

"He's improving, as far as I know. At least he was when I saw him yesterday. It's...Josiah."

"Papa?" A different, horrifying fear filled her. "Has something happened to him?"

"No, he's fine. He's here, in Paris."

Papa in Paris! There'd been two more stiff letters between them, but she hadn't expected him to come here. Emotions warred in her—shock, joy, apprehension, remembered anger—such a confusing mixture that she didn't know how she felt.

"When did he get here?"

"He arrived yesterday. My brother in Boston told him how to find me, and he came to my place last night." Ted's eyes, magnified by his glasses, were sympathetic but questioning. "I haven't told him where you're living. He wants to see you. I promised him I'd ask. Will you see him?"

Joy and longing crowded out Sarah's uncertainties. "Yes, of course."

"I'm to meet him at the Café de Paris at three." Ted chuckled. "I don't think he liked my room. Do you want me to take you to meet him there?"

"No. I wouldn't like a reunion, with strangers looking on."

"Then shall I bring him here?"

Her first impulse was to say yes, to have Ted as a buffer. But if she were to be reconciled with Papa, they'd have to talk alone. She did want a reconciliation—more than she'd let herself know. "No. Please just tell him how to find me. And thank you, Ted, for everything. You've been a wonderful friend to me."

He took her hand and patted it in an avuncular way. "Josiah was shocked when he saw where I live. I'm not sure he approves of me enough that I'll see him again. Let me know how you get along, will you Sarah? I care what happens to you."

She stood on tiptoe and pulled his head down to kiss his cheek. "Of course I will."

By two o'clock that afternoon with still over an hour to wait, Sarah was ready. Her light green muslin dress had a modestly high neckline, full sleeves and a few gathers in back—a bit warm for July weather, but respectable. What a proper Boston daughter would wear. At two-thirty she started looking at her pocket watch. Finally at ten minutes after three, she put the watch firmly out of sight and sat down at the piano. She played the Schubert Impromptu in G-flat Major, which calmed her with its lyrical and tender melody. At the knock her fingers stumbled as her heart seemed to rise chokingly into her throat.

Josiah stood on the landing, a white-suited figure, more

familiar than any other person in the world, and yet strange. He had a new mustache and goatee. "Hello, Sarah," he said stiffly.

"Hello, Papa. Please come in."

When he was inside, he looked carefully around the room and finally back to her. "I heard you playing. I'm glad you haven't given up your music."

"May I take your hat and stick?"

"Yes, thank you."

She had never seen him so constrained before. Why, she thought, Papa's as nervous as I am. With that realization her own apprehensions dissolved. She dropped his hat and stick on a chair, then threw herself at him. As his arms went around her, tears of regret for their estrangement mingled with tears of happiness.

When they were both a little calmer, they sat together on the couch. "Sarah," he said seriously, "you were correct about several things when you left home. We'll talk about that, but not just yet. Now I want to hear about what you've been doing. And I want us to see the exposition together. It will be a vacation, like ones we used to take. Do you remember the good times we had together?"

"Oh, yes, Papa." Her heart was full with love and delight, and she was glad to postpone painful topics.

She told him about getting the first job at the Opéra Comique with Ted's help, and losing it. He scowled when she got to the part about Rivarol and declared, "He's an infernal blackguard. That's the kind of men you meet in the theater!"

"Most of the singers aren't that way at all," she protested and went on quickly before he could say more. "Anyway, I'm back there now and singing in *Esclarmonde*, the new Massenet opera. You must attend a performance." She gave silent thanks that her medieval costume was modest.

"Yes, of course I'll want to hear you," he said. She could

see from his forced smile he was still unhappy about her singing for a public audience. However, he was trying not to show his disapproval, and that pleased her.

She described her tutoring and her remaining pupil, making it sound lighthearted and funny. "You know you don't need to earn money," he interjected.

"But I want to," she said, and realized they were verging close to topics they'd agreed to put off. Retreating, she said, "I'm taking singing lessons from Madame Rabaud. She's very interested in how I'm doing, and she gives me a lot of help." She went on to list triumphs from Solange's singing career, omitting mention of her current status in the demimonde.

"I suppose you've made friends here," Josiah said, in a voice that was a little too casual.

Sarah understood instantly that he wanted to know about men. "Helene Lebout is in the chorus. She's been a good friend. And Madame Rabaud. Two cousins, Pierre de Tourbey and the Comte de Saint-Maurice, have escorted me to several places around Paris."

Josiah's thick eyebrows slanted downward in a frown. Cravenly she added, "Ted introduced me to them. They're really friends of his." She felt ashamed for her lack of courage. She had every right to male friends.

"That's kind of them," he said, the frown smoothing. "Perhaps I'll meet them while I'm here."

It was her turn to manufacture a smile. "Perhaps."

Josiah suggested they have dinner in the garden restaurant of the Hotel Ritz. While she was changing to something more formal, she consoled herself that she and Papa would have a long talk later. Pierre would be confined while he was recovering, and she had no immediate plans to see Armand. There was no point in spoiling her and Papa's first days together. That didn't mean she intended for him to run her life again.

* * *

Sarah became Josiah's guide to Paris. Although at first he seemed uncomfortable with the reversal of their previous roles, he followed her lead and praised her knowledge of the language and city. They visited the Eiffel Tower and ate in all four of the restaurants. Sarah saved her favorite for last—Brébant's, with its traditional French dishes and the best view of the exposition grounds. Their dinner included turtle soup, made from a recipe used by Charles VI, and pheasant as Marie Antoinette's chef had prepared it. "How did you like that?" she asked afterward.

"A little rich, I thought," Josiah said. "Next time, let's go back to the Anglo-American restaurant."

At the Universal Exposition they spent virtually all of their time in the Palais des Machines. Sarah's interest in industrial machines didn't match Josiah's, except for another intensely enjoyable visit to Edison's exhibit of phonographs. Josiah thought she was joking when she proposed that they try the mechanical horses and other amusement attractions. She didn't suggest the colonial section, with its erotic dancers.

Josiah attended three performances of *Esclarmonde* at the Opéra Comique. Afterward, he refrained from comments about the unsuitability of Sarah's participation, but it was an opinion his unhappy expression clearly showed he hadn't abandoned. One day he insisted on going with her for her singing lesson. Solange, warned in advance, was completely the opera diva, regal and condescending, employing none of her seductive glances, with only a wink to Sarah behind Josiah's back as they were leaving. Outside, Josiah said to Sarah, "Madame Rabaud seems very cultured, but what about her background?"

"She is an excellent voice teacher," Sarah said with a touch of fierceness in her voice.

He gave Sarah an uncertain glance and conceded, "Yes, I suppose that's what is important."

Emile and Madame Bourget met Josiah one afternoon. He

chatted with her and managed to imply that his daughter had no need of giving lessons but that he allowed it to indulge her whims. Sarah would have felt resentful except that he talked graciously with Emile, treating him as if he were grown. Watching them, she wished she'd had a brother. Josiah would have liked a son, and he might have been less concerned with what she did.

A morning toward the end of the first week of Josiah's visit, Sarah, feeling a little daring, went to see Pierre. Having her father in Paris made activities he would disapprove of seem more scandalous. When she arrived, Jacques led her through the lobby to the drawing room. Pierre was lying on the sofa, wearing a dressing robe, his face still bandaged along one side. Jacques went in and out of the room, so it was a much less intimate meeting than the one in the bedroom. Even so, Pierre captured her hand to press it against his lips for a longer-than-polite length of time.

Her hand tingling, she took a chair beside him. "I'm sorry I haven't been here sooner. My father is in Paris."

He managed a roguish wink with his uncovered eye. "I'm the one who's sorry you haven't been here, but I'm glad for you. Is he enjoying the visit?"

"Oh, yes."

He regarded her soberly. "Are *you* enjoying it?"

"Yes. Why do you ask?" She hadn't told him of her difficulties with her father.

"You never talk about him."

For a moment she considered telling him—but that was past. "We had a disagreement before I left home. Papa doesn't really like for me to sing in public. But he's been attending *Esclarmonde*."

"Lucky man." Pierre smiled at her, then winced.

"Oh, your wound," she said, dismayed.

"I just forget to keep a sober face," he said lightly.

Thinking how much worse the duel could have been, she

realized how grateful she was that he hadn't been more seriously hurt.

"Dr. Najac is here," Jacques announced, and was immediately followed by the doctor.

She rose. "I must go."

"Dr. Najac," Pierre complained. "You've just ruined my morning."

"That's good," the doctor said. "You're better off without visitors awhile longer."

Remembering that, Sarah decided she shouldn't try to visit Pierre again. Instead she sent him notes, describing what she and her father were doing. "On July fourth," she wrote, "we went to the cemetery to see Lafayette's grave. Papa had been told all Americans in Paris did that. There were a lot of Americans there and Papa was surprised I didn't know any of them."

Pierre sent back a drawing of a sour-faced man, held down in bed by three devils with features that suggested Armand, the doctor, and Jacques.

After Bastille Day she wrote him a description of the military parade at Longchamp. "I think Papa was impressed, though it's hard for him to think anything in France is as good as it is at home."

Armand sent her a pneumatic letter, asking whether he might escort her and her father to any of the exposition events. Not wanting to ruffle her father by letting him see how well she knew Armand, she gave the excuse that she wasn't sure of Josiah's plans.

Sarah and her father took two days in the galleries of the Louvre museum. During the second afternoon, when they were pausing on the staircase to admire the Winged Victory of Samothrace, she saw Armand and his mother coming down. Armand stopped, and they exchanged introductions. Though he was cordial, Nathalie was as frigidly polite to Josiah as she had been to Sarah.

When Sarah and Josiah went on up the stairs, Josiah said, "The French! They don't like Americans."

"Most French people aren't like that," Sarah protested. Josiah just smiled, and she could see he was pleased. After that encounter, she guessed, he felt reassured that Frenchmen weren't appealing enough to become important to her.

At Josiah's insistence, they spent most of a week exploring a side of Paris unfamiliar to Sarah. On the boulevards around the Place de l'Opéra were housed the Bourse, the Banque de France, the Ministries of Finance and Justice, and most of the insurance companies—Josiah's business. For two days she trailed Josiah from one insurance office on the Rue de Rivoli to another, translating for him as he introduced himself and inquired about business. Another day they went to the Bourse, the stock exchange, arriving just after the noon opening to join the bedlam of confusion inside. From the gallery they looked down on the railed-off parquet where brokers shouted and gestured. It seemed impossible to her that business could be transacted among such deafening noise, but Josiah stayed until the three o'clock closing, apparently making sense out of the turmoil. His favorite restaurant became the Café Champeaux, in the Place de la Bourse, with a garden where red-and-white striped umbrellas protected them from the sun while they ate.

During their visit to the Palais de Justice, the ancient palace of the French kings, he hurried through the chapel of Sainte-Chapelle, barely glancing at magnificent stained-glass windows framed in delicate iron tracery. Instead he sought out the courtroom that heard civil matters. "Lots of lawsuits in the insurance business," Josiah told Sarah. "I want to see how they handle that problem here."

At the end of an hour of her whispered translations, he agreed to leave. Outside he said proudly, "The French courts don't do as well as ours. Just a lot of delays."

Though Sarah thought she'd probably never go to any of

those places again, the comradeship with her father was precious.

At supper one evening in the Café Champeaux, he said, "I can't stay on in Paris any longer, Sarah," and she knew that it was time for them to discuss the issues between them.

"Would you like to come to my flat tomorrow for lunch?" she asked. "I've learned a little about cooking."

"You've been cooking?" He looked as if he'd already tasted her meal and didn't like it. "Sarah, there's no need for that. It's not suitable for someone brought up as you have been."

"Papa! I'm glad I learned about it. I *like* to cook." She didn't like to clean up afterward, but she didn't admit that.

"All right." He smiled indulgently. It was the way he'd looked when she was a child and showed him a puzzle she'd solved or a picture of a sun with spokelike rays hovering over a skewed house. She subdued a flare of irritation; she still wasn't grown up to him, but she couldn't expect his attitudes to change immediately.

After Josiah left Sarah at her flat, the uncertainties she'd pushed out of her mind had to be faced. If Josiah wanted her to go back to Boston, it would be painful to refuse him. From the perspective of almost a year in Paris she understood much better about him and Cousin Mabel, and she felt confident she wouldn't let him run her life anymore. But she had her career in Paris. And there were Pierre and Armand. She didn't know how much either of them meant to her, but she was certain she wanted to find out.

Lunch the following day didn't display her culinary skills after all. The veal fricassee burned, and she had to substitute meat pies from a *patisserie*. Although the asparagus tasted good, it had turned a strange color. Josiah complimented her on the pears and cheese, and Sarah felt like the child he thought her.

When they were in the drawing room, Josiah put down his coffee cup and looked at Sarah soberly. "I want you to return home with me, Sarah."

The brew of her conflicting desires was as distressing as Sarah had expected it to be. "You know I love you, Papa, and it means so much to me that you came here . . . and that we've had these three weeks together. But there are reasons I want to stay here. At least for now."

He put up his hand, as if waving away a minor objection. "There's nothing to keep you from coming home. I've thought about what you said last summer, and you were right. I shouldn't have waited so long after your mother died." He paused, then offered her his prize. "I'm going to remarry."

She jumped up in delight and went to kneel beside him. "Oh, Papa. That's wonderful news! And I know how happy this makes Cousin Mabel."

He frowned and a slight flush crept up above his high collar. "You've misunderstood. My intended bride is Mrs. Waltham."

"Mrs. Waltham!" Sarah sank back on her heels, staring up at his face. "The widow whose husband was your attorney?"

"Yes, of course. We know only one Mrs. Waltham."

"What about Cousin Mabel?"

Josiah got up, leaving Sarah sitting on the floor beside his chair. He didn't look directly at her as he spoke. "We won't discuss Cousin Mabel. This has nothing to do with her. Mrs. Waltham is a fine woman. She's well-bred and accepted everywhere. She's perfectly suited to be my wife and your mother."

Sarah got up from the floor, feeling ridiculous at her child-like posture and furious at his explanation. "I don't need a mother," she said hotly, "and this has everything to do with Cousin Mabel. What happens to her?"

The muscles around Josiah's mouth were quivering, but his voice was determined to be patient. "I'll speak candidly. Mabel is a fine woman, but she's not of our station. She appreciates this."

"You mean you cowed her!"

"Now, Sarah," Josiah said sternly, "if you consider this matter reasonably, you'll understand. Mabel isn't at ease with my business acquaintances and friends. She's chosen to go to Philadelphia to live with her sister." He hesitated, then added, "Of course, I've provided for her."

Sarah's stomach threatened nausea; for the first time in her life she felt ashamed of her father. In her pain and anger she lashed out at him. "Oh, but I do understand. You discarded her and then paid her off because she wasn't suitable. After all, she's the one you've been bedding. Or have you been in Mrs. Waltham's bed too?"

"Sarah!" Josiah's face turned red. "How dare you use such language! So that's what you've learned in Paris. The stories I've heard about the French being filthy-minded must be true."

The tide of her anger ran too deep to stop. "No, I suppose Mrs. Waltham is too pure to let you touch her. She always seemed that way to me. It's no wonder she and Elmer Waltham never had any children. He probably died of frustration."

Josiah picked up his hat and stomped to the door. Without turning he said, "I plan to leave late tomorrow. If you have come to your senses, you can reach me at my hotel until then." Just as the door was closing behind him, he added coldly, "Thank you for lunch."

Sarah barely restrained herself from hurling a coffee cup at the door. She paced furiously around the room. That "thank you" said everything. The surface of politeness must endure no matter what else. And Mrs. Waltham was all surface. Sarah had seen her quite a few times over the years—a woman who smiled a lot and never said anything worth remembering. But she was suitable. Cousin Mabel, modest and self-effacing, wasn't. And she'd lain with Josiah without being married to him. So she wasn't worthy to be his wife!

Sarah's conviction that her father was wrong didn't make her heartache less. After her anger receded, tears began. They made her feel worse, but she couldn't seem to stop them. When it was dark, she went to bed but sleep was impossible. Was she being unfair? There was only one person she could talk to. She'd never discussed with Ted exactly why she'd left Boston, but he'd grown up there, in the same narrow society as her father. Maybe he could explain the situation in a way she could accept.

She got up and dressed. At almost eleven o'clock, people were still about. It didn't take long to find a cab with the red carriage lantern that indicated it would go to the Passy-Batignolles area. As Sarah jolted along, she thought wistfully of her mother. What would she have said about a daughter who went to men's rooms at night? First Pierre, now Ted.

Even this late, the Rue Boursault no longer intimidated Sarah, nor the prospect of the dingy stairwell. At least she'd grown up that much in the past year, even if she still couldn't get along with her father. She did ask the cab driver to wait. If Ted were home and could talk to her, she'd go back and dismiss the cab.

When she reached the fifth floor, she saw a light under Ted's door. As she approached, she thought she heard a faint sound of voices and almost turned back. But her need was urgent. Maybe, she thought, a visitor was just ready to leave. She knocked.

The door opened to Ted's voice saying, "You're late, Roland."

But it wasn't Ted at the door. It was a very tall woman, garishly dressed in a ruffled orange gown. Her lips were painted bright red, matching the rouge spots on her cheeks. She looked as if she were about to perform in a circus. Earrings of glittering stones hung from her ears under long blond hair that was obviously a wig. Ropes of pearls and more stones almost covered the front of her dress, and her eyelids were thick with blue paint.

Embarrassment made Sarah cringe; she'd arrived when Ted was entertaining a prostitute. "I'm sorry," she blurted.

At almost the same time the woman said, "Sarah?" in a shocked voice. Ted's voice.

Sarah stared at him, trying to reconcile this woman with Ted. It was like looking at a canvas that had been painted over, with the image the artist hadn't liked still discernible under the new one. But the myopic stare, the bony nose and tall, thin frame inside the female shell all reinforced the voice. This was Ted, dressed as a woman.

She took a step back. "I'm sorry," she repeated, but whether for her intrusion or her new knowledge she wasn't sure.

He seemed as appalled as she, but he recovered more quickly. "Has something happened?" He opened the door wider, and she glimpsed beyond him someone else in a dress, but she didn't look long enough to find out whether it was a man or a woman.

"No . . . yes . . . I mean, I quarreled with Papa. And I thought you might talk . . . but I see you're busy." She turned to flee down the stairs.

"Sarah, don't go." He stepped farther out onto the landing. "It's too late for you to be out. I'll—"

"That's all right. My cab's waiting. I'll talk to you some other time." The polite phrases came as stupidly to her lips as her father's "thank you" had to his.

She had stumbled two flights down before she thought how inept she had been. How naive and unsophisticated, as if she were still a New England schoolgirl. But she couldn't go back and pretend to accept what she'd seen. Not until she could sort through her shock and confusion.

By the next day the only conclusion Sarah had come to was that she didn't know how she felt. Ted and her father

must be no different from what they had always been, but
she couldn't find her way through her disorientation. How
could life be so different from the way it had seemed to her?
And how to find her way in a world that could shift so
radically?

The only way, she decided, was to keep on with her
routines and give herself time to discover what was real.
Singing surely was. And she had a lesson with Solange.

When she arrived at the house on the Rue de Chazelles,
Solange opened the door. "Come in," she said gaily. "Berthe
is away for the afternoon, so I'm practicing being the maid.
In case I ever have to earn my livelihood that way."

Sarah knew she was supposed to protest that Solange
would never have to be a maid, but she felt too depressed
to respond. Silently she followed the trail of Solange's ver-
bena perfume into the drawing room.

Solange went over to the piano. "I think we'll begin
with—." Her words broke off as she turned and looked at
Sarah. Quickly she crossed the room and took Sarah's hand.
"My dear, you're very troubled. What's wrong?"

The sympathy in Solange's face and voice unleashed tears
that still hadn't been shed. Solange pulled Sarah to the settee
where she patted her shoulders and murmured soothing
sounds until the flood stopped. "Now tell me," she ordered,
"what is making you so unhappy."

Solange's motherly comfort and the relief of unburdening
herself were too great for Sarah to resist, even out of loyalty
to her father and Ted. And she'd already told Solange about
her father and Cousin Mabel. The events of the last day
tumbled out.

When Sarah finished her recital, Solange said, "You need
a glass of Cognac."

Whether from the brandy or from pouring out her distress, Sarah found she did feel better.

"Yes, I see why you're upset," Solange said in the diplomatic tone that portends an opposing point of view. "Perhaps, though, you are being too severe in your judgment of your father and of Monsieur Kearns."

"But Papa's being so unfair. He won't marry Cousin Mabel and instead he picks out a horrible prude of a woman."

"You know her well, this widow he's marrying?"

"No, not really well," Sarah had to admit.

"Voilà!" Solange lifted her hands in a gesture of a point won. "The trouble is, you keep confusing marriage and some romantic idea of love. There may be perfectly good reasons for your father to choose this woman. Maybe it's for his position in society. Perhaps she has money that will be useful to him."

"She's not even pretty," Sarah said and knew she'd retreated to being childish.

"I remember one of my lovers, a clever man, advising his friend against marrying a beauty. He said that if a wife was faithful, she wasn't beautiful. And a beautiful wife wasn't faithful."

Sarah managed a smile.

"You see, it's not a tragedy," Solange said. "As for Monsieur Kearns, when you're wiser, you'll understand."

"Does that mean that he . . ." She searched for the right words.

"Makes love with another man? Perhaps. But he may just like to dress up in women's clothes." Solange took Sarah's hand and stroked it. "You are so inexperienced, my Sarah. You know nothing about passion."

Solange's fingers stilled. She seemed to be looking back into memory, and the bones of her face stood out under the careful makeup. For the first time she appeared all of fifty years old. "Once I was young and very innocent. Like you. I could have stayed with my husband, turned into a woman like Berthe. I left him, but it was harder to make my way than I expected. Still, I had beauty. I've known many men.

Some of the things I did with them made me ashamed. Some of those men I hated!"

The violence in Solange's voice touched Sarah deeply. She pressed Solange's hand, trying to return some of the comfort she'd received.

Sarah's gesture seemed to recall Solange from the past. Her face softened, and she said, "Caresses from another woman can be as tender as from a man, sometimes better, because women understand each other." She laughed, her seductive charm well in place again. "I have a rule. With a woman, anything down to the waist is permissible. Below the waist is reserved for a man."

Sarah's sympathy was still engaged enough to cushion the consternation she felt. Some of it must have showed, because Solange got up and went back to the piano. "Come," she said briskly. "Enough advice. In love you probably won't listen to me anyway. But when you sing, you had better remember everything I tell you."

After the lesson, Sarah left in a state of almost as much confusion as when she'd arrived. Even so, she felt better. Solange was herself, different from anyone Sarah could have imagined before she came to Paris. She must accept what seemed distasteful about Solange along with what she liked.

Is that what she should do with Papa, and with Ted? It would be harder, and she didn't know if she could. She wasn't even sure how to greet Ted over their next lunch. Or if he'd want to see her. Her appearance at his door must have been as unpleasant for him as for her. At least there would be a chance to see him again. Papa would be leaving this evening. How could she let him go, with their lacerating words as a last memory?

She reached up and knocked on the roof of the hansom cab. When he opened the trap door, she said, "Hotel Terminus, please."

At the hotel she pushed her way through the throngs of

visitors to the reception desk where a clerk peered questioningly over gold-rimmed spectacles. "Please inform Monsieur Josiah Taylor that his daughter is here and wishes to see him."

The clerk's eyebrows quivered in obvious disbelief that an unescorted woman was any patron's daughter. "I'm sorry mademoiselle, but I can't—"

"I am Mademoiselle Taylor," Sarah said in her most imperious voice. "Please contact him for me immediately."

Frostily he said, "Just a moment," and disappeared behind the racks of key pigeonholes. When he returned, he said, with a hint of satisfaction, "Monsieur Taylor has departed."

"Departed! You mean, he's out right now?"

"I believe he has checked out."

She looked at the clock across the lobby. Four-thirty. With a hasty *"Merci,"* she rushed out of the hotel and ran across the Rue St. Lazare to the Gare St. Lazare. Once inside the huge railroad station she stopped to catch her breath. Finding her father, even if he hadn't already left, would be almost impossible. She hurried on to the long tables of the Salle des Bagages, dodging piles of luggage as she searched for a white-suited man of middle height. From there she ran to the departure area for trains to Le Havre. As the platform emptied, she gave up. Tears threatened again, but she held them back. She'd cried enough.

When Sarah reached home, exhaustion caught up with her. She lay down for a nap and slept so long she was almost late getting to the Opéra Comique. She had to rush into her heavy costume. While not as elaborate as those for the prima donna, it was made of embroidered satin, with long, tight sleeves, a narrow skirt edged with gold and a velveteen cape that imitated the long velvet train worn by Sybil Sanderson. In the sultry July evening, the close-fitting costume soon became stifling.

Usually Sarah paid no attention to such discomforts; they

were part of the price for singing. That night she found the heat oppressive. Though she hadn't noticed before, it struck her how fancifully romantic the story was: the princess Esclarmonde falling instantly in love with the knight, Roland. He betraying his oath of secrecy and having to compete in a tourney to win her. Special lighting gave the magical palaces and gardens of the settings a fantastical quality. The music, though much of it was simple and direct, had elaborate passages to portray the rituals of medieval courtly love. None of it resembled the real pain of living.

When the performance ended, Sarah declined Helene's invitation to join her and Marc at a café. Instead she went home and crawled into her canopied bed where her mind circled around the events of the past two days. Solange would say that Sarah's expectations of love were as quaint as the chivalric love of *Esclarmonde*. And it was true that she was inexperienced. But it wasn't true that she knew nothing about desire between a man and a woman. There had been times with Pierre when she'd felt aroused with passion. After the Incoherents' Ball, her feelings had been so strong that they'd frightened her. Pierre, she was sure, had desired her just as much. If there'd been no revelers coming along to interrupt that night, would she have drawn back?

If she hadn't, now she might understand this force that was so powerful.

She still could, if she had a lover.

What lover? In her speculations, she'd thought only of Pierre and not of Armand. Considering this, she realized that her feelings for Armand reminded her of the infatuations of growing up. Fantasies of romance. Like *Esclarmonde*. Different from the feelings Pierre aroused in her, which were both more exciting and in a strange way more comfortable. She could imagine Pierre as a lover; with Armand everything seemed more serious. Too much would be at stake with him.

The rules she'd been taught as a girl, the prohibitions against "letting a man have his way with her" before marriage, no longer seemed real. She hadn't questioned then that school mistresses and the mothers of friends were right. It was what her own mother would have said. But those precepts no longer seemed to fit.

Climbing out of bed, she lit a candle and took it to her dressing table where she tilted the mirror to show her body. As she watched herself, she pushed down the straps of her nightgown until she could see her breasts, then slipped the gown all the way off. Growing up she'd surreptitiously looked at her body, but the action had seemed shameful. Now she studied herself boldly, comparing her body to women in paintings and to the dancers in the Egyptian café. Compared to them she was thin, but her breasts were full. And Pierre had desired her. When she saw that look in his eyes again, she would say yes.

Almost triumphantly she left the gown discarded on the floor and walked naked back to her queenly bed.

CHAPTER
SIXTEEN

T HE NEXT MORNING SARAH FELT ANYTHING BUT CERTAIN
and queenly. It was one thing to decide with the protection of night, the time of dreams, that she would take
Pierre as a lover; it was another in the clear sunlight of a
July morning to put that plan into action.

What if he no longer wanted to make love to her? During
the past months, he'd flirted some, but he hadn't really pursued her. What if she asked and he acted embarrassed, or
refused? No—he wouldn't refuse. If nothing else, it would
make sure of Armand's interest. The idea chilled her. She
didn't want Pierre to agree because of Armand.

Solange would be eager to advise her. They had a lesson
that day. But Sarah didn't want to discuss her feelings about
this with Solange. She went off to the Rue de Chazelles
feeling unsettled.

It was an unsatisfactory lesson. "You're not paying attention," Solange scolded. "Your singing is stiff. That woman
you complain about—the one your father's going to marry.
Today she could probably do better than you. You're not a
Boston schoolgirl now."

"Yes, you're right," Sarah said, but that was exactly the trouble. The Boston girl still lived inside her.

That night she dreamed she was giving a concert at home, in the room where Papa had put a stage. When everyone in the audience began to laugh, she realized she had forgotten to put any clothes on.

The next morning she wrote Pierre three notes and tore all of them up. She was starting on a fourth when she remembered this was her day to meet Ted for lunch at the Café d'Orsay. It was a relief to worry about that instead. She wasn't sure whether he would come, and if he did, what they would say to each other about the scene in his room.

When she arrived at the café, Ted was already there. He looked like any other middle- or upper-class man—his clothes were the summer masculine uniform of tall hat, walking stick, and a lightweight suit that included a waistcoat. He greeted her with his usual affection. Only an unusual stiffness to his shoulders and tight lines around his mouth suggested anything different.

After they sat down, he asked, "How was the visit with Josiah? Did it go well?"

His intention was clear. They were to pretend she hadn't knocked on his door that night. Questions lay just under her tongue. But since she'd been the intruder, she didn't have the right to breach that pretense.

She smiled. "Yes, Papa and I had a good time together. We went to places I would never have seen if he hadn't been here."

As she chattered on, part of her mind returned to her dilemma about Pierre. Would she be like this with him—never getting to what she really wanted to say?

That night was the final performance at the Opéra Comique before the August recess. During the chorus's last entrance, Sarah stumbled on the edge of her heavy gown and would have fallen except for the quick grasp of the man behind her. When she thanked him afterward backstage, he asked, "Is something wrong? Are you feeling all right?"

"I'm fine. Nothing's wrong." What was wrong was that she was a coward.

A message came to the changing room that the director wanted to see her. She hurried into her clothes and to Cesbron's office. "I'm sorry I was so awkward," she began.

He waved aside her apology. "That was not important. I wish to tell you that I am very pleased with your work in the chorus. Both your singing and acting have been outstanding." He paused, beaming at her. "I need someone to understudy the mezzo-soprano roles. When we return after the holidays, we'll discuss it."

"Monsieur Cesbron! That's wonderful!" If he'd had full whiskers, to her at that moment he would have looked exactly like Saint Nicolas.

Sarah almost danced out of the theater that night. When she reached her flat, she did several extravagant turns around her living room, curtsying to her imaginary audience. If she could succeed at this, she could do anything, even approach Pierre!

In her dreams that night she was standing at the top of the Eiffel Tower. Pierre stood at the bottom, gesturing to her. She knew he wanted her to jump, and that he was promising to catch her. With a great swoop of her arms, she flung herself off. She woke as she was plummeting through the air, before she knew whether or not he caught her.

At midmorning her dilemma was either solved or worsened, she wasn't sure which, with the arrival of a message from Pierre. It read, "I tortured Dr. Najac by reading him my unpublished stories. So he's relented and released me from imprisonment. Can you meet me at one for a celebration at the Café Américain?"

Her first impulse was to stay securely in her flat. A fantasy about asking Pierre to be her lover was safer than seeing him. Instead, her heart pounding, she went resolutely to the bedroom to choose her most seductive-looking dress.

Pierre waited in front of the Café Américain, drumming his fingers on the table. Then he saw Sarah approaching along the Boulevard des Capucines and rose, savoring her appearance.

Men turned to look as she made her way toward the café. Her dress, a soft material that floated around her with each sway of her hips, was pale yellow, as if it had captured part of the sunlight. She held her parasol slightly to one side, so that it only half shaded her. Her hair lay around her forehead in soft waves that looked more gold than red. A wide straw hat curved up away from her face; a pink flower peeked over the edge of the brim, matching the color in her cheeks. Pierre imagined he could detect the fragrance of her favorite perfume.

She arrived, offering him a smile that looked both pleased to see him and shy at the same time. "Pierre, I'm delighted you're well enough to be out."

"And I'm delighted to be here and see you." He kissed her hand, wishing she weren't wearing the lace gloves.

They sat down, their chairs close together. She asked, "Is your cheek still painful?"

He touched the red line across his left cheek. "No, just a little tender. I have a notch in the top of my ear, but that doesn't bother me."

She tilted her head, considering. "Your scar isn't too noticeable from the front."

The waiter brought a bottle of Hermitage white burgundy. "Dr. Najac has forbidden champagne," Pierre said. "A stupid prohibition, but for a few days I guess I'll do what he says."

She lifted her glass. "To your recovery."

"Thank you. Is your father still here?"

"No, he went back to Boston."

Pierre relaxed. He'd been dreading an announcement that she was going home with her father. "Did you have a good visit?"

"Yes," she said.

He could see she wasn't comfortable with that subject, so he asked, "What's going on at the Opéra Comique?"

Her smile blossomed. "When performances begin again, Monsieur Cesbron will consider me for an understudy!"

"Congratulations! That's wonderful news."

After they drank another toast, Sarah's smile died. Puzzled, Pierre chatted on. "Dr. Najac wants me to go away, someplace out of Paris, for a week or so."

To his surprise, Sarah turned pale. For a moment she stared at him, her eyes dark and larger even than he remembered them. Then she looked down at her wineglass, twisting it in her fingers so that the pale wine swirled up the sides. "Is something wrong?" he asked.

Her fingers stilled. She pressed her lips together; when she released them, they trembled slightly. Finally she looked up. "I'd . . . like to go with you. Will you take me?"

His astonishment was so complete that words wouldn't come. Muscles all over his body tightened and centered in on his groin. Wait! he told himself. "Sarah, do you understand what you're asking?"

Color rushed back into her face, the vivid blush that was so characteristic. "Yes," came out in a whisper. She tried again. "Yes," she repeated in a firmer voice. "I know."

"Sarah, do you know . . . I mean, have you ever . . ." *Sacré bleu!* He sounded like a schoolboy.

"No, but I've made up my mind about this."

Fragments of thought skittered through his mind. How beautiful she was and how much he desired her. The uneasy thought that he might be in love with her. How Armand fit into this, and what he meant to both of them. It might be inviting trouble to become too involved with her.

"I suppose I have to agree," he said lightly as he tried to sort through his feelings. "I did tell you once that if you ever made me an improper proposal, I'd be too weak to resist."

Under the impetus of her fingers, the wine in her glass began to swirl again. It became clear to him what mattered most. He reached across and stopped the motion. "Sarah," he said softly, "nothing would make me happier than for you to come with me."

He saw emotions sweep over her face like waves succeeding each other—relief, embarrassment, pleasure. *Mon dieu*, she'd just proposed that they become lovers, yet how innocent she looked. If this were a game to her, he hoped she could play without getting badly hurt. He probably should be shielding himself. But even more, he wanted to protect her.

Over her shoulder he saw a familiar figure across the boulevard, coming toward the café. "Armand is about to join us. I forgot to mention he'll be here."

Her shoulders went back and she sat up very straight. When she smiled at him, only his knowledge of the past few minutes revealed that she wasn't as composed as she appeared. "You'll want to let him know," she said, "that we're going away together, won't you? That ought to make him even more attracted to me."

"I suppose so," he said, not liking the idea at all.

Armand arrived and bowed over Sarah's hand. "I'm very glad to see you." When he turned to Pierre, his usual melancholy expression became a warm smile. "Pierre, it's wonderful that you're out of your rooms."

"Yes," Pierre agreed. "No more daily visits to listen to me cursing at Dr. Najac."

"You can do what you like now?"

"Pretty much. He wants me to get out of Paris for a while."

This was the time to say more, but he didn't.

"Perhaps I can keep you entertained, Sarah," Armand said, "when you aren't singing."

"Thank you," Sarah said, "but the Opéra Comique will be dark for three weeks. I'll probably go somewhere out of Paris also." Another of her phenomenal blushes swept over her face.

"Yes, I see." Clearly Armand saw more than she'd intended. The muscles of his jaw stiffened, and he gave Pierre a glance that could only be interpreted as unfriendly. He said to Sarah, "August is the time to get away. I may join my mother in Trouville. Is your father still here?"

"No, he's left for the United States."

"That's unfortunate. I enjoyed meeting Monsieur Taylor and hoped to see him again."

Though Armand was looking at Sarah, Pierre was convinced his cousin's reference to meeting Josiah Taylor was aimed at him. And he could tell from his feeling of irritation that the intimation of a special connection to Sarah hit home. When he'd told Sarah of competition between Armand and him, he hadn't expected to feel its edge. For Armand's sake he'd been holding back, acting the casual friend. No longer. Armand could look out for himself.

Over the next two days Pierre took care of arrangements, including having someone pick up Sarah's baggage ahead of time. She sent a letter to Solange apologizing for missing her lessons and a message to Ted. In the note to him she said only that she would be away and hoped he would have lunch with her at her flat when she returned. Maybe then they could talk about her untimely visit to his room. After she packed, she had nothing else to do. It should have made leaving easy for her. Instead she had too much time to consider what a bold and unseemly thing she was doing.

She might be getting in too deep with Pierre without

knowing his real feelings. Taking him as a lover felt like a break with the past as great as leaving home. There would be no going back to her Boston self afterward. But if she didn't do this, it would be as if she didn't have the courage to be anything else.

On departure day, Pierre's groom came for her. "Monsieur Pierre," Michel explained, "has a last-minute errand. He'll meet you at the train station."

Pierre was waiting outside the Gare St.-Lazare. Instead of a hat and a suit with a waistcoat, he was wearing a loose jacket and trousers and a cap. He looked unfamiliar. As he hurried her to the platform and into an empty first-class compartment, he said happily, "We'll have this to ourselves. I was lucky to get it. The one twenty-two to Normandy is often crowded."

Sarah tried to smile with equal enthusiasm. But her stomach felt like a ball of tightly wound string. What was she doing here, with this stranger?

When she felt the first jolt of the train, she looked out the window, pretending the view absorbed her completely. The train left the station of Batignolles and headed across the flat area beyond the old fortifications. When it crossed the Seine at Asnières, she studied the boats as if she'd never seen one before.

She felt a touch on her hand and turned to find Pierre looking soberly at her. "Sarah, you don't have to stare out the window all the time unless you want to. Please don't worry. For the whole trip, there's *nothing* I expect you to do unless you want to."

He understood! Her discomfort shrank into a manageable anticipation that included lingering apprehension, but was mostly excitement. What she was doing was right—for her.

In spite of that assurance to herself, her feelings were like the train ride, sometimes smooth, then suddenly bumpy. Pierre was an enthusiastic guide, mentioning names she

would know. At Mantes he said, "See that Gothic church?
William the Conqueror fell from his horse beside that church
and later died in Rouen." When they reached Rouen, he
pointed out how much the brick chimneys of the factories,
belching a mixture of flames and smoke, resembled the
hundreds of church spires. But by then, all she remembered
for certain was that they'd crossed the wandering Seine more
times than she could count.

By a little before eight in the evening Pierre had to rouse
her from dozing with her head on his shoulder. "We're at
Fécamp on La Manche," he said.

He meant the English channel, she thought fuzzily. When
they left the train, she smelled a combination of salt water
and wharves—not quite the same as Boston, but similar
enough to recognize. "Will we stay here?" she asked hopefully.

"No. Guy de Maupassant was born here, but that's the
most interesting thing about it. We're going on about fifteen
kilometers to Etretat. It's a small resort and not as crowded.
Offenbach built himself a villa there and worked on *Tales
of Hoffman*, the opera you almost had a part in."

By the time Pierre located their baggage and a farmer who
would take them in his cart, the day seemed very long.
Though the cart had wheels with rubber tires, it jolted on
the cobblestone streets and even more on the country road.
She braced herself and tried to ignore the discomfort by
watching low wind-bent trees surrounded by tangles of
ferns, gorse and brambles. They passed a few small villages,
at any one of which she was ready to stop. By the time they
reached a cluster of buildings spread out around a wide bay,
Pierre had to lift her down.

The hotel was a new three-story building that faced the
ocean. "You'll be very comfortable with us," the reception
clerk informed them proudly. "We have all the modern
conveniences. Safe and dependable gas light. A bathroom

on each floor." Sarah thought to herself grumpily that perhaps France might catch up with Boston someday.

"Let's stop downstairs and have a light supper," Pierre suggested. "Then we can get settled in our rooms."

Sarah thought that she should be anxious again, but she was too tired to worry about anything. After barely tasting the fruit and omelette, she found that her eyes wanted to close. "Come on," Pierre said. "You're almost asleep."

Immediately she was wide awake. As they climbed the stairs, she felt cold even though the night was warm and her heart was racing. She glanced sideways at Pierre as he walked beside her, and the feeling of panic came back. She should turn around and go back to Paris! But her feet went on.

At the third floor, Pierre led her along the hall to the end room and opened the door. When she stepped inside, he handed her the large key. "Lock the door from the inside," he directed. "I'm across the corridor if you need me. But I think you'll be too sound asleep to notice anything."

He touched her cheek lightly, then ran his finger down across her mouth, pausing at the center of her lips. "Good night, Sarah."

As she watched in surprise, he went to the door across the way, unlocked it, gave her a grin over his shoulder, and went inside. It took her several moments to recover and close and lock her door.

Later, lying in a bed big enough for two large people, she thought hazily that making love couldn't be as compelling as she'd imagined if Pierre didn't mind waiting. Her final hazy reflection was that she ought to be insulted—if she weren't so sleepy.

The next morning she woke to the sounds of waves slapping the beach. Momentarily puzzled, she searched for the familiar canopy overhead before remembering where she was. Daylight filtered into the room through lace-curtained glass doors. One of them stood open a few inches, letting in the sound of the sea. Eagerly she scrambled out of bed and into a robe, then went to the doors and pushed them open.

A small balcony with a black wrought iron railing faced the water. The hotel appeared to be at the center of the shore that curved around the bay. On either side, like embracing arms, the land rose sharply to white cliffs. Directly below her was the stone terrace of the hotel. Beyond it the pale yellow beach sloped gently downward to the glistening blue of the channel. Waves broke on the shore in parallel rows of white foam, like ranks of troops marching forward, with none allowed out of formation. In front of the terrace dark gray change cubicles, their wheels sunk into the sand, were arrayed toward the water—the opposing army.

Pierre, wearing a white shirt and trousers and carrying his jacket, was walking up from the beach. She leaned over the edge of the balcony and waved. He looked up, and she thought of her appearance—the ruffled white muslin robe and her loose hair, both blowing in the breeze. She stepped back, but he had seen her and bounded up onto the terrace.

Cupping his hands around his mouth, he called, "Ready to come down?"

She nodded and waved, then retreated to her room. As she put on a simple muslin dress, she thought of her trepidations of the previous day. They hadn't completely vanished, but in the golden morning, they only added an edge of zestful excitement to her feelings.

During the day she and Pierre explored the seaside town. For her it was like a series of paintings with different settings but the same central figure: Pierre. They listened to the conductor of the salt water baths warning, "If you go into the sea itself, it is unwise to stay longer than five or ten minutes."

"A timid soul," Pierre murmured to Sarah.

Another setting was the new casino. A bill of attractions posted outside announced that games of chance were available nightly and that a ball was held every Friday. It also listed several musical evenings. On Sunday a Madame Peyre would sing. "See all the things you can choose," Pierre said. "Gambling, dancing. Listening to another singer. Would you like to hear her?"

"Yes, I would." Sarah felt indulged, as she'd been as a child. "Are we going to do everything I wish?"

He looked at her, his mouth curved in a half smile, his eyes inviting. "Everything."

The air between them seemed to vibrate with secret messages, ones that made her stomach tighten with quivers of excitement.

When they saw a squad of soldiers drilling, she imagined Pierre in the blue and red uniforms with high black boots echoing smartly on the cobblestones of the square. At one side of the bay were oyster beds; fishing boats came in to moor on a gravel-covered shingle nearby. Planks on wooden supports, weathered gray by sun and fog, formed a market of sorts where women sold their husbands' catches. Sarah wondered what it would be like to wait on the shore for Pierre to return from following one of the centuries-old occupations linked to the sea.

"Shall we try swimming tomorrow?" he asked as they walked back to the hotel in the late afternoon.

His question reminded Sarah of how they might spend the time before then, and she had to swallow once before she could answer. "Yes, I'd like that."

She dressed for dinner in a new gown she'd purchased impulsively in the Bon Marche department store. The material was a soft orange-red cotton, so smooth it felt like silk. Small ruffles edged the round neckline and the small sleeves that came just over her shoulders. The skirt pulled smooth across her hips in front and ended in a froth of more ruffles in back. Around her neck she tied a black velvet ribbon, with the bow in back under her upswept hair. Last she used a new fragrance, "Nuit d'Argent." A silver night suggested moonlight, mysterious and alluring.

Pierre, waiting on the terrace, knew before she reached him that her perfume was different. It was sweeter than her usual scent, more like the tropical flowers imported for greenhouses. In the breeze off the water, her dress floated behind her like plumes from a delicate, exotic bird. Nothing of the unsophisticated New England girl remained. But as she drew closer, he saw he was wrong. She still had the telltale flush of color and half-shy smile. Desire flooded over him.

"Come watch the sunset," he said. "It matches your dress, and is almost as beautiful as you are."

Salmon-colored streaks of clouds were slowly turning gold as the sun set, but Pierre hardly noticed them any longer. When they went inside to the dining room, he barely looked at the menu. At the end of the meal he wasn't sure what he'd eaten or how it tasted. He also didn't care.

Afterward on the terrace, they had coffee and Orgeat liqueur, diluted with water to a delicate almond flavor. At dinner they'd talked of the town and exhausted their limited interest in that topic. Now Sarah was silent, and the questions he wanted to ask weren't for so public a place. "Shall we walk on the beach until we . . . go upstairs?" he asked.

She rose without answering. A crescent moon, which had been hidden by the sunlight, shone above the western horizon, making a silver path across the water that moved, as they moved. At first Sarah's hand on his forearm felt as light as the touch of a bird she'd reminded him of. When they were close to the water, she stumbled and gripped his arm. "I have sand in my shoes," she explained with a nervous laugh.

"I'll help you take them off," he suggested and knelt in

front of her. She put her hand on his shoulder and lifted each foot in turn while he slipped off her shoes. The glimpse of black stockings and the feel of silk against his fingers accomplished the arousal he'd been disciplining himself to postpone.

He rose and stood, looking down at her upturned face, the shoes dangling from his hand. Her hand still rested on his shoulder, and he could feel the sudden pressure of her fingers. The shoes dropped to the sand as he put his arms around her and drew her close.

His lips found hers, soft and yet eager. She tasted of almond liqueur, but then just of herself, as if part honey, part salt. A mixture he thought he could savor without ever having too much. He felt her response, in the way she pressed against him, in her tongue touching his, in her hurried breathing when they broke apart. He slid his hands along her upper arms, stroking the warm, velvety skin.

"Sarah, I'd like to make love to you." Waiting the first night hadn't been bad; he'd expected that. Now restraint would be hellish. But it depended on her.

Her eyelashes shadowed her eyes, and her voice was just above a whisper. "Yes."

His pulse hadn't been faster for any duel. "Shall we go inside?"

He carried her shoes, but at the terrace, she put them on without his help. She didn't look at him while they went up the stairs. When they reached her door, he took her key and opened it, then stepped back. "I'll join you in a minute."

In his own room he found the bottle of iced champagne and glasses he'd ordered earlier. Briefly he considered one of the sheaths in his baggage. He disliked them. And how to introduce a virgin to sexual pleasures and protect her at the same time? Reluctantly he found the package. He couldn't take the risk for her.

After checking that no one was in the corridor, he crossed

and knocked on her door. When he heard her say, "Come in," he found her standing by the open glass doors. In the light from a pink-shaded kerosene lamp, her dress looked deep red. He put down the champagne and glasses and opened the bottle.

"Are you disobeying Dr. Najac?" she asked, and he was disconcerted to hear how composed she sounded. More than he felt.

"All prohibitions need to be broken at some time." He realized how banal he sounded and had to laugh. "Here," he said, giving her a glass. "I don't think you need this, but I do." He held up his wine. "A toast to lovers."

Sarah understood that this was the last moment to pull back. Pierre was looking at her, his eyes serious, faint lines of tension at the corners of his mouth. Her heart was doing a staccato rhythm as she raised her wine and drank. A second later, he drank also. They put their glasses down and moved together.

The kiss began where their embrace on the beach had broken off. This time she was more conscious of his body, hard and strong against her softness. His lips teased hers, setting off tremors that reached deep inside her. He released her to turn the lamp low and close the glass doors, then returned.

This time his mouth was demanding, hungry, creating a growing hunger in her, though she wasn't yet sure for exactly what. She was still waiting as he pulled the pins from her hair and let it fall loose. When he slipped one sleeve down off her shoulder and brushed the uncovered skin with his mouth, her body began to learn. He traced the vein along the inside of her arm and she knew even more.

Along with caresses, his words, more breathed than spoken, taught her as well. "How beautiful you are. I love to look at you. And touch you. Your skin is smooth and delicate. There's no velvet or silk as soft."

Though she was used to his teasing, this was a new and tender side to him. In his rapid breathing, she sensed his urgency, but his restrained gentleness reassured her. It let her feel her own eagerness and help him find the fastenings to her clothes. As he undressed her, each piece of clothing was like a layer of herself set aside, revealing not just her body but an inner, still unknown core. When she stood in her camisole and pantaloons, she stopped him. She had let him take the lead, but it was suddenly essential that she know him as well. "Not yet, until you . . ."

He began to remove his garments almost awkwardly, as if buttons were an obstacle he was too impatient to manage. He didn't stop until he was naked.

The sight of his body startled her into words. "You look . . . different." It was both as she'd imagined and yet not. With his clothes on, he was a strong looking man. Without them he was beautiful. The well-defined muscles of his chest and arms were an intricate network above his lean stomach. She wasn't prepared for the contrast of dark brown hair and creamy skin. The evidence of his arousal startled her and made her feel shy again.

"Come," he said, "I want to see you," and pulled her to the bed. As they lay together, he held her close, kissing her and smoothing her hair until she relaxed and helped him remove the last of her clothing. "*Ah, Dieu!*" he breathed. "You are even more beautiful than all the times I imagined you like this."

In their close embrace, feeling all of him along her length, she was able to let her new hungers build and sweep her along. The touch of his hands and his mouth on her breasts set up a rhythm that built inside her like a slow melody that became louder and stronger, its beat compelling. Heat built in her abdomen, growing and spreading. He moved so he could reach her back and leaned over, trailing kisses along her spine and across her hips. When she turned back to him, he stroked the inside of her thighs. His caresses, reaching her most intimate center, introduced her to sensations she had only dimly known existed. She felt as if she were made of wax and he was a fire that was melting her, down to her bones.

When she thought she couldn't feel more, he entered her carefully, then with a final urgent thrust. The pain mattered less than the rightness of being joined to him.

"Sarah," he said, his voice hoarse in her ear, "I don't know how long I can wait."

"Yes, yes," she said, not sure what she meant, but it seemed the only possible answer.

The tempo of his movements, slow at first, gradually increased, pulling her with him toward some still-unknown place until the fire inside her exploded, like an enormous pinwheel, whirling and shattering into a hundred embers. As she slowly returned to herself, Pierre gasped and shuddered and finally lay still.

He turned, pulling her with him so that they lay on their sides, still entwined. "*Ma chérie*," he murmured. "You're wonderful."

She didn't know what was wonderful—she or he or the two of them together, but she knew something was.

A movement wakened Sarah; it was Pierre getting up from the bed. In the light just filtering into the room she watched as he pulled on his trousers and shirt. When he had gathered up the rest of his clothes, he came back, leaned down and kissed her. "Until later," he said softly and was gone.

She stretched, drowsily trying to discover whether she felt different from the day before, but sleep returned before she could decide.

When she awoke again, voices floating in through the windows told her bathers were already using the cubicles. After finding a gown and robe, she stepped out on the balcony and looked for Pierre among the figures that made dark spots of shade on the bright sand. She saw him at the same time that he turned and saw her. When she waved, he started toward the hotel. With melodies singing in her head, she rushed through her toilette and went downstairs to find him pacing the veranda. She paused in the doorway, not quite sure how to greet him. But when he saw her, his face lit in such a smile of pleasure that her uncertainty vanished as readily as her modesty had during the night.

"It's a lovely day, isn't it?" she greeted him.

"Yes. Very lovely."

They both knew they weren't talking about the weather.

Later they engaged two change cubicles, and Sarah put on the black bathing dress that Helene had lent her. Though to be polite she'd accepted the stiffened tulle corset that went with it, she didn't consider wearing it. She'd never worn a corset for swimming at home, and she wouldn't do it now just so her waist would look smaller. When she emerged from the cubicle, Pierre was waiting. He had on one of the new bathing suits for men; the trunks came halfway down his legs and the top had only narrow straps over his shoulders. On the way down to the water, several of the women walking on the beach tilted their parasols so that they could keep him in view. Sarah was glad he didn't seem to notice.

She was surprised and pleased that she could swim more smoothly than Pierre. Being pupil to his teacher in bed had been intensely gratifying, but she decided she liked being the knowledgeable one part of the time. After they swam and rinsed and changed in the cubicles, she discovered she was intensely hungry. Pierre laughed at her appetite, but when they reached the dining room, he read the menu as eagerly as she. The choice was generous: vegetable and tapioca soups, oysters, pickled cucumbers, three kinds of fish, capon, fricassee of veal, spinach, endive salad, stewed apples, jam tarts, and Neufchâtel cheese. She ate some of at least half the offerings, and Pierre ate as much as she.

They had just started to walk the two blocks to the casino when dark clouds began gathering. Lightning streaked down, and the thunder grew louder. Announced by a wind devil whirling across the sand, the storm was on them. Men with large black umbrellas came hurrying from the smoking room of the hotel to rescue women with collapsed parasols. Mothers called in exasperated voices to children who preferred to stand with open mouths to catch the sheeting rain. Sarah and Pierre joined the hurrying lines that converged on the hotel and stood with their fellow guests in the lobby, each one contributing his private shower to the pools forming on the floor.

While voices around them debated the merits of organizing card games in the dining room or trying to find cabs to take them to the casino, Sarah and Pierre looked at each other and silently went upstairs.

There, in Sarah's bed, they created a storm of their own. Like the mythological gods within the clouds, whose turbulent collisions raged overhead as lightning and thunder, Sarah's and Pierre's desires built and climaxed in an electricity of passion.

Afterward they lay, listening to the wind and rain gradually diminishing. Voices in the corridor reminded Sarah of a question. "The maid called me 'madame.' Was that just customary, or did you register us as being married?"

"Hotels list couples as married, whether they think they are or not. This hotel may assume we're actually married because we have separate rooms. Any woman sharing a room with a man is presumed to be his mistress."

Puzzled, she said, "That sounds backward to me."

"In France, at least among people who have enough money to go to resorts, love and marriage aren't considered compatible. A lot of conservatives àre suspicious of a politician who's happily in love with his wife."

A politician handicapped by a happy marriage? It seemed a sad way of looking at things to Sarah.

In the days following, she had few sad thoughts. She and Pierre swam every morning and walked along the beach to the points of the bay where the sea had undercut the cliffs, leaving arches out into the water. One day he hired a cart to take them several miles inland to a stream where they fished and he rowed, an exercise he enjoyed as much as bicycling and did as vigorously.

They also talked. Sarah told Pierre of her quarrels with her father. She expected him to say, as Solange had, that she was too hard on Josiah. He listened thoughtfully, then commented, "I feel sorry for Mabel. She must have been unhappy about her situation and the way it ended."

He described his family, a brother and sister who both died as infants. "Armand was really my brother. Enough older and bigger that he stood up for me in fights."

"Then he and your aunt are your only family now?" she asked.

"Yes. Aunt Nathalie is a difficult person. But I have a lot of affection for her."

With their growing intimacy, Sarah felt almost bold enough to ask Pierre about being Solange's lover. But she couldn't quite do that. Instead she said, "Why did you object to my friendship with Solange Rabaud?"

"Solange has some lovers who are women."

"She told me."

"Yes, I suppose she would. Her ways are understandable. She must have known men who were . . . unpleasant. But I don't think that's the best way to live. Not for you. After all, you'll probably have a family someday."

Again Pierre had surprised her. She hadn't expected his disapproval of Solange's life, or espousal of a family for her.

The two weeks went quickly. One afternoon they gambled

at the casino, and on Sunday they heard Madame Peyre, who Sarah secretly thought didn't sing as well as she did. They went to the Friday ball, which was an excuse to wear elegant clothes for dancing. Most evenings, however, they stayed at the hotel in her room.

Earlier in the summer Sarah had seen a painting by Auguste Renoir. It was called simply, *Path Climbing through Long Grass*. When she came upon it, she thought there must be a hole in the roof of the gallery, letting in a ray of sunlight that shone directly on the figures in the center. The nights in Etretat seemed to her like the center of that painting—surrounded by joyful but less vivid days. She had wanted to find out about sexual desire. With Pierre, she discovered appetites in herself she hadn't imagined. She also learned that sensual pleasure had many moods—urgent and demanding, teasing and gentle. At first it seemed strange to sleep beside another person, but she quickly adjusted to it. She liked waking during the night, hearing the waves outside and feeling the warmth of his body next to her. The bed was lonely when he slipped out just before dawn.

Sarah's only regret was that the time seemed to seep away as swiftly as the grains of pale yellow sand that ran through her fingers on the beach. The day for departure came too soon.

It was not until they were on the train returning to Paris that she discovered something more about herself. Though they exchanged a few comments about the scenery, for the most part Pierre was silent and preoccupied. She guessed he was thinking about returning to his work in Paris. Perhaps about Armand. Pierre had said nothing about what might continue with her in Paris. She'd been bold enough to ask to go away with him. It was up to him to suggest anything about the future.

She thought about her activities: singing in *Esclarmonde* and other productions to come, friends to see at the Opéra

Comique, tutoring Emile, her own lessons with Solange. A rich, satisfying life—or so it had seemed. Now, in the face of Pierre's silence, that same life appeared disjointed, as if half its purpose were missing.

When the train reached the Asnières bridge, with Paris just ahead, he looked at her as if he'd settled something with himself. "May I come to your flat sometimes?"

The joy with which she said yes startled her. With sudden clarity she realized that she'd done one thing Solange would approve of: she'd taken a lover. But though she thought she was taking this bold, free step to learn about life, she hadn't understood herself. In opposition to Solange's advice, she'd chosen for a lover a man with whom she was foolishly, heedlessly, in love.

CHAPTER
SEVENTEEN

PIERRE PUT HIS COFFEE CUP DOWN ON THE TABLE IN
Sarah's dining room kitchen and rose. "I must get to
Le Combattant. Lots of work this morning." Since they'd
returned to Paris two weeks previously, he'd come to her
flat after performances at the Opéra Comique. Usually he
stayed a few hours, but the previous night they'd both fallen
asleep.

As he leaned down and kissed her, his hand drifted to
the top of her blue silk robe. Then he stopped with a rueful
grin. "If I touch you, I won't want to leave. But there's too
much to do before the elections."

She rose too and followed him to the door. "They're September twenty-second?"

"Yes, for the first round. Only three weeks away."

"Why are you worried? General Boulanger isn't even in
France."

"His supporters are still here, so we can't let up. If they
win big in the general elections, they'll probably try to bring
him back. They're still a threat." He picked up his walking
stick and hat. "Unfortunately, it means I may not see you
as often as I'd like to until this is settled."

After a last kiss, he checked the hall. She peered around him. No one was in sight, and he started down the stairs. Reluctantly she closed the door after him. It shouldn't matter whether someone saw him; this was Paris, where liaisons between people who weren't married were more acceptable than in Boston. But he seemed anxious to shield her from gossip by her neighbors, and she liked that.

In spite of the risk of his being seen leaving, sleeping with him all night had been satisfying in a way that went beyond sexual gratification. Maybe, she mused, it was because she loved him. She hadn't decided what to do with the knowledge of how much he meant to her, or the question of how he felt. For now, it was enough to know he desired her and to share the pleasures they had together.

Today, she reminded herself, she didn't have time for mooning about. There was a rehearsal this afternoon at the Opéra Comique, and before that a lesson with Solange.

Two hours later when she arrived at Solange's town house, she could hear Solange playing the piano and singing. Sarah stopped, startled. Except for demonstrating brief examples during lessons, she'd never sung when Sarah could hear her. Berthe's usual impassive face broke into a pleased smile. "Madame is in a happy mood today," she whispered.

Sarah stopped just outside the doors to the drawing room. The song was from *Don Pascuale*, in which the heroine sings of how easily she can turn men's heads and win their hearts with tantalizing smiles and pretended refusals. Though Solange's voice was rough, she sang with emotion and charm.

When she finished, Sarah entered, applauding. "Brava!"

Solange rose from the piano. "Ah, Sarah, if you could have heard me once, your applause would have been justified." She kissed Sarah's cheeks and then said, "You're looking very well. That striped dress is lovely. I always liked sateen. And turquoise is a wonderful color with your hair."

Sarah couldn't imagine Solange in sateen; it was far too

ordinary. But she smiled and said, "Thank you."

Solange briskly, "Let's begin with your exercises and then I think we'll work on Dorabella's music from *Cosi Fan Tutte*."

Sarah happily agreed. She loved Mozart's music, even though this morning she couldn't imagine that a girl would fall in love with someone else just after she'd parted from the man she'd vowed to love forever.

When Sarah finished the exercises, Solange surprised her again by saying, "I'll sing the maid's part. I've always thought that Despina is something like me. I agree with her philosophy—that women are put on earth in order to be loved. She thinks it's fortunate God provided men for that purpose." Solange laughed. "Of course, I know more about love than Despina, but I like the role."

At first it was strange to sing with Solange, whose experience and technique were greater. Soon Sarah overcame her hesitation and enjoyed their collaboration. When they finished, Solange applauded with the generous sincerity that Sarah admired. "You are the one who deserves the bravas now."

Warmly Sarah said, "I've learned so much from you. I'll always be grateful."

The cupid-encrusted clock on the mantel chimed twice. "Oh, dear," Sarah exclaimed. "The time went by so fast. I must get to a rehearsal."

"Don't go just yet." Solange's mouth twitched in an expression Sarah couldn't quite interpret—almost a sly smile. She took a folded newspaper from a table in the corner. "Have you seen today's *Le Combattant*?"

"No. I was late this morning and didn't take time to stop for one. Does it have an article by Pierre?"

"Yes, but that's not what I found most interesting. Look at Gille's column. The third page." She handed the paper to Sarah and sat down on the settee, as if she were in a theater, waiting for a performance to begin.

There was an article on the front by Pierre about changes in the election laws. Though she'd like to read it, Sarah passed over that page and turned to Roland Gille's column. The first items gave her no clue why Solange wanted her to read it. Gille discussed Guy de Maupassant's latest novel, *Fort comme la Mort*; he admired the writing but thought the subject, an old man's hopeless love for a young girl, depressing. He reported gleefully that audiences at the Eldorado music hall loved a song by Yvette Guilbert about the ineptness of an aristocratic Frenchman's attempts at seduction. A fight had broken out at the opening of a new play, which he judged as unworthy of that much attention. Some of his colleagues, he railed rather bitterly, were abandoning Tortoni's restaurant for the Café Napolitain.

Sarah looked at Solange. "I don't understand—"

"Go on," Solange interrupted. "You haven't read the last part yet."

Sarah skimmed on through references to books and poems and came to the gossip. A man, identified as Comte M, "The Count with the Onyx Death's-head Scarfpin," was rumored to have purchased the slippers of Lord Byron's last lover and the bedpan used by Napoleon after the battle of Waterloo. Odd, Sarah thought, but no reason for her to read the column. When a duke's mistress, it continued, stood outside his house in the middle of the night, screaming for his wife to give him up, his wife had a servant pour water on her. He was labeled "The Unavailable Duke." Surely this wasn't what Solange wanted her to see.

Sarah read on and found it:

Readers should not think that French women are the only ones who occasionally abandon their status as the frail sex. One of the most beautiful chorus members currently at the Opéra Comique is American. Mademoiselle T proved her mettle after a lovers' quarrel with the departed Monsieur R by wounding him with the oversized hatpin she carries, much as our ancestors carried rapiers.

The heat flamed in Sarah's face. "That's outrageous! It's mostly lies, and it happened almost a year ago."

"A year ago?" Solange raised her eyebrows. "You haven't finished the column."

Apprehensively, she read on:

Now Mademoiselle T has chosen a new lover. Could it be a recent dueling scar that recommends Monsieur de T to this tempestuous lady? They spent a holiday in Etretat, from which he returned without additional scars. Perhaps 'The Beautiful American' wore no hats.

Sarah felt stunned. She sat down on the divan and read the paragraph again.

Solange patted Sarah's arm. "Don't be so upset. It's a nice phrase, 'La Belle Americaine.'"

"Why would—" The words came out in a scratchy whisper and Sarah had to start again. "Why would he write about me? Who would want to read it?"

"You're interesting because you're American. And Pierre's a writer. They're expected to lead scandalous lives, so people like to read about them. Gille's stock in trade is providing scandalous tid-bits. Besides, he likes to invent labels for people."

"But it's cruel, to parade people's private lives like this. Even if it were all true."

Solange shrugged. "You shouldn't still be so naive. Think of it this way, dear. Pierre won't mind because it's good for his newspaper. And it's not so bad for you. A catchy nickname is very valuable for a singer. To be La Belle Americaine will probably help your career."

Her career! The potential disaster of the article struck Sarah. The newspaper dropped from her hands and slid to the floor. "Monsieur Cesbron! He'll be furious. Maybe dismiss me."

"What are you talking about?" Solange said sharply.

"He warned me there mustn't be bad publicity about singers at the Opéra Comique. Because of the government subsidy."

"That's madness! You tell that ridiculous man that no one expects singers to lead chaste lives."

Her hands fumbling with distress, Sarah collected her things. Solange obviously didn't understand. "Thank you for the lesson, Solange. I must go." As she fled, she heard Solange call something else after her, but she was too upset to find out what.

She ran to the corner and hailed a cab. "The Théâtre des Nations, please."

As she jolted along, a sick anger churned in her stomach at the thought of the question she didn't want to ask herself. Where had Gille gotten his information about her trip to Normandy with Pierre?

She had told no one; she hadn't even known where they were going beforehand. The obvious answer was Pierre, but she couldn't believe that. He wouldn't do anything he knew she would hate so much and might damage her career. Not even to boost his paper's sales. Or would he?

How well did she really know Pierre? She'd thought she'd known Papa, but she hadn't. And the same with Ted. There were two things she felt sure of about Pierre. He loved Armand and was concerned for his future. And he wanted to help preserve republican government in France. She didn't know just how he felt about her.

Love is blind. An old phrase—a cliché. But maybe true. Maybe she didn't believe Pierre would do anything so hurtful to her because she didn't want to believe it. She must know—must ask him.

When she reached the theater, she hurried to the director's office. Through his open door, she saw *Le Combattant* lying on his desk. He looked up, frowning.

"Monsieur Cesbron," she began before he could speak,

"I'm very upset about that article. I'm so sorry."

His frown changed to a look of worried sorrow. "It is very distressing, Mademoiselle Taylor."

She took heart from his dismay when she'd expected anger. "I don't know how it got into the paper. You warned me, I realize. But I hope you can still keep me here. I'll be even more careful after this."

He took off his glasses, then put them back on and picked up the paper again. She waited, her pulse racing so fast she had to make an effort to breathe. Finally he put the paper down and said, as if he were arguing with himself, "You are one of our best performers. I don't want to be unfair."

"Hasn't it been several years since the problem about the medals? Maybe people aren't paying such close attention to places that get government money now."

"That may be true."

She thought unhappily that even if he kept her, this would end her chance to be an understudy. It wasn't a question to bring up now.

His expression told her he'd made a decision. "Very well, Mademoiselle Taylor. We'll say nothing more about this. So long as there is no more mention of you in the papers."

"Thank you, Monsieur Cesbron." As Sarah left the director's office, she felt as if she'd walked through a tiger's cage and survived. But there was another trial ahead—to talk to Pierre.

Before rehearsal began, she noticed several curious glances, but pretended not to. The rehearsal was for *The King of Ys*, a Lalo opera that was unfamiliar to Sarah and required all her attention for singing. When the stage manager signaled they were finished, she dallied at the back of the stage. After most people had left, she started for the changing room to collect her parasol and purse.

Helene, already on her way out, stopped. "Are you all right, Sarah?" she asked.

This was the opportunity to confide in a friend, but Sarah found she couldn't. "I'm fine," she lied.

Helene hesitated, then said, "I think there's someone waiting for you," and continued toward the outer door.

Sarah walked on slowly. What would she say to Pierre? No—not say—ask. No matter—the important thing was his answer. The churning in her stomach began again. She went around a corner and could see a man standing beside the changing room door. It was Armand.

She felt both relieved and dismayed. A confrontation with Pierre was delayed, but with Armand she might have to pretend nothing was wrong. She wasn't sure she could.

When she reached Armand, he looked very upset. She wouldn't have to pretend. "I'd like to talk to you, Sarah, if you're free," he said.

After she had her parasol and purse, they went to the Taverne de Londres, opposite the Opéra Comique. It specialized in English food, and few Parisians went there. Sarah saw no one she knew from the theater, but she was glad Armand found a table in a corner. After they ordered, he said, "I saw today's *Le Combattant*. Have you read it?" At her nod, he continued heatedly. "Gille's column is disgraceful! It may sell papers, but that isn't enough reason to allow such trash."

She asked him her first painful question. "How did Gille find out anything about me? Not about Rivarol—that's so old—but about Pierre, and . . . Etretat? I didn't think anyone knew where we were."

"Pierre told me where he was going. I guessed you were with him."

Hope started up. She asked, "Did you tell Monsieur Gille?"

"No, of course not!" His shocked face and voice convinced her. "I abhor him. I don't speak to him if I can avoid it. I would never discuss anything with him."

The waiter returned with plates of boiled beef that Sarah

knew she couldn't eat. Apparently Armand couldn't either, because he sipped at his wine and ignored the food.

Sarah had another question, one she didn't want to ask. But Armand knew Pierre better than she did. "*Le Combattant*'s circulation during the election campaign is very important to Pierre. And I suppose that gossip, even about someone like me, sells papers. Do you think Pierre told Gille?"

"No." Armand shifted uncomfortably in his chair so that he wasn't looking directly at her. "I'm sure he wouldn't. He has . . . too much regard for you."

Armand's protest sounded forced, Sarah thought miserably. Of course he would defend Pierre. And he assumed Pierre's affection for her because of their affair. He didn't know that she, not Pierre, had actually initiated their liaison. "I'm sorry," she said, "but I'm not hungry after all. I'd like to go home."

In the cabriolet they were both silent. The noisy streets were crowded with carriages and pedestrians, still flocking to the exposition. But the first, vulnerable leaves had begun to turn from green to yellow, a warning that the vacation season was passing. It would soon be a year, Sarah thought, since she'd arrived in Paris, but at that moment she felt more like a foreigner than she had for many months.

When they reached her street, Armand dismissed the cab. "I need the walk," he explained, and he did look pale and nervous.

At her door, he took her hand and held it. "Sarah, you have become very important to me. I want you to know how sorry I am that you are Gille's target. There is one thing I can do. I can challenge him."

Horrified, she exclaimed, "No! I would never want you to do that."

He gripped her hand more tightly, as if to convince her of his strength. "Your name wouldn't come into it. With a man like him, it would be easy to find a pretext."

"No, Armand. I know that you don't think of duels the way I do. But I don't want anyone fighting for my sake."

Because he looked so distressed, she added, "Thank you for wanting to help me. I appreciate that. It makes me feel better."

"I'm glad. I care a great deal about your happiness." He smiled his melancholy smile, kissed her hand and started down the stairs.

As she went inside, she realized that she did feel better. She would never want a man to fight a duel on her behalf. But it comforted her a little that Armand wanted to defend her.

Pierre stood in the bookshop across the street from Sarah's flat. Though he'd picked up a book, he was looking out the front window of the shop. He felt like a fool—like a character in one of the bad novels displayed on the table close to the door—skulking here, spying on his mistress, waiting for a rival to leave.

It hadn't started that way. When he'd reached *Le Combattant* that morning, he'd gone to his own office without talking to anyone. A curious junior writer had finally interrupted him with a copy of the day's paper. In his first rage, he'd hunted for Gille. Their shouting match had accomplished nothing. Gille refused to say where he got his information. His sneering response had been that they could fire him. Pierre would have loved to do just that. But even if his partner would agree, he couldn't ethically fire someone because Sarah was the target of the same kind of gossip *Le Combattant* published about others.

Afterward he'd rushed to Sarah's flat and found her gone. Restlessly, he'd paced the street, then come into the bookshop for something to do while he waited for her to return home. When he'd seen her arrive with Armand, he'd stayed in the shop. He wanted to see her alone. What he didn't want were the feelings of jealousy that were plaguing him while he waited.

"Do you like Madame Rachilde's work?" It was the shop owner, a middle-aged woman with a tired but pleasant face.

"Madame Rachilde?" He wasn't expecting a literary discussion.

She pointed to the book in his hand. It was a copy of *Monsieur Vénus*. "Did you know," she said, "that a court in Belgium, where this was published, convicted Madame Rachilde of obscenity? She'd be in prison now if she didn't live in Paris."

"Yes, I knew that," he said impatiently, wanting her to leave him alone.

"I think," she continued indignantly, "that it's because in her book it's the woman who sets up her lover in her apartment. Men keep mistresses all the time, but those judges didn't like the idea a woman might do the same thing."

Across the way Armand came out and walked away down the street. "You may be right," Pierre said, and handed the shop owner the book.

"Don't you want to take it?" she asked as he started toward the door.

"Perhaps. I'll come back another day."

As he left, he heard her mutter, "Just like a man. Can't stand the idea of a woman who's better than he is."

Pierre dashed across to Sarah's building and took the stairs two at a time. When he knocked on the door, his heart was hammering from more than the swift climb up the stairs. As he waited for her to answer, he thought ironically that the woman in the bookshop was wrong. He wasn't afraid Sarah was better than he was. The idea he was having trouble with was one he'd been crazy enough to promote—that she might think Armand was better. Especially now after this business with Gille. The rage he'd felt when he saw the column flared again. Gille, that jackass!

When Sarah opened the door, he said, "I want to talk to you."

Her eyes widened and her eyebrows went up, then came together in a frown. "That's good," she retorted, "because I want to talk to you."

He realized his emotions had spilled over into his voice. "I'm sorry," he said, following her into the drawing room. "I didn't mean to snap at you. I'm angry at Gille, not you."

"Why?"

"What do you mean—why?"

"Why are you angry with Gille?"

Her question threw him off balance. She was nervous; he could see that in the way she kept smoothing the side of her skirt. He tried to modulate his voice. "I'm angry because I know you're upset by what he wrote."

"Then if it didn't bother me, you wouldn't object to his column?"

"Just a minute, Sarah." He was beginning to feel under attack. "I'm not sure what you mean. I don't let people like Gille affect me. I'm used to them. But you're not. What are you trying to say?"

She half turned, as if she were going to walk away, then turned back. After a moment's hesitation, she said, "How did Gille know we went to Etretat?"

Instantly he knew what she was thinking. A new, more disturbing anger mingled with the old. "Are you really asking if I told him?"

Her troubled face lost the last of its usual color. "Did you?"

That she would ask the question was painful to a degree that appalled him. But he was damned if he'd let her know how much. "No. I didn't tell him," he said icily.

"I didn't think you would," she said, distress clear in the shakiness of her voice. "But . . . no one else knew where we were going. Except Armand. He said he didn't tell Gille."

Her reference to Armand brought back Pierre's confused emotions when he'd been waiting in the bookstore. The feeling that he'd behaved in a humiliating way then added to his anger. "Apparently you believe him readily enough. Did he suggest I talked to Gille?"

"No. He said he thought you hadn't."

"Then I have a defender, but that obviously isn't convincing." Sarcasm was wrong, but he couldn't seem to stop himself. "Have you consulted everyone else about this? What do they say?"

He recognized the defiant lifting of her head that meant he'd goaded her and she wouldn't retreat. "Solange showed me the article. She pointed out that gossip helps the circulation of your paper."

"And we mustn't overlook increasing Armand's interest in you. From the way he rushed to your side, that's been accomplished already. Also, there's your career. Publicity can help that along."

She turned white. "Help my career! I had to plead with the director to keep him from dismissing me."

"Cesbron! I'd forgotten him." Pierre's anger waned. "Sarah, let's not quarrel. I didn't tell Gille. I don't know how he found out. But there's nothing I can do about it."

The tense lines around her mouth softened. "I believe you, but isn't there something you can do?"

"No. I don't edit Gille's column, and even if I did, I don't have the right to change its content."

"You fought with that other columnist—Vernoy."

They weren't resolving anything, but now he wasn't ready to back down either. "It doesn't do any good to challenge someone over gossip. A duel only makes sure that more people hear about it."

"Isn't that what you want? More readers for your paper?"

"Not at your expense."

The color was back in her face, and her eyes were giving

battle signals. But he didn't want to do battle; conflict with Sarah was too painful. Perhaps they'd become too involved. He should have stuck to his first ideas about her and Armand. Maybe that would be better for her, and for him too.

Quietly he said, "Gille and I have detested each other for a long time. He's really aiming at me. If you and I aren't linked, he won't bother you. The gossip will die down. Gille will find something else to write about. If you're seen with Armand, that will help."

"You mean that you and I just shouldn't go out in public together?"

He wanted to say yes, but meeting privately wouldn't protect her. "Since I don't know how Gille gets his information, the best thing to do is for us not to see each other for a while. I'll be busy on the elections anyway. It's probably a good time to work on upsetting Aunt Nathalie." He tried for a smile to go with the last comment, but he didn't manage it.

Sarah looked at him for several moments without responding. He thought he saw the beginning of a quiver to her mouth, but she pressed her lips together and it stopped. She sighed, reminding him of a colt who has been resisting a bridle but has finally given in. "I suppose you're right about not seeing each other. And about Armand—that's what you wanted all along, isn't it?"

At this point he wasn't sure what he'd wanted all along. He did know it wasn't what he wanted now, but it might be the best outcome for both of them. He hesitated, then said, "Yes, I suppose it is."

CHAPTER EIGHTEEN

A FANFARE OF TRUMPETS CALLED FOR ATTENTION AT THE Hippodrome de Longchamp. Near one end of the racetrack a jockey quieted a skittish horse. Men and women who waited in line at the betting booths or crowded the lawn in front of the grandstand turned to look. Officers of the Guarde Municipale, their dark blue uniforms set off by red braid, formed two lines. Between them, several men in black suits and tall silk hats walked solemnly to the Presidential Box.

"Is that President Carnot with his cabinet?" Sarah asked. She was standing with Armand on the lawn, near the railing around the track.

"No. They're members of the Paris Municipal Council, which sponsors today's prize. This race is not as important as the Grand Prix, and the president isn't here."

"I think everyone else must be." The dark suits of men predominated, along with a confusion of colorful dresses and parasols. Near Sarah a man with a mustache waxed to thin points talked to a woman whose dress had fur trimming on every possible edge or seam. Beyond them two young women in emerald and russet dresses consulted a list of horses.

A monotonous clacking, sharp and insistent, came from the machines which were stamping betting tickets. Over its constant noise the words that Sarah heard were mostly French-accented English. "Why are so many people speaking English?"

"The horse-racing terms are English," Armand said in French, "so it's fashionable to speak English at the track."

Sarah and Armand had spent afternoons and evenings together frequently during the past month, but she wasn't sure she knew him better. "Do you care about what's in fashion?" she asked.

He looked a little surprised, as if he'd never considered that before. "Yes, if it's reasonable. Other people's opinions do affect us."

Gille's and Monsieur Cesbron's had certainly affected her. But she'd promised herself not to think about that.

The mid-October day was cool but sunny. Earlier at the Café de la Cascade in the Bois de Boulogne, Armand had sent his carriage and his coachman back. "It's too crowded to arrive by way of the main gate," he'd explained, "and afterward we can have tea and listen to the waterfall and wait for the carriage to be brought around." That was typical of Armand; he planned activities carefully, always with thought to what would make her comfortable. They had walked to the Longchamp Hippodrome through the gardens, where the air had the pungent dry-leaf smell of autumn.

Now he said, "The procession will begin soon. Would you like me to place a bet for you?"

"I don't know anything about the horses."

"Well, let's see." He concentrated. "The last three years the horses of the Duc de Vertus have finished among the first three. His horse might be a good choice, but he has a new jockey and..."

Sarah quit listening. Armand nearly always told her more facts than she wanted to know. When he finished his recital, she said wickedly, "I think there's a horse whose name begins with an S. I'd like to bet on that one."

Armand's smile looked slightly forced, but he went off to the betting booths.

From Sarah's position at the rail, she could see jockeys lining up their horses for the procession past the grandstand. She admired the riders' silks and white pants, which set off the glossy browns and blacks of the horses. One jockey, in a brilliant yellow shirt with orange sleeves, was leaning down, apparently soothing a beautiful chestnut mare with a dramatic white blaze on her forehead. Sarah decided arbitrarily that the chestnut was her horse.

"Sarah." The familiar voice vibrated over her skin like the first lustrous oboe note of *Swan Lake*, promising the intoxicating music to come. She turned, her undisciplined heart beating rapidly, hopefully. Pierre looked as she had been imagining him too often: rebellious curls of hair over the back of his neck and above his ears. The dark, thick mustache. Straight eyebrows over eyes that knew so many intimate things about her. The scar had faded during the six weeks since she'd seen him. "Hello, Pierre," she said softly.

"Are you here with Armand?" His expression was guarded when she wanted eagerness.

She ignored her disappointed heart. "Yes. He just went to place a bet for me."

"Then he'll be a while. The lines are long."

Such an ordinary conversation, when there were a hundred things she longed to say! But her pride wouldn't let her. She clamped the words tight inside where they settled into a painful lump just below her breastbone. Instead she said, "Congratulations on the way the elections came out."

"I don't deserve credit," he said, but his pleased grin was less modest. "Did you hear the final totals? The Boulangists won only thirty-eight seats."

"So the Republicans are in control?"

"Until the next crisis."

She wanted to ask whether he regretted anything the campaign cost him, but that was a forbidden question. "I've been going to the Paris salons with Armand," she said brightly. "I've learned a lot. The Princess Mathilde Bonaparte doesn't like young painters and serves mediocre food. Madame Natanson encourages new artists and will pose for them to do her portrait. The wines from Madame de Loynes' cellar are the best in Paris. If a writer wants to be elected to the French Academy, he needs a wealthy and witty hostess who will promote him faithfully at her salon."

Pierre was looking at her with concern, but her words seemed to spill out without her control. "And there's always lots of gossip. I've been told the Prince de Broglie was only twenty when he married the Baronne Deslandes, who was forty, and that writers regularly fall in love with her. I also heard that a friend of one of the hostesses reproached her for taking an inappropriate lover. She excused herself by saying the weather had been too unpleasant to go out and that she had nothing else to do. And—"

"Sarah," he interrupted, "are you getting along all right?"

She felt the beginning of the blush she hated. Her ridiculous chattering had only exposed her disarray. "Oh, yes. I'm fine." She looked away from his perceptive eyes, as if keeping track of the horses. "Gille hasn't written anything more about me," she said, pleased she sounded so composed. She couldn't help looking back at him. "Do you think Gille's lost interest in me by now?"

A muscle twitched along the side of his face. "I'm not sure. I'm afraid that when I got so angry at him the day the column came out, I furnished him with a target."

Hope turned into dismay. That wasn't what she wanted to hear.

As she and Pierre looked at each other, longing swelled

inside her—to reach out, to touch his face, to trace the edge of his mouth, to feel again his soft mustache brushing her lips. His eyes changed into an expression she couldn't read. "How are you and Armand getting along?" he asked.

She had the sense that he wasn't asking exactly what he wanted to know. Regardless of her distress and yearning, she couldn't push herself at him again. "We're getting along very well." If that wasn't completely true yet, she would give herself the chance for it to be true.

A ripple of applause began, and a man near them said, "The procession is beginning."

Pierre's eyes retreated to casual friendliness. "I'd better be returning to the box."

The box. The meaning assaulted her painfully. He was with someone. Otherwise he'd be staying down by the railing.

"Since Armand's so busy," he said, "Aunt Nathalie called on me to be her escort. If she's not angry with me for leaving her alone now, I may see you at someone's Sunday afternoon. Good-bye for now."

He was here with his aunt! As she watched him disappear into the crowd, the day recovered its brilliance.

In a few minutes Armand returned and handed her a yellow and red ticket. It was for a wager of one hundred francs—twenty dollars! Once she wouldn't have been shocked, but she'd learned the value of money during the past year. "Thank you, Armand," she said, and wished she'd listened to his assessment of stables and jockeys. "Which is my horse?"

"Sans Peur is the black horse with the jockey in turquoise silks," he said stiffly.

"Fearless. That's a nice name." She guessed from Armand's face that he thought "Senseless" would be more appropriate.

The horses were moving past in procession to the starting post. Cheers greeted each mount. A black horse toward the end sidestepped skittishly as if determined to go back to the paddock. Sarah looked anxiously, but the jockey wore orange and black, not turquoise. After the horses passed them, Armand said, "Do you want to go up into the stands?"

They might see Pierre again. At the appeal of that prospect, she wavered in her resolve to give friendship with Armand a real chance. But she disciplined herself and said, "No, let's stay by the rail."

When the horses were lined up, a black horse made a false start, and the jockey wasn't able to get his mount settled back in line. Sarah was relieved to see it was not Sans Peur. It would be too embarrassing if her choice weren't even in the race.

The race began. She cheered wildly, but when the horses had thundered by and the winner had been decided, Sans Peur might as well not have started. He came in next to last. The winner was a horse owned by the Duc de Vertus. Armand didn't say anything, earning her gratitude. In all his actions with her he'd shown he was a kind man. For the remaining races, she contented herself with deciding silently which horse would win and concluded that she would have to have Armand's wealth if she wanted to gamble at the races.

As they were walking back to the Café de la Cascade, she thought of Pierre's question. Was she getting along all right? She should be. Her job and lessons, which she loved, hadn't changed. She wasn't sure if she enjoyed the salons. They weren't as interesting as quieter occasions with Armand. Then he talked about his ambitions for his country. He cared passionately that France should be strong and have a glorious future. At those times he lost his gravity and seemed very human. She could understand why Pierre cared so much about him. Then why wasn't she happy and content?

In hopeful moments she told herself that because of Pierre's love and admiration for Armand, he was unselfishly concealing his love for her. Someday he'd realize how much he loved her and . . . But she was foolish to yearn so for him when he seemed to get along well without her.

When she and Armand reached the café, several bicycles were leaning against the entrance. "Do you like to bicycle?" she asked him.

"Occasionally. Would you like to come to the Bois and ride?" he offered politely.

She thought of the zest with which she and Pierre had raced against each other. "Thank you, but I think not."

On a night in mid-October the boxes at the Paris Opéra were full of jeweled women and men in tuxedos, but Sarah couldn't have described anyone else there. She gripped the railing of the Saint-Maurice box, oblivious to everything but the music. It was *Otello*, the newest Verdi opera, based on Shakespeare's *Othello*, and she was enthralled. On stage Emilia was helping Desdemona take off her regal robes and put on her nightdress. Tears ran down Sarah's face, but she was hardly aware she was crying. Soon Desdemona would die, and Sarah thought that she could bear it only because the music was so beautiful.

She felt a hand on top of hers. It was Armand. Gently he held her gloved hand in his, offering comfort. When Otello's lifeless body lay beside Desdemona and the curtain fell, Sarah realized she had been digging her fingers into Armand's hand. "I'm sorry," she said, releasing it.

In the week since she'd resolved to know him better, he'd sought her company constantly. He attended every performance at the Opéra Comique and arranged for them to attend this *Otello*. Sarah thought at first he had a passion for music, but she'd decided it was interest in her. That pleased her, though at moments like this, she wished he understood better how compelling music was to her.

He moved her chair so that she could get up. The music

remained in her head, and she wanted to explain how she felt. "Every time I see an opera, I imagine myself playing the mezzo-soprano role. You thought I was sitting in the box tonight, but really I was Emilia. How I would love to sing that part, here at the Opéra. Or anywhere."

"Perhaps you will sometime," he said, but clearly he was only being polite. As they went into the anteroom and he helped her on with her cape, the music left her.

They crossed the enormous foyer and her spirits lifted again. She'd read in *Le Courrier Français*, the journal that loved to attack conventional arts, that the opera house was a demonstration of bad taste. But to her it was like a beautiful woman whose vulgar tastes were so extravagant that she had a style all her own. Sarah loved the paintings of classical figures representing Melody and Harmony on the ceilings and the ten glittering chandeliers. From the tall columns, crowned with gilt statues, to the parquet floors, inlaid with gold sunbursts, the room delighted her. In honor of this occasion she had indulged in a new black velvet dress. When she and Armand descended the grand staircase with its two sweeping sides and balconies rising three floors all around, she felt as if she were royalty.

She stole a quick glance at Armand; he looked distracted, as if he were thinking of something else. The yearly rental for the box they'd occupied was twenty-five thousand francs. Though her father was wealthy, they hadn't lived in a style that spent five thousand dollars so easily. Apparently the cost meant nothing to Armand's family, and he must have attended often. She shouldn't expect a night at the opera to be as exciting to him as to her.

Outside on the loggia she saw Ted Kearns and greeted him warmly. She and Ted still hadn't discussed her unfortunate visit to his room. For a while she'd felt uncomfortable, but he acted as if nothing had occurred to change their relationship. She realized that nothing really had; they still had the same memories from Boston in common and the ties from her childhood. He was the same friend who'd helped her here when she'd asked.

After a brief exchange of comments about the opera, she waited for Armand to invite Ted to accompany them to supper. However, they came to good-byes without the customary invitation. When Ted departed, Armand looked slightly uncomfortable, and he took her elbow with unusual firmness to cross the Place de l'Opéra and turn left into the Boulevard des Italiens.

When they reached the Maison Dorée, he said, "We're dining here. I hope that suits you," and escorted her inside without waiting for her response. After a waiter showed them upstairs to one of the private dining rooms, she understood. The room was the same one where they'd first dined together. She was touched by his sentiment in wanting to return.

The divan with its convenience for lovemaking and the door that could be locked from the inside no longer intimidated her. She felt confident she could discourage any attentions she didn't want, and Armand always behaved properly. At the moment he seemed the one who was uncomfortable. The faint circles under his eyes were more pronounced, making him look especially serious. He drank the first glass of champagne quickly and silently.

Apparently conversation was up to her. "You didn't say what you thought of the opera."

"Oh, yes. Lovely music."

There was no hope of talking about the performance with someone who called Verdi's triumph "lovely music."

She tried again with a topic that never failed. "Have you heard from your friend who's been sent to Algeria?"

"No."

Fortunately the waiter brought the first courses of fish paté and a consommé with eggs. They were both delicious, but Armand ignored the paté and had only a mouthful of his soup. She was perplexed. If he weren't a sophisticated man in his thirties, she'd think he was a boy uncertain how to talk to a girl he was infatuated with. He admired her, she knew, but not to the extent of being tongue-tied. When the roast partridges arrived and Armand looked at them with disinterest, she put down her knife and fork. "Armand, what is wrong?"

He flushed, a color worthy of the blushes she could achieve. "It's ridiculous, but I don't know how to tell you."

"Please try, or I won't be able to eat anything either."

He reached past the forest of wineglasses and took her hand. For several seconds he held it without speaking. Finally he said, "Sarah, I want to marry you."

Stunned, she stared at him. Her first unbidden thought was the wrong one—this should be Pierre. She pushed it away and waited for the excitement that should come. His desire to marry her was immensely flattering. She should be thrilled at having someone so attractive propose to her. Someone considerate and admirable. Though he hadn't said so, he surely loved her because she was hardly a suitable choice for someone with his social position and wealth.

"You don't have to answer now," he said, and Sarah realized she hadn't responded.

"I don't know how I feel," she said, and that was certainly honest.

"Of course. I know you weren't expecting this." He smiled, relaxed and confident, as if only her consent remained in question and that it was fairly sure.

Probing, she said, "I know that many French people think of Americans as outsiders. And I'm a singer. My profession isn't always considered respectable. What about your family? Would your mother object?"

Momentarily his mouth tightened into grim, almost bitter lines. Then the expression vanished. "I have honored my mother's wishes in many things," he said calmly. "She will accept my decision in this . . . matter."

Sarah wondered if *peccadillo* or *aberration* had come to his mind before he settled on *matter*.

Though Armand began to eat with pleasure, her appetite had vanished. She managed only a few bites of the rest of the meal, even the coffee parfait at the end, which she loved.

As he ate, he returned to her question about Algeria, his interest carrying the conversation with minimal responses from her. While he talked, she watched him. How strange, she mused. He had proposed to her, but he'd never kissed her as a man does a woman he desires. Did she want him to?

She wasn't sure she'd marry him or anyone, but yes, she did want to kiss him. Intimacy with Pierre had ended painfully, but when they made love, she had felt gloriously alive. Armand was handsome and elegant; according to those early remarks by Solange, he was a skillful lover. If she learned to love him, she might experience those wonderful sensations again.

Solange's advice was to take many lovers before marriage. She would certainly urge Sarah to let Armand make love to her. However, Sarah recognized, though the year in Paris had changed her, she couldn't picture herself with many lovers, or with Armand. Still, she was drawn to him. His love might be an antidote to the hurt of missing Pierre.

Later, when Armand and Sarah arrived at her flat, he kissed her hand in the ritual way, but this time he didn't release her. Instead, with his other hand he lifted her chin. "You are very lovely, Sarah," he murmured.

With a catch of excitement in her stomach, she waited for his kiss.

At first it felt strange, the light pressure of his lips against hers. The scent wasn't what her memory expected, or the angle of their lips. The mustache felt wrong—too soft. Then his mouth became hungrier; little shivers trailed down from where his fingers stroked her neck. She welcomed the heat of his lips and returned the kiss, letting the pleasurable warmth sweep over her skin.

When they broke apart, he said huskily, "I've been wanting to kiss you for a long time."

"I'm glad you did."

After another ardent kiss, he said reluctantly, "I suppose I'd better go. You can make me forget everything else."

For a moment she'd forgotten—no, not forgotten Pierre, but being without him hadn't mattered so much.

Nathalie, the Comtesse de Saint-Maurice, was accustomed to getting her own way by subtle means, but Armand had shocked her. "You want to marry a woman who's an opera singer—and an American? That is out of the question. I can't believe you have such complete absence of judgment!"

"Mother," he said, and she heard anger in that word. "I consider your wishes in most things. Perhaps in too many. In this matter, I have made up my mind."

They were in the anteroom of Nathalie's bedroom. It was designed as a sitting room, but she'd installed there the large desk and massive cabinets that were once in her husband's office. The furniture was patterned after pieces that had been in Napoleon III's study in the Tuileries. Nathalie claimed she kept it because it reminded her of her late husband, but secretly she still used it because of her conviction that she, unlike her husband, had the character to have been an emperor. If she were, she thought furiously, her son would not be sitting across from her, announcing he planned to ruin his life and hers with it.

"If you think about this for a time," she said, managing with great effort to speak in a reasonable voice, "the whim may well pass."

He gave her a look that had a frightening lack of affection.

"It's not a whim. I have spoken to Sarah. She naturally couldn't respond immediately, but I'm sure she'll accept."

"But you know nothing of her family."

"We met her father."

She dismissed that. "For a few minutes on the stairway in the Louvre."

"Sarah has also told me about her life in New England," he said coldly. "She comes from a very respectable family."

Nathalie started to reach for the pocket in which she kept her smelling salts and found her hands were trembling. She folded them in her lap. The fixed lines around Armand's mouth warned her not to produce the faintness of breath and pain in her chest that she'd used so well in the past. Her daughters had been so easy to manage. They'd obediently married the men she chose. Armand had balked at her arrangements, but he'd bowed to her will about his career and she'd been sure he'd eventually give in about marriage. Now this!

Her rage swelled like an enormous fire, threatening to consume her. Ruthlessly she suppressed it. Now was the time for reason, not emotion. A marriage, even to anyone as ill-bred as an American, couldn't be arranged overnight. If she couldn't override Armand, there would be other ways to save the situation. "Very well. Tell me all about Mademoiselle Taylor and her father."

Sarah and Armand followed the black and silver-suited footman into the ballroom of Madame Dubreuil's mansion. Like her drawing room, everything was black and white. On the dais at one end a woman at a piano waited while a violinist tuned his instrument. Sarah and Armand went to speak to Madame Dubreuil.

The countess, dramatic as always with her painted face and white flowing robe, greeted them cordially. Julien Lemaire, her much younger lover, was with her. To Sarah's eyes, more accustomed now to Parisian life, the age difference between them no longer seemed noticeable. "Please find seats," Madame Dubreuil said, "and enjoy the music."

After Armand located places on the side, Sarah saw Pierre with Nathalie Saint-Maurice sitting on one side of him and a woman Sarah didn't recognize on the other. He was talking to the strange woman. She had dark hair and eyes and an exotic, alluring face, like the Middle-Eastern dancers at the exposition. Pain wrapped around Sarah like a winding sheet, pressing on her until she felt as if she were no longer breathing. She looked down at her hands and willed the pain to subside.

It did no good to think of Pierre, she reminded herself sternly. In spite of what they'd shared, he'd turned her over to his cousin. No—that wasn't fair. Pierre was protecting her from Gille, and her involvement with Armand had been the plan all along. A plan she'd agreed to. And he hadn't initiated their affair. She had. So she had no right to complain. In spite of her lecture to herself, she couldn't keep from looking at him again. The strange woman had turned to a man on her other side and was speaking into his ear. It appeared to be the familiar gesture of a wife with her husband. Maybe she wasn't with Pierre. Sarah wanted to believe that.

Only then did she realize that Armand's mother was staring straight at her. Sarah had never seen such a malevolent expression. Fear slithered across her skin like a snake, leaving her shivering. She'd known Nathalie wouldn't like Armand's interest in her. That was the original purpose of her involvement with him. But she hadn't expected hatred.

She turned quickly to give her attention to the musicians. After the audience quieted, the music began. The pianist and violist played Liszt's "Liebestraum," but for once Sarah had trouble listening. When the music stopped, Sarah applauded as if she could keep the musicians playing by the force of her response. But after another bow, the violinist put aside his instrument, and he and the pianist left the dais. Armand got up from the chair beside her. Reluctantly Sarah rose also. Until the music began again, she would have to mingle with other guests.

"Would you care for wine?" Armand asked. At her yes he went toward the refreshment table.

Snippets of conversation drifted around Sarah. A woman in a hat with two stuffed bluebirds perched on it said to another woman, "Jeanne has a new lover."

"Yes, I know. But how can she stand him? Adolphe is so ugly."

"He gave her a coach and four, with jeweled bridles for the horses. No man with that much money is ugly."

A different pair of women were arguing about music. "Wagner doesn't write music," one said. "It's just noise."

Ordinarily Sarah would have wanted to join them, or at least listen. But she was looking for Nathalie and Pierre. She saw him, standing with Armand near the refreshment table. Armand had his hand on Pierre's arm, talking earnestly. The two men went into a small salon off the ballroom. Sarah looked farther and located Nathalie. Armand's mother was greeting acquaintances, circling the room but slowly getting closer. Sarah felt as if she were in the center of a spider's web.

She looked for someone she knew, but there was no one close. She decided to go back and speak to Madame Dubreuil again when Nathalie's voice behind her said, "Mademoiselle Taylor, how pleasant to see you."

Nathalie was wearing a dark blue dress trimmed with scarlet braid around the collar and cuffs. A little like the *gendarmes*, Sarah thought, and the ridiculous comparison reduced her nervousness. That, and the genuine-looking smile Nathalie was offering.

Unable to avoid the polite lie, Sarah said, "I'm pleased to

see you also." Could she have imagined the hatred earlier, or was it well concealed?

"I believe you've seen *Otello*," Nathalie said. "What did you think of the tenor? I understand that his opening music is difficult because the orchestra is playing very boldly at that time."

Surprised at the specific question, Sarah said, "The tenor's entrance was very well sung. I could hear Tamagno perfectly."

Nathalie nodded appreciatively, her regal stance relaxed. "I'm told Petrovich is very good as Emilia. I enjoy the mezzo-soprano range. Do you regret sometimes that you aren't a soprano? There are so many more important roles for sopranos." She appeared truly sympathetic.

Sarah smiled more easily. "That's true, but since I'm in the chorus, it doesn't make much difference."

"You never know what will happen."

Across the room in the small side salon, Pierre faced Armand, hoping he hadn't heard correctly. "You asked Sarah to marry you?"

"Yes."

Pierre felt as if, without knowing it, he'd been entered in a boxing match with someone who'd just landed a stunning blow to his midsection. "What did she say?"

Armand smiled happily. "Of course she was surprised. She said she didn't know how she felt." His smile faded into a look of concern. "You've been urging me to make up my mind about what I wanted, so I thought you'd be pleased. You and she were . . . close friends. But that was a while ago."

"I didn't know you were considering marriage." Pierre trusted he sounded more reasonable than he felt.

"Pierre, I'm in love with her," Armand said earnestly. "She's the most appealing woman I've met in years."

"Does Aunt Nathalie know?"

"Yes, I told her. She was shocked, of course. But she accepted the idea."

That didn't sound like Aunt Nathalie who, Pierre realized, might be with Sarah right now. "Let's go back to the ball-room," he said, and started without waiting for Armand's agreement.

When he spotted Sarah and Nathalie, he led the way quickly through the clusters of guests. Contrary to what he'd feared, when he reached Sarah, she looked at ease. Nathalie smiled serenely and said, "Mademoiselle Taylor and I were having a pleasant chat about music. We plan to continue it another time soon. Now it appears the musicians are ready to play again."

Armand looked reassured, but Pierre wasn't. After he settled his aunt in her chair, her smile still disturbed him. It looked to him too satisfied. He decided they must have a personal talk.

When the entertainment was over, he steered her away from Armand and Sarah. Later in the carriage on the way back to the gloomy Faubourg-Saint Germain house that Nathalie loved so much, he steeled himself to talk about the subject he'd rather forget. He began bluntly, always the best way with her. "Armand told me he's asked Sarah to marry him."

"So he says. A man often proposes marriage to a naive woman when all he intends is to make her his mistress." Nathalie's face was in shadow, so Pierre didn't have clues whether she felt as serene as she sounded.

"Perhaps Armand doesn't have enough to occupy him." Pierre didn't have to say more; Nathalie knew he believed Armand should be in politics.

What she didn't know, Pierre thought, was how much he hoped Armand would choose politics over Sarah. Then perhaps things would work out for Sarah and him—if it weren't already too late. Tonight Sarah looked happy, and Armand sounded like a teenager in love for the first time.

"You don't seem pleased about Armand's marriage plans," Nathalie observed. "Don't worry, Pierre. I'm sure things will work out well."

Something in her voice alerted him. She sounded too confident. It wasn't like her to give in about anything this readily. Uneasily he wondered what plans of her own she might be making.

CHAPTER
NINETEEN

I N NATHALIE DE SAINT-MAURICE'S DINING ROOM, CHANDE-
liers lit with a hundred candles enticed rainbows from
the cut crystal wine glasses. A footman in evening dress
stopped behind Sarah's chair and whispered, "Château Laf-
itte or Château Margaux?" She shook her head, and he
moved on. At the far end of the table, Pedro Gailhard,
Director of the Paris Opéra, was talking with Nathalie. For
most of the meal Sarah had been too agitated to eat, and
she didn't need more wine.

Before dinner Armand's mother had introduced her to
Monsieur Gailhard and mentioned that Sarah sang at the
Opéra Comique. He had acknowledged the introduction
with the superior cordiality of his position compared to hers,
and not a trace of recognition. Of course he wouldn't remember her after a year. But she remembered! Her vivid
memory of his disdainful rebuff could still evoke a feeling
of humiliation. Now, at the same table with him, she was
torn between contrary and delicious fantasies. In one she
enchanted him with her singing and then—while he grov-
eled on his knees, pleading for her to sing at the Opéra—

she refused. In the other she enchanted him and accepted.

Another source of her agitation was Armand. He knew Gailhard, or at least had met him, and had never told her or asked whether she'd like an introduction.

The thirty guests were a mixture of ages but in clothing so similar as to be uniforms: men in formal black evening wear, women in swirls of colored ruffles, with bare shoulders and boldly displayed bosoms, and jewels enough to finance the French army. Sarah's black velvet dress and strand of single pearls were almost abnormal. Most of the men seemed to be occupied by being wealthy. A few were businessmen. One banker, a tall, nervous-looking man named Adolphe Fuzelier, was especially attentive to Nathalie. Sarah wondered fleetingly if he could be Nathalie's lover, but it was impossible to imagine anyone as haughty as Nathalie making love.

The meal ended, and the women went into the main drawing room, leaving the men to smoke. Sarah followed reluctantly. This was the second time she'd been invited to dinner by Nathalie, and she guessed the conversation would be dull. Although the most aristocratic of the Faubourg Saint-Germain families didn't dine with Nathalie, she followed their customs. Science and literature were unacceptable topics for men or women. Even the gossip lacked spice. The taking of lovers and mistresses had gone on for most of human existence, and divorce had been legal in France for five years. But to judge by the talk, no one participated in any but the accepted rituals of birth, marriage and death.

Too restless to sit down, Sarah wandered around the room, examining the pictures, and on into the adjacent drawing room. As she paused in front of a tapestry depicting Mars and an adulterous Venus, caught in Vulcan's net, she heard the rustle of layers of silk. It was a large, rather stout woman who walked with a pronounced limp. She looked to be perhaps ten years older than Sarah. Her appearance was a curious mixture of opulence and simplicity. In the gas lights a jeweled collar glittered with the fire of what appeared to be dozens of diamonds. Brown hair was drawn back severely from her plain face. Sarah searched her mind for the name. They'd been introduced earlier but seated far apart at dinner. Madame Houdon—yes, that was it.

"Do the tapestries appeal to you, Mademoiselle Taylor?" Madame Houdon asked. She had a husky, pleasant voice.

"The love story of Mars and Venus has inspired a lot of artists," Sarah said diplomatically.

A mischievous smile transformed Madame Houdon's plain face into one of charm, like the difference between the masks of tragedy and comedy. She lowered her voice to a mock confidential whisper. "I am so misguided as to prefer works by Manet and Degas. But I don't offend Nathalie's guests by saying so."

Sarah laughed. It was a treat to hear something besides platitudes.

Madame Houdon said, "Nathalie has told me about you— that you're from Boston and how talented you are. I understand you're in the Opéra Comique chorus. Do you like it there?"

Sarah was surprised that Nathalie had spoken so kindly of her, but she responded happily, "Oh, yes, I love singing."

"I can guess that you would also love being in the chorus at the Opéra. I saw you watching Monsieur Gailhard at dinner," Madame Houdon said, in such a sympathetic voice that Sarah felt understood rather than embarrassed. "Once I dreamed of being an actress. I made up little scenes and acted them out with my friends. That was many years ago, but I remember that one day a traveling theater troupe came to the village near our estate. I felt about the manager the way I think you must feel about Monsieur Gailhard."

In the face of the other woman's obvious limp, Sarah felt uncertain how to respond. "I suppose lots of us have dreams like that when we're children," she said. "I always wanted to be a singer."

"And your dream has come true. You had better luck than I did." Madame Houdon's smile faded and tight lines pinched her mouth. She was looking at Sarah but as if she were really seeing scenes from the past. "I wasn't lame then. My father loved drink more than anything or anyone else. Once when he'd had too much brandy, he . . . there was an accident. It left me with a limp. Women who limp don't get a chance to act on the stage."

Appalled, Sarah said, "I'm sorry. That must have been terrible."

"Yes, it was," Madame Houdon said in a bitter voice. "My father came from a good family, but he spent all his inheritance on drink. So we were very poor. But we had to pretend we weren't. That was the only kind of acting I got to do. By the time his abuse had killed my mother, I was determined I would never live that way again. I worked as a servant and housekeeper until I married a man who was kind and steady. That made up for my dream."

She stopped, as if realizing what she was saying. Her face flushed with embarrassment. "I'm sorry. Please excuse me for speaking so intimately. Seeing you and Monsieur Gailhard took me back to years I never talk about. It's an unpleasant story, and I apologize for inflicting it on you."

The recital stirred Sarah's ready compassion. "You don't need to apologize. I admire your honesty."

Madame Houdon smiled again, in the way that illuminated her plain face. "Thank you. Nathalie predicted that I'd enjoy getting better acquainted with you, and she was right. Since I've told you my worst secrets, I hope we'll be friends. My name is Claudine."

Claudine—the feminine version of Claude. Sarah wished Madame Houdon had some other name. Claude Vernoy was the man who'd wounded Pierre in the duel. Ashamed of her reaction, she said warmly, "I would like that, Claudine. And I'm Sarah."

"I hear the men leaving the dining room," Claudine said. She and Sarah went back to the main drawing room just as the men arrived, bringing brandied smiles and the odor of tobacco with them. Monsieur Gailhard went to sit by Nathalie. Curious about Claudine's husband, Sarah studied Monsieur Houdon. He was slight, shorter and smaller than his wife, with dark brown hair and a narrow mustache. Gold-rimmed glasses sat above a thin, sharp nose. A nondescript-looking man. Perhaps, like his wife, he had charm that wasn't obvious in his appearance.

Armand joined Sarah. "Mama would like you to have a chance to talk to Monsieur Gailhard."

Surprised and nervous, she crossed the room to a seat beside Nathalie, who said, "I have been chiding Monsieur Gailhard for not getting better acquainted with you, Sarah."

The director smiled with polite but unenthusiastic interest. "How long have you been with the Opéra Comique, Mademoiselle Taylor?"

"Since last January." She was thankful for the limits on conversation that had irritated her earlier. No one would mention the hatpin incident with Rivarol or "La Belle Americaine."

"In what operas have you performed?"

"Everything they've done this year."

"They do present the less serious works very well," he said pompously.

Sarah was just phrasing her protest when he added, "We seldom have openings for our chorus, but I must remember to inquire about you when we do."

She swallowed her defense of the Opéra Comique. "That is kind of you."

"My dear *comtesse*," he said to Nathalie, "I must go. Thank you for a delightful evening. And for the opportunity to meet Mademoiselle Taylor. I won't forget her."

As he left, Sarah restrained her impulse to kiss him or else to run wildly about the room, asking everyone, "Did you hear? Did you hear?"

The next half hour passed in a fog in which Sarah nodded and smiled and spoke but without attention to anything but the exhilarating hope Gailhard's words had raised. When it was time to leave, she went to Nathalie with genuine feelings of gratitude. "Thank you, *comtesse*, for the evening, and for the introduction to Monsieur Gailhard."

Nathalie's regal demeanor unbent enough for her to say graciously, "I'll be pleased if something comes of it."

Sarah believed her. Armand's mother probably hoped that promoting Sarah's career would prevent a marriage with Armand. Her motives hardly mattered; the opportunity did.

Outside in the carriage, Armand said, "You look very happy. If I had known you wanted to meet Monsieur Gailhard, I would have arranged it."

"You didn't guess that I would?"

"No."

It occurred to her that his mother understood her better than he did.

Then he redeemed himself by saying, "It's not midnight. You're probably too excited to go home. Would you are to go to one of the music halls or café-concerts in Montmartre?"

"Oh, yes."

"We could try the new Moulin Rouge. Or there's a shadow-show at the Chat Noir. The Elysée Montmartre often has something new. I don't know what's there now, but we could see."

She debated. Helene had talked about the new Moulin Rouge pleasure garden. According to her enthusiastic description, the windmill on top was only the first of its imaginative decorations. The Chat Noir was known as a favorite of the Bohemian artists and writers, and for its presentation of picture-stories made by cut-outs held in front of a projector.

Before she could decide, Armand said, "We might see Pierre at either the Moulin Rouge or the Chat Noir. He's been going there with a woman who likes both those places."

Sarah's exhilaration drained away under a sudden thrust of pain. She managed to say brightly, "Let's try the Elysée Montmartre."

As the barouche rattled its way across the Pont des Arts, the reflection of the lights on the Seine from the Louvre didn't enchant her as they usually did. Twice she subdued her tormenting curiosity. Finally it overcame her. "The woman—Pierre's friend who likes the Moulin Rouge and Chat Noir—is she someone I've met?"

"I don't think so. Simone is a writer."

She hated writers! At least she hated women writers. No—she hated women named Simone. *Stop this!* she told herself. *Don't think about it.*

The Elysée Montmartre was a gaudy building near the corner of the Boulevard de Rochecourt and the Boulevard de la Chapelle. A poster outside announced: First Time in Paris. Watch Women Wrestling. Nightly.

Armand said doubtfully. "I haven't seen this kind of show. Women wrestling. It doesn't sound suitable."

Sarah wanted distraction, which this would be. "If men can wrestle, so can women. I want to see it." She started for the entrance.

Inside, the large room verified the advertisements for music halls as places where men could ignore the manners required in theaters and restaurants. Though there were women scattered through the audience, smoke from cigars and cigarettes drifted in blue-gray clouds through the room. Armand removed his formal silk hat, and Sarah saw other men in evening clothes who had done the same. But many men still wore their bowler hats. No waiter came to seat her and Armand, and they squeezed between the crowded chairs to places at the side.

On a small stage at one end of the room a man in a straw hat, striped shirt and checked pants sang a ditty about how cleverly he had avoided military service. Sarah glanced at Armand, thinking the song would offend his patriotic pride, but he didn't appear upset, and he laughed and applauded at the end.

The manager came out and bowed. "For your pleasure, we are presenting tonight a battle between two fair ladies. First, Rosette." After some introductory chords on the piano, a woman came out onto the stage. Sarah barely suppressed a gasp. The woman had on flesh-colored tights and ballet slippers, and a one-piece garment that looked like under-clothing a street-walker might hesitate to wear. It was red satin with narrow shoulder straps that barely held the low-cut bodice in place over her breasts. The garment ended with a strip of narrow black fringe at the top of her legs. She acknowledged wild cheers with a bow.

"And her opponent," the manager proclaimed, "Florette!" A second woman came out, and another roar of applause began. She was similarly dressed except that she wore blue silk with yellow fringe and had a ribbon of yellow satin around her neck.

Armand leaned close to Sarah's ear. "I'm sorry. Do you want to leave?"

"No." Other women nearby, the well-dressed ones and some who looked like working-class girls, were laughing and enjoying themselves. To leave would seem naive and unsophisticated. Besides, she was curious.

The wrestlers began circling, putting their feet out to trip each other, grasping at each other's arms. Soon they were grappling, pulling hairdos loose and howling in pain. Calls and cheers from the audience egged them on. After a fierce yank by Rosette, one strap of Florette's costume broke, leaving her bare breast swinging free. Shouts of "Take everything off," and "Let's see what Rosette has," accelerated to deafening levels. Florette attacked vigorously, and soon both of them were bare to the waist.

Finally, to Sarah's acute relief, Rosette succeeded in knocking Florette's feet out from under her and the match ended. Armand hadn't been yelling, but he applauded loudly at the end.

Sarah concluded the wrestling was designed so men could be titillated while watching women humiliate themselves. It disheartened her. What circumstances would bring women to perform such a show? She didn't know, and she understood even less why the women in the audience applauded.

After one more song from the man in the checked pants, this one about the faithlessness of women, she said to Armand, "I'd like to leave."

Outside, he said, "I wish I'd known what it would be like. We should have gone somewhere else."

"I was the one who decided," she said. He'd enjoyed it, but she couldn't blame him that she hadn't.

By the time they reached her flat, her dismay had faded. Women did lots of things to make money. If she hadn't been fortunate, what might she have tried? Not that, but she wasn't sure what.

Following what had become their custom, Armand stepped inside her doorway to kiss her good-night. This time he wasn't content with one kiss but held her closely, running his fingers along the back of her neck and returning to her mouth again and again. At first she held back. She felt as if she were a substitute for the women he'd watched wrestling. But then she found her desire responding to his.

"Sarah," he said, "you're so beautiful. You know I want to marry you. Can't you say yes?"

He did arouse her. She could feel it in her rapid pulse and tightened nipples. How good it felt to have his body pressed against hers. If he were passionate this time because of watching the wrestlers, she'd often responded to him because she was remembering Pierre. Foolish memories.

A yes trembled on her lips, but she didn't quite let it out. Not yet.

The wheels of Armand's landau made a crackling sound as they rolled over drifts of dead leaves on the graveled drive of the Saint-Maurice chateau. It was a week since the dinner and the evening in Montmartre. With the coachman driving, Armand and Sarah had made the hour's trip out from Paris, an excursion Armand had been eager for them to take. A few stubborn leaves still clung to the otherwise bare poplars and elms in the grassy park on either side. The odor of the leaves and of damp earth lingered in the air. Beyond a depression where the mist still resisted the midday sun she could see thick woods.

"Over there," Armand said enthusiastically, "we hunt fox and wild boar. And we have good fishing ponds and a stream for boating. I wish I had brought you to the chateau last summer. The flowers are beautiful then, especially the lilacs and roses. You'll see, next spring."

Sarah never knew how to respond to Armand's remarks that almost, but not quite, assumed that they would be together in the future. It usually seemed best to let them pass without comment.

The drive curved around and up a rise. At the top she saw a sprawling two-story stone building. "How old is the chateau?"

"Part of it was built in the sixteenth century. My great-grandfather acquired it in 1805."

"That's the one who was a general under the first Napoleon?"

"Yes," Armand said proudly, "the first Comte de Saint-Maurice."

The one Nathalie would like to pretend was of the old nobility, Sarah thought. Apparently Armand, too, took his ancestors seriously.

The carriage stopped between a large marble fountain and an entrance with elaborately carved columns on either side of massive double doors. Armand jumped down and helped her out before the coachman could leave his perch.

Inside, the house matched the entrance. "We'll see everything," Armand said, and went ahead of her like a child showing off.

"This is Mother's favorite room," he said when they entered a large drawing room crowded with Louis XV furniture. On one wall shepherds courted shepherdesses; another had paintings of men and women in white wigs at court balls. A clock stood on the parquet floor in front of a mirrored wall. It was taller than Armand, with an eagle at the top and a mosaic panel below the clock face depicting Napoleon I on a rearing horse. A smaller, adjacent room had black-lacquered tables, a Japanese screen across one corner, and scroll paintings on the wall. "I like this drawing room best," he said, but then hurried her on.

Though Sarah saw no servants, the house was impeccably cared for. Bouquets of roses and arrangements of hothouse orchids looked dew-fresh. In the ballroom she ran her fingers over the keys of a square grand piano that was perfectly in tune.

"Who takes care of all this?" she asked as they started up a curving staircase with a magnificent Persian runner.

"We have a large staff, but I sent them away today. I wanted to show you everything myself."

On the second floor they saw bedrooms with anterooms furnished as studies, a modern bathroom, and sewing and linen rooms. "As soon as electricity is available this far out," Armand said, "I'll have it installed."

The last room they went into was a large bedroom with

dressing rooms on either side. It overlooked a courtyard at the back where the woods came close to the house. Armand opened the windows. "Listen, and you can hear the stream."

She joined him and heard a soft murmur. He rested his hand on the back of her neck and rubbed it gently. "This will be our suite when we live here."

"Armand, I haven't—"

He didn't let her finish. "Of course, if there's anything you want to change, we'll do that. Workmen from the village are always eager for jobs."

She turned, pulling away from his hand, and faced him. "Armand! You must listen to me! You can't assume that I'll marry you. I don't know yet if I want to marry at all."

His eyes flared and the skin of his face tightened. He grasped her upper arms, as if he thought she would run away. "Sarah, I know at first I was a substitute for Pierre. But can't you see how much we would have here? I've given up things before that I really wanted. Not you."

"I'm not yours to give up," she protested, but his urgency stirred her.

"You must be." He pulled her close and lifted her chin. His kiss was both command and entreaty. She resisted the command, but the entreaty reached tenderness in her that was a twin of desire.

As he kissed her mouth, then her eyes and cheeks, her desire became less tenderness and more passion. He loosened her hair and pulled it aside to kiss her nape. At the touch of his lips, shivers ran along her spine. His hand slid under her breast, then brushed the nipple through her clothing, and she felt its instant response.

"I love you, Sarah," he said between kisses. "I know you love me too."

She supposed he was right because when his hands moved to the buttons of her dress, she didn't want him to stop.

His first touch on her bare shoulder set off quivers over

her skin, and at the same time felt a little frightening. The clumsy process of undressing called up a see-saw of emotions. His fingers lifting and caressing her naked breast made her impatient for more. When she saw the smooth skin of his bare chest, the sprinkling of blond hair around the nipples instead of whorls of dark hair seemed wrong. As she removed the last of her clothing, she was glad for the dim winter light.

Then they were together under the coverlet of the large bed. His naked body pressed against hers, his fingers discovered her secret places, and sensations obscured thought. The spiral began that carried her where only need existed— a need that was simultaneously a kind of pain and intense pleasure. When their bodies joined, it was as if she were still in her separate world. Only after her passion surged to its fulfillment and she felt his climax did she return to the sense of them together.

As sensation ebbed, her first thoughts were confused. She'd felt passion with Armand. Now she should feel—she wasn't sure what. Cherished, loved, loving. Convinced that she truly did love him. Not this apprehension that in some fundamental way she hadn't been true to herself.

They lay on their sides until she moved away. He brushed back her hair and kissed her. "This will be our bed," he said, "and we'll make love here and remember the first time." He sounded happy and satisfied—and triumphant.

"Armand, you mustn't count on marriage."

He laughed. "Yes, I know. You haven't agreed, but you will."

She slipped out from under the coverlet and began to gather her clothes. After a moment he rose also. She carried her belongings into the dressing room and closed the door. As she heard him moving around in the bedroom, she stood, trying to make sense of her feelings. When she'd lain with Pierre, she'd learned more about herself than she'd ever dreamed. Now she should know more, but instead she knew less.

A pitcher of water stood on the washstand. She filled the basin and started to wash then stopped as she realized what had *not* happened. Pierre had protected her against becoming pregnant. Armand had not.

A cold churning began in her stomach. One time didn't mean she would become pregnant. But it could. Why had she been so foolish! With Pierre she hadn't known enough to worry, and he had looked after her. She was less ignorant now. Solange had told her how to protect herself, but she hadn't been prepared here. Solange even warned her that most men once they're aroused don't think about possible consequences. She should have thought about the risk— insisted that Armand take precautions.

Shakily she resumed washing. The afternoon *had* taught her something. Passion could have a power of its own that was stronger than reason. At least she should understand her father better after this, but that thought didn't console her.

When she finished dressing and repinned her hair, she found Armand dressed and waiting. He smiled at her and said, "Do you want help with your buttons? I must get in practice, now that you're mine."

"I'm not a prize!"

"Of course I didn't mean you're an award. But I do prize you."

His response didn't satisfy her, but she couldn't offer a reason, so she went to straighten the coverlet on the bed.

"You shouldn't do that," he objected. "The servants will be back later. A maid will take care of it."

"The room is so lovely," she said. "It's a shame for it not to be neat." She didn't want anyone, even a maid, to know they'd made love there.

In the carriage the coachman's presence made intimate

conversation impossible. Armand, his half-melancholy expression obliterated in buoyant good humor, pointed out local landmarks. She looked and nodded and felt more and more depressed. He was right—she had been using him as a substitute for Pierre. How could she have misjudged herself so—to think that she loved Armand? Or that if she didn't, she could go to bed with him as casually as Solange had advised. She wasn't convinced he loved her either. Maybe her protest that she wasn't a prize missed the mark. Just as likely she was a weapon against his mother. That's what she'd agreed to be a year ago when she didn't know what it might cost her. She longed for the afternoon to end.

"Shall we stop at an inn for tea?" Armand asked. "There's a good one at Bézons."

"I have a performance tonight, so I have to go right to my flat." It was a relief to remind him.

He took her hand, and the message of his eyes was that if they weren't in the carriage, he would claim more of what he considered his. "Then I'll see you afterward."

"I'm sorry. Madame Houdon plans to attend tonight, and she's asked me to have supper with her and her husband."

"Oh, I see."

Quickly she grasped at the impersonal subject. "I've had supper with the Houdons twice. Claudine is charming, and her husband seems very pleasant. I believe she said he studied law, but I don't think he practices now."

"I didn't know you'd become such friends with her."

"Yes, she told me about her childhood. It was dreadful, but she obviously hasn't let that affect her. Everyone seems to like her, and she appears to be wealthy now." Sarah stopped, out of breath and things to say.

"Bernard Houdon is pleasant," Armand remarked, "but he's not too practical. His father is a retired general, but he didn't teach his son discipline. It's common knowledge that Bernard has mismanaged his income."

"Oh, poor Claudine! That's what her father did," Sarah said, and then realized she'd talked imprudently. "I shouldn't have said that, Armand."

"You haven't betrayed a confidence. Madame Houdon will have quite a lot of money when some difficulty over an inheritance from someone who adopted her is settled, but she's had to borrow against it. My mother has lent her money, so I'm aware of her background."

"She doesn't act as if she has any worries."

Armand looked amused. "People who have to borrow must live well or no one will want to lend money to them. And of course she has to pay high interest since the case is contested. But she'll be very rich eventually, so she might as well enjoy some of her money now."

Sarah thought that her New England ancestors would never understand living off money they only expected to have, no matter how sure. But she could understand why Claudine would do that. With her background, having money could be an obsession. Besides, Sarah didn't feel like criticizing anyone's actions. Outside of singing, she was terrible at managing her own life.

When they arrived at her street, Armand escorted her to her door. He kissed her once more—a lingering, contented kiss. "You've made me very happy today, Sarah."

A smile was the best she could do. After she closed the door, she walked disconsolately into her bedroom and stared at herself in the mirror. "You," she said aloud to her reflection, "are a fool. Maybe it's good you made someone happy. You aren't doing it very well for yourself."

Pierre closed the last fastening on his white canvas and leather suit and pulled on his fencing glove. Carrying his mask and foil, he walked from the changing room of the fencing studio to the practice hall. It was empty except for two fencers using the cork strip and Armand, who stood to one side, watching them.

One fencer was a wiry man who thrust and lunged energetically while his larger opponent moved heavily, parrying and only occasionally attempting a riposte. They made Pierre think of a terrier attacking a bear. He was glad he and Armand were well matched; it made their weekly fencing practice more challenging. And challenging was what it had been the last weeks since Armand announced he wanted to marry Sarah.

He put his hand on Armand's shoulder. "Are you ready for defeat?"

Armand turned, his face more light-hearted than Pierre could remember seeing him since they were boys. "Today that's not possible. I'm sure to win."

Pierre had a painful premonition of the reason for Armand's good humor. "You've learned a new plan of attack?"

"If I can win Sarah, I can win a fencing match."

Pierre's gut told him to avoid any more questions, but he couldn't stand not to know. "She's agreed to marry you?"

"She hasn't said so, but after the way we spent yesterday afternoon, I'm sure she will."

The meaning came across clearly. Their fencing match hadn't begun, but Armand had scored the first touch. The wound was sharp and deep.

Before he could guard himself, Armand thrust again, "I wouldn't know her except for you. You've done me a favor I'll always be grateful for. I realize you're attracted to Sarah, but I knew you wouldn't mind. We've shared other women before."

"Sarah isn't *other* women!"

The surprise on Armand's face told Pierre how much of his feelings he'd revealed.

"Pierre, I thought . . ." Armand's face clouded with genuine distress. "I wouldn't have said anything, but I didn't think it would bother you if Sarah and I—"

"It seems she's decided," Pierre interrupted. He didn't

want to hear about anything she and Armand had done. "What does Aunt Nathalie think of your plans?"

"She was upset at first. You know that. But she's being reasonable now. And very gracious."

Pierre could believe she was gracious, at least on the outside. Reasonable? No.

"If you're worried," Armand continued, "that I'm not serious about marrying Sarah, you're wrong. I love her, and I'm sure she loves me."

If Armand was only "sure," Pierre thought, then Sarah hadn't actually said she loved him. And she hadn't agreed to marry him. Maybe she didn't love him. Pierre intended to find out! If she didn't, he'd find a way to silence Gille, unethical or not.

On the cork strip, the laborious fencer called out, "Touché," in an exhausted voice. The two men raised their foils in salute, shook hands and relinquished their places.

Pierre started toward the strip, then turned back to Armand, who was following. "Shall we use sabers today?" The saber, with its use of horizontal cuts as well as thrusts, better fit the savage mood that was building up in him.

"Yes, if you like. I'll get them."

While Pierre waited, he took deep breaths, concentrating on quelling his turbulent emotions. His first fencing master had drummed into him the essentials for success: surprise, timing and distance. Today Armand was already ahead in surprise and timing, but he'd better watch his distance. In matches with his cousin, Pierre didn't often use the *flèche*, the running attack combined with the lunge that increased his reach. With a saber it could result in too hard a hit. But this was a match Pierre intended to win.

When Armand returned, they took their positions. His salute was given with the camaraderie of a friendly contest, but it didn't lessen Pierre's determination. On his first lunge he got to the left of Armand's guard and scored a touch.

Armand said *touché* in a surprised voice that gave Pierre some satisfaction but not enough.

Pierre's mood translated into a series of fierce attacks and ripostes that capitalized on his slightly greater speed. Despite the advantage Armand's height gave him in reach, he had little room to parry and riposte. After he called the third *touché* without having scored against Pierre, his face behind the mesh mask looked grim. His thrusts and cuts began to breach Pierre's guard. He scored twice in a row, and their match became more equal.

When Armand had to acknowledge receiving a fifth touch, the chests of both men were heaving and sweat was dripping under their masks. Silently they saluted and exchanged the briefest of handshakes. Without speaking, Armand turned and walked away.

Pierre stood, trying to get back his breath. Though he'd won the match, it didn't give him the satisfaction he'd expected. He'd never thought of himself as a vengeful man. Especially not toward his cousin, whom he loved. It was an unpleasant feeling.

CHAPTER TWENTY

SARAH PEDDLED HER BICYCLE ALONG THE ROUTE DE LA Longue-Queue in the Bois de Boulogne, then glanced back to see where Helene and Marc were. There was a strange man on a tricycle behind her, but not her friends. She circled back and found them stopped beside an entrance to the Bagatelle palace. "What's the matter?"

"It's too cold for riding," Helene complained.

"Not if you ride fast."

"You won't give up because you like to wear your new rationals too much."

Sarah laughed. It was true; she loved the freedom of the loose trousers patterned after knickerbockers, and they were designed to wear without a corset.

"Rationals." Marc said derisively. "That's just a fancy name for bloomers." He gave Helene a look that warned her never to wear anything so outlandish.

Amused, Sarah said, "You two could go to the café in the Jardin d'Acclimatation. I'm going to ride as far as the Grande Cascade. Then I'll be back to join you."

Helene said, "Marc, you ought to ride with her."

"Oh, no." Sarah wouldn't inflict herself on him. Someone might think the woman in the tweed jacket and pants that showed a disgraceful amount of black-stockinged calf was his wife. Before Marc had to make a polite offer, she wheeled around and started off, calling over her shoulder, "I'll see you in a little while."

She peddled as fast as she could, relishing the feel of the wind against her face and the effort for her legs. Wanting the exertion that kept her from thinking. At the Grande Cascade she had to stop to get her wind back. Only two other people, a couple wrapped in bulky clothes, had braved the November chill. Sarah watched the frothy spray from the thirty-foot waterfall and listened to its roar, pretending she was on a stream in Maine where she'd gone as a child when her life was serene and uncomplicated.

The pretense didn't last. Instead her thoughts came back to the fear that was always just below the surface. Avoiding it the past week had kept her frantically rushing from one place to another. Solange had been delighted to give her an extra singing lesson, and Claudine Houdon had welcomed several visits. This was the third time she'd been bicycling. Altogether she'd managed so that when she got home she was exhausted enough to sleep readily. But it would be another two weeks before she knew whether she would have to marry Armand. At pauses like this, her spirits felt as battered as the rocks at the bottom of the waterfall.

"Sarah."

She turned, and her heart did several somersaults.

Pierre stood, holding his bicycle by the handlebars. His face was flushed, and he was breathing rapidly.

Her tongue felt paralyzed, but she swallowed and got it working. "Hello, Pierre. You look as if you've been riding fast."

"I saw Helene, and she told me you'd be here. I didn't want to miss you."

The somersaults turned into cartwheels.

He cocked his head on one side, studying her clothes, and grinned. "I like your outfit. It almost matches mine."

She hoped his appreciative expression meant she looked as good as he did. His tweed jacket narrowed from his broad shoulders and chest to a snug belt at his waist. His knickerbockers fit his legs closely enough to show the muscles of his thighs. Desire swept through her. Hastily she bent and looked at her bicycle, as if concerned about the chain.

"Could we go over there?" Pierre pointed to a bench several meters away. "We could talk more easily where it's quieter."

She shouldn't. It would be too painful. But she wheeled her bicycle to the bench and leaned it against a tree, then sat down.

When Pierre was sitting beside her, he didn't speak immediately. Nervously she asked, "Are you still busy at the paper?"

"Not so much now. I'm going away for a while."

Those words, "going away," pierced her with chilling intensity. With him away, Paris would be like a glass paperweight that could be shaken to create the illusion of falling snow, but was really lifeless. An even more hurtful thought struck her. The woman writer Armand had mentioned— was she going with him? An image of Pierre, naked in the room at Etretat, was so vivid Sarah feared he could read her thought in her face. Would he be naked with someone else?

She felt almost faint. It would be unbearable to know, but she asked anyway. "On a vacation?"

"Not exactly. Every year I spend six weeks where I grew up, near Cannes. I look after the property and the people who depend on it. Since I'm alone there, I also get some writing done."

She breathed again. "What a coincidence that you came bicycling today."

"I've been looking for you. I didn't want to come to the Opéra Comique, and you haven't been home. I remembered you like to bicycle."

Had she come to the Bois so often because she knew he did? That was too dangerous a question to ask herself in her unsettled state. "You should have sent me a message."

"I wasn't sure you'd answer."

And that was too dangerous a reply. "I haven't been home much," she said, resorting to her usual nervous conversation in an uncomfortable situation. "I've been working hard on improving my singing with Solange. And your aunt introduced me to a woman I like who's been very kind to me. I've spent a lot of time with her. Claudine Houdon. Maybe you know her."

"No. I've heard her name, but I haven't met her." Pierre frowned. "Sarah, remember that Aunt Nathalie probably doesn't have your best interest in mind. If she introduced you to Madame Houdon, it might be better if you weren't too friendly with her."

Sarah welcomed irritation and fanned it. Anger might protect her against wanting him to take her in his arms. "You're not being fair. Nathalie also introduced me to Monsieur Gailhard. He said he'd try to give me an audition for the chorus at the Opéra. Do you disapprove of him too?"

"I don't know him at all," Pierre retorted. "Of course I'm pleased you might have a chance you want. But you must see that Aunt Nathalie would have her own reasons for hoping you get on with your career. It could limit Armand's interest in you. An introduction to anyone else could be a trap."

She worked at being furious and succeeded. "How ridiculous! You're trying to dictate what I should do again. The same as before. You wanted me to stay away from Solange. And you pushed me at Armand."

Her blow landed. Pierre's face turned pale and his eyes

narrowed. "My advice about Armand seems to have worked out well," he said angrily. "You're in line for his name and money. But then you'd better forget about a career. He'll never let you keep on singing."

Sarah jumped up and started toward her bicycle. In a moment he followed and caught her arm. "Sarah, don't leave." The anger was gone from his voice and face. "I didn't come to quarrel with you. Please stay so we can talk."

She looked at him, at his eyes that seemed a more beautiful blue than any lake or sky could be, at his mouth she longed to kiss. Her mostly manufactured rage drained away. Silently she walked back to the bench. If he asked her, she'd probably lie down on the grass, in sight of the shocked eyes of anyone who might come by, and make love. Except, of course, that he wouldn't ask. And even if he did, the uncertainty about whether she was pregnant remained an impossible barrier between them.

Pierre didn't sit immediately but stood looking off at the waterfall. Finally he sat down and looked directly into her eyes. "Sarah, are you going to marry Armand?"

The awful, revealing blush rushed up her neck and face. "I'm not sure. I may."

"Then you love him?"

She didn't think he'd intended to trap her, but he had. Thoughts raced through her mind. She longed to say, *I love you*. But she remembered how powerful the sexual attraction had been between Pierre and her. If she had to marry Armand, she and Pierre would be relatives and see each other at times. Maybe often. Could they stay away from each other? If Pierre knew she didn't love Armand, it would be almost impossible. She wanted to be a faithful wife. Marriage in France might not be like marriages at home, but she still had the values she'd grown up with. She'd already learned she couldn't escape them. And a breach with Armand would rob Pierre of his only family. The only protection for them both would be Pierre's belief she was happy with Armand.

Pierre was looking at her, waiting for her answer. She hated lies, but this time the truth could be worse. "Yes, I think I love him."

His face set into a mask, revealing nothing. But when he spoke, his voice had an undertone, like the sound of a bass violin that underlies the melody. "Sarah, I want you to know that I . . . care what happens to you. If you need help, ever, will you ask me?"

Her resistant heart told her that he'd almost said he loved her. Though it would do no good, she wanted to believe her heart a little longer. "Yes, Pierre. Yes, I will."

He stood up. "If you're ready to go back to the Jardin, I'll ride with you."

They rode together along the Route de la Longue-Queue, past the naked oaks and linden trees. Though they were riding slowly, now the wind seemed cold and hostile. The hope that Pierre loved her was like a bitter orange. It had only the possibility of sweetness. And there was nothing she could do now. Maybe never. If she didn't have a child, would Pierre want her, knowing she'd lain with Armand? He had a friendship, perhaps more, with another woman. There was a difference, she was painfully finding out, between accepting the idea of freedom to make love and practicing it. Perhaps uncertainty about whether she were pregnant was her punishment for not having learned that sooner. If only the punishment were no greater!

A little over a week later Sarah stood in the doorway of the manager's office at the Paris Opéra and waited gleefully for Monsieur Lebeau to notice her. He was wearing brown instead of the nauseating green he'd had on at their last encounter over a year ago, but when he did look up, his expression was no more cordial.

"Mademoiselle Taylor." He rose. "The director is expecting

you. I'll show you to his office." His disdainful tone attempted the message that she was wasting Gailhard's time, but Sarah could see that he was impressed with the director's agreeing to let her audition.

"Thank you, Monsieur Lebeau," she said in her most gracious voice and accompanied it with a seductive smile that would do credit to the temptress in *Samson et Dalila*. Lebeau's face colored, and he didn't look at her again as he led the way past other offices and up a flight of stairs.

As she followed, Sarah's pleasure in her minor triumph with the manager vanished, replaced by a knot in her stomach and the rapid acceleration of her pulse. Her legs felt cold and leaden. Four days previously the director had sent a message that he would give her an audition. He'd included a copy of the selection he wanted from *Boris Godunov*, a Russian opera that had never been performed in Paris. The words were not translated into French. She was to sing in Russian, a language she couldn't even decide how to pronounce from looking at the score.

At the top of the stairs Lebeau stood aside to let her enter a small salon. A large, elaborate desk and a grand piano dominated the room. Monsieur Gailhard came from behind the desk to greet her with a perfunctory bow. "You are ready, mademoiselle?" Though less obvious than Lebeau, his polite impatience indicated that he was reluctantly doing a favor for a friend.

She clutched her copy of the score to keep her hands from trembling. "Yes, Monsieur Gailhard. I am ready."

A young man approached from the corner and sat down at the piano. The director chose a blue velvet upholstered chair and made himself comfortable. He folded his hands over his stomach and rested his head against the high back, as if preparing for a nap. She laid her sheet of music on the piano and looked past him, out the window at the buildings of Paris, pretending they were the Kremlin in Moscow, and took a deep breath.

After the introductory bars she began, concentrating on being Feodor, the czar's son. With her voice she became the teen-aged boy, who teases his sister with a mischievous song about a hen hatching a calf and a pig laying an egg.

When she finished, Gailhard was sitting up in his chair with an expression on his face that was half-surprised and half-admiring. He rose and said with genuine approval, "That was well sung, mademoiselle. Your Russian is quite good."

"Thank you, monsieur." Silently she sent her most fervent thanks to Claudine Houdon, who had recruited a Russian friend to teach Sarah the meaning and pronunciation of the words, and to Solange who had coached her on the music.

"Have you sung trouser roles?" he asked.

Momentarily she thought regretfully of the hatpin she'd embedded in Rivarol. "No, I haven't, but I know many of them."

Monsieur Gailhard kissed her hand with a respect Sarah felt she'd earned. "When I am in need of new members for our chorus, I shall consider you."

Sarah left the Opéra feeling as if she could float across Paris. How she wished Pierre weren't away. Even though she shouldn't, she would find him and tell him of her triumph. At least she could tell Claudine and Solange. And of course Armand. When she reached the Houdon mansion on the Champs-Elysées, she ran up the steps and rang the bell with all the force of her jubilation.

Her exuberance brought an unauthorized smile to the face of the footman who directed her to the greenhouse, where she found Claudine tending to a large collection of orchids.

"Monsieur Gailhard liked my singing!" she said before Claudine could greet her. She caught Claudine's hands and danced her around until she remembered Claudine's limp and stopped. Breathlessly she said, "He'll consider me for the chorus! And it's partly thanks to your help."

"Sarah, that's splendid."

Not until she'd described every detail did she realize that after Claudine expressed her congratulations, she seemed subdued. Sarah said contritely, "I've been talking just about myself and haven't asked about you."

Claudine's face settled into worried lines. "It's just some difficulties about business."

"Oh, Claudine, I'm sorry. I wish I could help. I don't know much about business, but maybe just explaining it to me would be useful."

"That is dear of you but . . . well, maybe it would." She smiled wryly. "You know almost everything else about me anyway. Come, let's sit here."

After Claudine set her watering can beside a pot of orange and bronze orchids, she and Sarah sat down on a white wrought iron bench. "I told you," Claudine began, "that after my mother died, I worked as a servant for an American living in France. You may know his name since he was from a wealthy New England family. William Appleton."

"Yes, I've met some of the family. My father had business with their shipping firm. The Appletons are well known in Boston."

"Monsieur Appleton was an old man, and I loved and admired him." Claudine's face softened. "I often wished my father had been like him. I became more like a daughter to him than a servant. I met Bernard while I was working for Monsieur Appleton, and he provided a grand wedding for me." She paused, and Sarah wondered if she also wished her husband were like William Appleton.

"Monsieur Appleton never married," Claudine continued, twisting her garden gloves in her fingers. "When he died six years ago, three wills were found. One will was very old, leaving his estate to a relative in the United States. The other two were dated the same day. I think he must have been making up his mind which one he wanted. One named me as his heir, and the other named an illegitimate son who was born in France but raised in the United States."

Though from Claudine's description, the legal details were complicated, Sarah listened intently and thought she understood. The old will didn't count, but the ones from the same day were both equally valid. Claudine located the son, Georges Royer, who'd taken his father's name of Appleton. Like his father's relatives, Georges Appleton had a shipping business. He and Claudine agreed that she would have three-fourths of the six-million-franc estate and Georges, who was wealthy in his own right, would take one-fourth. Bernard Houdon used his training as a lawyer to draw up a legal contract to bind their agreement until the real property could be appraised. Claudine was to keep the land titles and take care of the stocks and bonds until the settlement was completed.

"But then I had bad luck again," Claudine said bitterly. She stood and walked back and forth agitatedly, her limp very pronounced. "Within a few months Georges Appleton lost several ships in a hurricane. He changed his mind about sharing the money and hired an attorney to challenge the contract. By then Bernard and I also needed the money, and we wouldn't agree to a change. So we hired an attorney."

Distressed, Sarah rose also. "Has the case been decided against you?"

"No, certainly not." Claudine picked up the watering can and went back to the orchids; she seemed calmer now. "It won't be. The contract is plainly legal. The court has confirmed that. But Georges Appleton's attorney does everything possible to delay the settlement, and we have to live until we receive the money. That means borrowing, and when one lender needs his money, another must be arranged. Just now one of them, a banker, is pressing me. I hate all the juggling."

Prodded by her Yankee training, Sarah ventured, "Is there some way that you could manage without borrowing?"

Claudine frowned. Just as her smile changed her from a plain woman to a charming one, her frown made her look a little sinister. "You've always had enough money, Sarah," she said sharply. "Here in Paris you've had good luck. You don't know what it's like to be really poor."

"Yes, you're right," Sarah said guiltily. She wasn't responsible for her father's money, but her question had been pompous and insensitive. Her economies when she came to Paris were nothing compared to Claudine's impoverished childhood.

Claudine's frown smoothed to a worried expression. Absently she put the watering can down again. "I'm sure that the Appleton family won't let Georges become destitute. They don't object to his using the name, and they'll help him get started again. But the Appletons aren't well-known here, not like Jennie Jerome who married Lord Churchill or the Astors or the Goulds. If my creditors understood how wealthy the Appletons are, it would be easier to get the loans I need."

"Then there is something I can do," Sarah said. She *could* repay some of Claudine's friendship and help. "I don't know Georges Appleton, but I certainly know that the Appleton family is wealthy. If there's someone whom I can reassure about that, I want to."

"Oh, Sarah. That is an offer of real friendship." Claudine took Sarah's hands and kissed her cheek, then drew back and said ruefully, "I told you this depressing story when we should be talking about how much Monsieur Gailhard liked you."

"It doesn't matter." The glow Sarah felt was even better by thinking she might do something for her friend.

"Madame." It was the footman calling from the doorway. At Claudine's gesture, he came closer. "Guests are arriving for your afternoon."

Claudine gave a cluck of dismay. "Heavens! I forgot the time. Sarah, please excuse me. You will stay, won't you?" She hurried out without waiting for an answer.

Sarah made her way to the large Japanese-style drawing room where she lingered a short while to be polite and then slipped out. In the lobby she met Nathalie coming in. "Good afternoon, Sarah," Nathalie said pleasantly. "Are you leaving? Armand just brought me, and he's still outside. I'm sure he'd be delighted to escort you wherever you're going." She turned to a groom and said, "Tell the Comte de Saint-Maurice to wait."

Sarah had been avoiding Armand with the excuse she was too busy, but she said, "Thank you, *comtesse*," to Nathalie and went outside.

He looked delighted to see her, and that eased a little of the fear she would have for a few more days. If they had to marry, surely she would learn to love this handsome man who had so many good qualities.

He was driving his small elegant phaeton himself. "Where shall I take you," he asked when she was settled.

"To Madame Rabaud's. I have good news to tell her."

"About what?"

He'd forgotten something so important to her! Irritated, she said, "About the audition with Monsieur Gailhard. I told you about it when I saw you after the performance two nights ago."

"Oh, yes. Before you went off with the Houdons and their Russian." He sounded somewhat aggrieved. "How did the audition go?"

"Monsieur Gailhard liked my singing. When there's a vacancy in the chorus, he'll consider me." She savored the words again.

"Sarah, that's wonderful. I hope the vacancy is soon. Once we're married, it would be too late."

"Too late?" She'd given up protesting about references to marrying him.

He gave her a perplexed glance. "A married woman doesn't work. After we marry, performing in the theater will be out of the question."

"Women all over Paris—all over France—work to earn money," she protested.

"We're not talking about women of that class."

His assurance silenced her. She knew he was right for most upper- and middle-class women. It was the same way at home. If she married him, he'd expect her to give up her career. And with a baby she'd probably have to do what he wanted. But she wouldn't add to her fears by worrying about that now.

He seemed to have dismissed the question because he looked at her with a familiar message in his eyes. "When shall we go back to the chateau? Tomorrow?"

"No. I'm not sure when."

"You're very busy," he said a little sharply. "Are you going to see that Russian again?"

"Perhaps. It would be a good idea to learn more Russian in case I need it again."

A hint of color crept up above his high collar into his face. "Were you ever alone with him?"

"You sound jealous." It felt good to argue with him when she couldn't talk about what really bothered her. "What you're really asking is whether I've made love with him. Do you think I have so many lovers?"

His lips compressed into a tight line. "You must have had lovers when you were in the United States."

"That doesn't deserve a response!" Anger felt even better.

"Who were they?" He was looking straight ahead, his aristocratic profile pronounced. "I'm going to be your husband. I'm entitled to know."

Recklessly she said, "Well, if you insist, I'll tell you. There was Miles Standish. And Cotton Mather. Let's see. I think his father, Increase. Yes, definitely Increase. It's so hard to remember. And just before I left home, there were Thomas Hendricks and Grover Cleveland. They were really at the same time."

His head snapped around. "The president and vice-president of the United States?"

She glared at him. "Did you really think I was going to answer? You don't have the right to ask me such questions!"

He looked ahead again, his face a definite red. For a moment he paid all his attention to the horse, as if the smoothly moving muscles were all that concerned him. Finally he said, "Yes, you're right. I don't usually let my feelings sway my judgment. With you I have. Forgive me."

Helplessly she said, "Yes." It was difficult to be angry with a man who admitted his faults. And there was still the uncertain future.

He left her at Solange's door without pressing her as to when they would meet next. Her spirits lifting again, she ran up the steps and rang the bell.

"Berthe," she said to the impassive face when the door opened, "I have exciting news. Is madame here?"

Berthe nodded toward the drawing room and Sarah hurried on to find Solange coming toward her. "Gailhard liked you," Solange guessed.

"Yes!"

Solange embraced Sarah, holding her close and kissing her cheeks. Though the fervent embraces no longer made Sarah uneasy, she usually avoided them. Now she drew back but let Solange pull her down to a seat on the settee while she went over all the details of the audition. When she finished, Solange jumped up, clasping her hands excitedly. "This is the eighteenth of November. Monsieur Gailhard won't get in touch with you until after Christmas and New Year's. We'll work every day, and you'll be ready."

It wasn't fair not to let Solange know that her plans might have to change. "I'm not sure just how things will work out. I may decide to get married."

"Married?" Solange sounded alarmed.

"Armand wants me to marry him, and I'm considering it."

"Oh, Armand," Solange said dismissively. "That's all right. Being a wife does have some advantages. He'll be a good husband for you."

"He says that as his wife, I couldn't have a career."

"You can manage him. He'll be so happy making love to you that he'll do what you want. When you get tired of him, you can discreetly take lovers. Like Pierre."

An explosive mixture of anger and unhappiness erupted in Sarah. "I don't need anyone else telling me how to run my life! I'll decide for myself. Armand is just asking what most husbands expect. If I marry him, I'll probably have a child."

"A singer has her music," Solange said in an irritated voice. "You don't need a child. And I've explained how you can prevent that."

"Maybe what I really want is to be a wife and mother— to have an ordinary life."

"Ordinary life!" Solange's voice rose to a shriek. "I haven't done everything so that you can give up singing!"

"I'm grateful for the lessons but—"

Solange's face was ugly with anger. "I'm not talking about lessons. Who do you think got Gille to write that article about you? It was my idea to call you La Belle Americaine."

Horrified, Sarah stared at Solange. "*You* told Gille about Pierre and me?"

"Yes." Solange spoke defiantly but in a tempered voice. "You must understand. It's dangerous for a woman to be in love with someone like Pierre. I was afraid you'd sacrifice yourself and get badly hurt. But I was sure you wouldn't give up your career for someone like Armand."

Sarah felt almost ill. She had to get away! As she turned to leave, Solange caught hold of her arm. "Please, listen. I was thinking of what was best for you. You mustn't give up your music. That's what really matters."

Too furious to speak, Sarah shook off the hand on her arm and rushed into the foyer. Standing there with a startled look on her face was Solange's friend, Eleanore. She must have heard their shouts, but Sarah didn't care. She pushed past Eleanore.

Outside she started along the street, then stopped. How did Solange know that she and Pierre had gone to Etretat? She resumed walking. It didn't matter. The damage was done, and she wasn't going back to talk to Solange—not ever.

When she found a cab, she refused to let herself think until she was home. Once inside her own flat, she let go the flood of rage and hurt. Shaking, she crawled into bed and faced her thoughts.

Solange had betrayed her. But she had helped in the betrayal herself. The first wedge between her and Pierre had been her doubt of him over Gille's column. And now the afternoon with Armand and the consequences she still feared stood between them. Even though Pierre hadn't taken a woman with him to Cannes, one might be waiting for him here. Maybe one he was learning to love.

It was dark when Sarah finally got out of bed and started to undress. She really did feel ill now. Rage was exhausting, she decided forlornly. As she removed the last of her clothing, she discovered that fate had been merciful and had spared her further waiting. She wasn't pregnant.

Wrapped in her robe, she sat beside her window for a long time, listening to the sounds of Paris. Voices. The crack of whips. Horses neighing. Footsteps on the cobblestones.

She listened as well to her inner voice that told her to have courage. Her painful folly with Armand had at least taught her what she really wanted—to be with Pierre. If Gille wrote about them and Monsieur Cesbron wouldn't have her at the Opéra Comique, she'd sing somewhere else.

There was another question. She hoped Pierre wanted her—but she didn't know whether he did. When he came back to Paris, she would go to him and tell him that she loved him. It would be difficult. The most difficult thing she'd ever done. But if he rebuffed her, it couldn't be worse than the way she felt now.

CHAPTER TWENTY-ONE

A SIGN OVER THE INN AT BEZONS SHOWED A PROFILE OF a man's head. Underneath it large letters proclaimed, Restaurant Rossini. Smaller letters listed Soups, Fried Fish, Private Rooms, Gardens, Boats for Rent, and at the bottom a last line boldly announced, A Favorite of Giacomo Rossini.

From Armand's cabriolet Sarah looked up at the sign. "I wonder," she said to him, "which of that assortment of services Rossini favored. If he actually came here at all."

"I'm sure he did," Armand said shortly. "I thought you would appreciate this place since you admire his operas so much."

"Yes, I do. It's very pretty here."

It had been four days since Sarah discovered she wasn't pregnant. This was her first afternoon with Armand since then, and he had wanted to go to his chateau. She'd refused. She didn't fear she would succumb and make love with him, but it would be too cruel to say what she must at his home. Instead she'd reminded him of the inn he'd recommended. Though he'd agreed, his disappointment was obvious.

After Armand helped Sarah down, a servant led the horse

332

and cabriolet away. Behind the inn a large yard ran down
to the Seine. Several tables rested under the trees, and a
swing hung limply from the branch of a bare chestnut tree.
No other patrons were about; she could begin the talk she
dreaded. No, not yet. She started toward the river, and
Armand followed. Small waves lapped indolently at the
shore, as if the Seine had fulfilled its holiday duties in the
summer and felt entitled to laziness. A skiff bumped softly
against the dock of a wooden boathouse in rhythm with the
waves.

Delaying, she asked, "What kind of fish are good to catch
here? Could we go fishing?"

"They catch gudgeon in the summer. I doubt that we'd
catch anything this time of year, but we can try if you wish,"
Armand said unenthusiastically.

"Then let's go rowing for a little while," she persisted.

While he went to find oars, she waited, her emotions in
turmoil. Her feeling of reluctance she understood; she didn't
want to hurt him. What surprised her was her feeling of
regret.

Armand came back with the oars, and they set out up-
stream in the skiff, with him in the middle to row and her
facing him from the seat at the stern. "We'll stay fairly close
to shore," he said.

"Yes, I'll watch ahead," she assured him. As he rowed,
however, she found herself looking as often at the push and
pull of his shoulders as in the direction they were going. It
would be easier, she thought sadly, if she did love him and
wanted to marry him. Easier than hurting him and risking
Pierre's rejection. But the stakes for her were too high; she
must have the courage to try for what she really wanted.

The boat gave a sudden lurch, and she had to grab the
gúnwales to keep from sliding off the seat. They had banged
into a limb that was sticking up out of the water.

"*Dieu!*" Armand swore. From the expression on his face,

he would have liked to say something considerably stronger. He shipped the oars and bent down, examining the boat.

She should have seen the limb. Her face began to flame. "I'm sorry. Is the boat all right?"

He sat up and took up the oars, then said, in a tone of controlled exasperation, "Yes."

"Maybe it would be better if I rowed," she suggested. "Then you could look out for where we're going."

He didn't answer, only maneuvered the skiff around to go back downstream to the boathouse.

"I did lots of rowing on lakes and in the harbor at home," she assured him, hoping she sounded cheerful. "I'd like to row."

"No," he snapped, "that would not be proper."

"You don't always want me to do what's proper," she retorted, and then gave a silent "damn!" When would she learn to think before she spoke?

They finished the abbreviated boating excursion in silence. Walking up to the inn, Sarah looked longingly at the swing. She loved the motion, pumping higher and higher until it became a contest with the resisting air. But it would also flip up her petticoats, and this certainly wasn't the time for that.

Inside, the inn's proprietor showed them to a table in an alcove with a window facing the river. No one else was in the dining room.

The waiter, a stout young man who looked like a more recent edition of the proprietor, bustled over to them. "Good day, monsieur, madame," he said. "Do you wish a menu? Today the matelot is very good."

"That's a mixture of several kinds of fish with a sharp sauce," Armand explained.

Sarah had lost any hunger the fresh air had given her. "Whatever you choose is fine."

"Or you might like the fried gudgeon," the waiter said.

"It was caught just this morning."

Armand looked uncomfortable. "We'll have matelot and a salad. And a bottle of Montrachet."

When the waiter left, Armand said, "I was wrong about the fishing. I apologize. I was feeling out of sorts. This isn't the place I really want to be with you."

Sarah glanced around at the empty room, then back at him. Her respite was over. She put her hands down so that the edge of the linen cloth concealed the fact that they were trembling. "Armand," she said. To her dismay, her voice was trembling too. She took a breath and began again. "There's something I must tell you. I don't know any good way to say it. I'm sorry if it makes you unhappy, but I don't want to marry you."

The bones of his face seemed suddenly more prominent. "I don't understand. Why?"

"I'm not in love with you."

"I don't believe that. That afternoon at the chateau, you acted like a woman in love!"

With her feeling of shame the blush she hated returned. "Yes, I know," she said, resisting guilt. "I thought I was in love with you, but I'm not. I . . . love Pierre."

"That's not a reason," he rejoined. "I know you were lovers. But that's over."

His words hurt, not because he said them with anger, but because they might be true. "Maybe. I have to find out. Even if it is over, I won't marry you."

Armand leaned across the table and said forcefully, "Don't decide now. You said you don't know if Pierre loves you. I do love you. I want to marry you. Does he?"

His question was a band around her heart, squeezing until she wanted to cry out.

The waiter coming across the room with the wine gave her time to breathe. When the bottle had been examined, tasted, and approved, she was in control of herself again.

She'd vowed to be honest with Armand. There was more she must say.

After the waiter left, she said, "Pierre had a reason for introducing me to you. He had a plan—that if your mother thought you were seriously interested in an American woman, she might give up her objections to your political career."

All the color drained out of Armand's face. "And that's why you lay with me—for a scheme of Pierre's?"

His contempt cut as if he'd stripped away her skin and left raw flesh. "No!" she protested. "That wasn't part of any plan. That was because . . . I was drawn to you. For a while I thought I did love you. And you made me feel . . . well, I wanted you to make love to me."

He looked a little less wounded, and she hurried on. "You must understand about Pierre. He loves you and admires you. He thinks you should be in government and that your mother is wrong to oppose you."

"And that I don't have enough courage to stand up to her myself." His bitterness was back.

She'd gone this far. Anything was easier than what she'd already said. "Why don't you stand up to her?"

"I made a vow to my father that I'd never do anything that would really hurt her."

"Pierre told me about that. But you were only eight years old. It wasn't fair of your father to ask you to swear to something then that affects your whole life."

"Perhaps you're right," he said wearily. "I've thought about that a lot lately."

Their meal arrived. Sarah tried a bite and couldn't eat. After a few efforts, Armand put down his fork also. "Shall we leave?" he asked, and she was relieved to agree.

They rode silently through the lengthening shadows; before they reached the center of the city, lights were being lit. In the early-evening crowds, Armand had to watch for pedestrians and for other carriages, so conversation was impossible. When they reached her flat he didn't help her out immediately. Instead he turned and studied her face.

"Shall we keep up this pretense of romance?" he asked, and added caustically, "If you stop being seen with me now, it will waste all your efforts."

"Armand, I'm sorry. I never intended anyone to be hurt, but I know I've bungled things. Of course I'll continue going places with you if you want me to."

His voice softened. "Yes, I want you to. And I won't give up about marriage."

After he got out and helped her down, he escorted her to her door, but he left without any move toward the customary kiss. She felt both relieved and sorry. Ironically, after their painful talk, she felt closer to him now than she ever had before.

"Sarah," Helene said, "Marc and I are going to the Folies Bergère tonight. If your friend isn't here, would you like to go with us?"

She and Sarah were in the changing room at the Théâtre des Nations. It had been three days since Sarah and Armand's afternoon at Bézons. The following night they were to go to dinner at Nathalie's, but he hadn't asked to see her before then. She was both glad to postpone their next meeting and unhappy for the distress that probably kept him away. That concern, along with her ever-present longing for Pierre had made her spirits troubled. She smiled gratefully at Helene. "Yes, I'd like to go. But I'll pay my own way."

"All right, but hurry," Helene said impatiently. "The next show starts soon, and Marc doesn't want to miss the boxing kangaroo."

"Yes, I'm almost ready." Sarah put away the white wig she'd worn in *Mignon* and took her coat and hat from their peg. She had been slow changing after the opera. The leading role was for a mezzo-soprano, and it had taken Sarah a little while to shrug off her dreamy state of imagining herself as Mignon, being rescued from fire by the hero and winning out over her rival. Since Armand had told her about Pierre's woman writer friend, winning out over a rival was a more poignant fantasy.

Outside the theater Sarah and Helene joined Marc, who had a cab waiting. When they reached the Folies Bergère, lights blazed over the four streets that met in front. Their cab had to jostle for position among all the others before stopping near the entrance.

Marc pointed to a poster that read, Le Kangourou Boxeur. "That's what I want to see."

"I hope we haven't missed the bearded Burmans," Helene said as they passed another poster. "They're descended from the ruling family of Burma."

The two men pictured on the poster peered out from beards that grew over their entire faces. The women pictured with them did look Oriental, but Sarah thought that the beards were probably no more authentic than their supposed lineage. She didn't say so to Helene.

They paid their two francs each and went inside. The wide gallery that circled the auditorium was full of people visiting and going back and forth between the boxes and the three bars. Tall mirrors behind the bars reflected men in business suits, an occasional man in a tuxedo and top hat, and well-dressed women. How many times had Pierre come here? Sarah wondered. Had one of the shoeshine boys doing business in front of the imitation Greek statues shined his shoes? Prostitutes, painted with thick white makeup, made their rounds through the crowd. Maybe one of them had approached him. She didn't like that thought.

The red-carpeted boxes were open to the gallery at the back and the auditorium at the front. At box number seventeen a portly man in a black suit already occupied one of the four chairs. He grudgingly got up to let Sarah and Helene squeeze through to the ones closest to the rail. Marc sat behind them. Onstage seven acrobats climbed to a pyramid while the orchestra blasted out chords, competing with talk, shouts of program hawkers, and applause. Haze from cigarette and cigar smoke dulled the light from the chandeliers and almost obscured the gold and ocher colors in the tasseled fabric that decorated the ceiling. Everything smelled of tobacco, beer and dusty carpets.

If only Pierre were with her. . . . No, she scolded herself. She mustn't spoil the evening by her longings. Her impressions could be stored up—funny incidents to describe to him when they were together again. If they were.

An Indian snake charmer followed the acrobats, then a woman singing English songs. "You can sing better," Helene whispered generously, and Sarah silently agreed. Three men in red tights rode velocipedes, and after them two clowns engaged in a pantomime duel. They shook with fear, tried to run away, and finally accidentally shot their own toes. Remembering Pierre's wound, Sarah couldn't laugh with the others.

A drum roll sounded and Monsieur Lallemard, the manager, introduced the boxing kangaroo and his trainer. The man wore a regular boxing outfit, black trunks and tights and a striped shirt. The kangaroo, who was as tall as the man, had on boxing gloves. The two danced around each other and sparred, the man obviously careful not to damage the animal. Marc cheered wildly, but the bout seemed tamer than Sarah had expected. After the kangaroo was declared the winner, Helene suggested they go into the gallery for a drink.

At the nearest bar a barmaid with blond bangs and white roses tucked into the lace trim of her black jacket rested her hands on the edge of the marble counter. She waited for the next customer with a look of sad disinterest, as if nothing could occur that she hadn't seen before. The yellow and pink roses in the vase in front of her seemed delicate and, like her, a little out of place. Pierre might have talked to her. Sarah suppressed a ridiculous desire to ask the sad barmaid if she knew him.

Marc ordered anisette for all of them, and Sarah insisted on paying her sixty centimes. He and Helene had no more money than she.

As Sarah waited, she saw a man and woman who seemed familiar reflected in the mirror behind the bar. She turned and saw Wilhelm Hotter and Eleanore Matrat—both of Solange's lovers. Seeing them brought back the anger and hurt of her betrayal. Sarah glanced quickly around; their shared lover wasn't anywhere in sight. Hoping Eleanore and Wilhelm wouldn't notice her, Sarah turned the other direction.

"Mademoiselle Taylor," came from behind her. Reluctantly she faced Eleanore, who was approaching, a cordial smile on her face. Wilhelm was following.

"Madame Matrat. Monsieur Hotter," Sarah acknowledged. "Do you remember my friends, Mademoiselle Lebout and Monsieur Simon?"

To Sarah's amazement, during the comments about the acts they'd seen, Eleanore joined in amiably, talking more than she'd done in the several times Sarah had been in her company before. Though Wilhelm didn't say much, he didn't give Sarah his usual sullen appraisals. At a pause in the conversation, she asked casually, "Is Madame Rabaud here this evening?"

"No," Eleanore said. "She's home with a headache."

Sarah felt intense relief.

Marc had been looking at Helene, obviously interested in activities they couldn't begin until they were alone. "We've seen the best acts," he said. "Are you ready to leave, Helene and Sarah?"

"I haven't seen the bearded Burmans yet," Helene objected.

"We'll come back another time." Marc plainly didn't intend to stay longer.

Helene said, "All right," but she didn't look pleased.

With painful longing, Sarah imagined how she would feel if she were with Pierre and he was eager to make love to her. Helene was fortunate.

"Monsieur Hotter and I were just on our way into the garden," Eleanore said. "Perhaps you'd care to join us, Mademoiselle Taylor. We can see you home later."

Sarah didn't want to share a cab with Helene and Marc and think about what they would be doing when they reached home. Also, she was curious about Eleanore's uncharacteristic volubility. "Yes," Sarah said. "I'd like to stay longer."

Although the air in the garden was cool, it was pleasant to be away from the smoke and noise. Two ugly fountains in the center were dry, but evergreen yews with spiky leaves and fragrant thuja cedar trees made it seem like a garden, even in late November. Wilhelm chose one of the zinc-topped tables and ordered Roederer champagne. It didn't surprise Sarah that he would so readily spend twenty francs for one bottle of wine. She'd decided when she met him that his wealth must be at least part of his appeal for Solange.

It did surprise her that he, like Eleanore, was relaxed and friendly. "The English singer had style," he remarked, "but a harsh voice. Solange tells me that you have a fine voice and that you progressed rapidly with her." He surprised Sarah even more when he added. "You must find another teacher and keep working."

Eleanore said, "Wilhelm, you're startling Mademoiselle Taylor. Sarah, let's speak candidly. I'm sorry for your estrangement with Solange." She didn't look sorry at all. "But it's for the best. Wilhelm and I have learned to share everything, and we have a good arrangement. I was afraid you would disrupt that. Solange is very intense about music, and you're a beautiful young woman."

Now Sarah understood. Underneath this cordiality was a warning. Poor Eleanore and Wilhelm—one, in Solange's words, her lover above the waist and the other below. Sharing must already be difficult; to them she represented a threat. In her new awareness of the pain of loving, she sympathized and was willing to speak with equal candor. "I appreciate and admire Solange. She's a fine musician. She fascinates me because she's so different from anyone I've ever known before. I respect the way she says what she thinks, but I don't have a . . . special affection for her. And I resent the way she interfered in my life."

Wilhelm shook his head and sighed. "Solange must be accepted the way she is. I know why she likes me. My money. But I have more than I know what to do with. She helps spend it."

"Yes, that's true," Eleanore agreed. "But she's worth more than the money. Do you have another singing teacher, Sarah? I know of some who are good."

In case Sarah hadn't caught on before, that message was clear: don't go back to Solange. "I haven't decided what to do about a teacher," she said.

Wilhelm signaled for another bottle of champagne. He'd be paying what a working girl could have dined out on for two months. Would he and Eleanore be so indifferent to money, Sarah wondered, if they didn't each have so much? If they were poor, they might be like Claudine.

Claudine! "Do you really have more money than you can spend?" Sarah said boldly to Wilhelm.

"Yes."

"I have a friend who needs to borrow money until her inheritance is settled. She pays interest, of course. I don't know all the details, but I do know the American family the arrangements depend on. They're wealthy and very respected in Boston. If you want to find out more about it, I can give you my friend's name."

He looked a little startled, but he said, "Certainly. I'll look into it. Who is it?"

"Claudine Houdon."

"I don't know Madame Houdon, but I know of her husband's family. His father is retired from the army and was once the Minister of War. A very good man. Yes, I'll get in touch with her."

"That's a good idea," Eleanore said. "Perhaps I'll do the same."

The quick agreement startled Sarah. She noticed that Eleanore's amiability had been replaced by a strained expression. It occurred to her that they might think she was putting subtle pressure on them to follow her suggestion—with the unspoken threat that otherwise she might be reconciled with Solange. She started to reassure them, and then stopped. They would use their own judgment about lending money to Claudine. All she'd done was suggest they investigate it. She had the happy feeling that this time she had done something that might turn out well.

Nathalie swept across her drawing room as if clothed in royal robes. Sometimes Sarah could almost see small boys, dressed in the regal colors, carrying the imaginary train. A short middle-aged man with cheerful eyes and a bushy goatee followed Nathalie, who spoke imperiously to Sarah. "I wish you to meet Signor Castelli." To the man beside her she said, "Mademoiselle Taylor is a very close friend. We hope someday soon she'll be one of the family."

With this startling bestowal of imperial favor, Nathalie moved on. Sarah felt dismayed and unsettled. Pierre's plan was that Nathalie would object if she thought Armand was serious about Sarah. That was the reason Sarah was still here. She glanced at Armand, a short distance away, wondering if he'd heard his mother. But he was listening to Bernard Houdon.

Signor Castelli bowed over Sarah's hand and said in Italian-accented French, "It is my great pleasure to meet you, mademoiselle."

"And I to meet you."

It turned out that though Signor Castelli lived in France, he was from Bergamo, a town in northern Italy Sarah had never heard of. "It is not far from Milan," he explained. When he learned that she was a singer, he described for her some of the performances he'd heard at La Scala. She was envious when he said he'd attended Verdi's *Otello* on its opening at the famous opera house. "You really must go to Italy, mademoiselle," he told her. "It is the best place for opera."

"Perhaps I will," she said. If Pierre rejected her when he returned from Cannes, she might not want to stay in Paris.

Signor Castelli continued to talk enthusiastically about music, and Sarah was grateful. Armand hadn't referred to their conversation at Bézons, but there was a stiffness to his behavior that reminded her she had made him unhappy. She'd expected a difficult evening, but she was enjoying the voluble Italian. During dinner he entertained her with a seemingly endless series of anecdotes about operas. The conversation was more relaxed than usual among the small group of guests: Giovanni Castelli and his wife, the Houdons, Adolphe Fuzelier, the banker who paid his usual attention to Nathalie, and a young couple, the Charcots. Madame Charcot was Monsieur Fuzelier's daughter, and her principal interest, Sarah had learned at a previous dinner, was whether the house of Worth or Laferrière had the best fashions.

When the women left the men to tobacco and cognac, Claudine sat beside Sarah. Claudine's face had the cheerful expression that so transformed her plainness. She said, "Two friends of yours came to see me this afternoon. Monsieur Hotter and Madame Matrat. We had a very pleasant conversation. Thank you for mentioning me to them."

Sarah had already guessed from Claudine's relaxed demeanor that her affairs were going better. "I'm glad I've been able to help." She was surprised and a little amused that Eleanore and Wilhelm had acted so hastily. They didn't realize she was no threat to them.

"Do you want more Russian lessons?" Claudine asked.

"Not right now." Sarah knew she should do something about a voice teacher and her career. But until she could talk to Pierre, decisions seemed beyond her. She had been moving mechanically through her days, as if she were no more than the doll in *Tales of Hoffman*, waiting for her Hoffman to return. Then he would wind the key that brought her to real life—or smash her into bits of metal and china that would fly in all directions.

The sound of low-pitched voices preceded the men's return to the drawing room. Bernard Houdon came across to Claudine and Sarah. "Excuse me, please, Mademoiselle Taylor," he said, "I need to speak to my wife privately for a moment."

"Of course," Sarah said, rising. "Please take my chair." She didn't see Signor Castelli, so she wandered into the adjacent room. Nothing had changed since she'd seen it last; Mars and Venus still struggled in their tapestried net. Outside the alcoved window a December wind was bending the branches of a willow tree that grew close to the building. Periodically the branches brushed against the glass panes, as if the tree were asking to be let inside. Sarah went to the window and looked out at the swaying tree, black against the silver of a moonlit sky. What was Pierre doing now? If only she could send him a message on the wind that would reach all the way to Cannes.

Behind her the rustle of a dress and the sound of several footsteps told her two people had come in from the hallway. She leaned closer into the alcove, preferring her thoughts to conversation.

"But I don't want to wait," a man said in an irritated voice. It was Adolphe Fuzelier. "I have all the information I need."

"Don't be so impatient." That was Nathalie, sounding equally annoyed. "Just a few days longer. It takes a little time, even for someone so trusting—"

Nathalie's voice broke off. Then she said, in a slightly high-pitched tone, "Sarah, I didn't see you there."

Sarah turned, a little embarrassed at overhearing what was clearly a private argument. "I was just enjoying looking out the window." She smiled and walked past Fuzelier's and Nathalie's immobile faces. As she started back to the drawing room, she decided that whoever they were talking about would be foolish to trust either of them. Then a little guiltily she reminded herself that she owed her audition at the Paris Opéra to Nathalie and should be more charitable in her thoughts.

After a pause, Nathalie and Fuzelier followed. When they all reached the drawing room, Signor Castelli greeted Sarah with another story, about an Italian tenor who was singing the role of Don José in *Carmen* in a small French town near the Spanish border. Between the first acts he mistakenly went through an outside door and was locked out of the opera house. Deciding he might as well have a glass of wine before he returned, he went to a nearby café. The local gendarmes were looking for an army deserter, and since the tenor was wearing a uniform, they decided he was their man. They were halfway to the jail before angry members of the audience, whom the opera impresario had sent in all directions, rescued the tenor. The group was small enough that everyone listened and rewarded Signor Castelli by laughing. Sarah stored away the anecdote in her mental hope chest of funny stories to share with Pierre.

The conversation turned to the judicial system, with Monsieur Fuzelier criticizing the tactics of lawyers. Bernard Houdon waved his hands indolently. "True, Monsieur Fuzelier.

Though I'm trained in law and should defend my colleagues, my wife's unfortunate case proves your point."

The banker looked at Claudine. "Are you no closer to settlement, Madame Houdon?"

Sarah was surprised that Claudine's legal tangles were so well-known, but perhaps the banker was one of her creditors. Claudine didn't look offended. "Indeed, I should be," she said. "By good fortune it turns out that Mademoiselle Taylor knows the Appleton family. She can vouch that with their position, they will certainly help Georges."

Fuzelier looked at Sarah. "Is that correct, mademoiselle?"

Sarah hesitated. She had no way of knowing whether the Appletons would actually help their illegitimate relative. "Of course I can't say what they'll do. But I know they're in a position to help. They're wealthy, and they are very generous in aiding worthy causes."

"A reputation like that is a good recommendation," the banker commented.

"When they help Mr. Appleton straighten out his affairs," Claudine said, "surely he will instruct his lawyer to desist from the tactics that have obstructed justice for so long."

"I read of a case of disputed property that lasted seventeen years," young Mr. Charcot volunteered.

"Oh, don't say that," protested Claudine. "Seventeen years would be intolerable."

After that everyone but Madame Charcot and Sarah seemed to have heard of some instance of justice either aborted or delayed, each one more distressing to Claudine. The evening ended with the consensus that the less anyone had to do with the legal system, the better.

Armand's coachman was driving the landau that evening, so Sarah waited until Armand escorted her upstairs to her flat to tell him, "When your mother introduced me to Signor Castelli, she practically said I'm to be your bride."

"Yes. She told me she won't oppose me on this."

"But that means she won't bargain with you."

Armand looked serene. "There will be time for politics later."

Exasperated, she said, "But you ought to *do* something. Use your knowledge of colonial affairs to influence policy."

"I am doing something. I'm waiting for you to give in and marry me."

She wanted to shout at him, to stir him up. "You could also wait until your mother dies to have your own life, but that might be a long time. I don't think your mother would give in to death if it meant you'd be free."

His serenity was jarred now. He gave a curt good-night and left.

Inside her flat, her irritation evaporated, leaving her remorseful. She, more than other people should understand how easy it was to let a parent's wishes dominate. What she'd said was cruel. But she knew Armand well enough to appreciate how much ability he had. He could absorb and analyze facts rapidly, and had a good grasp of political problems. If he'd apply the same insights to his personal life— but he seemed blind about his mother. And about her.

After she undressed, she looked at the calendar on the stand beside her bed. Though she didn't know just when Pierre would be back, each morning she crossed off another day to wait until she might see him—talk to him. At the thought her heart pounded with a mixture of eagerness and apprehension. She wanted to see him and she feared it.

Restlessly she wandered back to her drawing room and sat down at the piano, letting her fingers lie on the silent keys and wishing it weren't too late to disturb the other tenants by playing. Music had always been her consolation. She stood up, impatient with herself. Instead of just waiting for Pierre, she should be busy. A careful assessment of her money—something she hated to do but had learned— would tell her how much she could pay a voice teacher.

She would accept Claudine's offer to arrange more Russian lessons, and she'd study Italian and German on her own. She would also talk to Cesbron.

The next day she put her plan into action. Claudine agreed to contact her Russian, and an appointment was arranged for the following Monday. At the bookstalls near the Odeon Théâtre Sarah bought books to help her with Italian and German. After that, buoyed up by determination, she went to see the Opéra Comique manager.

"Yes, Mademoiselle Taylor?" he said, leaning back in his office chair, his chin resting on his fingers.

"You told me you had planned to let me understudy the mezzo-soprano roles," she reminded him. "There's been nothing more about me in the newspapers."

"Yes, that's true."

"Will you consider me again? I think I deserve the chance." She waited, her heart racing along like one of the runners who practiced on the track at Longchamp.

Monsieur Cesbron sat up and riffled through some papers on his desk. "We'll be doing *Romeo et Juliette* in February. If you want to work on the role of Juliette's nurse," he said cautiously, "we might use you if we need an understudy."

She wanted to tweak his white sidewhiskers and kiss the shiny top of his head. Instead she said, "Thank you, Monsieur Cesbron. I'll study very hard."

The next day, stimulated by her success with the manager, she spent a morning at her dining table, carefully going over her finances. At the end she had to face the discouraging recognition that any voice teacher who would accept what she could pay probably knew no more about singing than she did. Maybe this was why Claudine was so obsessive about money. Sarah decided that when she went to Claudine's house to meet the Russian again, she would be more sympathetic if her friend mentioned financial worries.

But on Monday the majordomo at the Houdon's mansion

said, "I'm sorry, Mademoiselle Taylor. Monsieur and Madame Houdon are not home."

"Did they leave a message?" she asked, disappointed.

"No, mademoiselle. They departed quite suddenly."

"Do you know if Monsieur Vesenkha is expected?"

"He was here briefly, but he didn't stay."

Sarah left a note for Claudine, asking her to send a message when she returned, and spent the rest of the day studying the music for *Romeo et Juliette*.

By evening a storm had come up. The gusts of rain that blew against the windows matched her lonely spirits. Waiting was so hard! That night she let herself cross off the following date on her calendar instead of waiting until morning.

The next day she was drinking her breakfast coffee when a pounding on her door startled her. Halfway to the door she heard, "Mademoiselle Taylor." It was the concierge's voice, sounding urgent.

"Yes, I'm coming," she called and hurried to open the door.

Behind the concierge stood a tall gendarme. Rain dripped from the bill of his cap and off the edge of his cape, splattering onto his boots. The concierge turned to him and said, "This is Mademoiselle Taylor." Then she retreated partway down the stairs and lingered there.

Sarah's first thought was that something had happened to Pierre. But she stilled her alarm—she wouldn't be the person contacted.

"Mademoiselle Sarah Taylor?" the gendarme asked.

It seemed a strange question when the concierge had just identified her, but Sarah said, "Yes. What do you want?"

"I must ask you to come with me."

"Go with you where?"

"To the Palais de Justice."

That made even less sense. "But why?"

He glanced once at the listening concierge, then said, "You are under arrest, mademoiselle."

CHAPTER TWENTY-TWO

RAIN SPATTERED THROUGH THE BARRED WINDOWS OF THE police van as it jolted over the cobblestone streets. Sarah sat, grasping the edge of the wooden bench to steady herself, too stunned to care about the rain. The gendarme had given her only the additional information that she would be questioned at the headquarters of the Sûreté. The Sûreté was the criminal investigation division of the Paris police! This had to be a dream. A nightmare.

The van stopped and the door opened. They were on the Quai des Orfèvres in the Ile de la Cité. The Palais de Justice loomed menacingly above her. Sarah had seen it often from the Opéra Comique, just across the Pont au Change. Now its gray stone turrets with their steep conical tops called up images from its medieval origins, not just as a palace, but as a place of dungeons and torture.

Inside, the gendarme led her to a room with dark wooden chairs around the walls, three of them occupied by men. Two other policemen stood, one on each side of the door. "Wait here," her escort told Sarah.

She stepped in front of him, stopping him from leaving.

"What is this about?" she demanded.

"The *juge d'instruction* will tell you," he said and went around her.

Sarah started after him, but one of the policemen at the door barred her way. "Sit down, mademoiselle," he ordered.

She sat down and tried to sort her thoughts. She'd done nothing to be arrested for. This had to be some appalling mistake!

Someone coughed, and she looked at the men sitting with her. Two of them wore the caps and rough coats of working men. The third looked like a shopkeeper. She supposed they were here because they'd been arrested. Did they know as little as she did? The shopkeeper, a middle-aged man, was looking at her sympathetically. "Please," she said to him, "can you tell me what a *juge d'instruction* is?"

"That's the magistrate who presides over the investigation of a crime."

"I see. Thank you."

He waited expectantly, obviously curious about her. When she didn't say more, he asked, "Are you in trouble, mademoiselle?"

That she was even here answered his question. He really wanted to know why. "I don't know," she said.

The gendarme who had brought her to the waiting room returned. "Mademoiselle Taylor, come with me."

"If you see the judge this soon," the shopkeeper said enviously, "you must be someone important."

She wasn't important, but if it cleared up the mistake sooner, Sarah hoped the judge thought so.

In the large office where the gendarme took her, two men waited. One was dressed in the same dark blue uniform as the policeman, but with medals across his chest, more braid, and a commanding air. The other, a large man with a small mustache and a somber expression, had on a black robe. Facing these stern-looking officials, Sarah felt her alarm growing to a chilling fear.

The black-robed man rose from behind a desk with a sheaf of papers on it. "Mademoiselle Taylor," he said, in a high voice that didn't match his bulk, "I am Henri Ibert, the *juge d'instruction* in this case. Monsieur Nohain here is the chief of the Sûreté. Under our direction an investigation is being prepared. I must inform you that you are being accused."

She understood the words he was saying; they just didn't make sense.

"Before you confront your accusers," he continued, "you have the right to be represented by counsel. Is there someone you wish?"

"What are you talking about? I haven't even been told why I'm here. What am I accused of?"

"Swindles and fraud," the Sûreté chief said. "You are suspected, mademoiselle, of aiding Bernard and Claudine Houdon in a scheme to defraud their creditors."

Stunned, she could only stare at them. Then shock gave way to dismay for her friend and relief for herself. "Monsieurs, I think you're mistaken about Madame Houdon. But I'm not involved in her affairs. All you have to do is ask her."

The magistrate looked even more stern. "We would like to do that, if you will tell us where we can find Madame Houdon."

"Why at her ..." Sarah began, then remembered. Suddenly everything began to seem terribly, frighteningly real. "I don't know where she is."

The magistrate looked as if he didn't believe her. "Do you wish to arrange counsel before we proceed?" he asked. "If not, I shall ask for the accusing witnesses to be summoned. When they arrive, I shall summarize the evidence."

Sarah tried to think rationally. Did she need an attorney? She didn't know anyone, even by reputation. And if she heard what the evidence was and who had accused her, she could explain. Then she wouldn't need legal help. Her desire for this to be over became paramount. "I want to go ahead now."

The policeman found her a place to wait in a small room on the second floor. She couldn't sit, but instead paced back and forth between the door and the window. Claudine, guilty of fraud? Sarah couldn't believe it. Though she realized her feeling was irrational, Claudine's limp seemed to guarantee her innocence. A lame person was surely trustworthy.

She stopped at the window and looked down on the rain hitting the stones of the courtyard and lashing at the umbrellas of people hurrying in and out. The only time she'd been inside the Palais de Justice she'd gone through the elaborate iron gates on the other side with her father. At the memory, she had to clamp her lips together to keep back the sobs that threatened to burst out. If only Pierre were here! He'd know what to do. No—she must stay calm. Wishing for impossibilities could lead to hysteria. Soon this would all be cleared up, she assured herself, and when she told him about it, he would be tender and sympathetic that she had gone through such a horrible day.

After a time that stretched out to an impossible length, the policeman returned for her and they went back to the magistrate's office. Seated on chairs inside were Eleanore Matrat, Wilhelm Hotter, and the banker, Adolphe Fuzelier. Eleanore looked angry. Fuzelier gave Sarah a haughty, accusing stare. Only Wilhelm appeared sorrowful; the glance he sent her held more distress than reproach.

When Sarah sat down, Monsieur Ibert began. "An investigation has been begun to determine whether Bernard Houdon and Claudine Houdon, with the help of accomplices, have attempted to defraud and swindle their creditors. Suspected accomplices are Georges Royer, also known as Georges Appleton, Sarah Taylor, and the following notaries and attorneys . . ."

After the chilling sound of her name Sarah didn't hear anything more for a few seconds. When she could listen again, she didn't recognize any of the names. After that came the evidence. It was long and complicated, beginning with the results of a private investigation of the Houdons by Adolphe Fuzelier. He had found that the American address for Georges Appleton would have put his office in Boston Commons. This evidence led to a charge of fraud and a search warrant, not for the agreement which had been debated in the civil courts for six years, but for the property titles, stocks and bonds of the purported estate. When the warrant was served, the lockbox that was supposed to contain the papers was broken open. It was empty. So was the Houdon mansion. Bernard and Claudine had disappeared.

During the reading, doubt began to chill Sarah. An address that turned out not to exist. Claudine and Bernard vanished. Sarah felt as if she were wading into an icy stream, going deeper all the time.

The magistrate read on. "Evidence suggests that Georges Royer, or Appleton, entered into a conspiracy with the Houdons to commit fraud and swindles. Sarah Taylor also entered into that conspiracy to urge creditors to lend money to the Houdons. Evidence for this charge is the sworn testimony of Adolphe Fuzelier, Wilhelm Hotter, and Eleanore Matrat."

He stopped reading and looked at Sarah. "That is the portion that concerns you. Do you wish to confirm these charges?"

She'd been afraid she wouldn't be able to force words past her constricted throat, but anger at the unfairness of the accusation saved her. "No. They aren't true!"

"Then we'll hear from the witnesses."

With a beginning of panic she couldn't afford, she said, "Monsieur Ibert, I know what they will say. I don't remember my exact words, but I did tell them what I know—that the

Appleton family in Boston is wealthy. The Appletons probably would help a relative, even an illegitimate one. But I didn't know more about it than that. I was just trying to help Madame Houdon."

The Sûreté chief said skeptically, "You're saying, mademoiselle, that it's just a coincidence? That out of all the people in Paris you, who are personally acquainted with the Appleton family, happened to meet Madame Houdon."

"Yes, that part is a coincidence, but many people from Boston would know the Appletons. They're a prominent family."

"And solely from sympathy for Madame Houdon," Monsieur Nohain continued, his voice disdainful, "you supported her claims about this family whose name was used to give a facade of legitimacy to her scheme?"

She had to fight off panic again. "Yes, but—"

"You did say that they would probably help Georges Royer?"

"No, I didn't. I said they would help a relative. I've never met Georges Royer."

"That's not so," Eleanore Matrat interrupted. "Madame Houdon told Monsieur Hotter and me you were acquainted with Georges Appleton. She said you knew he was on very good terms with his wealthy family."

As if Adolphe Fuzelier were just waiting to get his turn, the banker said impatiently. "It's clear that Mademoiselle Taylor did urge the soundness of the Appleton family and their willingness to aid relatives. In addition to Madame Matrat and Monsieur Hotter, Signor Giovanni Castelli and my son-in-law and daughter can swear to that. The supposition anyone would make is clearly that Mademoiselle Taylor was urging her listeners to lend money—I might say offer it to be stolen—to this fraudulent scheme."

"It hasn't been proved that any scheme was fraudulent," Sarah said furiously. "When Madame Houdon returns, she'll tell you how ridiculous the charges against me are. And I'm sure she'll clear herself." Sarah was no longer sure she believed in Claudine's innocence, but she wouldn't admit that to Fuzelier.

"We are equally anxious to hear Madame Houdon's testimony," the Sûreté chief said sarcastically. "If you know where she is, you should tell us."

Sarah's anger was no longer enough to ward off fear. She didn't answer.

Judge Ibert dismissed the witnesses. Fuzelier and Eleanore walked past Sarah as if she weren't there. Wilhelm Hotter paused, his face troubled. "I'm sorry," he said, and followed the others.

The Sûreté chief gestured to the policeman waiting beside the door. "Mademoiselle Taylor is to go to Saint Lazare."

The prison! What had seemed fear before was nothing to the terror that enveloped Sarah. She turned to the magistrate. "Why? I'll be here—at home. Can you do this?"

"Our laws are not the same as American ones," Monsieur Ibert said disapprovingly. "You will be confined for the present. If you are correct about Madame Houdon, she will shortly return and confirm your innocence and you will be released."

She should have asked for counsel. Anyone. Someone walking down the corridor! No—she must think rationally. "I'm an American citizen. You must notify the American Embassy. And I want to send some messages."

"Very well. Write your messages and I'll have them delivered."

If only she knew how to reach Pierre—but he was far away. In handwriting that barely resembled her own, she wrote notes for Armand and for Ted. Then the gendarme led her back to the van, black and glistening in the rain that continued to pelt down.

The prison of Saint Lazare had been built in the seventeenth century as a hospital for lepers. St. Vincent de Paul had worked and died there. After the Revolution it had been converted to a prison, and later designated for women. Sarah vaguely recalled these facts from guidebooks she had read. They didn't prepare her for the reality of the terrifying wall of stone that faced her when she emerged from the van.

The wall was high, broken by an occasional roof and a grim front side with small, mean windows. Except for two gates, the only entrance was an arched tunnel. In the rain, no light penetrated far enough to indicate that once she entered, she would ever come out at the other end. It might go on endlessly, like corridors in nightmares. Yet when she reached the end and heavy iron doors clanged open, she wished for the uncertainty of the tunnel.

She was in a large guard room. Several policemen greeted the man with Sarah. A woman wearing the black habit of a religious order came forward. "I am Sister Thérèse of the order of Marie-Joseph," the nun said to Sarah. "Follow me."

A guard undid the heavy iron bolts of a door on the opposite side and let the sister and Sarah into an inner courtyard. Behind them the door closed with a reverberating boom, as if to make final the separation from ordinary life. On either side, four tiers of barred windows looked down like malevolent eyes. Woodenly, trying not to think or feel, Sarah followed Sister Thérèse across the courtyard into a corridor on the other side. Their footsteps were the only sounds in the hall, as if the prison were empty. But the room they entered held a second nun and a lay sister in an apron and a lace cap with a large bunch of keys at her waist. Three other women appeared to be prisoners. One of them was pulling on a gray petticoat while beside her the aproned woman was laying earrings and a necklace of glass beads on a table. The two other prisoners stood against the wall. They wore identical dark gray dresses. One of them was sobbing. The other had her hand on the sobbing woman's shoulder, as if trying to comfort her.

The aproned sister looked at Sarah and said, "A new one. Strip off your clothes."

"But what—" Sarah began.

"Be silent!" ordered Sister Thérèse. "The rule here is that no prisoner speaks except in response to a question from the guards. And never to another inmate."

With the words "prisoner" and "inmate" seared into her mind, Sarah finally understood that this was real. She was in prison.

Along with the horror a fierce anger burned inside her— an anger that took her through the humiliation of being searched and prison clothes substituted for her own. She was allowed to keep only her shoes. In silent fury she did as she was ordered; she unfastened her hair, pulled it back from her face, braided it, and pinned the long braid at the base of her neck. Then, with the other three prisoners, she followed Sister Thérèse up to the second floor. They passed a laundry where she could see women folding and stacking linen and entered a long room with rows of tables and benches. An enormous crucifix hung on one wall. A sister sat at a table opposite seven or eight women, who were writing. A large group of prisoners doing needlework sat at another table.

To Sarah the worst thing was the silence. In the face of it her rage softened to the hysterical feeling that all these women in identical dark gray dresses with identically braided hair were wraiths in a tomb. And that she was being buried alive with them.

Sister Thérèse led the way along another corridor lined with doors that had heavy wire mesh over square openings in the upper halves. She stopped at one of them and opened the door. "This is your cell. You'll be assigned work to-morrow." The cell had gray walls, a stone floor, a tiny window, and four pallets, each with a shelf above it. Sarah followed the others inside, and the door closed behind them.

As the sister's footsteps receded, the prisoner who was being searched before Sarah gestured toward the fading sound and hissed, "Bitch!"

"Calling the sisters names won't do you any good," the prisoner who had been comforting the sobbing one said coolly. "They aren't all bad, and at least it's better than having men for guards."

The woman who had cursed lay down on one of the four narrow cots. "You're crazy," she said. "It was better with men. Then you could trade your body for cigarettes and wine."

"We don't have to be silent?" Sarah asked.

"This must be your first time here," the more collected woman said. "The sisters don't bother about talking in the cells. There are too many of us."

Sarah felt as if she'd been granted a partial reprieve. She would have to be here until someone—Armand or Ted or an American Embassy official—responded and found a lawyer for her. Or until Claudine returned and exonerated her. To be silent, cut off from even ordinary conversation with her cellmates, seemed unbearable. Then she'd have nothing to think of but the fear that Claudine might not come back.

The composed woman introduced herself as Louise. With an air of telling a faintly interesting story, she said, "I used to work in an office. My lover worked there too. He embezzled money from my employer. When the theft was discovered, he blamed me, and the police believed him. That was my first sentence to Saint Lazare."

Sarah couldn't imagine what it would be like to have to return here. "This is the second time?" she asked, hoping it wasn't the third.

"Yes. This time is for murder," Louise explained calmly. "When I got out before, I killed my lover. But this sentence isn't long. Men think women can't help committing crimes of passion because we're so weak."

Sarah thought she should feel revulsion or fear, but she didn't. Louise seemed no threat here, and Sarah had learned a great deal in a few hours. She didn't think she would kill in revenge for being sent to prison, but she was beginning to understand how hatred might be that strong.

Cecile, when she finally stopped crying, said that she was a seamstress. She had helped her lover break into a wine shop by crawling through a window and unlocking the door. He had run away, but she had been caught. She had never been in prison before.

"You were stupid," the woman who had called the nun a bitch said to Cecile. "You should have claimed you were drunk. They'd probably have let you off." When Cecile began to sob again, the woman shrugged and turned to Sarah. "I'm Marthe. A seamstress, like her. I've done a few sentences before. I borrowed some money from a . . . friend who was visiting me. The bastard came back with the police and had me arrested for theft."

Sarah noticed that Marthe, for all her foul words, didn't admit the obvious—that she was a prostitute and had stolen money from a client.

The need or desire for money—that was what had brought all of them here. Her too, indirectly.

"My name is Sarah," she said. "I'm here because of a mistake. Someone thought I helped in a swindle."

She could see that none of the others believed her.

Dinner was held in the rectory, the long room with the tables. Sarah's eerie feelings returned in the hall where the only sounds were the dull rustle of clothing and the clink of spoons in bowls. The food was some sort of brown soup. Prisoners around her ate every bit, but Sarah knew she would be sick if she forced down even one spoonful.

The worst time came in the cell when lights were extinguished. Louise and Marthe went to sleep readily, and Cecile cried until she too was asleep. Sarah lay on her pallet, and all the horror of the day inundated her like a wave thundering in, sucking up all of the Atlantic to pour over her. If she could somehow turn time back! To summer, the exposition and her father's visit—and the trip to Etretat.

The memory of those two weeks to Etretat brought her back to the terror of the present, as brilliant sunshine gives shade a blacker cast. Pierre might not want to see her again. She might never have more than those two weeks.

Tears of despair and rage flowed from her eyes and ran down, dampening the hair beside her face. When the silent weeping had exhausted her, determination remained. She would endure Saint Lazare and clear herself. And she wouldn't cry again.

The next day Sarah was assigned to the laundry to fold sheets. She kept her mind occupied by observing other prisoners and listening to her cellmates. These activities provided more trenchant lessons than the religious books in the prison library. How little she knew of the lives of poor women. According to Louise most of the sisters who acted as guards were also from impoverished backgrounds. Like the inmates, a few were cheerful but most acted as if they expected the worst from life.

Sarah told her cellmates that she was a singer. "So am I," Marthe volunteered. "I used to sing at a *beuglant*." That was a slang name for the most squalid of the cafe dance halls. To illustrate, she sang in a raspy voice a song of several verses praising the "tender apples" of a country girl's lover. "The jackass of a manager had a rule. To keep a job there, you had to be available after the show," Marthe said, abandoning her pretense she wasn't a prostitute. "I quit singing. I found out that I could love any man who was generous."

Sarah remembered that she'd heard that same philosophy expressed by a society woman.

At mid-morning of Sarah's second day at Saint Lazare, the names of prisoners who had visitors had been announced. Sarah's name was on the list. She had to wait four and a half anguished hours for her turn. A sister escorted her to the rectory. When they reached the locked door, the sister said, "No physical contact with the visitors is allowed," and then opened the door.

Prisoners sat at specific intervals along the tables, with visitors placed precisely across from them and monitors behind. Sarah could see her place; Armand was sitting opposite an empty space. Relief swept over her like a river breaking through an ice jam. He was proof that she really existed. She hurried joyously toward him.

As she reached her place, Armand rose. He looked sober and tired. "Sarah, I can't tell you how sorry I am about this terrible situation."

"Thank you." She appreciated his concern and sympathy but she was in even greater need of information. "Do you know if the American Embassy has done anything?"

"Ted talked to them. They said they would do what they could, but things are difficult and move slowly."

She felt shaky inside. That wasn't what she wanted to hear.

"Ted wanted to visit you," Armand continued, "but only one of us could come today. And he wants to send a cablegram to your father."

"No! At least, not yet. But I do need a counsel. I don't know anyone. Can you suggest one?"

"I've already talked to Leo Jondinet." Armand had been thinking about her and doing something. Her distress eased a little. "He'll take your case if you wish."

With no prospect of immediate results from the American Embassy, Sarah knew she needed someone very skillful. "Is he good?"

Jondinet is an excellent lawyer. He's already asked a friend in the Sûreté about you. Though he's less certain about the accusation of swindles, he's sure you won't be charged with fraud. The minimum sentence for fraud is five years in prison, but that's the maximum for swindles."

Up to five years in Saint Lazare! That he could say it so calmly shocked her. "Do you think you're comforting me by telling me that?"

He looked taken aback, and she felt contrite. Her troubles weren't his fault, and he was trying to help. "I'm sorry, Armand. This is such a terrible place." Stop, she warned herself. No whining. "I'll manage though, because I know I'll be released soon."

She waited for him to agree with her, but he said, "I left money with the sisters. For you to use at the cantine. I understand you can buy food and stamps and paper. Is there anything else I can get you?"

"Thank you, but all I want is for the police to find Claudine."

"They're doing the best they can."

Armand's words didn't reassure Sarah. If the police had done the best they could, she shouldn't be here.

After he left, she realized that he had said nothing affectionate to her. Not that she expected protestations of love in the rectory of the prison, but she longed for something special that would make her feel cherished, or even human.

The next day Sarah's name was on the list for visitors again. This time she was one of the first to be called, and she went to the rectory breathless with hope. Her visitor was Nathalie. Her elegant fur-trimmed dress and cape made Sarah's prison garb feel even more intolerable.

Sarah sat down, the last of her excitement vanishing at the barely shrouded satisfaction in Nathalie's eyes. But she put on a pleased expression as if this were a visit from someone concerned for her welfare.

"I wanted to see for myself how you are getting along,"

Nathalie said. The polite words of concern, spoken smoothly, didn't disguise a nuance of gratification.

"It's not a pleasant place," Sarah said, lifting her chin defiantly, "but being here is an education. And I won't be here long."

Nathalie didn't bother with the courtesy of agreeing with Sarah. "What a coincidence that you are from Boston and so is Claudine's supposed benefactor."

Sarah's expression felt brittle. If anyone touched her face it might shatter. "That's all it is—a coincidence."

For a moment the hatred Sarah had seen at Madame Dubreuil's musicale contorted Nathalie's face. Then she said smoothly, "The coincidence must be what made the police suspicious. It was one of the first things I noticed about you. When I pointed it out to Claudine, I didn't imagine it could get you into difficulty."

Nathalie's meaning was clear. She had taken advantage of that coincidence. Sarah felt a rage so great it was as if her lungs had stopped functioning. She had to force a deep breath before she could speak. "Then you knew that Claudine was under suspicion," she guessed.

"How could I have known that?" Nathalie's hatred was concealed again, but not her enjoyment.

A memory returned to Sarah—of the fragment of overheard conversation between Fuzelier and Nathalie in the room with the tapestries. "Adolphe Fuzelier! I think he knew something and told you." From Nathalie's slight surprise, Sarah had made another accurate guess.

"You'll be free eventually," Nathalie said coldly, "after a lesson in how unpleasant gullibility can be. And unfortunately your reputation will be ruined."

Loathing overwhelmed Sarah, as if it were part of her bloodstream, filling every fragment of her brain and body. She felt an intense desire she'd never experienced before— to strike someone. To inflict as much physical pain on Nathalie as possible. "Aren't you worried that I'll tell Armand?"

"He wouldn't believe you. After all, I lent Claudine a sizable sum of money myself, and now I'll lose it."

Sarah thought she was going to be violently sick. But not in front of Nathalie! Fiercely she contained her nausea and said contemptuously, "You would do anything to control Armand."

All pretense of amiability was gone. Nathalie's eyes were those of a predator that already held the prey in its claws. "My son means everything to me."

Summoning all her acting skill, Sarah said in an assured voice, "Oh, but I think you've forgotten how much *I* mean to *him*." She paused and let a suggestive smile grow on her face. "Under certain circumstances, which Armand is always eager to repeat, he'll believe exactly what I tell him. Especially when it's true."

Nathalie's face lost its color. Her imperial posture sagged as fear filled her eyes.

Sarah's surge of gratification lasted only a moment; then her spirit recoiled from an ugly contest with this woman. The period for visiting wasn't over, but she rose. Without looking back, she walked to the locked door and waited for someone to take her back to her cell. The women there were more honorable company than Nathalie.

Sarah spend that night raging—at Nathalie, at herself for not having been more wary, at Nohain and his Sûreté who hadn't found Claudine. By morning her fury had exhausted her to a weary calm. Somehow she must endure the prison for now. She wouldn't think about how long.

It was the day for baths. A week before, Sarah would have shrunk from undressing in front of strangers. Now modesty was unimportant compared with the chance to be clean. It was only a little uncomfortable when several women eyed her with interest. She'd already observed that the pairs of women who passed notes and risked exchanging murmurs during the exercise hour acted more like sisters or mothers and daughters than lovers. Some of them must be lesbians, she supposed, but many of the special relationships in the prison didn't appear to result, as outraged moralists claimed, from wicked lascivious desires. They developed from the women's need to love and receive affection in return. She understood that very well.

During the baths she was startled to see a few women with tattoos. Two had images of a madonna and child; several had pictures of mothers with children surrounding them. One declared the woman, or at least her right breast, was the "property of Henri Joly." Unclaimed property. Sarah felt unclaimed too.

The fresh gray dress Sarah put on after the bath felt good, but she combed her washed hair resentfully. It had just enough wave that she had to pull it tight to achieve the prescribed severity. Small ends that had broken off around her face curled stubbornly, refusing to stay in the braid. The previous day a sister had reprimanded her for the wisps around her face, as if she were a child. As much as the silence and being herded by the sisters, she hated that reminder of her loss of freedom.

Sarah had just finished pinning up the braid when Louise came in. "Your name is on the list for visitors again," she said enviously.

"It must be Leo Jondinet, the attorney who's going to be my counsel," Sarah said, as much to herself as to Louise. "Or someone from the American embassy." It couldn't be Nathalie, come to gloat again.

She tried to keep her conviction during the two hours she waited for her turn, but when she followed the sister to the rectory, the muscles of her neck and shoulders ached from the effort of appearing calm. Inside the large room, the nun who waited said, "The middle place at table two. Come along."

Table two was at the far end of the large room. The concrete posts that supported the roof and the tall black stove that provided meager heat blocked Sarah's view. She walked stiffly forward. When she passed the iron cylinder of the stove, she could see a man sitting across from the spot that waited for her. The man looked like Pierre.

She stopped. It couldn't be! She saw him because she wanted to so desperately.

He saw her at the same time and rose, starting toward her. The sister behind him put out a hand to stop him.

It was Pierre. It was! Sarah wanted to run, to fly across the table that would be between them, to feel his arms around her, holding her close. But her legs barely managed to carry her to the bench across from where he stood, waiting for her, his eyes on her as if she were the only thing he could see.

His eyes. Suddenly she became aware of what he was seeing—the ugly prison uniform, her hair pulled severely back without anything to soften the lines of fatigue she knew must be in her face. Everything that proclaimed her shame and humiliation. She put a shaky hand up to her hair, but nothing would help. Heat scorching her skin, she took her place on the bench.

Instantly he reached across and grasped her hand.

"No touching!" the sister said sharply.

He released her hand, but that touch was the sunshine she hadn't seen for a week. He smiled at her, the wonderful quirky smile that teased and caressed her at the same time. "You look beautiful. Even here." She felt like a flower opening under the sunshine.

Now she could talk to him, as if she were a normal person instead of a ghost. "You weren't supposed to be back in Paris yet."

His eyes sobered to a hard glint. "Ted got my address in Cannes from *Le Combattant*. He sent me a telegram." Pierre tried a smile that didn't make it through his anger. "It was the slowest train in France."

"I'm glad you're here." The most inadequate statement she'd ever made.

"Who is your attorney? What does he say? What about the American Embassy?"

"Armand arranged for Leo Jondinet to represent me. I haven't seen him or anyone from the embassy yet."

Pierre said a word under his breath that Sarah knew the sister wouldn't like. "I'll talk to Jondinet. He or some other lawyer will be here tomorrow," he promised grimly. "I'll go with Ted to the embassy and find out why you haven't seen them. And I'll find out what the Sûreté is doing to locate the Houdons. It may be necessary to hire private investigators to look for them."

His anger and determination enveloped and nurtured her as if he'd made love to her. It was a kind of lovemaking— or at least of loving.

"Sarah." He took a breath as if preparing for something he didn't want to say but must. "Did Aunt Nathalie have a part in this?"

Her first impulse was to tell him about Nathalie's visit. But she knew that he dreaded her answer. His cousin and aunt were his only family. If she told him about Nathalie's intentions, it wouldn't help free her from prison, and he would blame himself for getting her involved with Armand and Nathalie. No—she couldn't repay his kindness now with hurt. "I met Claudine at your aunt's house. But she didn't ask me to tell people I know the Appletons or that I suggest anyone talk to the Houdons. That was my own doing."

The flash of relief in his eyes rewarded her.

"When I got into Paris last night," he said, "I saw a friend in the parquet. That's the prosecutor's office. He told me a little about the case. Adolphe Fuzelier's bank was in trouble, and he couldn't get their money back from the Houdons.

That's why he got suspicious and started an investigation."

"I knew he'd done that."

"Some of the people who lent money to the Houdons received five percent interest. That's well above the going rate—and they were promised a fifty percent bonus when Claudine gets her inheritance. That amounts to usury. Some of them tried to stop the official investigation. A couple of newspapermen got hold of the story. They've published rumors that the Houdons were warned to flee."

She began to feel cold again. People usually "flee" when they're guilty.

"The evidence against you is very weak," Pierre said angrily, "but the Sûreté is anxious to show they're not being influenced to go easy. They don't have the Houdons so they're holding you. And they've arrested the attorneys and notaries who handled the civil proceedings over the fortune Claudine claimed she's to inherit."

Pierre's use of the word, *claimed* banished the last of the optimism his appearance had brought. "Then you think she's guilty?"

"I don't know. I do know you're innocent."

Those wonderful words restored her hope again. "I'm not sure anymore what I think about Claudine Houdon, but surely she'll say I didn't know anything about her affairs."

"There may be other things to do while we look for her. What about your father? Can he get the American Foreign Service to put pressure on the French authorities?"

"He's so far away," she temporized. "He knew President Hayes, but that was more than ten years ago." She hesitated, and realized that she didn't have to pretend with Pierre. "I'm frightened. But I don't want Papa to know unless that's the only chance. He'd be so upset. And maybe he'd be ashamed of me."

"I don't think he would," Pierre said gently. "You haven't done anything to make anyone ashamed of you."

His gentleness almost released the tears that she had hidden since the first night. A confession trembled on her lips—about loving him. But she stored it inside along with her tears. She couldn't tell him she loved him, not now. It would be like a demand that he respond because of her need.

As if he could read her thoughts he reached across the table again and clasped her hand. The sister behind him started forward, her mouth open to speak, but he ignored her, his voice shutting out hers. "Sarah, I love you."

The room shrank to the warmth of his hand and his tender eyes, separating them for a moment from the red-faced sister. With a great rush of joy, Sarah knew his words had strengthened her for whatever she had to endure. She wasn't positive whether he spoke from real love or from kindness. Just for this while, she wouldn't question.

CHAPTER
TWENTY-THREE

SARAH SAT ON A WOODEN CHAIR IN A WAITING ROOM IN the Palais de Justice and tried to ignore her tight throat. It had been eight days since her arrest—eight days since she'd been taken from here to Saint Lazare. Would she be freed today, or disappear again behind its sinister walls?

Leo Jondinet sat on her left. He was a stocky, vigorous man with dark hair, large ears and a full beard streaked with gray.

Pierre, sitting on the other side, asked her, "Shall I get you something?"

"Thank you. I don't want anything." Except for this to be over. Until then she wouldn't be able to swallow even water.

The previous day agents of the Sûreté had located Claudine and Bernard in a hotel in Le Havre and found the mysterious Georges Appleton with them. Judge Ibert, the magistrate presiding over the investigation, had called a hearing to be held as soon as they were in Paris. When Jondinet had come to Saint Lazare and told Sarah, she had been exultant, sure that meant her release. Overnight her uncertainties and fears returned.

The lawyer said, "I'll go downstairs and see whether the Houdons and Monsieur Appleton have been brought in yet. The train from Le Havre should have arrived half an hour ago."

"Yes," Sarah said, "please do. It's so hard to wait."

Jondinet looked at her somberly. "Remember my warning, Mademoiselle Taylor. This hearing may not settle everything you're hoping for. The evidence is not conclusive one way or the other. Monsieur Ibert may need time to investigate further, particularly in regard to Georges Appleton. Little is known about him. That will mean delays in checking on him because of the time involved in getting information from the United States."

"Yes, I understand," she said quietly. Inside she was screaming, *No, that can't be true! I can't stand to go back to Saint Lazare!* But she might have to stand it.

Jondinet's black robe ballooned behind him as he left.

"You look lovely, Sarah," Pierre said.

Gratefully she turned her thoughts to him. He had gone to her flat and brought a modest blue walking dress and a hat to the prison for her. That morning she'd had a bath, all to herself, and had been able to coil her unbraided hair in her usual way on top of her head. But she didn't feel lovely. Nothing seemed quite right. The dress no longer fit properly, and her hair felt insecurely fastened. Her hat was an uncomfortable appendage. She had the feeling that during the days in Saint Lazare she had become a stranger to herself.

But she smiled at him and said, "Thank you for saying that." He squeezed her hand gently, returning her smile. Armand had found Jondinet for her. She appreciated his help for that, and for his first visit. But Pierre's spirit had sustained her.

The small anteroom where Sarah and Pierre waited was austere, with dark chairs set against the walls, like an outer room to any government office. But it wasn't. It was next to the courtroom for criminal trials. "Monsieur Jondinet told me so many things I'm not sure I have it all straight," she said nervously to Pierre. "Please explain to me again why the hearing is in the Cour d'Assises."

"They need the courtroom because so many people are involved," he said patiently. "A lot of people lent money to the Houdons. They're all potential witnesses. The police interrogation room isn't big enough. But this is an investigative hearing, not a trial."

"Yes, I see," she said, but she couldn't ignore the possibility that she might come back to the courtroom as a defendant in a trial. And no matter which way she looked, she found her eyes coming back to the policeman who had brought her from the prison. He was standing with his hands behind his back and a bored expression on his face, as if marking time before the return journey.

Pierre said, "I've been thinking about Georges Appleton. You've never met him. But Eleanore Matrat says Claudine told her that you knew him."

"Yes, that's what Eleanore said in the hearing." Sarah and Pierre had spent his visits to the prison going over all the circumstances of her arrest.

"If Appleton couldn't identify you," Pierre said, "that would tend to discredit whatever Claudine says."

Sarah could feel her hands begin to tremble and clasped them together in her lap. "I think Claudine will tell the magistrate that I don't know anything about her affairs. It won't help her to involve me. Georges Appleton will surely say the same thing—that he doesn't know me."

"I hope you're right," Pierre said. She could tell from his careful tone that he didn't agree with her. "But things may not turn out that way. Just in case, I think we should be prepared."

His immediate assumption that he shared her problems had comforted her enormously. However, today it wasn't enough to stem her fears about the hearing. "Remember what Jondinet told us," she said, trying to convince herself. "If I were in England or the United States, I'd be free on a writ of habeas corpus because there's so little evidence." Pierre didn't say anything, but at least he didn't point out that the American Embassy hadn't been able to get her released.

Monsieur Jondinet came back and sat down. "The Houdons and Monsieur Appleton are in the building," he reported. "It won't be much longer."

Pierre asked, "Could Mademoiselle Taylor sit with the witnesses so that she doesn't stand out?"

Jondinet looked thoughtful. "I probably could arrange that. But why?"

"She's never met Monsieur Appleton. But Madame Houdon claims she has. If Appleton were asked to point out Mademoiselle Taylor and he couldn't, that might discredit Madame Houdon and support Mademoiselle Taylor's innocence."

"Hmm. Yes, that might be useful."

"Wouldn't everyone turn around and look at me?" Sarah asked. She imagined the heads turning curiously. The accusing faces. "Then he'd know who I was and the magistrate would think I was the one who lied."

"If you slipped in at the last moment and sat just behind the witnesses," Pierre maintained, "everyone would probably be looking at the Houdons."

Jondinet frowned. "What about the newspaper stories? There have been sketches of Mademoiselle Taylor in all of them. Appleton may have seen one of the drawings."

Sarah felt a flush of humiliation. Pierre hadn't told her about the newspapers. She must have been described as a criminal!

"The articles," Pierre responded, "have been about 'La Belle Americaine.' The writers like that phrase. I'm sorry about that, Sarah. But it has an advantage. All the drawings have pictured you dressed in costume for an opera. Wig and all. None of them looks like you."

Jondinet's face cleared. "In that case, asking Appleton for an identification might work. However, Mademoiselle Taylor, if you do as Monsieur de Tourbey suggests I will be seated in front and not beside you. Do you wish to do this?"

She hesitated. Pierre wouldn't be there since only people involved in the case could be at the hearing for the investigation. It would be even more frightening to sit alone. Could she do it? "Yes."

"If there's some question we must discuss that seems more important than leaving you unidentified, I will have you join me immediately," he assured her.

She breathed a little more easily. "I understand."

"I'll go speak to Monsieur Nohain so that you can slip in without the policeman calling attention to you." Jondinet jumped up and hurried out in his brisk way.

Sarah couldn't sit any longer. Pierre stood up with her, taking her hands and holding them. His warmth seeped through her gloves, but she still shivered. "How are you feeling?" he asked.

"I'm terrified," she confessed.

"Good, then you'll do fine." His smile offered warmth too. "Isn't the bravest person the one who's terrified and does what's necessary anyway?"

Jondinet rushed back in, followed a little more slowly by Monsieur Nohain. The Sûreté chief said to the policeman, "Monsieur Jondinet will be responsible for his client in the courtroom. You do not need to accompany her." He acknowledged Sarah with a perfunctory nod, and left.

Jondinet went to the small window in the door that led into the courtroom and looked inside. "Mademoiselle Taylor, please come and point out the witnesses who know you."

He stepped aside. Sarah stared into a large, dark room.

Just to the right she saw the rows of chairs where the witnesses sat. About a third were women. "Madame Matrat and Monsieur Hotter are in the front. The Comtesse de Saint-Maurice is near them. I don't see Monsieur Fuzelier."

Pierre spoke softly from behind her shoulder. "All the women except my aunt and Madame Matrat and one other have their veils over their faces. Sarah, if you pull yours down, you'll look just like the rest."

She began to unfasten the loops of veil from around the wide brim of her hat, but it snagged and her trembling fingers couldn't get it free. "Here," Pierre said, and finished freeing it, then pulled it down across her face.

Jondinet opened the door a crack. Sarah could hear the murmur of hushed voices. "The door to the corridor is opening," he said. "I see the Houdons and Appleton just outside. In a moment everyone will be looking at them and you can go in. Sit in the last row for witnesses. I'll come in after a minute or two."

In spite of the presence of the lawyer and the policeman, Pierre gave her a fierce, reassuring hug. "I'll be watching through the window."

The volume of sound from the courtroom increased sharply. "Now," the lawyer said. She slipped through the door into the courtroom.

As quietly as possible she walked to the last row of chairs for witnesses. Two men she had never seen before already occupied seats there. Though her heart sounded to her like a gong in the orchestra being struck repeatedly, no one noticed her. Everyone was watching the far end of the room where gendarmes were entering with the Houdons. In what seemed like a long time but must have been no more than a minute, Maître Jondinet came in from the anteroom. After he reached the front and took a seat, Sarah could look at Claudine and Bernard.

The Houdons were seated at a long narrow table. Two

men Sarah hadn't seen before were with them. One, seated across the table, was large, with a full gray beard. The other, a slight man sitting beside Claudine, was clean-shaven except for a narrow goatee. He appeared nervous, stroking his goatee with one hand and rubbing the table with the other. Both the Houdons looked angry. Though Sarah couldn't see their faces in detail at that distance, Claudine was frowning and her back was rigid. Bernard was talking to the large man, punctuating his words with short, forceful gestures.

Sarah decided the large man must be the counsel and the nervous man Georges Appleton. She strained to see whether he resembled any of the Appletons she had met in Boston, and realized such a farfetched attempt only indicated the intensity of her fear. Deliberately she looked away and steeled herself to wait for the proceedings to begin.

The courtroom was designed to reflect the dignity of French justice. Intricate carvings decorated the ceiling. On the walls sunken panels displayed a sword and balanced scales. The bench for the three justices who presided over criminal cases occupied the highest level in the room. On the level just below, an elevated box with tiered seats for the jury suggested they would also be above the fray. Sarah decided an isolated seat behind and slightly above the table where the Houdons sat was for the defendant. Anyone sitting there would be completely alone. Sarah shuddered.

At the rustle of a woman's garments she looked to her left. Madame Charcot and her father, Adolphe Fuzelier, stood at the end of the row of seats. Sarah felt frozen in place. Her veil didn't obscure her face enough to keep them from recognizing her at this short distance. When they saw her, Monsieur Fuzelier frowned. He looked around, and Sarah thought he was about to call for a policeman. At that moment the double doors to the corridor at the end of the chamber opened. Monsieur Nohain, in his intimidating Sûreté uniform, came in. Fuzelier said something to his daughter, and they sat down. Sarah's blood began to circulate again.

Judge Ibert entered, followed by a clerk carrying several large folders. The two men joined Nohain at a table near the Houdons, and the room quieted.

Sarah's hands were damp inside her gloves. If the Fuzeliers pointed her out, the plan to trap Appleton could go against her. *Sarah*, she told herself sternly, *Pierre said you would be brave. You will not give in to fear!* She stared at the magistrate, refusing to look at the Fuzeliers again.

"Bernard and Claudine Houdon," Juge Ibert began, "the evidence—"

"These proceedings are outrageous!" Claudine interrupted, her voice high and shrill. She pushed her chair back with a violent motion and stood, glaring at the magistrate. "This is a scheme by Adolphe Fuzelier to attack me and my husband. He pretended to be my friend. He even sent a spy, a footman with a sad story, to my household. Fuzelier knew I would be soft-hearted enough to hire the man. His plan was for the man to fabricate evidence." The forcefulness of Claudine's denunciation revived a little of Sarah's hope that the Houdons were innocent.

"Madame Houdon," said Ibert. "You will have your opportunity to answer once the evidence is detailed and witnesses give their testimony."

Claudine went on as if the magistrate hadn't spoken. "Fuzelier's plan didn't work the way he expected. Once the footman knew us, he refused to do his dirty work. Instead he told us about this disgraceful attempt against us."

"And you fled rather than bring charges against Monsieur Fuzelier?" Apparently Ibert, red-faced, had temporarily abandoned the effort to restrain Claudine. Sarah was astonished that the French system allowed Claudine to argue so freely.

"We did not flee." Suddenly Claudine was an icy aristocrat.

"We happened to be leaving for a vacation in England."

"Why were no papers found in your lockbox? No wills. No titles to land. No stocks and bonds."

"You'll have to ask Monsieur Fuzelier. The footman undoubtedly wasn't the only spy in our household."

"Madame Houdon," Ibert said sternly, "you are asking us to take your word about a very serious charge."

"You have taken too many other people's word," she said hotly.

To Sarah's left Adolphe Fuzelier started to rise, and Sarah's breath pounded painfully in her chest. If he spoke, everyone would look this way. But then Jondinet rose to his feet. "Monsieur Ibert," Jondinet said, in a moderate voice. "I have a question for Madame Houdon. Depending on her answer, I believe I can suggest a way to establish her truthfulness."

"Very well, Maître Jondinet," the magistrate responded.

"Madame Houdon, I'm sure you know Mademoiselle Taylor has been detained until it is determined whether she is to be charged with conspiracy in this case. She says she did not know anything of your affairs other than that the Appletons are a wealthy American family. If you can clear her of suspicion, that will be justice for her."

The rotation of Sarah's earth stopped while she waited for the answer.

"Justice! I can't clear her. I can't *clear* anyone because there is no conspiracy. That is what must be recognized here. That is the justice I want."

Sarah wanted to cry and scream, but she could only clench her hands and wait.

"Monsieur Ibert," Jondinet said. "I have a request for Monsieur Appleton."

"But—" Claudine began.

"Madame Houdon," Ibert thundered. "You will sit down and be silent now or you will be removed from this hearing. Monsieur Appleton, please stand."

The slight man rose hesitantly, rubbing his hands together. He looked in Jondinet's direction, but at the floor instead of the lawyer's face.

"Monsieur Appleton, Madame Houdon has told two witnesses that Mademoiselle Taylor knows you. Mademoiselle Taylor is in this room. Will you please point her out to me?"

People seated in front of Sarah began to turn and look at each other. Fuzelier and his daughter swiveled and stared directly at Sarah.

Appleton said in French, but with an American accent, "I can't see their faces. Most of them are wearing veils."

Jondinet turned toward the witnesses behind him. "Will the madames be so kind as to put up their veils." After a pause, women began to lift their hands to their chins.

For a second the room seemed to Sarah to be filled with a gray fog. Then her vision cleared. She folded her veil up over the brim of her hat.

Georges Appleton, his face visibly pale even from a distance, stared at each woman in turn. When his appraisal reached the last row, he frowned. Then slowly he looked over all the women again, his gaze finally returning to the last row. "There." He pointed an unsteady hand toward Sarah. "That woman with the man on the end. The one in the brown dress."

He meant Fuzelier's daughter!

"That is not Mademoiselle Taylor," Jondinet said, and his voice held a tiny fraction of the exhilaration Sarah felt.

Claudine was on her feet again, her face as red as Appleton's was pale. Her strident voice boomed out. "I never claimed Monsieur Appleton and Mademoiselle Taylor knew each other. Whoever said that misunderstood me. I said Mademoiselle Taylor knew the Appleton family. I was trying to tell you that but you wouldn't let me."

"If that is so," Ibert said equally stridently, "why, Monsieur Appleton, did you attempt to identify Mademoiselle Taylor?"

"Monsieur Appleton," Claudine snapped, "is not well, and the outrageous treatment we have received has confused him."

Ibert had abandoned the majesty of his position in the furor Claudine had created, but he had force on his side. "Monsieur Appleton will speak for himself and you, Madame Houdon, will be quiet."

She sat down. Appleton looked from Claudine to Ibert and said in a faint voice, "I'm not well. I didn't understand." He sat down as if his legs wouldn't hold him longer.

Ibert didn't press for a further answer. Sarah felt the walls of Saint Lazare closing in, crushing her.

Now Bernard Houdon was on his feet, not shouting as Claudine had been, but saying in a cold, hard voice, "It's enemies of my father who are responsible for this infamous attack on my family." Light glinted off his glasses, making his eyes as hard as his voice. "Those people who are secret workers for Germany." A mutter went around the room at the word that always roused French hatreds.

He ranted on, but Sarah didn't listen. Instead in her mind she heard Georges Appleton. He spoke French with an American accent. That fit with Claudine's account that he had spent most of his life in the United States. But there was something about his accent that prodded at her.

Bernard Houdon had finally finished. Ibert looked at Georges Appleton. "Do you wish to say something now?"

Appleton said, "I don't feel well. But everything is as Madame Houdon . . ."

Appleton's voice trailed off as Sarah rose and started toward the front. Everyone stared at her as if they could see that her legs were barely negotiating the distance. She reached the table where Monsieur Jondinet sat and said softly to him, "I want to say something."

He hesitated, then rose and addressed the magistrate. "Monsieur Ibert, Mademoiselle Taylor also has a request."

Ibert nodded grimly. "I suppose Mademoiselle Taylor is entitled to a turn."

She took a steadying breath and said, "I would like Monsieur Appleton to tell us about his business in the United States. And I would like him to speak in English."

The magistrate looked at Appleton. "Monsieur, please do as Mademoiselle Taylor requests."

After a pause, Appleton began nervously. He spoke in English with only a modest French accent. "Because my business is shipping, I don't spend much time in the United States."

"But you grew up in New England?" Sarah asked.

"Yes. My father took me there and I went to school in Boston." He went on with convincing details about the shipping business, but Sarah wasn't listening for the sense of his words. She was listening to the way he pronounced them.

When he stopped, she rested one hand against the table and clenched the other at her side to keep them from shaking. Watching Appleton's face, she said, "Monsieur Ibert, Monsieur Appleton is not pronouncing English the way we do in Boston. He speaks as people do only in the southern part of the United States."

From Appleton's complete loss of color and the trembling of his lips she knew she was right. At her side Jondinet, on his feet as well, said in an accusing voice, "Monsieur Appleton, I think you must tell the truth."

The flesh of Appleton's face seemed to slip downward until his forehead looked shrunken and his jaw heavy. "Yes," he said, in a voice that was close to a whisper. "It was part of the scheme. There never was a Georges Appleton."

"He's lying!" Claudine was screaming now. "It's all part of the plot against us!"

Sarah sagged against the table. No one would believe Claudine now.

While Jondinet went to confer with Ibert, Sarah sat at his

table, unable to let go of the fear entirely. Behind her, whispers hummed sibilantly, but she didn't look around. At the front the Sûreté chief moved Appleton to a different table away from the Houdons. Claudine was talking to the attorney with her, making furious gestures. After a single malevolent glare she didn't look again at Sarah, as if she'd dismissed her from any place in her thoughts.

Jondinet returned, his jubilation breaking through his usual contained expression. "Monsieur Ibert has concluded that the charges against you are without merit."

Sarah felt a joy so fierce that for the first time in her life she thought she might faint.

Monsieur Jondinet put a supporting hand under her elbow. "I'll get all the papers from Monsieur Ibert later." An exultant smile escaped his careful legal demeanor. "Come," he said, "Monsieur de Tourbey is waiting for you."

He held her arm as they started back to the anteroom. She leaned on it until they were almost there. Then she ran ahead to the door and through it into Pierre's arms.

"I'm free! I'm free!" It was all she could say.

Behind her Jondinet closed the door. "Mademoiselle, I admire your courage. Monsieur de Tourbey, I wish you could have heard her. You would have been proud."

"I could see, and I am proud." Pierre held her as if he would never let her be anywhere but in his arms.

"I'll take care of the formalities," Jondinet said. "You don't have to worry about anything more."

"Will Mademoiselle Taylor be needed to testify?"

"No. Monsieur Ibert is convinced she knows nothing of the Houdons' affairs."

"Then we'll be going to my property in Cannes for a week or so," Pierre said. He released her enough to look down at her. "Is that all right with you?"

She nodded, too overwhelmed with emotion—relief, love,

an exhausted anguish, she wasn't sure what—to speak. The ordeal here was over. Being with Pierre would be joy mixed with a different uncertainty. If she had courage for Saint Lazare, she could have courage to be honest with him.

CHAPTER
TWENTY-FOUR

T<small>O SARAH'S EYES HER FLAT LOOKED NEGLECTED, LIKE A</small> house whose owners had been away for a long time. She resisted the impulse to dust and polish, but she touched her piano, then the chair next to the stove where she liked to sit and read. In the dining room she greeted the dishes. "I'm free! I'm home!"

Was she home? No sure answer occurred to her. Monsieur Cesbron would have had to replace her in the Opéra Comique chorus, and he probably wouldn't have her back now. If he'd been upset about a reference to her in a column, he might have had a heart attack from reading newspapers the past two weeks. Maybe she would have to leave Paris to continue singing in opera at all.

That was for the future. Now she must pack. She would take only clothes in bright colors. Nothing gray or black. In Cannes there would be wonderful, glorious sunshine. And Pierre. Singing the "Habañera" from *Carmen* softly to herself, she began to fold a pale green dress.

A knock interrupted her song. It wouldn't be Pierre. He'd gone to make arrangements for travel to Cannes and then to get what he would need from his flat. Momentarily she considered not answering. No—she couldn't live that way, fearful that a policeman waited every time someone knocked. She approached the door warily. "Who is it," she called.

"Madame Loti."

The concierge. She'd brought the policeman. "What do you want?"

"I have messages for you, Mademoiselle Taylor."

Letting out the breath she hadn't known she was holding, Sarah opened the door.

Madame Loti's smile was artificial. "I saw you arrive. While you were . . . away, these came for you." She handed Sarah four envelopes.

"Thank you, Madame Loti, for saving them for me."

Sarah closed the door on the concierge's expression of disappointed curiosity and stood for a moment, regaining her composure. Facing people who knew she'd been imprisoned, even unjustly, wasn't going to be easy.

Two of the messages were from Ted, and one was from Helene. The fourth envelope was addressed in Solange's elaborate handwriting. Sarah wasn't sure she could face an emotional outpouring. She put it aside and opened the ones from Ted.

He had sent word to the prison through Pierre, telling her of his concern and support. These were additional reassurances that he was eager to see her and talk to her. "After this," he wrote, "you should consider going back to the United States." That might be good advice.

Helene sent love and a muted description of the effect the news of her arrest had at the Opéra Comique. "Monsieur Cesbron was quite upset. He replaced you in the chorus. But everyone else wants you to come back as soon as you can." The "but everyone else" confirmed Sarah's guess about the manager's reaction.

Picking up Solange's envelope, Sarah decided that the ordeal she'd just been through made what Solange had done seem less important. People's behavior, Sarah realized, including her own, was more complicated than she'd imagined before she came to Paris. The city had been her teacher. The lessons, sometimes terrible, sometimes wonderful, had changed her.

Solange's note was dated the day after Sarah's arrest. It was brief: "This monstrous injustice can't be allowed to damage your career. There are things we must do. I expect you at my house right away so that we can get started."

Solange's arrogant conviction that she knew what should be done also carried the unquestioned assumption of Sarah's innocence and quick release. The confidence outweighed the arrogance. Sarah felt a rush of her previous affection for Solange. At the bottom of the note under the embellished signature she noticed a final sentence: "Please come." It was as humble a plea as Solange could make.

Hastily Sarah wrote notes to Ted, Helene, and Solange, explaining she would be away and promising to see them when she was back in Paris. Then she returned to packing and added her prettiest underclothes to the dresses. As anticipation brought the inevitable blush to her face, she also gathered the things Solange had explained how to use. In Etretat Pierre had taken care of protection against pregnancy, but she must be prepared this time herself. The future with him was uncertain, and she didn't want either of them trapped into marriage. Or was it really his reluctance she worried about? She wasn't sure.

She had just closed her case when she heard the expected knock on her door and glanced at her pocket watch. Yes, it was time for Pierre to be back. She carried the case into the drawing room and answered without hesitating.

It wasn't Pierre.

Armand said, "May I come in?" '

"Yes, of course." He had come twice to the prison, as her first visitor, and a few days afterward when he brought Leo Jondinet to meet her. Now he looked just as usual, tall and elegant in his black frock coat, his eyes faintly melancholy. But she had the same feeling as she'd had about her apartment—that she hadn't seen him for a very long time.

When he was inside, he grasped her hands and said, "I just heard that you were released. I'm relieved and delighted."

She stepped back, releasing herself. "Thank you again for persuading Monsieur Jondinet to be my counsel. By doing that, you helped free me."

"It's enough thanks that you've been exonerated. I wish I could have done more. Your welfare is very important to me."

She could see the truth of his words in his eyes and hear it in the slight unsteadiness of his voice. She responded with genuine warmth, "Your friendship means a great deal to me."

He noticed her case on the floor, then looked questioningly at her. "I'll be away for a week or so," she explained. "Pierre and I are going to his property near Cannes."

The lines of Armand's face deepened to unhappiness. "I see."

The knocking that sounded on her door again was sharp and impatient. She could barely get it open before Pierre was inside, saying, "We don't have much time. Are you—" He stopped, looking at Armand.

"You're taking Sarah to Cannes?" Armand asked challengingly.

Pierre's "Yes!" bristled with a responding challenge.

"I want to go away from Paris for a while," Sarah said, but neither man looked at her. "I don't think I can stand anything more unpleasant to happen now."

For a frozen instant it seemed to her as though they had

all stepped out of the painting by David in the Louvre of *The Rape of the Sabine Women*. Pierre and Armand were the warriors, girded for a deadly struggle. She was like Hersilia in the center, pleading against bloodshed.

Finally Armand said stiffly, "I won't delay you." He turned to Sarah. "Good-bye for the present, Sarah. I shall see you when you return to Paris." Now he was a Roman emperor, commanding with his voice the obedience of the civilized world. He kissed her hand and left.

Eyebrows meeting in a frown, Pierre looked after his cousin. Sarah put her hand on his arm. "I'm ready to go with you."

He turned back to her, his face smoothing into a smile that seemed to Sarah to hold both tenderness and love. As he took her bag and they closed the door behind them, she prayed she was right.

The only accommodations on the train Pierre had been able to secure were in a compartment with three women—a middle-aged woman and two elderly sisters who were apparently her aunts. The sisters made constant demands on their niece and then complained when she didn't please them, which was most of the time. When the sisters were finally quiet, Sarah dozed, leaning against Pierre's shoulder.

By the time the express train arrived in Cannes in late afternoon of the following day, Sarah was too exhausted to care about her surroundings. She had an impression of fading sunlight, of the carriage climbing up a hill with gates and drives disappearing into pine trees. Each motion of the carriage swayed her tired body until she gave up and slumped against Pierre. Her next conscious feeling was of arms about her, lifting her, and the movements of his body as he carried her. She couldn't force her eyes open as he put her down. Then everything faded away.

*   *   *

When Sarah awakened, she found she was nestled in a soft comforter in the middle of a large bed. The flannel lining of the quilt felt warm against her bare arms and calves, and she realized she had on only her camisole and drawers. Faint pearl-gray light was coming in tall arched windows that also let in the fresh smell of pine trees and morning dew. She stretched cautiously and discovered she felt whole and renewed. Like mornings in childhood when she had been ill, and awakened to the wonderful knowledge she was well again.

As the light grew and changed, colors and shapes became more distinct. The wood of a high chest took on a reddish gleam. Gray draperies turned to rose brocade. Blots on the wall were transformed into pictures of boats with ghostly sails, like images emerging on a photographer's plate in its bath of developing fluid.

She sat up and slid off the bed, holding the comforter around her. Now she could see that the crouching animal at the foot of the bed was her portmanteau, and the sprawled body on a chair her petticoats. When she stepped off the rug beside the bed, the wood floor felt cool under her bare feet. At the window she looked out at a vista of trees and rooftops sloping down toward a mist penetrated by indistinct spires and towers. That must be the town. Along with the pungent smell of pine, she could smell the dusty, bitter odor of eucalyptus. A rooster crowed and was answered by the faint challenge of another rooster, but she heard no voices, outside or in.

She found her robe and exchanged the comforter for it, then went to the open door and looked out into a dim, silent corridor. No one was stirring.

A draft along the hall sent a shivery finger under the robe onto her bare legs. It reminded her that the previous night someone had taken off most of her clothing. Pierre had said he lived alone here, though that didn't mean there weren't servants. She wanted to think it was he who had undressed her—removed her dress, unfastened her petticoats and unlaced her corset, touched her skin. At the image of his hands, a quiver began low in her abdomen.

Somewhere nearby was Pierre's bedroom. In a house that was strange to her, she was sure he would have put her in a room close to his. He would be asleep, perhaps naked.

Her breath came fast, her whole body tensing with desire for him. She wanted to touch him and have him touch her in turn. She wanted the caresses that made them both wild with passion. She wanted him to thrust deep inside her until they experienced again that ecstatic frenzy and its climax.

She hadn't talked to him about her feelings, as she'd determined to do. But this wasn't the time for waiting. Or for words that might come between them. She went back and hastily made the preparations she'd learned from Solange, then started along the corridor.

The door to the next room was open. She knew by the soft sound of breathing that someone was asleep there. As she tiptoed inside, the familiar scents of hair and skin told her the sleeper was Pierre. With fingers that could barely manage the ties, she discarded her robe and underclothes. A breeze puffed out the lace curtains at the open windows and sent shivers over her bare skin. Quickly she went to the bed, lifted an edge of the covers and slid underneath, into the cocoon of warmth from Pierre's naked body.

He stirred and his hand bumped her naked thigh. "Sarah, what—"

She leaned over him, stopping his words with a kiss.

Pierre, still half asleep, thought for a moment that his dreams of Sarah had become even more realistic than usual. But the hair falling around his face as her lips lingered, the brush of her breast against his shoulder convinced him she was real. He'd never managed so vivid a sensation in his sleep. She had come, naked, to his bed. Desire shot through him like a flame catching in dry tinder. The tightening of his muscles spread instantly to his groin.

"Sarah, Sarah." He almost groaned the words, his male organ already throbbing. Control—he must keep himself under control.

But Sarah wouldn't let him. She kissed him, her lips teasing, demanding, her tongue dancing inside his mouth and inviting him to taste hers. He turned her to her back and leaned over her, savoring the wonderful honeyed flavor of her mouth. She responded with a hunger equal to his. Her breath teased his ear as she nipped at his earlobe. He kissed the side of her neck, then moved lower to the edge of her collarbone. His hand found her breast, the nipple already erect against his fingers. Then he did what he'd longed to do for months and took the nipple in his mouth. He heard her sharp gasps, and she clutched at the back of his neck.

He lifted his head. "Sarah, I don't know if I can go slowly. It's been too long. I want you too much." Even as he got out the words, his fingers, as if with an intention of their own found the soft center of her sex.

Sarah heard the urgency in his voice, and it was no greater than her own. "I don't want you to wait!" Her hips thrust against his hand as she found his rigid member to guide it toward her.

As her legs opened for him, he mounted her and thrust inside. His breath came in great rasps in her ear, matching the drumming of her heart. The music of passion began, not with a slow movement; they were already beyond that. This was a frenzy of wildly accelerating notes, each thrust of his body welcomed and answered in the rhythm of hers. Their passion became a crescendo until together they reached a climax that reverberated for shattering seconds before it slowly diminished.

Sarah felt Pierre still inside her, and knew that part of

her had been missing. Now she was whole again.

He turned, pulling her against him so that they lay on their sides. They remained, not speaking, and his slower breathing sounded as content as she felt. Even when she moved and they were no longer joined, she felt as if they were still connected.

Pierre laughed, a wonderful soft, tender sound. "This wasn't what I'd planned," he said. "I was going to be careful and patient our first time again after all you'd been through. Let you rest and tell me when you were ready."

"I was ready," she said, and felt her skin grow warm.

His hand, which was brushing a strand of damp hair away from her face, stopped. "Sarah, you're blushing."

The blush progressed from warm to hot. "Yes. I can't help it. I hate blushing so easily."

He laughed again and kissed her. "Sarah, shy and bold at the same time. I love you. And your blushes. I love everything about you."

Joy vibrated through her like a reprise of passion. It released the words that had taken so long for her to voice. "Oh, Pierre. I love you."

In the pleasure of discovery they remembered and disputed. When had love begun? Who had known first? "I realized on the train back to Paris from Etretat," she said. "But I didn't know how you felt, and I'd been the one to ask. So I couldn't tell you. Later I tried to convince myself I'd been mistaken."

"Before we went to Etretat I knew," Pierre said. "But I really didn't want to believe it for a while. I guess I'd been happy being a bachelor. There was the business about Gille. And then Armand. I didn't know how much he meant to you."

This was the time to tell him about Solange and about Armand. She began bravely enough. "I shouldn't have doubted you about whether you gave Gille his information."

"I was angry about that at first," he acknowledged. "But when I thought about it, I could understand. The paper and the campaign had become more important than almost everything else. Not more than you, but you didn't know that."

His understanding encouraged her to go on. "Later," she explained, "I found out that Solange was the one who talked to Gille. She had some idea the publicity would help my career. She seemed to think she should arrange my life for me. I'd told her how Cesbron felt about publicity, but she didn't believe me."

He settled her head in a more comfortable place on his shoulder. "How did Solange know about Etretat? Did you tell her?"

"No, and I was so angry that I left before I thought to ask her. So I don't know. I haven't seen her since, but I'm going to when I'm back in Paris."

"When we're back in Paris. No more misunderstandings and separations. I was miserable."

Now was the time to tell him about Armand. But she couldn't. Not when his fingers were brushing the side of her face and across the curve of her neck to her shoulder. The breath to speak deserted her as she waited for his hand to make its slow, tantalizing way to her breast.

His lovemaking this second time seemed to Sarah like the first low E flat in the bass violins at the opening of *Das Reingold*. As in Wagner's music drama, their passion built its careful way, repeating and expanding the familiar gestures, promising the tumultuous sensations to come. The knowledge of shared love enriched each caress. When the promise of the climax had been fulfilled, Sarah felt that she and Pierre had created their own elemental myths of love.

Several hours later they stood on the terrace. Below them the villas gleamed white in the morning sunshine. The gray town had become a bright crescent along the edge of the bay, ending at a jetty on one side and a promontory on the other. "Those are the Iles de Lérins," Pierre said, pointing to two islands that resembled huge green sea animals, floating on their backs. The far side of the bay looked as if a giant hand had carelessly jumbled a row of mountain peaks into an irregular horizon. "That's the Estérel."

Sarah tried to listen and look, but her real attention was on the sentences she was practicing in her mind, choosing one, then discarding it for another equally inadequate. It was heaven to know Pierre loved her, but it made telling him about Armand even riskier. Maybe she didn't need to say anything. But what if he found out later? He and Armand were as close as brothers.

"Sarah," Pierre said, "are you worrying about something?"

"No. I mean, well, maybe I . . ." It was so hard to begin.

"If it's this morning, I know I didn't take any precautions. But you surprised me and that wasn't what I was thinking about."

"Oh, no." That was easy to talk about. "I had already done something."

To her surprise he didn't look pleased. "That's good," he said unconvincingly.

"Solange explained what to do." His disappointed expression perplexed her. "Don't you think a woman should know about contraception and take care of it herself when she can? You act as if you're sorry."

He gave a wry grin that mocked himself. "If you were pregnant, you'd have to marry me."

"Have to marry you?" Her knees felt as if they belonged to some smaller person.

"I didn't intend to bring it up this way. I want to marry you, but it wouldn't be fair if you had to. So I think I'm glad you took care of things this morning."

"You want to marry me?" She sounded stupid, even to

herself, repeating him. "But Armand said—that you have a woman friend, a writer." Though Sarah remembered the name, she wouldn't say it.

He did. "Simone? She's only that—a friend. It's you I love and want to marry."

She still couldn't quite believe words that filled her with such incredible joy. "After all that's happened, maybe you feel sorry for me. It might make you think you want to marry me."

His teasing smile appeared. "I had hoped for enthusiasm from you. But I can wait. We have a week here. By the end of the time you'll know you can't live without me."

When she didn't respond, his face sobered. "I know how much singing means to you. And that you have your father in the United States."

Neither of those was the uncertainty that dismayed her. Now she couldn't wait. She must tell him about Armand. "Pierre, there's something I need to tell you." She stopped and sighed, and he began to look concerned. Before she could delay again, she rushed on. "When I hadn't seen you and I was with Armand so much, I thought—" No, no excuses. "One day we were at his chateau and—" This was terrible!

He took hold of her hand. "Sarah, stop. I know what you're trying to say. Armand told me."

Sarah felt as if she'd just jumped off a precipice and found out it was only a step down. "Armand told you?"

"Yes."

"You mean—you didn't mind?"

"Of course I minded. I was furious—and jealous. But it's past. I love you the way you are. Even when you do something I wish you hadn't."

He stood, drawing her up with him. "Enough. I don't want to talk about that. We'll explore the country while you make up your mind that I'll be the perfect husband."

She looked up at him, the sunshine making gold lights in his brown hair, his eyes more blue than the bay. "I know that now. It just seems too much happiness to be real."

"We'll make it real."

Cannes and the surrounding hills reminded Sarah of an enormous park with trees and gardens and the Mediterranean Sea as its lake. One day she and Pierre took the Antibes road halfway around the bay and watched tall-masted sailing ships skirting gracefully around squat iron steamships, like ballerinas showing up the clumsy antics of dancing bears. On the way back they stopped at a restaurant on the water and ate a spicy soup of crab, mussels, clams, and several kinds of fish that Sarah hadn't heard of before.

"Do you want to go to the casino?" Pierre asked.

"No. I like staying at the villa better." He laughed, knowing exactly why she liked the villa so well, and of course she blushed.

On Christmas Eve they traveled several kilometers inland to the manor where Pierre had grown up. Pierre showed her over its farms and orchards, and he talked to the tenants of those and adjoining farms. Everyone greeted him jovially and gave sly winks behind his back after being introduced to Sarah. But when he discussed land and crops with them, their faces grew serious and respectful.

The manor house was old and solid, and Sarah could see that Pierre loved it in spite of its old-fashioned design and lack of conveniences. "My parents moved to the villa in Cannes," he explained, "when I was about fifteen. I really grew up here."

Before dark, Pierre cut a small pine tree that they decorated with pieces of candied fruits, tinsel and paper stars. Sarah unwrapped the *santon* Zola had given her the previous year—the poor peasant woman who gathered firewood for her living. She put the figurine on the mantel in a cluster of Christmas candles. "Now I know a little more about the kind of life she leads," Sarah said to Pierre.

At midnight they listened to carols being rung on the bells of a village church and feasted on their own small Christmas midnight supper of food they'd brought from Cannes—goose, with salad and fruit, and a bottle of champagne. Afterward they went to bed in the bedroom where he had slept as a boy. Making love in the narrow bed gave her a special joy that made physical pleasure even greater. Sarah knew that Pierre's love was the greatest Christmas gift she could ever have.

During the quiet times at the villa Pierre didn't bring up the question of marriage, but they talked of many other things and particularly of Claudine. One evening was cool enough for them to be sitting on the sofa watching a fire in the fireplace. "How could I have been so gullible?" Sarah lamented.

"You were too trusting, but not greedy," Pierre comforted her. "Lots of other people were both. I got a long letter from Jondinet. He learned a lot about the Houdons that would explain their success. Bernard knew how to manipulate the legal system, and they also traded on his father's good name."

"But it had gone on for such a long time! Six years, I think."

"They never defaulted on a loan. When someone pressed them to repay, they would send another friend—Claudine had a way of inspiring confidence—to offer to buy the loan. So the lender generally decided it was a good investment to keep. If not, they borrowed from someone else, always promising high interest and part of the inheritance."

"Who is Georges Appleton?"

"A childhood friend of Claudine's. He was a sailor who learned English on trips to Louisiana and Georgia. Claudine picked a name from New England because she and Bernard wanted the excuse of a shipping business to explain why no one was ever able to get hold of the fake Appleton. It was just a coincidence that you knew the family. And she took advantage of it."

"Yes. An awful coincidence for me." And one Nathalie had taken advantage of, Sarah thought, her anger rising at the memory.

Pierre gave her a sharp glance and frowned. "That day in Saint Lazare—you said Aunt Nathalie had nothing to do with your troubles. Are you sure the introduction to Claudine was all there was to it? I want to know!"

From the grim line of his mouth she realized that her thoughts must have shown on her face. Reluctantly she said, "Your aunt did know that an investigation of the Houdons' affairs was going on. I think Adolphe Fuzelier told her."

"And so she introduced you to Claudine, hoping you'd become involved." His voice was husky with anger and dismay.

This time Sarah couldn't deny the truth. "Yes. She admitted it to me."

Lines deepened around his mouth. "It was my fault too, for involving you with Armand. Why didn't you tell me?" he demanded.

"Because it wouldn't have helped me, and you'd have blamed yourself, just as you're doing now." She put her arms around him, looking into his face. "You couldn't know how far she'd go. You told me that anything I did in the past is over. That's the same for both of us."

He said yes and stroked her hair, but it wasn't until she'd convinced him with kisses that the unhappy look left his face. The pain she felt for Pierre didn't keep her from being glad that he knew of Nathalie's treachery. She hoped that losing his affection would hurt Nathalie too.

The day before they were to leave, they were on their way back to the villa from a walk in the last of the day's sunshine.

As they walked, Pierre said, "We've never discussed what it was like for you in Saint Lazare. I wasn't sure you'd want to talk about it."

"I don't want to think about just how I felt, but I learned a lot there. Some of the prisoners were criminals who'd done terrible things. But the trouble for a lot of the others was mainly that they were poor. For poor women, life is just work and babies. Some of them who were servants worked fifteen or eighteen hours a day."

Remembering, Sarah grew agitated. "One woman told me she made feather pillows. Even with her three children working too, she didn't make enough to live. No wonder she stole. Some women wear men's clothes to get jobs because men are paid more. That way the women can earn enough to keep from starving. A lot of them are drunkards. I suppose they think life has to have some pleasures."

Pierre paced beside her, his fists jammed in his pockets. "Paris is a city full of entertainments for people with money. Working men have a hard time. Most of them can't afford the fifteen centime minimum at the worst cafés."

"It's even harder for women," Sarah contended. "They have almost no rights. Some women were in prison for adultery. That isn't a crime for a man. Women aren't treated fairly!"

"You're right." He punctuated the air with an angry finger. "France had the first universal manhood suffrage in Europe, but we won't let women vote."

Sarah looked at him in surprise. "You're in favor of that? Armand told me giving women the vote would be turning the country over to the church."

"Maybe some women are too influenced by the church, but they still should be able to vote. And have a lot of other rights."

They reached the villa and climbed the steps to the terrace. He continued talking heatedly, as if she were opposed to his ideas and he had to convince her. "When I go out on stories in the working sections of Paris, I see drunks lying on tables in Cafés and in the streets. Prostitutes who don't look more than ten years old. People in the Faubourg Saint-Germain are demanding cleaner air and water. They should have them. But the working-class sections need them most of all."

"Pierre, why aren't you in politics?"

He looked at her as if she'd said something startling. Then he shrugged. "I'm a journalist, not a politician."

"You're wrong." Why hadn't she realized this before? "You believe in different goals from Armand, but they're just as important. Decent work is probably *more* important to most people than colonies and glory."

"I'll use my influence as a writer."

"But politicians can do more!"

"Hmm. I'll think about it. For now," he said, "look at the sunset." He pointed across the bay.

The sun was sinking behind the mountains, streaking the clouds with red that faded to salmon and then gold. The air turned cool, and Sarah welcomed Pierre's arm around her as they watched.

When the clouds began to lose their gold color, he said, "We'll leave tomorrow on the one-thirty express. We haven't talked about marriage again. Is this enough time to make up your mind?"

From his confident tone he felt sure of her answer, but their earlier discussion troubled her. "I don't want to give up singing, if there's still a chance the Opéra Comique will have me. It might be bad for your career to have a wife who's an opera singer."

"A newspaper man has no reputation to worry about," he said lightly.

"But a politician does."

"I'm not a politician," he repeated, but she thought he

didn't sound quite as definite as he had before.

"You should be!"

He ran his finger along her jaw. "Don't look so stubborn. You're making too much of this. I'm probably never going to get into politics. And Monsieur Cesbron won't be such an idiot as not to take you back. We'll have everything we want—if you'll marry me. You haven't answered yet."

"Yes, of course I want to marry you." She pulled his head down and kissed him, for the pleasure and in gratitude for his confidence in her. But he'd just used the word "probably" about politics. He must want to at least consider it. She wasn't as sure as he seemed to be that they both could have everything they wanted.

CHAPTER TWENTY-FIVE

"**A**RE YOU SURE YOU DON'T WANT ME TO STAY?" PIERRE asked. He and Sarah were sitting in the back corner of the Café Bonvalet near her flat.

"No, I must talk to Armand by myself."

They had returned to Paris from Cannes the previous night and found a message from Armand at Sarah's flat, asking to see her. She had sent a reply, suggesting he come to the café on the Rue Lafayette.

"All right," Pierre said reluctantly. "I'll leave when he gets here."

The waiter arrived with their breakfast. The nutlike aroma of the coffee and the yeasty smell of the bread sharpened Sarah's hunger. She savored the combination of bitter liquid and crusty roll. Food seemed to taste better in Pierre's company.

Though she had her back to the entrance, she knew by the appearance of faint lines around Pierre's mouth when Armand arrived. The two men greeted each other with restraint.

Armand's greeting to Sarah was warmer.

whether his assurance wasn't easier for him to give now that he didn't have the choice to make.

Sarah rang the doorbell at the Rue de Chazelles town house with anticipation. Since she had no intention of letting Solange try to arrange her life, she looked forward to seeing her again. A harried-looking Berthe opened the door.

"What's the matter, Berthe?"

"I swear the devil puts ideas into Madame's head!" Berthe went on grumbling to herself as she took Sarah's wraps and disappeared along the hall.

"Sarah." Solange's musical call came from the drawing room. "Please come in."

Solange was sitting on the settee with a stack of music scores on her lap and a large box on the floor. "I'm delighted to see you, but I can't get up. I'm sorting scores. Here, I'll make a space for you." She moved another stack from beside her onto the floor.

The room looked as if a burglary had taken place. The cupid-encrusted clock was gone from the mantel, as were other ornaments from tables around the room. The corners held only half as many plants as usual, and they looked neglected.

"Is something wrong," Sarah asked. "Berthe looked upset."

"I'll tell you later. First you must tell me how you are." Solange's expression hardened with anger. "That horrible business with the police! How could they have made such an insane mistake? After this I won't ever believe any claims by the Sûreté. Was Saint Lazare very bad?"

"Yes, it was bad. I don't want to think or talk about it anymore. I'd rather tell you good news. I'm going to marry Pierre."

"Good heavens!" Shock was followed by dismay. "But, my dear, that is dreadful."

Sarah laughed. "I don't agree. I think it will be wonderful."

Solange threw her hands up in a despairing gesture. Part of the music scores slid unnoticed off onto the floor. "It will be a disaster, but you'll probably be convinced you're happy."

Sarah knelt down, gathering up the scores and put them back on the divan. "The room looks as if you're getting ready to move."

"Yes, I am."

"No wonder Berthe is unhappy. Where will you be living?"

"I'm going to Germany with Wilhelm. We're going to be married." Solange's face flushed a faint pink. "Don't bother to say what you're thinking."

Sarah was too astounded to say anything.

"I know," Solange continued, "that I'm being as foolish as you. Still, Wilhelm is a good man. He's kind." Her voice softened and the lines of age in her face were more apparent, as if she'd relaxed some kind of control she ordinarily kept in place. "I've known too many unkind and selfish men."

"I hope you will be very happy with him," Sarah said sympathetically. "When will you go and where will you live?"

"We'll leave in a few weeks. His home is someplace in Bavaria. It's not near any of the cities, so I'm not sure just where."

Solange, in a rural village, without an audience for the charm she enjoyed exerting? It was difficult for Sarah to imagine such a different Solange. Curiously, she asked, "Does Eleanore Matrat plan to visit you in Germany?"

"Oh, no. Wilhelm doesn't use the title, but he's a baron." Momentarily Solange looked annoyed. "He didn't even tell me about it until recently. His mother, the baroness, wouldn't care for Eleanore."

So there was a title involved. Solange hadn't changed so much as it seemed at first.

Solange got up and went to a small desk and took out a piece of paper. "I haven't told you the most important news.

I have talked to Signor Marchesi." She paused dramatically. "You remember him, don't you?"

Excitement quivered along Sarah's spine. "Of course. The voice teacher. He's famous."

"After I described what you and I have accomplished, he agreed—enthusiastically—to give you an audition. If he likes you, he will take you as a pupil. And of course he will like you. About music, my judgment is impeccable."

"Oh, Solange," Sarah said, and found she was so overwhelmed no more words would come.

"Now, don't object because of the cost. I will pay for the lessons." She hesitated, then added, "I know how unhappy you were because of that newspaper business. This will advance your career, and I want to do it."

Sarah put her arms around Solange and hugged her. This kind of "arranging" was generous and unselfish. Pierre could afford the lessons, but it clearly made Solange feel better to do it. "Thank you, Solange. This makes me very happy."

Solange kissed Sarah's cheek, then gave a sly smile, like a child with a special secret to tell. "I have heard something very exciting. Jules Massenet is working on a new opera. It's based on Goethe's poem about young Werther. What voice do you think he intends for the heroine?"

She paused dramatically, but not long enough for Sarah to respond. "A mezzo-soprano!"

A new leading role for her voice range! Fantasies sprang up in Sarah's mind, like fireworks shooting up in thin lines and exploding to fill the sky.

"Monsieur Massenet," Solange said gleefully, "took Sybil Sanderson and made her famous because she was beautiful and was Marchesi's pupil. And of course because she could sing well. After your lessons, you will be in the same position."

Tears began to gather in Sarah's eyes. Solange had understood her dreams and was offering a way to fulfill them.

"I'm grateful for everything you've done for me. I'll miss you when you go to Germany."

"I expect to come back to Paris to hear you in the premiere. It's too bad it's not a trousers role. I never did see you in one. You would make a delightful young man."

"That's what you told me the first time I came here for lunch," Sarah reminded her, and they smiled at each other.

"Have you been back to the Opéra Comique yet?" Solange asked.

"No, but I intend to see Monsieur Cesbron this afternoon. Helene told me there's no rehearsal today, so it's a good time to go. Monsieur Cesbron is almost always at the theater. It's practically his home."

"Tell that prudish director not to make any petty objections about you. All that worry about scandal just because of the government subsidy. What madness! You tell him I say you are the perfect mezzo-soprano for trouser roles."

"I will."

"Then get along and see him," Solange said brusquely. Her eyes had a sheen of tears, and Sarah realized Solange was as moved as she.

Pierre insisted on going with Sarah to the Opéra Comique. As they walked across the Place du Châtelet toward the Théâtre des Nations, he predicted, "Everything will be fine. The director knows I'm a journalist. I'll assure him that the papers will give you favorable notices."

"Notice of any kind is what Monsieur Cesbron objects to," she said nervously. "Do I look all right?"

He paused and took a slow, appreciative look. "Beautiful, as always."

"I mean—do I look respectable?"

Her wine-colored wool suit was the most stylish thing she owned. It had a fashionable gored skirt, slender at the waist and smooth across the back, without the gathers that were remnants of bustles. The sleeves of the snug jacket puffed at the shoulder and narrowed to tight cuffs at the wrist.

Pierre gave her an exaggerated bow. "As respectable as the Queen of England."

She smiled at him, but the smile felt the way she imagined circus clowns felt behind their paint.

Except for a man in the ticket office, the lobby of the theater was deserted. As Sarah and Pierre walked along the quiet corridor to Monsieur Cesbron's office, she almost hoped for one of the rare occasions when the director was away.

A thin line of light shone under his door. Her pulse thrumming nervously, she paused in front. After Pierre squeezed her hand encouragingly, she took a shaky breath and knocked.

"Come in."

Monsieur Cesbron sat behind his desk. It was cluttered with papers that could have been the same ones as on the day Sarah first saw him. When he looked up, he exclaimed, "Mademoiselle Taylor!" and his face lit up with a pleased smile. He rose and came toward her, his hands outstretched to grasp hers. "How good it is to see you!" His voice was tremulous with emotion.

"I'm glad to see you again, Monsieur Cesbron."

For a moment she thought he was going to embrace her, but he kissed her hand, then nodded to Pierre. "Good afternoon, Monsieur de Torbey. Please, sit down." He pulled one chair forward and shifted several books from another, balancing them precariously on an already crowded cabinet.

When they were all seated, he took his glasses off and wiped his eyes. "A dreadful business. Dreadful. I hope you are recovered, mademoiselle."

She smiled at him, touched by his emotion. "Yes, thank you. I'm fine, and anxious to be singing again. I came to talk to you about rejoining the chorus."

"Hm, yes." His face sobered. "That is a difficult matter. The newspapers ran many articles about your arrest."

She could feel the muscles tensing in her neck. "I understand about the subsidy and how careful you must be. But I'm innocent. I was cleared. The newspapers also reported that."

"Yes," the director said uncomfortably. "I read about the decision not to indict you."

"My paper, *Le Combattant*," Pierre asserted, "has pointed out that Mademoiselle Taylor should never have been held. That there was too little evidence for anything more than questioning."

"I assure you, Monsieur de Torbey, that personally I am delighted for Mademoiselle Taylor."

Pierre leaned forward, his hands resting on his knees. "Restoring her to the chorus will benefit the Opéra Comique. Just because there *has* been so much publicity, the name La Belle Americaine now represents the best of French justice."

"That's the way it is in the United States," Sarah said. "It shows that the system protects innocent people."

"That's right," Pierre said. "If you give Mademoiselle Taylor her position, Frenchmen will understand that you respect justice. Sarah will be an asset to the Opéra Comique. And to your personal fairness. Journalists will continue to write about La Belle Americaine for a while. Reports that you support her will be the best kind of publicity, the kind you'll prefer." There was a subtle note of warning in Pierre's voice.

"Yes, I see. You may be right," Monsieur Cesbron said thoughtfully.

Sarah felt elated. Since she and Pierre were a good team, she might as well be audacious. "You said you would let me understudy a mezzo role. Now might be a good time."

Monsieur Cesbron took off his glasses again and polished them, this time doing it absently, a habit to let him think. Sarah tried to read his face. Doubt there. But interest too. And excitement.

He got up and walked to the window where he stood, looking out, for what seemed five minutes. Finally he turned. His white whiskers quivered with purpose. "We are presenting *Tales of Hoffman* in five weeks. I believe, Mademoiselle Taylor, that you were rehearsing for the part of Nicklasse—before you felt obliged to use your hatpin to fence with Monsieur Rivarol." He chuckled at his own wit. Sarah managed a small laugh.

"As it happens," he went on, "the mezzo I had engaged has been so foolish as to marry a colonial. She's going to Asia with him. Would you care to audition for the part? I could listen to you now."

A few minutes earlier Sarah would have said she couldn't force a single note from her throat. "Yes, of course. I would love to sing for you."

As the three of them walked along the corridor to the practice room, Sarah felt as if a sorcerer had transported her back in time to her first audition. This time Pierre, not Ted was with her, smiling at her with love and confidence. When Monsieur Cesbron sat at the piano, that confidence became her own.

"We'll do Nicklasse's song from Act Two," the director said. "Begin with 'Yes, I know. Everything is physical.'" He played a few bars and hummed the line that was Sarah's cue.

When he finished, she began. "*Oui, je sais, tout pour la physique, pour la physique.*" The melody floated from her as she went on with the mocking song, making fun of the mechanical doll who has enthralled the poet, Hoffman. When she reached the final lines, she sang them to Pierre. "*Je t'aime! Je t'aime!*"

His eyes repeated the same words to her: *I love you. I love you.*

Monsieur Cesbron rose from the piano, then turned back and played a crashing chord, as if he needed that outlet for his excitement. "Brava! You have improved your technique since you sang that for me before, Mademoiselle Taylor. Yes, when we open on February fourteenth, La Belle Americaine will be my Nicklasse." As if so much enthusiasm were uncomfortable, he put on a more sober expression. "Of course, you will have to practice very diligently."

Delight was a whirlwind, spinning Sarah into dizziness. "Oh Monsieur Cesbron! Thank you so much!"

Pierre laughed exuberantly. "Monsieur Directeur, Paris will know and appreciate your fair-mindedness."

"You understand, Mademoiselle Taylor," the director said with a gruffness that didn't conceal his pleasure, "that you must demonstrate that you have this role because your singing warrants it."

"I will! I will!"

After they left the Opéra Comique, Sarah and Pierre went to the Café Americain. "This seems the right place to celebrate," Sarah explained. "I came here often when I was first in Paris and was a little homesick. It reminds me to be grateful for my good fortune."

Pierre touched his glass of champagne against hers. "To you. 1890 is just two days away. And then the last decade of this century. In the nineties you'll be a successful singer and my wife."

After they drank, he said more soberly, "What about your father? Will he be pleased that you're marrying a Frenchman?"

Thinking about her father wasn't painful any longer. "I'm not sure. I've written to him, telling him what happened and that we're going to marry."

"Fine. Now let's decide the date. How about tomorrow?"

"Tomorrow! I can't be ready that soon!"

His grin let her know he was mostly teasing—but not altogether. "All right. Next week."

She started to protest again, but she knew she didn't want to wait longer either.

* * *

Exactly a week later Sarah stood with Pierre before a magistrate in the Hotel de Ville, holding a nosegay of yellow rosebuds. Her wildest girlhood fancies hadn't pictured being married in the Paris city hall. But she'd never imagined either that the husband vaguely pictured in her dreams could mean to her what Pierre did.

The magistrate said, "Congratulations, Monsieur and Madame de Tourbey."

Pierre gave a great laugh of delight, lifted her veil, and kissed her until she felt that her toes must be blushing. After that it was a confusion of embraces.

Helene gave her a tearful kiss and said, sobbing, "This is a happy day."

A beaming Ted kissed her on only one cheek as an American relative would. "Sarah, you are a beautiful bride."

"Yes," Armand agreed, "beautiful." He kissed her on the mouth—not as an American relative would.

Before Armand could kiss her again, Pierre grabbed Sarah's hand and pulled her along with him. "It's time for the celebration."

Paris had refused to cooperate with sunshine. But to Sarah the rain was a silver shower, making the gray stones glisten as ornaments for her wedding day. On the steps of the Hotel de Ville they put up umbrellas and dashed to the closed carriages that waited in the Rue de Rivoli. "Where are we going?" she asked Pierre. He'd refused to tell her earlier, but she guessed that like a boy with a secret, he couldn't hold out much longer.

"The Café Anglais," he said, succumbing to his own exuberance, "to a private room—the Grand Seize."

Astonished, she said, "That's only for royalty."

"What's suitable for the next king of England will do for the next queen of opera."

"Don't say that. I haven't even made my solo debut yet,"

she protested, but on this day anything seemed possible.

As they went upstairs, she caught a glimpse of herself and
Pierre in a large mirror, she in her dress of crushed yellow
satin with extravagant fur trim on cape and hem and he in
morning coat and striped trousers. A distinguished couple,
she thought delightedly. The second floor room, elegantly
decorated in gold, white and red, was as opulent as its
reputation had led her to expect. Its famous sofa was discreetly sheltered in an alcove. What pleased her most were
the people already there.

Solange, with a patient Wilhelm beside her, was lecturing
Monsieur Cesbron. Members of the Opéra Comique chorus
mixed with people she recognized as friends of Pierre. For
a moment she wondered if Armand knew why Nathalie was
not among the guests, but then Hector Lunel saw them and
raised a cry, "The bride and groom!" and she dismissed that
brief thought as the celebration began.

Later, when all the toasts had been drunk and songs sung,
she and Pierre went back to her almost empty flat. They would
live in his apartment, but she wanted to sleep this night in
her canopied bed where she'd wondered so often if they
would ever be together again.

They drank another toast to the future. "We'll be so happy
everyone will envy us," he predicted.

"Not everyone. You have a wife who's a singer," she reminded him. "Lots of men wouldn't like that."

"It doesn't matter. I'll be famous as your husband." He
said it lightly, but she couldn't imagine that.

"No. You'll be my famous husband. I think you won't be
happy unless you're successful in what you do."

"You're right." He sounded thoughtful, and she wondered
if he were remembering her urging that he consider politics.

She thought of something she'd been intending to mention. "I'd like to visit Papa in the summer when the opera
houses are closed."

"Opera houses?" he teased. "You're planning to be singing at the Paris Opéra as well as the Opéra Comique by then?"

"I can dream about it. Will you go with me to Boston?"

"Of course." He hesitated. "We haven't talked about where we'll live. You do want to come back to Paris, don't you?"

"Yes. I feel like a Parisian now."

He picked up his glass. "A toast to La Belle Americaine and her triumph in *Tales of Hoffman*. After that and the triumphs that follow, she'll be La Belle Parisienne."

She caught his hand. "No—no toast yet. Wait until opening night—if it all really happens that way."

Laughing, he put down the glass and pulled her into his arms. "Come to bed now. I think I know how to make you forget to worry about the opening."

He was right.

Sarah wore a path in the carpet of the small dressing room. Fear of getting caught in a snarl of horses and cabs and missing her opening night as Nicklasse had brought her to the theater very early. As a result she had too much time to be nervous. It felt strange not to be in the changing room, surrounded by the chatter of other chorus members. Pierre had come with her, but he was off somewhere, banished when the costume mistress had come to help her dress.

For the dozenth time, Sarah stopped in front of the mirror. Could she be this eighteenth century dandy she saw reflected here?

Her black wig was tied at the back in a queue. Below her chin a white froth of lacy ruffles spread over the high-standing collar of her silk waistcoat. More ruffles showed at the bottom of the sleeves of the coat, almost covering her hands. The coat nipped in at the waist but was loose enough to conceal her breasts. It disguised her hips by flaring out, ending just below her knees at the bottom of her breeches. The waistcoat was gray-striped silk; the coat and breeches a blue-gray, cut silk velvet. White stockings and black buckled shoes completed her transformation into a young man.

She tried out her walk, lengthening her stride, keeping her hips from swaying. After her hours of practice, it had to look right.

Pierre leaned around the door. "Is it safe to come back?" Without waiting, he came in. "Madame de Tourbey," he said admiringly, "I prefer you as my wife, but you make a beautiful man."

He came closer with a look she recognized. "I've never wanted to kiss a man except in greeting, but—"

"No!" she warned. "You might spoil my face paint. Afterward. As many times as you like."

"That's probably best." He gestured toward the door. "Ted is outside. So is Solange. They'd each like to speak to you. Do you want to see them, or would it distract you too much?"

She hunted for her pocket watch. It wasn't where she thought she'd left it. "How much time?"

"Almost an hour."

"Yes, let them come in. I'd like to be distracted for a little while."

Ted arrived first, beaming behind his glasses. "Did we dream of this, Sarah, when we came to the Opéra Comique that day?"

"I did, but I don't think you did."

"Perhaps I was a little doubtful," he conceded. "I had a letter from Josiah. He thanked me for standing in for him at the ceremony."

"He sent me a cablegram, wishing me good luck tonight."

"I wish you the same."

After Ted left, Solange swept in on a wave of perfume, gold brocade and glittering jewels. She stopped inside the door, as if too stunned to move. "Sarah, my dear, you look wonderful! That costume—it's marvelous! I always knew you would make a perfect man."

"On the stage," Pierre interjected.

She ignored him and advanced into the center of the room. "I saw Signor Marchesi. He was very pleased with your audition. He congratulated me on how much you had improved with me."

Sarah felt amused. Since the singing teacher had never heard her before the audition, he couldn't know how much she'd learned from Solange. But Sarah herself knew. "I'll always be grateful to you," she said warmly. "I'm glad you and Baron Hotter postponed leaving for Germany long enough to be here tonight."

"Now you must *not* be nervous," Solange commanded. "I saw Jules Massenet in the lobby. He'll love you because you will sing magnificently."

After revealing the fact most likely to make Sarah nervous, Solange swept out again.

Before Sarah collected herself, Armand appeared. "May I come in?" he asked.

"Yes," Sarah said.

"Just for a moment," Pierre said. "Then we all have to leave Sarah alone."

"I wanted to wish you good luck, Sarah," Armand said. "And to tell you that I've decided I want to run for a seat in the Chamber of Deputies at the next election. I'm talking to people about it now."

Sarah laughed delightedly. "That's the best kind of news."

"What did Aunt Nathalie say?" Pierre asked.

"Nothing. No seizures or attacks." Armand's smile was faintly self-mocking. "Since she recovered from her silence, she's been making a list of the families with respectable names who have daughters and no money. She's given up on the old nobility. I let her make the lists. She knows I'll do what pleases me."

Pierre looked at his watch. "It's half an hour until the performance begins. We'll go now, Sarah." He came over to her and took her hands. "Solange is right about one thing. You'll be a marvelous Nicklasse. I know it."

His eyes and smile offered her the caresses that her painted face didn't allow.

As he and Armand started out, Pierre said to his cousin, "So you expect to be in the Chamber of Deputies? Maybe we'll be there together."

"But you're married to a singer and—" Armand began, then stopped.

"Times are changing," Pierre said confidently as they disappeared into the corridor.

Briefly Sarah thought about Pierre's intentions, glad that he was considering politics after all. But that could wait until later. She had to concentrate on her music as Nicklasse now.

Half an hour later she stood offstage in the wings, wondering whether she would be able to hear the orchestra over the pounding of her heart. The tenor in the costume of the poet, Hoffman, stood beside her, waiting with her for their entrance. Then the first F-minor chords thundered out as the curtain rose on the wine barrels and tables of a Nuremburg tavern, and the music began to resonate in her head.

Behind the scenery the Opéra Comique chorus began a lively song about the virtues of wine. The muse spoke from the back of the stage, followed by the bass viols in the orchestra, with their somber music of foreboding. She heard the deep voice of the sinister Lindorf, singing his boast that he will triumph over Hoffman. The men of the chorus, dressed as students, streamed past onto the stage. Their boisterous exchanges began, praising Stella, Hoffman's love. Finally came the lines to announce the entrance of Hoffman and his friend, Nicklasse: "Vivat! C'est lui!"

She waited a half second for the tenor to get a step ahead of her. Then, to the music of the cheering students, Sarah strode onto the stage.

Barbara Keller is the author of three previous historical romances. She lives with her husband in Southern California and the Sierra Nevada.